# HAWK AT THE CROSSROADS

# HAWK AT THE CROSSROADS

## AJ ABERFORD

This edition produced in Great Britain in 2022

by Hobeck Books Limited, Unit 14, Sugnall Business Centre, Sugnall, Stafford, Staffordshire, ST21 NF

www.hobeck.net

A CIP catalogue for this book is available from the British Library.

ISBN 978-1-913-793-87-6

Cover design by Spiffing Covers

www.spiffingcovers.com

Printed and bound in Great Britain by Clays Ltd, Elcograf S.p.A.

# PRAISE FOR BODIES IN THE WATER

'I thought I knew everything about murders in the Med – not so – this series is a fantastic read!'
Robert Daws, bestselling author of the *Rock* crime series

'What a fantastic debut thriller from AJ Abeford! *Bodies in the Water* gives the real lowdown about crime and corruption in the Mediterranean, in an adventure that ranges from the tourist enclaves of Malta to the war-torn deserts of Libya and weaves together an intricate tale of murder, human trafficking, money laundering, terrorism and organised crime. In the centre of it all is Detective George Zammit, an intriguing new character on the crime thriller scene who is sure to become an instant fan favourite. Meticulously researched by someone who clearly has a deep understanding of the subject matter, *Bodies in the Water* rattles on at a supercharged pace, leaving the reader waiting expectantly for the next novel in what is destined to be a hugely popular new series.'
J.T. Brannan, bestselling thriller and mystery author

'I am definitely a fan of George and 100% will look forward to reading the next in the series.' Alex Jones

# AUTHOR'S NOTE

Although the plot points are inspired by the political circumstances and certain events at the time of writing, the story is the product of my imagination and not intended to be an accurate account of any such real-life events or a comment on any of the people who may have been involved in them.

Malta is a small island and three-quarters of the population share the same one hundred most common surnames. As a result, there's a chance I have inadvertently given a character the same name as someone alive or maybe dead. If that is the case, I apologise. The events, dialogue and characters in this book were created for the purposes of fictionalisation. Any resemblance of any character or corporation to any entity, or to a person, alive or dead, is purely coincidental.

# ARE YOU A THRILLER SEEKER?

Hobeck Books is an independent publisher of crime, thrillers and suspense fiction and we have one aim – to bring you the books you want to read.

For more details about our books, our authors and our plans, plus the chance to download free novellas, sign up for our newsletter at **www.hobeck.net**.

You can also find us on Twitter **@hobeckbooks** or on Facebook **www.facebook.com/hobeckbooks10**.

*To my granddaughters, Eva and Isabel. May your love of books exceed your love of chocolate!*

# CHAPTER 1
# O. R. TAMBO
## INTERNATIONAL AIRPORT –
## JOHANNESBURG

SOUTH AFRICAN DIAMONDS are legally exported in secure containers with specifically numbered and government-validated certificates. This regulates the trade in stones mined in the warzones of Africa that have caused misery to so many, for so long. It is for good reason that such stones are often referred to as 'blood diamonds'.

Cristina Cassar had passed through the security scanner of O. R. Tambo International Airport, overseen by a lethargic, slack-jawed woman whose glazed eyes only occasionally drifted towards the screen in front of her. Cristina gathered her blue cabin bag, cosmetics, jacket, and slipped her feet into her expensive sandals. She took the soiled grey plastic tray and headed towards the stainless-steel packing table. They were in no hurry, having plenty of time left before their fifteen-hour flight back to Malta, via Amsterdam. She and her boyfriend, Nick Walker, had spent the last week at an industry conference at Sun City, the large resort one hundred and forty kilometres to the north west of Johannesburg.

There, Nick had attended a relaxed programme of presentations and workshops, meeting colleagues and friends from the world of online gaming. During the day Cristina read at the poolside and, when Nick was free, they had visited the Madikwe Game Reserve, played golf and enjoyed the resort's spas and pools. At night, they had dined, taken in shows at the big hotels, and Nick had even taken Cristina onto the gaming floors of the casinos, explaining why it was odds-on she would never get her money back once she had converted it into chips.

He was at an adjacent security scanner, putting his belt back through his trouser loops and repacking his laptop, when he noticed a group of four Hawks walking slowly down the security hall. South Africa's Priority Crime Investigation brigade, the Hawks were a much-feared branch of the police and their appearance usually meant trouble for somebody. They wore black berets, short-sleeved blue shirts, stab jackets, and their trouser legs tucked down inside high, black lace-up boots.

Cristina's cabin bag had glided through the scanner. She had not noticed the security woman, apparently watching the endless parade of personal items passing before her, signal to a colleague with a nod. He had helpfully corrected the position of the blue cabin bag on the conveyor belt and, in doing so, deftly slipped a paper envelope into one of its external pockets.

When diamonds are traded in Amsterdam, Surat in India or even Kinshasa, it is traditional to package them in a small paper envelope with a waxy blue interior finish. *Briefke* is the Flemish word for this envelope, which is used by everybody in the diamond trade. Cristina did not realise it, but the *briefke* inside the front pocket of her cabin bag held about one thousand carats of diamonds, or two hundred and forty grams, with a retail value of over one million US for accredited stones.

Nick saw the Hawks looking over at the scanner where Cristina was fussing, repacking her cosmetics. He zipped up his briefcase and noticed one of the policemen tap a colleague on the arm and point in Cristina's direction. Two of them walked slowly towards her, their thumbs tucked under the shoulder straps of their stab jackets. One was smiling and started engaging her in conversation. He watched as she produced her passport and boarding pass, which the Hawk took from her and inspected. Nick smiled to himself. He knew Cristina had nothing to fear, but she would be petrified by the big, intimidating police officers in their military-style uniform.

Nick was walking towards her when the second officer started gathering her things from the packing area. He took her cabin bag, her purse and her jacket, while the first man laid his hand on her arm. Nick was becoming concerned. He arrived in time to hear his agitated girlfriend saying: "What are you doing? Those are my things."

The first officer put her passport and boarding pass into the pocket of his stab jacket, then looked at her with an expression that had curdled.

"You must come with us."

Cristina saw Nick approach and stepped towards him, fear on her face.

"Nick, they want to take me with them. They've got my things."

Confused, he spoke to the officer who seemed to be in charge, noticing the sergeant's stripes on his epaulettes.

"Hey, what's going on? You can't take her away, she's done nothing wrong."

He had made to take her hand and pull her towards him when the two Hawks who had initially stood back quickly moved in and grabbed his arms, roughly pulling them behind him. The man with the sergeant's stripes spoke loudly in his ear.

"Who are you to her? Are you two travelling together?"

"Yes, we live together. Now let us go! Get off me!"

There was a brief scuffle as he tried to shake himself free, until he realised he was making things worse for both of them. He forced himself to relax and turned to Cristina, saying, "Let's go with them and get this sorted out – whatever they think it is."

Turning to the sergeant who was holding him, he said: "It's OK, we're coming with you."

The police officer relaxed his grip and said: "Sensible of you. We go this way."

He nodded to his colleagues and they set off. Cristina grabbed Nick's hand and the pair of them were marched, closely surrounded by the four Hawks, through the endless corridors of the airport. Heads turned and people sidestepped as the Hawks paraded the couple through the terminal to the airport police station. There, they were split up and held in separate, stifling interview rooms.

The sergeant interviewed Cristina first, after placing her cabin bag at his feet. He looked at her for a while, then said: "Is there anything you want to tell me?"

"No. I don't understand what this is all about."

With a shrug, he reached down to her case and slipped his hand into the front pocket.

Cristina gasped in horror and put her hand to her mouth when he produced the white *briefke* and let a small stream of glittering stones tinkle onto the metal table between them. His gaze met hers as, without a word, he slowly gathered up the stones and put them back into the envelope.

The sergeant sighed deeply and closely studied the shocked and tearful young woman, sitting shaking on a wooden chair bolted to the floor. She was a pretty, slightly built woman, with short, pixie-cut blonde hair, clusters of freckles on her cheeks and piercing blue eyes. Tears had smudged her mascara and reddened her lids. Her tip-tilted nose was running slightly. She looked and felt very small in the presence of the bulky law enforcement officer across the table from her.

Sergeant Enzokuhle Lubanzi was not a man given to pity. He had seen too many tears and heard too many cries of innocence. If he had any sympathy, it was for those who were forced into wrongdoing by threats from organised crime gangs, or else by desperate poverty. He had seen plenty of that, but here sat a well-dressed white woman, returning from a week in Sun City, with a business class ticket to a destination halfway across the world, smuggling what could be a million dollars' worth of blood diamonds. If compassion had been in his makeup, he would not be wasting it on a person such as this.

He said: "You won't know this, but the nickname for the Women's Correctional Facility in Johannesburg is also Sun City. Ironic, hey? You won't see much sun, but there's gambling and the inmates are very like the wild animals on the Madikwe Reserve."

IT WAS the night of the new moon, when its dark side faces the earth and the cold, rocky satellite becomes all but invisible in the night sky. In the darkness on earth, the inky waters of the Mediterranean gently lapped upon the rocky shoreline of the suburb of Gargaresh, twelve kilometres west of the centre of Tripoli, Libya. The blackness of the sea and sky stifled the weak light from the few lampposts along the sea front. The night effectively concealed the approach of the eight-metre-long, open fishing boat that was slowly approaching the land.

Between the shore and the coast road lay an old nine-hole golf course that had been built by expat oil workers on top of a former rubbish tip. There, the oilmen could play a few basic layouts, using compact oil and sand 'browns' as putting surfaces. Like most of the infrastructure of the once-fashionable suburb, the golf course had fallen into disrepair, following the evacuation of the expats after the death of Gaddaffi over a decade before.

The evening, and the situation favoured the arrival of Jamal and his group of six heavily armed fighters, who crouched low in the boat, their hearts beating fast. Jamal was now in his early twenties and had grown up in Libya, knowing nothing but a country at war with itself. His father had been exiled during

Jamal's early teens, but had reappeared several years ago, backed by the Americans, to become a militia leader in western Libya.

In Jamal's opinion, the man who had returned to a hero's welcome, had now capitulated to the Islamist Government of National Unity, the UN-recognised GNA. He had turned soft and become more interested in the money to be made from helping the big oil companies protect their operations across the western deserts; had opted for an easy life and lost touch with what mattered most to his country. Jamal was angry and believed it was now his turn to fight for the principles their family had once held dear.

He knew the GNA could not survive without the Turks, linked to them through their common affiliation to the Muslim Brotherhood. Turkish influence had now permeated the government of Libya. In exchange for weapons and protection from General Boutros's breakaway rebels in the east of their country, the cowards in Tripoli had given the Turks the right to exploit the oil in Libyan territorial waters and allowed the promotion of political Islam.

Outraged by the meddling of these foreigners, Jamal had joined a group, the Free Libyan Militia, who sought to rid the country of this Turkish influence and move to a government based on a more liberal, modernist view of Sharia. Truth be told, they had more in common with the army in the east than those in power in the west of Libya, but loyalty to his family would never allow Jamal to join the Libyan National Army of General Boutros.

Jamal's aim that dark, moonless night was to strike a blow against the Turks and rid Libya of one of the most high-profile foreign representatives in the country, Hakan Toprak. He was a known powerbroker and an associate of Jamal's father. Everyone in the Libyan oil business knew Toprak. It was he who had negotiated the handover to Ankara of Libya's rights to exploration and exploitation of the seabed around her shores. His death would be a blow to Turkey that would reverberate throughout the Mediterranean. Of this, Jamal was certain.

Life in Tripoli was always difficult and, at times, perilous. If General Boutros's troops were not bombarding the outskirts, the militias would fight between themselves, harassing and bullying neighbourhoods so as to extend their territories. Some militias protected their enclaves from the criminal gangs who were given to carjacking and kidnapping. Ironically, these 'protected' areas were the ones Libyans considered the safest to live in.

In Gargaresh, the Tripoli Deterrence Force had made the district relatively secure and that was why Jamal and his group had arrived by sea. It would have been impossible for them to make their way through the checkpoints and grid of residential streets unobserved. It was crucial that they arrived at Hakan Toprak's residence without the Deterrence militia being altered to their presence.

Jamal saw the skipper's mate at the bow signal to cut the engine. The mate lowered himself over the side of the boat, gasping in the cold, chest-high seawater. He took the bow line and towed them nearer to the shore. When the water was waist deep, he said: "OK, that's as near as we can get."

Jamal turned and saw the tense young men lined up behind him.

"Weapons and rucksacks above your heads. We gather at the top of the beach, under the carpark."

Two streetlights shed a sickly orange light over the entrance to a small concrete parking area on the edge of the golf course. The short drop down from it to the beach lay in deep shadow.

One by one, the young men slid into the chilly sea and Jamal handed them their automatic weapons and rucksacks, which they held high as they waded onto the rocky foreshore. He peered across the golf course and along the coastline. It was early in the morning. Other than the occasional car making its way down the local road, it was quiet.

Satisfied all was as it should be, Jamal raised one fist and said to the skipper: "Be ready to move quickly when we return. All hell will break loose!"

"May Allah be with you. *Inshallah!* I'll be here."

Jamal entered the water and the skipper handed him the long tube of the grenade launcher. He gingerly made his way ashore, struggling to keep his balance, as he crossed the rocks towards the golf course. Here, the guys were stripping off their sodden shorts and trainers changing into dry jeans and boots, taken from their rucksacks.

They had located Toprak's house by following him from his offices in Tripoli and then doing screen prints from Google Earth. Like all houses in Tripoli, this one was surrounded by a high wall and the entrance was via a heavy steel gate, secured with a chain and padlocked from the inside. The walls were covered with razor wire and inside the compound they expected to encounter armed guards and possibly dogs. They guessed the guards from the private security firm that protected the villa would either be asleep or lounging around watching DVDs or late-night television. The demand for night-time security was so great here, the quality of those providing it was notoriously poor.

Jamal hunkered down next to the boy he knew as Marwan.

"OK, when you're ready. Text me when you're in. Remember, wait for the signal before you start the engine."

Marwan nodded. With a last glance around at his nervous accomplices, he casually shouldered his rucksack, climbed up the bank onto the golf course and went across the car park in search of a suitable vehicle. It did not take him long to find one of the sort he had in mind, a Toyota flat-bed truck. He knew the make and model and exactly how to break in and get it started. The Toyota's engine had good torque, chunky tyres and a tow bar.

He used a 'slim jim' tool to slide through the window seal and release the car door. The alarm immediately started to honk, urgently and loudly. He quickly put his hand under the dash to locate the onboard diagnostics port used by garage technicians. He attached a coding device to disable the alarm, unlock the other doors and start the engine. The whole process took less than fifteen seconds. He sat quietly in the driver's seat and waited until he was certain nobody was coming to investigate the alarm. Then, he started the engine.

He drove the car slowly around the block, to warm it up and get a feel for the vehicle. When he was happy all was in good order, he drove down one of the wider dirt streets that led to the golf course. He stopped outside Toprak's large house with its high, black steel gate, secured by a metal chain. There were no lights on in the house or garden and up and down the street everything appeared quiet.

He texted Jamal's phone.

*Ready. All good.*

After several minutes, he saw several crouched figures hurrying over the golf course and across the road, keeping to the shadows. They made their way up the dirt road towards him and stood, weapons in hand, with their backs pressed against the high walls, either side of the gate. He watched as Jamal took a rucksack from one of the older boys and unfurled a length of chain, which he doubled up and threaded through the handles on both leaves of the gates. Marwan then started the engine and backed the truck towards them. Jamel took a shackle from his pocket and quickly secured the loops of chain to the truck's tow bar. He banged twice on the roof and ran towards the gates, taking up his place nearest to the entrance.

Marwan revved the engine and the truck lurched forward. Its wheels spun madly, tyres smoking, engine screaming, sending up a spray of grit and stones that loudly clattered against the gate. All pretence at staying undercover was now gone. Lights started coming on in windows all over the street. Jamal knew they had only minutes in which to complete their task.

The Toyota strained and heaved, the chain went taut, then finally, the gate buckled and the hinges were ripped away from the stone pillars. The Toyota shot forward, pulling the metal gates behind it, colliding head on with the high stone boundary wall of the house opposite. Marwan had not put on a seat belt and his evening ended abruptly as his head slammed into the windscreen, snapping his neck. Later, Jamal was to consider him the lucky one.

The shock of the Toyota smashing into the wall stunned the entire team, who all hesitated, staring at the crumpled truck, steam pumping out of the radiator. Their hesitation probably saved their lives, as at the exact moment they should have been storming the entrance, through the gap left by the missing gates, a hail of high-calibre bullets from several automatic weapons was fired from the windows of the upper storeys.

They cowered outside in the street, unable to charge the house. They waited for the right moment. Jamal, who had a loaded RPG launcher over his shoulder, poked the weapon around the corner, aiming to fire at the front door of the house. As soon as the tip of the weapon appeared, another stream of bullets forced him back. They started looking at each other, realising the futility of the attack. The eldest of them, Ramzi, shouted from the other side of the gateway: "Jamal, we can't get in! We should run – now!"

But Jamal could not countenance such loss of face. He had not come this far, and spent so much money, to fail now.

"Wait! I'll fire and we go in after three!"

He counted, then leaped from behind the pillar, steadied himself and fired the RPG. Bullets seemed to bounce around him but one sailed straight into his shoulder, spinning him around. As he screamed in pain, he did not see the grenade blow in the front door and smash windows across the front of the house. He did manage to lift his head high enough to see his team fleeing down the dirt road, back towards the golf course, just as three Tripoli Deterrence Force 'technical' vehicles sped past the house, armed militia fighters hanging on to the rear decks.

He lay there, as four armed Turkish soldiers appeared, through the smoking wreckage of the porch, looking down the sights of their weapons as they carefully started a sweep of the front yard. A window opened on the first floor and a heavily moustached man, wearing a white singlet, looked out. His eyes met Jamal's, who heard him shout something in Turkish to the soldiers. The man watched as the young Libyan was dragged to his feet. Despite the excruciating pain from his wounded shoulder, they bent his arms behind his back and roughly secured them with a plastic tie. One soldier then pivoted on his feet and rammed his fist hard into Jamal's solar plexus, a blow that bent him double. The soldier followed it up with a knee planted firmly in the wounded man's face.

Down the road, on the golf course, there was the sound of heavy machine gun fire, as the Brownings mounted on the back of the technicals cut down the remaining boys trying to run, adding their blood to the oil and sand of the 'browns'.

# CHAPTER 3
# ARTICLE IN MALTA TELEGRAPH

Reporter: Amy Halliday
2 June 2021

*Turkey and Greece in dispute over territorial waters*

Turkey has submitted a series of claims to the United Nations in an attempt to establish Exclusive Economic Zones in the eastern Mediterranean. These conflict with applications already made by Greece for zones in the same area. An Exclusive Economic Zone is an area recognised by the UN Law of the Sea, which gives a sovereign state special rights to explore and use marine resources, namely oil, gas and wind energy.

The Turkish claims include a sea zone extending west of the Aegean Island of Rhodes and south of Crete. They were made in an official letter sent by Turkey's Permanent Representative to the UN, and reflect Ankara's policy of establishing a 'Blue Homeland'.

Turkey has already angered the Greeks by signing an agreement in principle with the Government of National Accord in Tripoli, Libya, to carve up Greece's oil- and gas-rich waters between them – despite the *fact this area is already recognised by the UN as a Greek Exclusive Economic Zone.*

*Turkish Special Energy Envoy, Hakan Toprak, announced earlier this month that a drilling vessel will start oil exploration operations immediately south of the Greek island of Crete 'within three to four months'.*

# CHAPTER 4
# GEORGE ZAMMIT
## BIRKIRKARA, MALTA

GEORGE'S WIFE, Marianna, turned the knob on the gas ring and a strong jet lit under her dented, aluminium pasta pan. In itself, an everyday occurrence but, in Malta it had only been a year or so since the whole of the island had started to enjoy the convenience of cheaper Libyan gas, piped directly into their homes. Before that, the population had to lug heavy green gas canisters up staircases and along corridors, scraping their shins and bruising their toes.

Marianna was only too aware of this. Every time she approached the hob, it reminded her of how badly her husband, George and her whole family, had been treated on his return from Libya, where he had more than played his part in securing this wonderful amenity for the island.

The formerly exalted Superintendent George Zammit was now merely Inspector George Zammit again. His wife felt the shame of it keenly. Unable to hold her head up in the high street, Marianna was certain that, behind her back, her neighbours talked of little else but the humiliation the Zammits had suffered. More importantly, George's demotion in rank meant she no longer received the prestigious invitation to the Police Commissioner's Garden Party, or to the Christmas Drinks event held at the best hotel in Valletta. She had protested loud and hard at the unfairness of it all, but her husband seemed serenely unperturbed by the turn of events.

In fact, he had been left with little choice by Assistant Commissioner Gerald Camilleri, but to accept a two-year secondment to MalTech Energy, where he had worked alongside his friend, Abdullah Belkacem, and the woman Abdullah referred to as 'the Lady Mantis', Natasha Bonnici. After some manoeuvring, MalTech Energy had joined forces with the American oil companies to establish the VertWay gas pipeline from Libya to Malta, and George's role had been to manage the immense deposit of Libyan dinars Natasha had stolen from the Russians, her former partners in the venture. The annexed funds were used to support Abdullah's militia in protecting the wells and pipelines in the desert.

All had gone well. Six months ago, at the end of his two years of secondment, George had demanded that Camilleri reinstate him in the Malta *Pulizija*, so he could return home to Malta. He had, however, made it clear that he did not wish to go back to working directly for Camilleri, in his Organised Crime and Anti-Money Laundering Command. For too many years, he had been manipulated by the AC who, besides presiding over police business, quietly ran the affairs of the island on behalf of a variety of interests, the most prominent being the Family, a shady organised crime group based in Milan, but also with a presence in Malta. Following a bloody coup, several years previously, the Family was now headed by the same Natasha Bonnici who ran MalTech Energy.

Over the years, George and Camilleri had been involved in many investigations where the senior officer had steered events and outcomes in favour of those he served, which were not always as stipulated in the *Pulizija*'s Code of Ethics. Camilleri had come to accept that George's preference for a quiet life meant it was unlikely he would turn whistleblower and upset the delicate balance that had arisen between them. However, he was not about to take any snub to his Organised Crime Command lying down, and made his point by agreeing to accept George back in the *Pulizija* only in the rank of Inspector, in the distinctly unglamorous Community Policing section.

In fact, this position suited George perfectly and he was happy breezing around, liaising with the various councils, charities and special-interest groups, listening to people's concerns and feeding them back up the line. He always had time to return home for lunch and, afterwards, could usually find thirty minutes for a short nap in his chair, in the shady back yard. Sometimes, during his after-lunch snoozes, he would journey back through the deserts of Libya, to gunfights with ISIL militants, imprisonment in a concrete hut in the Chadian wilderness, or else a perilous crossing of the turbulent Mediterranean Sea. But then he would wake and hear the gentle buzzing of insects, Marianna chatting in the kitchen to their daughter Gina, and the neighbour's radio, playing increasingly incomprehensible 'popular' music. With a sigh of relief, George would rouse himself and head off to a school, to deliver a short presentation on the evils of drugs to an audience of bored teenage students or talk to a dazed-looking group of recently arrived migrants about their duties as prospective Maltese citizens.

George was happy and the night terrors from his adventures over the past few years had started to recede. So, it came as a surprise when his mobile rang and he saw the name 'Abdullah Belkacem' pop up on the screen. He could tell immediately that something was wrong. His smile of pleasure on seeing his old friend's name swiftly faded as he realised Abdullah was not making a social call.

"My friend, George! It has been too long since we talk, no? How are you and the good lady wife?"

But there was a shakiness in Abdullah's voice and a fake *bonhomie* that belied this apparently jovial greeting.

"Abdullah, how's it going in Libya? And where are you… Marsabar?"

"Yes. Yes, I am home. George, I am sorry to call with bad news but, once more, I must plead for your help. I wish to talk about better things, but I have problems and they are all I can think about."

George heard the distress in his friend's voice.

"Mela, tell me what's up. What can I do?"

George and Abdullah had known each other for nearly six years, over which time their friendship had been tested, and endured, on several occasions. When in Libya, George had often stayed with Abdullah and his wife, Rania, and had happily worn the traditional male Berber dress for men of long cotton, hooded tunic, the *djellaba,* plus a *cheche,* a Tuareg cloth turban. With his oiled beard and desert tan, he had enjoyed walking alongside Abdullah, two Berber brothers together.

Now he heard Abdullah sigh deeply, as he braced himself to tell his friend what was on his mind.

"It is my stupid boy Jamal. He has been arrested – they've taken him to Abu Salim. You know how bad that is? I am sick to the stomach and Rania... she has not stopped crying for three days. And, of course, it is all my fault!"

George inhaled sharply. Abu Salim was Tripoli's infamous, high-security prison where inmates all too often disappeared and unspeakable acts took place. A journey to Abu Salim was a fate every Libyan dreaded. In Gaddaffi's time, in one terrible day, the regime had murdered over a thousand prisoners, an event only discovered when a surviving inmate recalled being ordered to wash the wristwatches that had been removed before the shootings began. He had counted approximately twelve hundred of them.

"What has he done, Abdullah?"

"Oh, the stupid boy got it in his head that the Turks were taking over our government. He thinks they would bring the Sharia to Libya and cut down freedoms for the young. He and some friends, they give themselves a name, you know? They say we are 'the Free Libyan Militia', or some such, and attack the house of Hakan Toprak, the Turkish Special Energy Envoy. It is very bad. He is important man."

George was stunned.

"Mela, Abdullah, no!"

"Yes, George. His friends died, only Jamal lived. Toprak's house was filled with Turkish soldiers. Stupid boy! I could have told him the Turk would never rely on a few sleepy security guards."

"And Toprak?"

"He lives. No Turks were injured."

"That's something."

"But my boy is in Abu Salim! He will die in there. They will shoot him for what he has done – but I cannot even think about that. What I fear the most is what will happen to him before death. Libyans can be cruel, but Turks are worse."

"I'm so sorry, but I don't see how I can help. What can I do? I am just a policeman in Malta."

"George, you must find a way…"

At that moment, the phone was snatched away from Abdullah and, after a pause, George heard Rania speaking to him. George knew her well. He liked and respected her. She was the strong and steadying hand that balanced Abdullah's often impulsive behaviour.

"George, are you there?"

"Yes, Rania, I'm sorry for your troubles."

She wavered briefly, but had the strength to gather herself together.

"Listen, George. You know the minds of stupid Berber men; they think everything can be solved by guns and fighting. Abdullah taught this to Jamal. It should be him that is in Abu Salim, not the boy. He is to blame for all this. Now we must think, George! How can we get our son out? You know the old policeman and the Lady Mantis – both have important friends in our country. You must try to find a way to get them to help us."

"Mela, Rania, Jamal tried to kill Hakan Toprak – the most

important Turk in Libya. You know the influence he has! He brings money, weapons – everything. The government can't let Jamal walk free. If they did, Toprak would kill him, himself."

"We get Jamal out and we look after the Turk. George, we have no one else to ask. If we do not find a way, I fear Abdullah will storm the prison himself."

George knew his friend well and could see that as a definite possibility.

They talked for an hour as Marianna busied herself around him, trying to listen in on the conversation. When they had finished speaking and George collapsed back in a chair in the kitchen, his wife rounded on him. She was no friend of Abdullah, whom she correctly blamed for leading, cajoling, or forcing her husband into trouble, on more than one occasion.

"I heard most of it. Sounds like he got what he deserved. Like father, like son. Don't think you're going to do anything foolish, George. You're not going back to Libya – over my dead body do you ever go near that place again! Things are starting to get back to normal here and you're not doing anything to damage your chances of promotion. I want to be a superintendent's wife again!"

George picked up his phone and left the house to walk to the small park at the end of their street. He sat on a bench in the shade of an ancient gum tree, sheltering from the early-summer heat, and passed his phone from hand to hand, searching for the courage to make the call.

# CHAPTER 5

# NATASHA BONNICI
## CASTELLO BONNICI, MALTA

NATASHA BONNICI LAY BACK against the blue-and-white striped cushions of the sun lounger, adjusting her large floppy hat and oversized dark glasses. She towelled her long, wet hair and dabbed her face, noticing Luke blatantly ogling her from the nearby poolside table. She had just finished her morning swim. She lay stretching out her long limbs, beads of water glistening along the lines of her body, slowly drying in the June sunshine.

"God, I hate having to leave with you lying there, looking like that!" he said.

Natasha smiled at him and said: "I think you've enjoyed enough of me for one weekend, don't you?"

She liked Luke van der Westhuizen, but only as much as she liked Earl Grey tea or cashmere sweaters. Meaning, she could take him or leave him. He was a fast and energetic lover, which suited Natasha, and he had houses in Johannesburg and Turkey, where he kept his young, good looking Azerbaijani wife, which also suited her.

Luke van der Westhuizen, however, was fascinated by powerful, mysterious Natasha Bonnici and had fallen completely under her spell. As one of the most eligible women in the European business community, Natasha could have had her pick of partners, married or not. For the time being, she had chosen Luke.

He was an unsophisticated South African, originally from a farm south of Johannesburg, who had made his way in the diamond and gold mines of Gauteng province. Luke quickly realised that selling the stones was easier and more lucrative than digging for them in the earth's depths. He was short and stocky, with a wide chest and shoulders and the pronounced forearms and calves of the rugby forward he had once been. His chunky body, head of blond hair and ruddy complexion made an odd contrast to Natasha's slender build, olive skin and cascading, glossy black locks.

Luke was well known on the wrong side of Africa's diamond trade and had access to rough, uncut diamonds from Angola, Liberia, Ivory Coast and the Democratic Republic of Congo. Despite efforts to stop the trade in illegal diamonds, there was still good business to be done in unregulated gems. He took the stones to the back streets of Surat, Western India, or to one or two less scrupulous shops in Ramat Gan, Tel Aviv. There, they were cut and polished and, if necessary, legitimised with fake certification. Most of his buyers did not ask too many questions about provenance. In fact, most of his buyers did not ask any questions at all, as the majority exchanged Afghani heroin in payment for the stones. He preferred the processed product to the bulkier opium or poppy straw. Luke took the heroin and concealed it in freight containers in Istanbul's Haydarpaşa port. From there he shipped it via the Suez Canal to Durban, to be distributed across South Africa.

Heroin for gems diversified the risk for his buyers and avoided the difficulties of 'washing' large amounts of cash. Luke's payment in heroin was multiplied tenfold when he sold the drugs on to gangs in South Africa.

Of all the world's riches, diamonds are the easiest to smuggle, due to their size and the fact they cannot be detected by airport scanners. Luke would casually pack them in cotton wool and hide them inside a false bottom of his briefcase or stitch them into the lining of his jacket. He never used 'mules' as they were unreliable and, like all operations involving people, too much trouble. He was well known at Oliver Tambo International Airport and paid good money to ensure that whenever he walked through security, it was without interference.

Smuggling heroin was trickier, and his deep connections with the Turkish police and administration were a fundamental part of his distribution chain. That was why he lived in Istanbul, in the bijou district of Cihangir. He had to keep his powerful friends close and, in the turbulent world of Turkish politics, that meant being amongst them, and changing them as their fortunes rose and fell. It was no coincidence that he had a Muslim wife. Although he had never attended the mosque, he was well versed in and respectful of Islamic custom and tradition.

The final piece of his business involved Natasha Bonnici, who had agreed, for a price, to launder his profits through the Family's Malta-based i-gaming platform, BetHi. Natasha had formerly been CEO of this company, having ousted her ex boyfriend, Nick Walker, to prove to the Family's governing body in Milan that she was ready for advancement. She had thanked them for their recognition of her abilities by seizing control of the organisation, some two years later, in a process that left most of the old guard dead.

It was time for Luke to leave and he reluctantly rose from his chair. He took one last lingering look at Natasha and then allowed his gaze to drift across the hills of northern Malta, towards the church spires and domes on the neighbouring island of Gozo. He couldn't decide which sight pleased him more.

They were at the Castello Bonnici, the two-hundred-and-something-year-old family seat that nestled quietly in the hills behind a tiny village called il-Wardija.

"Putting the pool in was a fantastic idea. You say your father was against it?"

"Yes, for years he argued it would spoil the traditional feel of the *castello*. You've seen inside, it has hardly been touched in two centuries."

The venerable building had long, polished stone corridors and unplastered limestone-block walls, hung with tapestries interspersed with suits of armour. The double front doors were made from thick hardwood, with black iron nails securing the planking. The vaulted entrance hall contained a grand marble staircase, which split into two, halfway up, accessing the galleries running around the first and second floors. Its crenellated towers and adjacent chapel gave the *castello* a fortified look, though in reality it had always served as a family home.

The way in which Natasha had taken control of the Family had shocked her father. Marco Bonnici was appalled by the ruthlessness of her behaviour. In the wake of the takeover he had chosen to retire, leaving the island to spend his days developing their estate in Serbia. He had sold the *castello* and its contents to an unknown buyer, not realising that the purchaser was a company owned by his daughter. Natasha felt that gave her the right to please herself as to how she chose to modernise the property. She didn't feel bound by its history, or anything else for that matter.

Luke checked his watch.

"OK, Simon is coming for me in five minutes. Let's decide: what shall we do with the woman in Jo'burg? It's been three days. They can't hold her forever."

"Why not?"

"Because she's done nothing, that's why!"

"But she's a gem smuggler."

"I've told you, she's not. It's not an offence to travel with an envelope full of cushion-cut cubic zirconia – they're fakes!"

"Oh, come on, just a little longer?"

"I can't, I'll lose the goodwill of my contact at Oliver Tambo – any longer and I'm messing him around. Enzokuhle Lubanzi would have known those stones were fake the minute he saw them. When I get back, I'm going to make a call, all right?"

Natasha tutted in disappointment.

"Oh, OK. Do it if you must."

"Hey, a thank you would be nice. I went to some trouble to set that up for you."

"I think I've thanked you several times this weekend already."

He looked at her, acknowledging the truth of the statement.

"So, are you finally going to tell me why you hate this girl so much?"

"I don't hate her. I don't even know her. It's her boyfriend who needs to be taught a lesson."

"What for? What's his crime against the beautiful Natasha Bonnici?"

"He preferred her to me."

Luke was taken aback.

"Really? I don't see how that's possible! I'd better watch my step then."

She lifted her sunglasses and smiled broadly at him.

"You don't know how right you are."

At that moment, Simon, Natasha's head of security, arrived and stood waiting, holding Luke's well-travelled cabin bag. Moments later they were driving down the hill towards St Paul's and taking the coast road towards the airport. Sitting in the back of the car, Luke thought about that last conversation and admitted to himself, it had mildly unsettled him.

Natasha had decided to stay on the terrace for a little longer, determined to finish this week's *Economist*, when she noticed her phone was vibrating on the wicker table next to her.

She picked it up to see the name of the caller and smiled to herself. Her instinct was to reject the call, but curiosity got the better of her.

"George, how nice to hear from you. I've missed our little chats. What can I do for you?"

GEORGE WAS SITTING at his desk, so engrossed in a new road-safety proposal for a pedestrian crossing in one of Malta's busy villages, that he did not notice his immediate superior, Superintendent Lino Grech, entering his office.

He told George, with raised eyebrows, that Assistant Commissioner Camilleri was looking for him. There was a time when such a message would have thrown George into a total panic, while he tried to guess what fresh angle the slippery Assistant Commissioner might be pursuing. George was older and wiser now, and able to put such worries to one side. He had no doubt, however, he was going to receive a dressing down for having the cheek to make a direct appeal to Natasha Bonnici for help in securing Jamal's release. George had accepted Camilleri was bound to find out about the call sooner or later. He just had not expected it to take less than twelve hours.

He had rung Natasha almost immediately after speaking to Abdullah and Rania. She had listened without interruption. Once George had stopped talking, there was a short, unnerving silence until she said: "OK, let me get this right. Abdullah's son, Jamal, leads a team of militants on a raid, into the centre of Tripoli, armed to the teeth, and tries to kill my friend and valuable business associate, Hakan Toprak. Correct?"

"Mela, yes, that's about what happened."

"And you want *me* to help get the boy out of prison?"

George had gulped. Even as he was explaining the situation to her, he had realised that it sounded like a lost cause.

"Umm. Yes, that's about the size of it. His parents are frantic! They're sick with worry that he's being held in Abu Salim, it's a dreadful place."

"George, it's only because you looked after my affairs in Libya so well that I haven't slammed the phone down on you already. I'm surprised the boy hasn't been put up against a wall and shot. That would be a perfectly reasonable outcome, considering what he's done. Is there anything else you want to say before we finish this conversation?"

"Er, no, Miss Bonnici, I don't think so."

"Tell Abdullah Belkacem that you did your best, and I respect your loyalty in trying. But please, say to him from me that he should examine his parenting skills to find out where he went wrong, because at some point, he obviously did."

George had immediately rung Abdullah back, who had listened in silence as he recounted the conversation with Natasha, omitting the bit about the need to examine his parenting skills.

George had felt his friend's hopes deflate during the call and, even though she had said nothing, could sense Rania listening, probably crouching next to the handset. With a heavy heart, when there was nothing more to be said, George put down the phone, disappointed he could do nothing to help them. He thought about Natasha's response and, in his heart, realised that any hope she would be inclined to help had been badly misplaced.

As he climbed the staircase to Camilleri's large, austere corner office, he was reconciled to taking the rebuke he knew was coming, and then he would try to put the Belkacems' misery out of his mind. In many ways, the situation was all the boy's own making and probably a tragedy common to many families in that war-torn country. Attacking Hakan Toprak, of all people, was a suicidal thing to do.

Camilleri was sitting at the head of his large rosewood conference table. The windows were open and the faintest smell of iodine and salt wafted in on the breeze from Marsamxett Harbour below. George had noticed that over the years, as Camilleri had aged, he seemed to have shrivelled slightly. George tried to work out how old he was, hopeful that retirement might soon beckon.

Camilleri's head had become more skull-like; his grey hair had thinned until his pate showed beneath it. His pale blue eyes had gone slightly milky and developed a pinkness around the lids, while his lashes had all but disappeared. He was immaculately dressed, as always, in a grey, double-breasted suit, and, although George could not see them under the table, he knew the black Grenson brogues would be polished, mirror bright. It occurred to him that the Assistant Commissioner was starting to fade and, for a moment he felt that, maybe, the hint of threat his superior carried was diminishing with him.

It was known that Camilleri had refused the role of Commissioner of Police when it had been offered to him, pleading that the political and ceremonial aspect of the job would detract from his ability to effectively lead the fight against crime on the island. George knew enough about Camilleri to realise that he could never move too far away from the operational side of the job, as too many people depended on the delicate balance he maintained in upholding order on the island, if not always the law.

The Assistant Commissioner directed him to sit at the bottom of the table. Camilleri sat three metres away, right at the head. The lack of subtlety in the arrangement was not lost on George.

"Well, *Inspector*, you appear to have overstepped yourself."

George accepted the snub. Being addressed as 'Inspector', no longer 'Superintendent', was a deliberate ploy to remind George how much power Camilleri retained over him. But he was not going to be intimidated.

"I'm sorry, I don't understand," he said firmly.

"You telephoned a private citizen and asked her to involve herself in perverting the course of justice in a foreign country. That probably justifies my referring you to the Internal Affairs section, would you not say?"

George had not seen that coming and started stuttering.

"Mela... I... I... didn't see it quite like that."

"No, probably not. Tell me, George, how did you see it?"

"I w-was trying to help Abdullah Belkacem. His son is in Abu Salim, you know. It's bad."

"I know. He is charged with terrorism offences and attempted murder. He is most likely facing a death sentence and you are trying to get him set free. Not very policeman-like, is it?

"I am tempted to suspend you, refer you to Internal Affairs and recommend you be dismissed. Obviously, you would lose your right to a pension, as well as suffering the humiliation of being drummed out of the force. I am sure your wife would be most understanding of the predicament your unsuitable friendship has landed you in."

George was stunned.

"I don't understand! Why would you do that?"

"Because it is what you deserve, George. Did you forget about consulting me? Did it not occur to you to share your dilemma, to seek wise counsel? That would have been the most sensible course, would it not? But no, instead you rang one of the island's most powerful women and tried to get her to bend the rules of a foreign country, so you could ride to the rescue of your friend."

"I'm sorry. I didn't think."

George was crushed. Surely Camilleri was not serious. What would he tell Marianna?

"No, you did not, did you? What did you think Natasha Bonnici would do, in any case? Speak to Toprak and get him to forgive the man who tried to kill him with a rocket-propelled grenade? Send him home with a slapped wrist and a stern warning? Come on, George, not even you are as stupid as that!"

He felt diminished. The Assistant Commissioner glared at him from the top of the table. Any suspicion George had entertained about Camilleri's powers fading vanished, as the AC's pink-rimmed eyes fixed him with a viperous stare.

Camilleri broke the spell by standing and walking over towards the open window. He turned and faced back into the room. George looked at him piteously from the far end of the table.

"There was a time, George, when I thought you had changed. You acquitted yourself well in Libya, and your two years with MalTech Energy, reining in Belkacem, were a success. I admired you for that. Your heroics in the desert, if reports are to be believed, were remarkable. Which only makes me more disappointed that all you have done since your return is to idle away your time in Community Affairs."

Camilleri paused and looked out of the window at the hundreds of yachts and power boats, gently rocking off the pontoons.

"So, you really want to help your friend, Belkacem, get the threat of a death sentence lifted and move his son out of Abu Salim?"

George slumped in his seat, recognising how unlikely it sounded.

"Yes, I do," he mumbled.

"Well, it may be that Natasha Bonnici is able to help, after all. She is a good lateral thinker, that woman. There is something she needs doing, apparently. A glimmer of hope on the horizon, George, but everything comes at a price. Are you prepared to pay it?"

"I don't know, do I? I mean, how much is it? What's the price?"

"Well, for once, this is nothing to do with me. Others are

taking the lead but, if you want this wretched boy to dodge a bullet, it is the only chance you and Abdullah Belkacem are likely to get. The same proposal has been put to Abdullah himself. Understandably, he asked for photographic evidence of proof of life – as you say, Abu Salim does not have the best of reputations. I am told his son is being kept in one of their 'grave cells', a concrete enclosure two metres long and one metre high. Unpleasant, I would imagine."

George shut his eyes, as he imagined Abdullah's horror on learning about that. There was no choice left.

"OK, whatever it is, I'll do it. Tell me."

"I have already said, I really do not have the details, it's very hush-hush. Neither does Abdullah, nor does he know that you are involved. Get packed, George. You leave for Libya tomorrow. In Tripoli, you will meet with Ali Taher Fetori of the Libyan Resources Corporation. There is a room reserved for you at the Athina, so it is not all bad. Tell Marianna it is a desert-skills refresher course.

"I will send a car at noon. Chin up. This is your chance to be a hero again!"

# CHAPTER 7
# LUKE VAN DER WESTHUIZEN
## MALTA INTERNATIONAL AIRPORT

Natasha's bodyguard dropped Luke off at the main terminal of Malta's only airport and watched him swagger off, into the building, without a word of thanks. Like a lot of short, well-built men, Luke rolled his hips as he walked, making his short legs look slightly bowed. Simon had often wondered what on earth Miss Natasha was doing with a man like that, but he was wise enough to keep his own counsel. An ability to keep his mouth shut as well as his Polish military training and imposing physique, all made Simon Michallik admirably suited to his role of head of security at the castello.

In their own way, he and Miss Natasha enjoyed a good relationship and were relaxed in each other's company. Simon knew his place and rarely overstepped the mark. He knew Miss Natasha had a ruthless, even cruel aspect to her character and had no intention of getting on the wrong side of it.

Before Luke left Malta for his flight to Turkey, there were two things he needed to do. The first was relatively straightforward – making a call to a bank in Turkey and releasing the best part of a million US dollars to an agent who was buying a ship for a newly established charity, Rescue at Sea.

The *Samaritan* had been built forty years before, as a salvage vessel, but the four hundred-tonne, forty-metre ship, with its distinctive blue-and-yellow superstructure, had since then become a regular visitor to Malta's Grand Harbour, where it disembarked groups of maritime migrants it had rescued from the dangerous waters between Libya and Europe.

The directors of the charity that formerly owned the *Samaritan* had become tired of watching tragedy after tragedy unfold in the southern Mediterranean. They despaired of the corruption and callousness of the Libyan government and the open hostility shown to humanitarian operations by the Italian and Maltese authorities. They had conceded defeat and decided to direct their efforts, and their money, elsewhere in the world, where they might be better received. The charity was delighted, however, when it received an offer to buy the *Samaritan*. It had come from an anonymous, philanthropic South African, who had pledged to continue their good work.

The only disappointing aspect to the deal was that the purchaser had been adamant that he had a skipper and new crew ready and waiting, so was, unfortunately, unable to take on any of the existing team.

The second item on Luke's list was to take coffee with Assistant Commissioner of Police, Gerald Camilleri. Luke had asked Natasha to set up the meeting and had been coy as to why he was interested in meeting the policeman. When she pressed him for a reason, Luke had shrugged and said it was always prudent to introduce yourself to any 'movers and shakers' when the opportunity arose – who knew when it might prove useful?

Natasha had her doubts about his motives, but decided that the only way to discover more was to let the meeting play out. She had asked Gerald to report back to her and stressed that, whatever Luke said, he was not Family and nothing he did was Family business.

The two men met in the executive lounge on the second floor of the terminal and took secluded seats outside, on the shaded terrace, so Camilleri could smoke. Luke explained he was a

South African businessman with a special interest in Turkish imports and exports, who was looking to expand his area of operations.

The Assistant Commissioner listened to this nonsense politely, but without comment.

"So, that's it, Gerald. I'm looking to put a face to the name. I get the feeling nothing happens around here without you being involved and, if I get round to doing something, it might be best if we know each other."

Camilleri sat back and took a drag of his cigarette, which he held in the tips of his fingers.

"Why do I think there is something you are not telling me? Nice though it is to meet new friends and drink airport coffee, I cannot help thinking that, at some point, you are going to want something from me. I would rather know now than be surprised later."

"Natasha told me you were a wily one! Listen, I've something here. Look upon it as a 'hello' gift. If, in the future, I do happen to need some advice or legal help, then this'll help you put a face to my name."

Luke reached inside his navy blazer and pulled out a small *briefke* that he placed on the table, pushing it towards Camilleri.

The policeman did not even look at the envelope but stared at Luke, before twisting his mouth in a sour expression.

"Look, Mr van der Westhuizen, that" – he pointed to the *briefke* – "sets all my internal alarm bells ringing. It might be how you do business with the Turks, but not with me. Stay close, sir, and be careful what you do on *my* island.

"Luckily, the coffee in the executive lounge is free, otherwise I would most certainly have paid for my own."

# CHAPTER 8
# NICK WALKER
## ST JULIAN'S, MALTA

NICK WALKER SAT on the terrace of his penthouse flat overlooking picturesque Spinola Bay. This was in fact a small inlet, tracked by a busy road that followed the promenade and climbed the hill into Paceville, the island's entertainment district. Alongside the road, a solid line of apartment blocks, food outlets and hotels squeezed against the few remaining older buildings that had comprised the original fishing village.

He sat nursing a drink and talking with his guest, Amy Halliday, a journalist from the *Malta Telegraph,* with whom he had become friendly over the last four years or so. Nick and Cristina had arrived back from South Africa three days earlier, after their harrowing experience in the 'Inad' detention facility at Oliver Tambo International Airport.

He was furious about the treatment they had endured and had called Amy to asked if she was interested in doing a piece on their experience.

"So how are you both holding up?" she asked sympathetically.

"I'm OK, just bloody angry! Three days in a filthy cell, sleeping on the floor. People coming and going the whole time. I was kept in the place they use to detain people who are 'inadmissible for entry' – hence 'Inad' Facility. It's designed to hold people for a few hours – I was there for seventy-two! Cristina was sent to 'Sun City', the women's prison in Jo'burg. You can imagine what that was like! She's really screwed up. Can't bring herself to talk to you. She's taken to her bed."

"God, Nick, it sounds dreadful. How did the diamonds get into Cristina's case? Any ideas?"

"Well, they weren't real diamonds, remember – they were zirconia. Each stone would cost about twenty US dollars as opposed to fifteen hundred for a real diamond the same size. Somebody must have slipped them into the front pocket of her cabin case. It would have been easy. It's an open pouch, you know, no zip or anything, sort of where you keep a magazine or a newspaper."

"You didn't see anything or leave the case lying around?"

"No, we've been round and round that one. We've no idea how they got there."

"Did you see anybody from the embassy – lawyers?"

"No, we weren't allowed any outside contact. There was this sergeant, Lubanzi, who organised everything. He took our phones stripped and searched us... had his hands all over Cristina, down her pants, everywhere. Then he disappeared."

"What then?"

"The other guards wouldn't talk to us or even look at us. They kept saying 'Wait for Lubanzi'. One man propositioned Cristina, saying he would let her use her phone. He kept grabbing her hand and rubbing it on his crotch.

"Eventually, three nights later, while I was sleeping on the floor, I was woken, taken to the desk, given our stuff and told they had checked the diamonds and they were fakes. The airport police said I could leave and wait outside for Cristina to be brought – just like that. We weren't allowed to leave the airport so we booked the first flight out, to London, spent a night at Heathrow, got cleaned up and came back here the next day. A complete nightmare."

"Sounds like it. Also, very weird. It feels to me like a setup, designed solely to make your life unpleasant."

Nick nodded in agreement.

They sat in silence for a few moments. After another sip of her drink, Amy said: "You don't think *she's* behind it, do you?"

Nick glanced back at her to be sure they were on the same wavelength. The look on Amy's face assured him they were.

"It had crossed my mind," he admitted, with a sigh.

Amy had been persecuted by Natasha Bonnici after she had run a series of articles in the *Malta Telegraph*, investigating the ownership and sources of funding behind BetHi and MalTech Energy. The numerous court actions she had been hit with, for criminal defamation, libel and actions to protect reputation, had nearly ruined the journalist personally, and all but got her fired from the paper. Finally, she had been forced by its management to back off from her investigations, but Natasha had one final flourish, to show Amy how far she was prepared to go to silence her.

It had been late one evening when Amy had finished work at the paper and had gone to the almost empty multistorey carpark. As she had turned on her car's ignition and reversed out of the space, she was nearly overcome by choking blue smoke. She had flung the door open and fallen out, coughing violently. Almost immediately, there was a loud explosion and a blaze of metallic light surged from beneath the car. Shock waves reverberated through the solid concrete floors of the building, quickly followed by further explosions that threw blinding yellow, red and blue lights across the low ceiling. Amy had cowered, crouching against a concrete pillar, shaking like a frightened dog.

The police had said the explosion had been caused by a large firework, probably left over from a village festival and placed under the car, as part of an elaborate prank. They refused to accept it was in any way related to the ongoing legal disputes Amy was engaged in with the Bonnicis. Her car had suffered some damage to the paintwork, but otherwise was mechanically sound, so she had reluctantly driven it home.

Any doubt in her mind that the explosion was the work of Natasha Bonnici was soon dispelled when she had returned, shaken and frightened, to her apartment, much later that evening. She had hardly dared open her triple-locked front door but, when she did, the first thing she saw was a plain buff A3 envelope lying on the tiled floor. It contained a single sheet of paper with a message that simply read: 'Cease and Desist'.

Nick also had history with Natasha. He had returned from Gibraltar some years previously, at her request, to run BetHi, while Natasha took the chair of MalTech Energy and, more importantly to her, became the head of the Family. They had been lovers some years earlier, but things had gone very wrong between them when Natasha had lost her temper one night. He had made it a condition of his return from self-imposed exile in Gibraltar, that their new relationship was to remain strictly professional. The previous one had ended with him seriously injuring her with a heavy, Murano glass vase, in fear for his life, after she'd stalked him around their villa, gun in hand.

On his return to Malta, he had found that Natasha was simply not prepared to allow anybody to dictate terms to her and would not accept that he was reluctant to be drawn back into a personal relationship with her. He had started to refuse her advances and, twelve months previously, had told her that he found it impossible to run BetHi for her. To avoid her, he had taken another job with a smaller, unconnected, online gaming company.

Natasha had been beside herself with rage. Nobody had ever rejected her so comprehensively and she found the anger, disappointment and frustration almost impossible to bear. Her emotions had swung between a feeling akin to bereavement at the loss of him, to paranoia that she was hated by everybody in her life and, finally, an enduring, driving urge to destroy everything that gave Nick Walker happiness. Recently she had found out that he was involved with Cristina, daughter of Joe Cassar, who owned a chain of Maltese supermarkets. Natasha had called Nick at his new place of work and screamed down the phone at him that he would be sorry he had ever set eyes on the girl.

Amy Walker said: "You don't want this story to be purely about being wrongfully locked up in South Africa, do you? You want me to point the finger directly at Natasha Bonnici's involvement?"

"No, I don't want to cause you any more trouble in that direction, but I've no one else I can talk to about it. Amy, I'm scared and I daren't tell Cristina. Natasha could ruin me professionally, no matter where I went. I always knew that was a risk, but now she's attacking Cristina, as well as me. That's not fair – she's not involved."

"She is, though, isn't she? With you. Natasha won't be able to stand that."

"I'm thinking of leaving the island."

"How long has it been since you left BetHi?"

"About a year."

"And Cristina? How long have you been together?"

"Not long, a few months."

It's early days. Maybe Natasha will get over it sooner or later."

"I'm not so sure. Apparently, she's got a new guy. A South African."

Amy's head jerked.

"South African?"

"Yep. Coincidence, isn't it? I was hoping you could find out some more about him. What he does, who he is. If I knew it was her who set me up on the smuggling rap, that would at least be something. Not having a clue is worse."

"Aren't you tempted to tell me some specifics about her and her businesses? You know what she did to me. There's unfinished business between me and Natasha Bonnici. Give me something I can take off island, to a newspaper that won't be intimidated by her."

"Amy, d'you think I'm crazy? Don't provoke her, for God's sake. You know all too well what she's capable of." He thought for a moment. "But I'll tell you one thing – if it comes to it, I know enough to put that woman away for the rest of her life."

Amy's journalistic instincts were buzzing. She would stay close to this man, do her best to get his story – and, once she did, she could finally bring down the woman who had done her and her career so much damage. For the time being, Amy realised she had to play it cool.

"OK, let me see what I can find out about this mysterious South African. We'll see where he leads us."

# CHAPTER 9

# ARTICLE IN MALTA TELEGRAPH

*Reporter: Amy Halliday*
*15 June 2021*

**Tensions mount between Turkey and Greece over island disputes**

*Turkey has issued a formal notice of its intention to start exploring a section of the eastern Mediterranean on its continental shelf, for potential oil and gas reserves. A continental shelf is the edge of a continent lying beneath the ocean. This shelf extends from the coastline of a continent to a drop off point where the underwater edge of a continental shelf begins to rapidly slope downwards towards the ocean floor depths.*

*The United Nations Convention on the Law of the Sea stipulates that every nation's continental shelf over which they have exclusive economic sovereignty shall not be exceeding two hundred nautical miles from any given nation's coastline. Widths of continental shelves vary, but their average width is forty miles before giving way to deeper open ocean waters.*

*The NAVTEX notice serves as a warning to other vessels to steer clear of the area due to the sensitivity of the work being carried out, and signals Turkey's claim to sovereign exploration rights. The long-standing dispute arose as Greece has said the area being explored falls within its maritime boundaries, not Turkey's.*

*Greece bases its claim on the fact that it is entitled to an Exclusive Economic Zone of two hundred miles around its huge number of islands. Many of these remote and barren outposts are far distant from Athens, but near the Turkish coast. If the Greek claims were to stand, Turkey would effectively be blocked out of Mediterranean exploration. Turkey, on the other hand, argues that these islands should not form part of the Exclusive Economic Zones that are authorised to coastal states, but that their economic rights should be limited to a twelve-nautical-mile exclusion zones. Turkey claims its own rights derive from the contested area being on its continental shelf, which it says gives it rights to oil and gas deposits beneath the ocean floor.*

*The Turkish Foreign Minister has gone so far as to say: 'The Greeks talk about a continental shelf around its islands. There is no such thing around the islands, no Exclusive Economic Zone, there is no such thing. There are only territorial waters.' If the Turkish argument is accepted, the Greeks would only be able to exploit an area 12 nautical miles say, from the coast of Crete.*

*Crete is Greece's largest island and the fifth-largest in the Mediter-ranean. The Turkish argument that it does not merit an Exclusive Economic Zone, and that it sits on the Turkish continental shelf, is an assertion likely to be hotly disputed by Athens.*

# CHAPTER 10
# ABDULLAH BELKACEM
## TRIPOLI, LIBYA

ABDULLAH WAS MAKING the two-hour drive from Marsabar to the offices of the LRC, the Libyan Resources Corporation, in Tripoli. The LRC managed the oil business in western Libya. He was always cautious on leaving Marsabar, as nowhere in Libya was safe these days. Even with the backup of his own militia, it would only take one bomb, bullet or grenade for him to be be dead in an instant. A convoy of three SUVs contained his heavily armed escort and they travelled as fast as the traffic allowed, down the busy Airport Highway, towards the LRC's white cubist offices, near Tripoli's seaport.

Some years before, the UN had decreed that any sale of oil or gas not approved by the LRC, was in breach of sanctions and therefore illegal. This had infuriated the rival regime in the east of the country, run by General Boutros. He had refused to recognise the LRC and started his advance towards Tripoli, aiming to depose its Islamist government, unite east and west Libya, then take control both of the LRC and of the country's lucrative oil and gas business.

It was now the job of Abdullah's militia to police the westward Coastal Road from Tripoli to the Tunisian border, keeping it safe and free from local roadblocks and interference. More importantly, they also guarded the large coastal refineries at Marsabar and Az-Zawiyah. In the south west, he worked with the Tuareg tribes, for whom he had secured lands and political autonomy. They, in turn, guarded the wells and pipelines on the Sharara and Wafa oil and gas fields, keeping them secure from militia incursions from the Sahel.

ISIL terrorists and bandits had previously enjoyed easy pickings in this area. They would cross the borders from Chad, Mali and Niger, damaging and raiding the plants, as well as kidnapping, ransoming and harassing the workers. The Tuareg now zealously controlled those borders and the raids had all but ceased, as had the flow of migrants from the sub-Saharan countries. Abdullah's role was crucial to the LRC and, by implication, to what was left of the Libyan economy

The offices were near the centre of the city and, as Abdullah was driven there, his convoy passed uncomfortably close to Abu Salim prison. He tried to put his thoughts of what might be happening to Jamal out of his mind, but could not. After his normal business was finished, he was determined to talk with the head of the LRC, ask him to use his influence to at least arrange the transfer of his son out of the grave cell. Just the thought of it made Abdullah feel ill.

His own helplessness made him desperate. He had resolved, that if nothing could be done through the LRC, he would abandon the west of the country to the bandits and jihadi, while he attacked the jail himself, with as many men as he could muster. It had been done before; there had been mass breakouts. He had to do it there was no other option. If he did not try he would not only be failing Jamal, but also Rania. She had become listless and silent, spending her days in their darkened bedroom, stupefied by the doctor's medication. He considered it his failure as a man if he allowed his son to rot in the hellhole of Abu Salim.

Abdullah was dressed in the traditional *djellaba* and a cloth turban that looked out of place on the landing of the executive floor, which was filled with people in Western-style business suits. The earlier meeting was finishing and the suits were filing out. One or two glanced at the strange and slightly threatening figure, standing quietly by the doorway, his two bodyguards behind him.

As the crowd disappeared towards the lifts, Abdullah entered the boardroom and stopped dead in his tracks. There were three men seated at the top of the long, highly polished table. One was his usual contact, Ali Taher Fetori, the second he did not know, and the third was Hakan Toprak.

Ali immediately came to greet Abdullah and tried to usher him into the room. Abdullah shrugged off the guiding arm and stood at the door, his dark eyes blazing at Hakan Toprak.

"*As-salaam 'alykum*, Abdullah Belkacem," the Turk addressed him.

Abdullah reluctantly replied to the traditional Arab greeting: "May peace be upon you, also."

Toprak's next words were spoken evenly and calmly.

"I have not met you before, but I am well acquainted with your son."

Toprak was well built and not a particularly tall man. He had a full head of thick, black, curly hair, streaked with grey, that added several centimetres to his height. He also had a thick, black moustache, flecked with grey, that drooped over his top lip. His unblinking dark brown eyes were slightly protuberant, but he could hold any man's gaze without looking away. Abdullah knew this man's nickname was 'The Hawk', and had visualised someone entirely different. In his mind he had seen a hooked Arab nose, narrow eyes and a sinewy build, not this well-built man with the melancholic, staring eyes and luxuriant, bristly moustache.

"I am sorry we have to meet in such circumstances, as I have admired your work for some time. Please, come and sit with us. I hope I may be able to be of help," said the Turk.

Abdullah was confused and struggled to control his emotions. He had no personal reason to hate this man, yet had to quell the urge to rush at him and strangle him with his bare hands, since Toprak was the reason for Jamal's imprisonment in that hellhole. Breathing deeply, he went and sat midway down the long table.

Ali Taher Fetori nervously messed with a coffee pot while saying: "Abdullah, Toprak *bey* has a proposal for you. He is prepared to help Jamal. You should listen to what he says."

Abdullah was delighted to be able to take his anger out on someone.

"Of course, I will listen to him, you fool! Why would I not, eh?"

Hakan took control.

"Yes, I cannot forget that the boy made a good attempt to try and kill me. It cannot go unpunished, you know that. However, I can make it known that I do not seek the ultimate punishment. You do realise the usual reprisal for a crime such as this is a single bullet, fired in the prison courtyard?"

Toprak let this image sink into Abdullah's head.

"But I have sufficient influence to ensure that he avoids that fate. I can also have him removed from Abu Salim to a more appropriate facility, with a more lenient regime. That is, so long as you do a small job for me and promise not to interfere in his captivity."

Abdullah could not believe what he was hearing. *Mercy*? He had not believed the Turks were capable of such a thing.

"Hakan Toprak, Jamal is my son and his safety is the only thing I can think of. He has behaved stupidly, without my knowledge or encouragement. He has brought shame on our family and caused us much grief. I apologise for the disturbance."

Abdullah cast his eyes down and brought his hands together in front of him, to rest on the tabletop. He let his shoulders droop and paused, humbling himself before Hakan Toprak. When a suitable amount of time had passed, he briefly glanced upwards to see if the performance had won over the Turk. Toprak sat impassively, his unflinching gaze fixed firmly on the supplicant.

"I thank you for your apology, which is accepted. Now, I will tell you what I need from you, to complete our agreement."

Abdullah could not prevent a sour expression from spreading across his face. The corners of his mouth set and his eyes narrowed.

"What is it you want of me?"

"You have heard of the island of Crete, of course. But, you will not have heard of the island of Gavdos, I expect. No?"

Abdullah shook his head. Toprak continued speaking.

"It is fifty kilometres south of Crete and has only one hundred inhabitants. Now, it has twelve extra people, Greek soldiers. The Greeks are fortifying the island, so they say. It will bolster their argument for extending their territorial waters into the Ionian Sea."

Abdullah looked at the Turk and shrugged.

"And this makes your country angry? I understand, but what has it to do with me?"

"Well, it should make you angry, too, as your employer, MalTech Energy, has just been granted a concession by the Turkish government to survey the area for hydrocarbons, with the right to exploit any finds of oil or gas it may make. Signorina Bonnici has finalised the lease on a drillship. It should arrive in the area in a matter of weeks."

Abdullah looked at Ali Taher Fetori.

"Is this true?"

Ali smiled and said: "It is. The Signorina was furious when she heard the Greeks were trying to block her debut into offshore oil exploration. She wants them off Gavdos. As does Mr Toprak."

Suddenly, the penny dropped and Abdullah saw where this conversation was leading.

"So, you want me to go to this rock and clear out twelve Greek soldiers. Then, you can pretend it is nothing to do with Ankara? Hah! Do they die?"

Hakan Toprak looked at him closely.

"No. That is not how it will be. Gavdos, is in fact a Turkish island, originally part of the Ottoman Empire. Many years ago, it was known as Gondoz. The Greeks illegally took the island and now its rightful owners want it back.

"You, and fifty or so of your men, are fishermen and, more importantly, relatives of the original dispossessed Turkish residents. When you land, you make a big fuss. We will tell you how. You have some men who can sail and fish?"

Abdullah hesitated; he could neither fish, nor sail nor swim, and nor could most of his men.

Toprak pressed on.

"Never mind. We will supply you with islander names and Turkish passports. You will not harm the Greeks. You will not argue with them unless you have to. Put them in a boat and make them leave. The Turkish government will make it known we support the heroic efforts of our fishermen, to retake what is rightfully theirs. In the event of any trouble from the Greeks, we will land our own troops, together with anti-aircraft batteries and land-to-sea missiles; to fully support our fishermen."

He smiled for the first time since Abdullah had entered the room.

"Oh, and one more thing. Signorina Natasha was quite insistent on this. She says you always deliver your best work when you have the support of your special adviser, so she has arranged for him to accompany you."

Abdullah furrowed his brow in confusion.

Ali Taher Fetori jumped to his feet, saying: "Ah, yes, I'd nearly forgotten!" He hurried to a door at the back of the room. Opening it, he waved at somebody to come into the boardroom.

Abdullah's mouth fell open and a half smile glimmered across his face, when he saw the slightly portly figure of his friend, George, poke his head around the door.

Indeed, today was full of blessings. *Inshallah.*

# CHAPTER 11
# ASSISTANT COMMISSIONER GERALD CAMILLERI

## VILLA BOLOGNA, ATTARD, MALTA

GERALD CAMILLERI WAS STROLLING through the public gardens of the grand Villa Bologna, one of Malta's finest eighteenth-century Baroque houses. As he wandered, he was enjoying the gentle early-summer warmth and the faint waft of citrus scent in the orange garden. He was on his way to see the ornate Nymphaeum, a limestone grotto built into the walls in the far corner of the gardens, when he heard rapid footsteps on the rough stone paving behind him. He checked his watch and turned towards the sound.

The American CIA man, Mike Lloyd, was speed walking towards him. Camilleri glanced behind and, sure enough, there was Mike's usual security detail, casting narrowed eyes over the morning visitors to the gardens. A few years previously, Camilleri had used his considerable political connections to have the CIA officer exiled to a low-status, undesirable posting in Lima. This seemingly spiteful act was in revenge for Mike Lloyd telling the Russian security service, the FSB, about Natasha Bonnici's involvement in the theft of a container of Libyan currency bound for General Boutros in Benghazi. Mike Lloyd's information leak had led directly to the death of Sergio Rossi, a senior member of the Family and relative of the Bonnicis, who was murdered in a car bomb meant for Natasha's father, Marco.

Mike Lloyd was an abrasive, impatient black New Yorker, with short grey hair and a carefully trimmed matching beard. He always moved as though he was late for something or other. Camilleri wondered how he had enjoyed the posting in Lima.

"Gerald, you look older! They're working you too hard."

The pair did not shake hands. Camilleri gave Mike his best smile. It had a duration of less than one second.

"And how was Lima? To your liking? A suitable chance to reflect on past mistakes, perhaps?"

"It was shit, thanks. Fortunately, I wasn't there long. Quality always rises to the top, Gerald, you know I hear you turned down the Commissioner's job. Too few opportunities to keep up your fingers in the pie, or what?"

Camilleri kept a straight face, concealing the irritation he felt whenever he had dealings with this man.

"I believed I could better serve my country in my current role. So, are we going to stand here and insult each other, or is there something you want to talk about?"

"OK, look, I've come in peace, Gerald. I chose these fly-infested gardens because I remembered how much you enjoyed meetings out in the wild. See what I do for you?"

"This is hardly 'the wild!' these are the finest formal gardens in Malta and, yes, thank you, it's a most pleasant spot. So, what ails you and brings you back to our shores?"

"What ails me? Friggin' Turkey ails me, Gerald. Nothing but trouble, those people. Stirring up the Muslim Brotherhood shit with Egypt, the UAE, screwing about with NATO, getting their hands all over Libya – and, now, claiming half the eastern Med and pissing off the Greeks! They've had a chip on their shoulder since the Greeks wheeled that horse into Troy. But, the real kicker is they're going to throw us out of the Incirlik Air Base. We've been operating out of there since, well, forever! That's how we blasted ISIL in Iraq and Syria."

Mike sighed and breathed in deeply.

"Anyway, I can see you guys need them to keep the Malta pipeline deal sweet, but what's the Bonnici woman up to, acting as drilling proxy for the Turkish Energy Corporation? I ask you – drilling in the Greeks' back yard? Only going to cause more trouble."

"Hmm. So, the Turks are not your favourite people. Unlucky for them. But there is not a lot I can do about it, Mike. Independent power and all that. Why exactly does this mean we get to spend this very pleasant interlude in the Villa Bologna gardens?"

"Cos, Gerald, there is more than one way to skin a cat. While the politicians huff and puff about it and the navy boys sail their ships up and down, I've been asked to screw up the Turks' energy plans. That's why I'm back here."

He folded his arms, leaned back and smiled broadly.

"Excellent. Good to know, Mike. I trust that will not involve any interference in Malta's energy interests."

"No, you Maltese carry on doing what you're doing, you're just small fry. I'm here because I like the weather, and because I need to get my hands on that little jerk, Savi Azzopardi. You know where I can find him?"

"What on earth do you want with him? You put people into space, you spend more money on security than any other country on the planet and, yet, you want a pimply Maltese youth to do your dirty work?"

"Exactly! A 'non-attributable' pimply youth! You've missed a trick, these last few years. Our Savi's been a busy boy and moved up the hacking food chain. You've heard of a cyber group called the Prairie Dogs, I expect? A real pain in the butt. That's him, and it seems he ain't worried who the hell he upsets. In hacker HQ, he's the real deal!"

Camilleri was genuinely surprised.

"I had no idea. Very well, I will see if we can find him for you. I do feel a little guilty about your trip to Lima. Tell me, did you find time to learn any Spanish?"

# CHAPTER 12
# SAMARITAN

## MALTESE MARITIME SEARCH AND RESCUE ZONE, SOUTHERN MEDITERRANEAN

THE MALTESE MARITIME Search and Rescue Zone begins where Libyan territorial waters end and stretches from Tunisia eastwards, nearly as far as Crete. It is a vast expanse of water and when calls are picked up from desperate migrant boats by coastguards on the Italian island of Lampedusa, or from NGOs like Alarm Phone, rescue is by no means certain. Panicking migrants, using GPS-enabled smartphones, misread coordinates; changes in the weather can easily swamp an overcrowded, leaking rubber dingy; sometimes there are no vessels in the immediate vicinity able to respond to a call for help before disaster strikes. It also takes time for one of the small number of Maltese or Italian coastguard vessels to reach a stricken boat, and time is never on the side of those in trouble at sea.

The *Samaritan* was currently patrolling twenty nautical miles outside Libyan territorial waters, heading for an inflatable raft containing forty-eight adults and twelve children that had reported itself as being in difficulties. The coastguards on Lampedusa had seen on their tracking systems that the *Samaritan* was in the vicinity of the stricken raft and had asked it to lend assistance, on condition they disembarked the migrants in Malta.

For once, the captain obtained the agreement of the Maltese authorities, who had a deserved reputation of avoiding their maritime obligations towards those in trouble on the crossing from Libya. Maltese coastguards were more likely to 'push back' the rafts, or allow the unfortunate occupants to board, then return them to Libyan concentration camps, than they were to bring them to safety.

On that particular night, the weather was calm and the moon nearly full – good conditions for a crossing. However, information from the boat was that it was leaking and taking in water. The crew of the *Samaritan* were busying themselves to accommodate the new passengers, stacking plastic cases of large foil blankets, energy bars and bottled water, ready on the deck.

Despite the fact visibility was good, due to the waxing moon, the *Samaritan*'s two camcopters were flying ahead, using thermal imaging technology to try and locate the exact position of the raft. Eventually, a slight change of heading brought the *Samaritan* gently alongside the inflatable vessel, filled with desperate people, shouting and waving. The coastguards had said that, as they had no other vessel nearby, the *Samaritan* should bring the migrants aboard if they thought there was risk to life.

A gangway was lowered from the rear of the ship and the crew helped the throng of relieved, but nervous, migrants aboard. The last four, all young males, stayed seated in the raft while the rest of the passengers gratefully received their blankets, energy bars and water. Two of the *Samaritan*'s crew then assisted the youths up the gangway and took them round to the other side of the ship, down a companionway, to below decks. A third crew member jumped into the raft, took a Stanley knife from his pocket and slashed three long cuts in the raft's fabric, before quickly hauling himself back up onto the gangway. He stood and watched as the air left the floats and the weight of the engine pulled the raft under the surface. Soon, all that was left of the scene was a surge of bubbles, a scattering of sports bags and discarded clothing, and a dozen large plastic water bottles, that floated on the water.

In the cabin below, the crew helped the four youths remove their orange life jackets, which they hung on a rack beside several others. The youths then rejoined their fellow travellers on deck. Once the ship had berthed in Valletta, the forty kilograms of white heroin, with a street value of five million US dollars, which had been stitched inside the life jackets' lining, would be collected.

A call was later made from Mersin, a port in eastern Turkey, only one hundred and eighty kilometres from the Syrian border, informing Luke van der Westhuizen that the collection of the goods had been successful, and they would be into Malta within the next twenty-four hours. The new route from Turkey to southern Europe, via Benghazi, had been established. He smiled, knowing that when the *Samaritan* arrived at Boiler Quay, in Valletta's Grand Harbour, as it would do on many future occasions, the assembled officers from Frontex, Europol and the Maltese *Pulizija* would have enough work on their hands, processing the new arrivals, to worry about whatever else the ship might be carrying.

There was only thing that annoyed him. He had the full protection of the Turkish law-enforcement agencies and elements of the political establishment. It had also been easy enough to secure the cooperation of the police and customs officials in Tripoli. In Malta, the failure of Camilleri to take the bait was a problem. Luke did not understand why his gift had been so rudely refused. He intended to try and bring Natasha around to helping him. If he could only secure Malta, Luke would have built himself a fully protected new route by which to traffic Afghan heroin into western Europe. He had linked up with a well-connected Austrian, Matthäus Schober, who wholesaled the goods for him and promised Luke he could handle as much product as could be supplied.

What Luke did not realise was that Matthäus Schober's father had been a Wise Man of the Family, murdered by Natasha's Uncle Sergio some four years earlier, while she had callously plotted her way to power within the Family.

# CHAPTER 13
# GEORGE ZAMMIT

## OFFICES OF THE LIBYAN
## RESOURCES CORPORATION,
## TRIPOLI

GEORGE HAD BEEN WAITING in the small rear conference room, padding up and down and periodically pressing his ear to the door, trying to listen to what was being said. He was sure he could hear Abdullah's deep, resonant voice, but could not make out the conversation. Camilleri had told him he genuinely did not know what they wanted with him and, no matter how hard George tried, he could not imagine what his usefulness might be. Whatever it was, he knew from experience, he was not going to like it.

After what seemed like an age, Ali Taher Fetori had opened the door and ushered him through into the main boardroom. George was prepared to see Abdullah, who welcomed him with a surprised grin, but shocked to see Hakan Toprak, the Turkish energy envoy, who had a reputation in Tripoli as a ruthless operator and who currently held Jamal's fate in his hands. George was disconcerted to note that Toprak seemed to know exactly who he was.

"Well, please do not hide behind the door, Inspector George Zammit *efendim*. We are all friends here. Aren't we, Abdullah *bey*?"

Toprak half smiled at them, eyes moving from one to the other.

"No introductions necessary, I assume."

George and Abdullah looked at each other, George desperately searching his friend's face for a clue as to what was happening.

Abdullah scowled at Toprak and glanced back at George.

Toprak lifted a phone and asked somebody to bring black Turkish tea for two people. He then gathered his papers and case and, with Ali Taher Fetori, stood up and moved towards the door.

"Inspector, you no doubt want to know why you are here. Your friend knows the details of what we want and will explain them to you. Once you have heard him out, if you agree to help with our plan, tell Ali Taher Fetori and he will have Jamal Belkacem moved out of Abu Salim, into a military facility. There, he will be expected to work during the day, cleaning vehicles and such like, but he will be safe, fed and, most importantly, spared the execution otherwise scheduled for tomorrow morning. If you do not wish to assist us, that too is fine, but..."

Toprak shrugged and left the room.

The two men stood shocked to silence by what they had heard. Neither George nor Abdullah knew what to say. George turned to his old friend, whose frown had heavily creased the lines on his brow and hardened his jaw.

"What? Did he just say..."

"*Ibn al Kalb!* That son of a dog, I swear I will take his life myself... I will tear him... may his father be cursed... may his mother be taken..."

"Abdullah, shut up! What does he want us to do? What's happening here?" George interrupted.

His friend paced the room, up and down, muttering to himself and rubbing his hands together. George watched, waiting until Abdullah had calmed down a little. The double doors to the boardroom opened and a young man in a white jacket entered gingerly, balancing a tray on which stood two glass cups, a sugar bowl and a silver teapot.

Abdullah screamed at him.

"Get out, get out! May God take your soul – go!"

The boy jumped, nearly dropping the tray, then nervously, and very quickly, started backing out of the room, but collided with the closing door. The teapot toppled off the tray, clattering onto the tiled floor.

"You… I said, get out, now!"

Abdullah headed towards the boy with clenched fists and a murderous expression on his face. The boy fled, leaving a steaming puddle and a heap of silverware on the floor behind him.

There was a short silence before George said: "Mela, now you've shouted at somebody and you're feeling better, tell me, what is all this about? What do they want us to do?"

Abdullah slapped the table, hard. The unexpected noise made George flinch.

"Hakan Toprak wants us to go to Greece and take an island."

"A whole island?"

"A small island."

George waited. He did not understand.

"How small?"

"Small, with a few Greek soldiers on it."

"How many Greek soldiers?"

"Not many."

"How many is not many?"

"Not many is not a lot, eh?"

"Do they have guns?"

"By the Prophet, may peace be upon Him, 'Do they have guns?' These men are soldiers! Yes, they have guns!"

"So, there will be fighting?"

"George, please, sometimes you annoy me more than Rania does! Tomorrow, they shoot my son. If they said I must capture America, I would try and you would help me, no? So, stop with the stupid questions. How big? How many? All that. It does not matter! Not one bit!"

Abdullah grabbed a phone from the end of the table and flicked through a directory, running his long fingers down the list of names and numbers. "There." He pushed it towards George. "Ring that number and say, yes, you will go with me."

George paused. Abdullah approached him and brought his face up very close, saying softly: "If you do not do it, you will have to tell Rania that you let her son die."

George's mouth dropped open.

"No!"

"Then tell me, yes!"

He held out his phone, daring George to refuse it. With Abdullah's dark eyes drilling into him, George reluctantly took the phone and rang Ali Taher Fetori's number.

"It's George Zammit. The answer is yes, I'll go with Abdullah Belkacem."

He gave the phone back to Abdullah, whose whole posture immediately relaxed, as the tension flooded out of him. He broke into a wide smile.

"There, you see, my friend, the right thing is always easy to do. Allah makes it so." He came round to George's side of the table and clapped him, hard, on the shoulder. "It is exciting, eh? You and me, back together, guns in our arms, doing good work! It is a long time since we have enjoyed the fighting, no?"

George did not want to do any fighting. In fact, the last thing he wanted was to be thrown together with Abdullah and sent off on some fool's errand. Capturing an island, indeed.

"Which island do they want us to seize?"

"I don't know. There are many islands in Greece. It cannot be too hard."

"So, an island, somewhere in Greece? But , you don't know where?"

"Yes. Hakan Toprak is a Turk and I think he wants to make

war on Greece and for us to start it. So, can you fish and can you make go the boat?"

"I don't fish, I can't swim and I hate the sea, but you already know that. A Greek island. So, we have to take a boat there?"

"Yes, we are Turkish fishermen, coming home to take what is rightfully ours."

"And do you think there will be much fighting?"

"No! What I know of Greeks, they do not like the fighting. But do not worry. I will pick some men who like to cut throats and, when we land, I make sure we will not get the wet feet and there will be a pile of dead Greeks. No, wait, Toprak said no killing the Greeks. We must send them away. So, no killing."

"What happens then?"

"I do not know – but we stay until Toprak says 'come back'."

"Abdullah, I don't want any harm to come to Jamal, but why am I involved in this?"

Abdullah looked hurt.

"You and I are always together in such times! Remember the crossing of the sea to Malta? The ambush at the café? The shooting of Abu Muhammed... I would not be alive without you! I am Maverick and you are Goose. It is how it should be."

Abdullah laughed loudly; he loved the *Top Gun* analogy. "Maverick needs his Goose, eh? It is Allah's wish that you are here, so all will go well."

George slumped down on a chair and put his head in his hands.

"Oh, God! What have we got ourselves into now?"

Abdullah flopped into the chair next to his, emotionally exhausted.

"Yes, oh, Allah! You have saved Jamal, my friend. It was because of you, pleading with the Lady Mantis. She must have spoken to the scorpion Toprak and this is his idea of a joke, to make us do his dirty work in Greece. But, as always, we will have the last laugh, eh? We will do his work and, when we come back, we will get my son free and Rania will talk to me again. I cannot go home without him – she has said so."

Abdullah stroked his long, oiled beard and studied George, who was looking pained. He felt nervous already and it was interfering with his digestion.

Abdullah said: "I am now even more in your debt. If I live to be one hundred years, I cannot repay you."

George replied:

"As long as I live to see one hundred years, I won't care. But that's not very likely with you around."

# CHAPTER 14
# ARTICLE IN OIL AND GAS WEEKLY

*Reporter: Amy Halliday*
*2 July 2021*

*Malta company to commence exploration within disputed Libyan and Turkish maritime area*

*Turkey has further inflamed tensions in the eastern Mediterranean by granting new concessions in exploration blocks to a Maltese company, MalTech Energy.*

*The blocks in question sit within the maritime boundaries agreed between Libya and Turkey in 2019, but which Egypt has dismissed as 'illegal'. Greece has also described the accord as 'geographically absurd' because it ignores the presence of the Greek island of Crete between the coasts of Turkey and Libya.*

*Until now, the only two countries to recognise the agreement as valid are its signatories, Libya and Turkey. But Malta, which has a successful relationship with the Libyan Resources Corporation, supplying gas through the VertWay pipeline, appears to be adding its weight to the argument, recognising the Libyan/Turkish accord.*

*Greece contends the exploration blocks are within its UN- recognised Exclusive Economic Zone that stretches two hundred nautical miles from its coastline and, furthermore, that an island the size of Crete should have its own Exclusive Economic Zone. Turkey is the only country not to recognise Exclusive Economic Zones, as set out in the UN's Laws of the Sea.*

*The Chairwoman of MalTech Energy, Natasha Bonnici, said: 'We are very excited by the concession, which will give us the opportunity to exploit resources within the agreed Libyan/Turkish area. The blocks start well beyond Crete's twelve-mile territorial waters, so we see no reason for conflict.'*

*Miss Bonnici was hopeful that the drilling would start within a few weeks and said, given the heightened emotions in the area, MalTech's drillship would be accompanied by a Turkish naval frigate.*

# CHAPTER 15
# LUKE VAN DER WESTHUIZEN
## ISTANBUL, TURKEY

THERE IS A POINT, off the peninsula in the city of Istanbul where the narrow channel of the Bosphorus meets the fjord of the Golden Horn and the Sea of Marmara. It was in the sheltered waters of the Golden Horn that the Byzantine and, later, Ottoman fleets had rested at anchor, before sailing out on the business of empire. History flows through these waters, as the opposing forces of Europe and Asia, Romans and Greeks, Islam and Christianity, Allies and Axis, have all, at various times, encountered each other at this crossroads.

It was from here that in 1565 Suleiman the Magnificent launched his ill-fated attack on the Maltese Knights of St John, whose galleys persisted in harassing Ottoman shipping in the eastern Mediterranean. What became known as the Great Siege of Malta had ended in ignominious defeat for Suleiman and secured the island as home to the Knights, and to Christianity, for the next two hundred years.

Overlooking this turbulent confluence in Istanbul was a rooftop restaurant that caught the cool evening breeze and afforded views across the Galata Bridge, onto the historic Old City. The distinctive domes and slender minarets of the subtly lit

Hagia Sophia and Blue Mosque stood out prominently against the evening skyline.

Luke van der Westhuizen had finished dinner, during which he had enjoyed his self-allotted two glasses of wine. His Austrian companion, on the other hand, was getting himself quite drunk. Luke had first recommended a white, from Eastern Anatolia, which had gone down well. That was followed by a bottle of Turkish Syrah, then another bottle of the Syrah, and now Matthäus Schober was extolling the virtues of vintage *raki*, the triple-distilled Turkish liquor made from grapes and aniseed.

Luke had met him a few years earlier when they were introduced by a mutual business contact. The slight, pale-haired Austrian needed money, a lot of money, and had been forced to sell a valuable collection of diamonds that had been in his family for generations. He had told Luke his father had died unexpectedly and that he had been robbed of his share of a profitable business by its double dealing partners. The Schobers lived in great state in their ancestral home, an old schloss in the wine district of Burgenland, twenty kilometres south of Vienna. After his father's death, Matthäus had discovered the estate barely generated enough income to meet his extended family's considerable day-to-day expenses.

Matthäus's ailing mother, his two sisters, their families and several others, all expected to be kept in the manner they thought appropriate to their status, as former Austro-Hungarian nobility, a class that had been formally abolished in 1919. The practicalities did not concern them in the same way as maintaining their rank did. Matthäus was charged with the dirty business of running the estate and providing the means for life in the schloss to continue in the same way it always had, without concerning the broader family with the sordid details of how he did it. Luke recognised an opportunity when he saw one and recruited the impecunious Austrian as part of his Malta operation. He formed a perfect link, distributing the heroin arriving from Libya across Europe.

For the past few years, however, when not rebuilding the family fortunes, Matthäus had made it his business to look into the circumstances surrounding his father's untimely death, and frequently regaled Luke with tedious stories about his investigations. This evening, however, Luke was fully attentive to his friend's revelations, as the saga had taken an unexpected turn. Matthäus was mumbling into his *raki* about the company his father was involved with.

"I finally got Mother to talk. She's refused to discuss it for years. Vows of silence, made under threat of death... or so she says. But I told her, 'There's no bloody money left!' *That* woke her up, I can tell you. She said that my father's partners referred to themselves as 'the Family' apparently. Ridiculous – 'the Family'? Like the Mafia, isn't it? But no, this lot are something different, originally a bunch of aristos who went around medieval Europe, pillaging mortgaged land and lending cash to kings... stuff like that. The vultures associated with popes, counts, great landowners, all sorts... Mind you, probably all *Böckchen*."

He belched.

"Anyway, Mother said they murdered him... They killed Father. And not just him; someone killed all the old guard of this Family thing. All of them copped it, except for one. Mother spoke to the man who survived. She's known him for years. He retired, ran off and took a load of cash to keep quiet. Said it was better than the alternative. But you know how it is with secrets – they always come out."

Luke looked at Matthäus who sat sadly pondering his empty glass.

"Wow! Did you involve the police?"

"Never involve them. Too dangerous. Some woman did it all. Took everything. From an old Maltese family, apparently. You know what *they're* like... all pimps and murdering bastards, the Maltese. Wouldn't trust them."

It was at this point that Luke sat up straighter in his chair.

"Tell me more. Who was this woman, exactly? You say she was Maltese? From which family?"

"Yes, she murdered Father, or her people did. Mother would never say how. Must'ave been nasty. She's protective like that, Mother. But, yes, the woman came from Malta. You know the place? It's a shithouse! Maybe you can help me find the bitch. I'll kill her…"

"Yes, but who is she? You must have a name?"

"Oh, yes, Mother knew it… Can't remember it now. Anyway, this Maltese woman murdered Father, stole the business and our money and left us with fuck all. Bitch!"

Luke felt the warm glow from his carefully calibrated alcohol intake fade away, as he absorbed all the implications of Matthäus's story.

A few days after the *Samaritan* had docked in Malta, a member of the cleaning team collected the assembled life jackets, concealing them in bin liners, and removed them from the ship. The cleaner took them with the rubbish to a refuse collection point, where the bin liners were picked out of the fetid piles and transferred to a small warehouse in the Grand Harbour, rented by a shelf company formed by Luke's Turkish attorneys.

There, the heroin was packed into standard two hundred litre steel drums, beneath circular plates that formed false bottoms. The plates were then welded into place. The drums joined others that had not been tampered with and all of them were filled with the liquid clarifying agent that Matthäus used in his loss-making winery. Loaded onto pallets and collected by a haulier for transportation through a variety of hubs, they made the trip north to Burgenland, Austria.

Upon delivery to the Schober vineyard at the schloss, the white heroin was retrieved from the doctored drums and middlemen wholesalers, from across Europe, emailed their orders for cases of Schloss Altersdorf wine. They received boxes of special opaque bottles, some of which were filled with product from a unique *terroir* that had more to do with the poppy than the vine.

Each box contained up to nine kilos of processed heroin, depending on the size of the order. The boxes were collected and faithfully, and unwittingly, tracked across Europe by FedEx.

Luke waved at a waiter, pointing to the empty *raki* glasses and holding up two fingers.

"So, I suppose, if you find this woman, you can not only get your revenge, you can also get your father's money back?"

"Hmmm. Dunno. Can't take on a killer like that, can I? Quickest way to end up dead."

"What does your mother say?"

"Find the father."

"Whose father?"

"The woman's… the killer… she's a father; we all have. Or I did… not now. Dead. He, the father, was part of it too. But he disappeared. Somewhere in Serbia."

"So?"

"Leverage, maybe. But I dunno where he is, not sure about his name… something Italian sounding."

Luke hesitated but could not resist the prompt.

"Does the name 'Bonnici' mean anything to you?"

Matthäus had slumped back in his chair. He stared at the tabletop, considering his outstretched hands.

"Bonnici?" He paused. Then, suddenly alert, exclaimed, "Yes, that's the name! You're a genius! Bonnici. Bonnici! All murderers!"

"Shush! Not so loud, Matthäus."

"You know the Bonnicis?"

"No, I've only just heard the name. You're right, though. People like that would kill you, if they thought you knew their business. Forget them. You're better off working with me. We're making good money, aren't we?"

"Yes, money. Never enough money for Mother and the rest of them. Money, money, money. Parasites."

With that, Luke paid the bill, generously tipping the waiter and asking him to put Matthäus into a taxi. After leaving the restaurant, Luke took a walk across Galata Bridge and along the ancient limestone walls on the south side of the Golden Horn. The further he walked, the more sense Matthäus's drunken ramblings made to him. Natasha Bonnici: chair of upstart energy company MalTech Energy, alleged murderess and now head of this shadowy Family. He had underestimated her; he had not appreciated with whom he was dealing.

The implication that Matthäus might be thinking about kidnapping Natasha's father, in a bid for revenge, amused Luke. He would like to see how far someone as ineffectual as that would get with such a plan. Matthäus Schober taking on Natasha Bonnici? No contest.

# CHAPTER 16

# SAVI AZZOPARDI
## SLIEMA PROMENADE, MALTA

SAVI AZZOPARDI WAS SITTING on a bench on the Sliema promenade. From here, he could look over the waters of Marsamxett Harbour towards the walled fortress city of Valletta. At least, he could have done, if he were not engrossed instead, in the latest high-end game designed for his oversized iPhone. Savi's morning power walk, taken to keep Danka off his back, always ended at the same bench, two hundred yards down the promenade. There, he would have a kebab for breakfast. Or brunch, or even lunch. Whatever the time, it did not matter, he ate kebabs.

Savi had, by now all but forgotten about his spell locked up in the Bonnicis' clifftop chapel. While he had been imprisoned there, Natasha had forced him to use his considerable hacking skills to divert a container, with one billion Libyan dinars in it, en route from the Russian mint to the alternative Libyan government in the east of the country. It had dropped into her waiting hands instead. Savi had made a fool of Mike Lloyd and the CIA, who were also trying to intercept and appropriate the money. The hacker had switched the shipping identification codes on the container in transit and, to his embarrassment, Mike Lloyd had ended up with a container full of 'puffa' jackets, not the container full of dinars he was expecting.

Lloyd had eventually forgiven Savi. The kid was an idiot. A gifted idiot when it came to computers, but still an idiot. It was Natasha Bonnici coercing him into making the switch on her behalf that he could not forgive.

Camilleri had told Mike that Savi lived in an expensive penthouse in Fort Cambridge, a new highrise complex overlooking the entrance to Marsamxett Harbour. But the fact was, Savi did not much like living alone and preferred to stay in the single bed in Danka Bijak's box room. This did have the drawback of having to listen to Danka and Simon's occasional, but vigorous, bouts of lovemaking. When the two of them collided, Savi thought, the sex sounded more like the clashing of rhinos, than the sweet music of love.

Danka was a muscled, stocky, short-haired blonde, with a liking for stylish tattoos and kettle bell work outs. Her penchant for tight athletics vests and sleeveless tops showed her broad powerful shoulders and highly developed, well-inked biceps. She had a long-standing but relaxed relationship with Simon, a fellow Pole. The hard-nosed ex-military policeman had no problem cracking skulls, but for some reason, had taken an almost fraternal liking to Savi. When his boss Natasha had suggested it might be time for the hacker to take a one-way dive off Dingli cliffs, Simon had done the unthinkable and disobeyed her, hiding their former prisoner with Danka. And there he had stayed.

With Savi's ill-gotten gains from ransomware, his landlady had moved her kettle bell exercise studio out of the converted basement garage and into a purpose-built gym, off the promenade in Gizra. The gym had a café and a small shop, selling supplements and vitamins, together with an under-the-counter trade in steroids. Business was good.

As a flatmate, Savi was a nightmare; he was idle and dirty. She had thrown him out numerous times but, like a stray cat, he always made his way back. He was incapable of putting a pizza box in the waste bin and continually stubbed out his cigarettes in his food, something Danka found particularly repulsive. Nevertheless, with Simon perpetually away, travelling and attending on Natasha Bonnici, often spending weeks on end at the castello, Danka had got used to Savi's company. Together, they spent hours on the X-Box, watched countless TV series, and zoned out on lager and the weed that Savi grew in tubs, behind the rooftop washroom.

Mike Lloyd spent ten minutes watching the kid, who was totally engrossed with his phone while rocking his skateboard back and forth with one foot. He was amazed that a feared and renowned international hacker could be so oblivious to approaching danger, which was how Mike liked to think of himself.

He sat down on the bench next to Savi and casually crossed his legs. Savi was still the same scrawny, long-haired, slacker man-child that Mike had strongarmed two years ago. He must have been in his late twenties by now, but looked and acted like a seventeen year old.

Seeing his arrival had gone totally unnoticed, Mike banged on the slats of the bench with his fist. The noise attracted Savi's attention. Lazily, he turned his head. On recognising Mike, he instantly leaped to his feet, sending the skateboard shooting away across the promenade.

"Sit down, Savi, sit down, I'm not going to hurt you."

The kid stood there, wide-eyed and open-mouthed with shock. He immediately wondered if Mike could have brought a team to abduct him or worse. He frantically scoured the early-season tourists walking the promenade, looking for black-suited CIA operatives.

"Relax, I'm alone and I come in peace. Sit down."

"Yeah, peace! You guys don't know the meaning of the word."

Savi kept flickering his eyes warily back at Mike, as he

slouched away to retrieve his board. After quickly checking the
route ahead for suits, in a deft movement, Savi hopped on the
board and kicked off. He managed to get three metres down
the promenade before a large man in a black suit materialised
from behind a drinks kiosk, and casually swept him to the
ground with a firm body check. Savi lay there breathless,
tourists sidestepping around his prone body. He picked himself
up, glaring at the grinning pile of muscle and shouted, loudly:
"Fuck you!"

Sheepishly, he returned to the bench.

"What the fuck? Why do that? You said you were alone!"

"So, I lied. Just as well I wasn't alone, you were going to do a
runner! Here's me thinking we'd got past all this mistrust stuff."

"Huh! What do you want? I'm not doing anything for you, no
way. Remember last time? You said you'd look after me and I
nearly got killed."

"Yeah, darn' right – that's because you double-crossed me.
Your own fault, like everything else in your sad little life. OK,
listen to me now. How d'you want to make some big money?"

"Big money?" Savi shook his head. "You've got me all wrong,
man, I'm not into that these days. I'm already loaded. I'm so
loaded, it's untrue. I've even got a financial adviser guy at the
bank. He keeps everything tight."

"Yeah, so you won't mind me telling the bank where all that
dirty ransom cash came from?"

"I worked for that money – it's clean."

"Sure, it is! Bet the *Pulizija* would agree. Ransom shake-
downs? Extortion? No biggie. Sorry, my mistake."

"Hey, I'm guided by principles now. I do the right thing and
make sure others do too. Eco stuff, XR, Occupy Wallstreet,
Animal Liberation Front! Real causes that make a difference.
Yeah, stuff that you just don't get!"

"OK, Batman, you really are the Caped Crusader. So, now
you've filled your pockets, time to save the world. All great, but
how would you like to stick it to an autocratic state? One that

silences free speech, bullies its neighbours, persecutes its citizens, fucks up internet access… and *still* make big money?"

"Hmmm. I dunno… those Chinese dudes are dangerous."

"I'm not talking China."

"Who then?"

"Turkey. More particularly, the Turkish Oil and Gas Organisation. TOGO."

"TOGO? Isn't that, like, a Roman skirt thing?"

Mike Lloyd rolled his eyes, but kept on talking.

"They aren't the bad guys really, but they're owned by the Turkish Sovereign Wealth Fund and account for a big whack of Turkish government revenues."

"What've the Turks done to piss you off?"

"They're screwing over the Greeks, our NATO partners, shit-stirring in Libya, throwing their weight around in the eastern Med, firing up the Muslim Brotherhood, cosying up to the Russians… and, generally, being a pain in the ass! They need someone to teach them a lesson."

"And you don't want your fingerprints all over it?"

"Savi, you're really coming on… proud of you, man! I'm giving you a steer on where to make your next shakedown."

"Then don't, because I still don't see why I should do any of this bullshit for you?"

"OK, let's say I have a tasty little morsel that you might like in return. A nice bit of payback. Interested now?"

Savi eyed Mike suspiciously, while bouncing one leg on the paving.

"Might be. What is it?"

"All in good time. So, if I wanted to make life unpleasant for our friends at TOGO, what would be on the menu?"

"I'm not saying I'll do anything yet, OK?"

"Sure."

Savi fiddled with his hair, twisting a fingerful of greasy strands into a topknot.

"You heard of Dragonfly 2.0?"

"Sort of. Screwed up the Ukrainian utilities a few years back."

"And the rest. It's a big-deal program. But, listen up – I've got access to Dragonfly 4.0. Yeah! Hackers are, like, businessmen now, professionals. We do things for a reason, not just screwing around for the hell of it."

Savi waited smugly, expecting congratulations; a gasp, a reaction of some sort.

"So?" said Mike, after an awkward lull.

"Disappointing. You haven't a clue what any of that means, have you?"

Seeing Mike was unimpressed, Savi continued.

"OK, if – and I mean *if* – I choose to do this, the oil and gas industries will be wide open to the new software. The IT systems they use are probably decades old. And Turkish IT? Can't see that being up to much. I can attack individuals first. People are pretty dumb. I'll need to recruit a Turkish speaker for that, but there are plenty of pissed off people in Turkey.

"The way it works is, you go phishing and get an employee to open an email, maybe an attachment, a social media post. That's your infection vector. Bang! We're in. The malware gives us the network credentials and we install those on our servers. Then, we've got a backdoor into the network. That's when we can really go to work.

"We can encrypt all the files on the servers – every one of them, all across the network, and extract them. Then we can send a ransom demand to the TOGO boys, telling them to pay up or their business will be paralysed. Also, because it's an oil and gas business, we can screw around with the operational technology – and there'll be a lot of that! We can attack them upstream, close down their drilling and exploration rigs, that sort of thing. But nothing kinda nasty to the environment, you know?"

"Then there's all the financial stuff. We'll download files, get into the employee system, stop wage runs, publish ID numbers and bank details. We'll get confidential documents … you know, future production details, field potentials and bidding documentation – send them to industry journos and every global oil major. That do you for starters?"

"Yeah, yeah, that's the sort of thing I had in mind. It all that great, but, you're right, we don't want oil spills or any eco problems, get it? That's bad news for everybody."

"Well, nothing's happening until you tell me more about this *tasty morsel* and give me guarantees on no blowback. Last time you hung me out, man! We also have to talk about money, serious money. I'm a big player now, it's not like it was back then, I can pick and choose what I do."

"'Course, you're the man now, I hear that. But I'm not paying you squat – take whatever ransom you can screw from them. I don't wanna know about it. Do your job properly and they'll shower you with Bitcoin, M&Ms... or whatever.

"You see, you think you're the real deal. Thing is, I know you. To me, you'll always be Savi, the overgrown, unwashed kid who can't hang on to his own skateboard. Now, listen up, you're going to like this a lot..."

THE AIR PEGASUS flight touched down at Northern Cyprus's Ercan Airport in the middle of the day. The flight from Malta via Istanbul had been uneventful – unlike George's conversation with Marianna when he had told her he could be away for several weeks on *Pulizija* business.

His big mistake was to make the call from Abdullah's SUV, upon leaving the LRC offices. When she realised what her husband was telling her, Marianna's reaction was predictable enough. She had demanded to know why an inspector in Community Affairs had to travel at all? What was he doing in Libya? Inspecting pedestrian crossings in Tripoli? She blamed Abdullah. He was nothing but trouble and had been since the day George first met him. Abdullah, sitting next to George in the back of the SUV, could not help but overhear every single word she screamed. George tried to quieten her, but to no avail. Once Marianna lost it, there was no way she could be diverted from a tirade.

She had finally slammed the phone down and the two drivers, Abdullah and George had all sat in embarrassed silence. Abdullah wore a hang-dog expression. He let out a long breath and said:

"By the Prophet, peace be upon him! I am upset. I always thought I was much liked by the lady wife."

The driver sniggered.

Abdullah barked at him in Arabic and the driver's smile instantly disappeared.

George sighed too. He should have expected her reaction.

"It's not your fault, Abdullah." George considered this statement. "Well, yes, it is, really. You always drag me off on these…" he struggled to find a word that would not offend " … trips!"

"Not this time, my friend. Tell your lady wife to take her complaints to the Lady Mantis, this is *her* doing! But it matters not, because you would be with me, despite her chiding. This is about Jamal. Do not tell me you would not help me rescue my son? I know you would. You have never let me down and my debts to you are many."

George looked at him doubtfully, without replying.

That was over a week ago and now they were landing in Northern Cyprus and making their way to Kyrenia, to meet the rest of Abdullah's men, who had flown in a few days earlier to prepare fishing vessels for the journey to Gavdos.

The Turkish Republic of Northern Cyprus came into being in 1974, when Turkish 'peacekeeping forces' arrived on the island to defeat the Greek-inspired military coup that was supposed to lead to the reunification of Cyprus with mainland Greece. The brief conflict resulted in the island being divided by the UN's Green Line, with the Turkish-speaking new republicans in the north and the Greek Cypriots in the south. To this day, Turkey remains the only country to officially recognise the new northern republic.

Kyrenia was the only sizeable port in Northern Cyprus and it was where the small fleet of three requisitioned Turkish fishing vessels were being fitted out for Abdullah's mission. They were mid-sized commercial ships, of between thirty-five and forty-five metres long, each with berths for at least twenty men.

The vessels were chosen for their stern ramps, to launch

fishing nets and haul the catch back up onto the trawl deck. These were now loaded with small RHIBs, inflatable boats, to enable the 'fishermen' to dash speedily from their vessels to the small port of Karave, the only settlement on the island of Gavdos. Or Gondoz, its original Turkish name, as they now had to call it.

The plan was that once Abdullah's men on the RHIBs had cleared the jetty of smaller boats, the larger fishing vessels would be able to dock. Then they would use the ships' cranes to unload the five SUVs they carried and go in search of the main expeditionary group, who would already have landed on the south of the island. That group were due to make a night-time, sea-borne landing and surprise the twelve unsuspecting Greek soldiers, who no doubt spent their time swimming off the deserted beaches and generally lying around, celebrating their good fortune on being posted there.

To say Karave was a small place was an understatement. The harbour boasted a mini-market that supplied summer visitors, drawn by stories of free camping, nude bathing and the hippy-hedonism the Greek islands were once famous for. It also boasted one taverna and the island's administrative office, grandly referred to as 'City Hall'.

The island's thirty square kilometres were divided by a windswept central ridge that rose to three hundred metres and, despite its exposed position, Gavdos had a covering of scrub and pine trees, which made it greener than might be expected.

But, all this was unimportant compared to its strategic position. The Greeks had been warned that Turkey was not unaware of the advantages that control of the island offered. In 1996, during the planning of a NATO exercise south of Crete, Turkey had announced that Gavdos should be kept out of the exercise, because it fell into a 'grey area', in so far as sovereignty was concerned. Greek efforts to exercise authority over it since then had been unconvincing.

In Tripoli, Toprak had explained that, despite the three days it would take them to cover the eight hundred kilometres from Cyprus to Gavdos, it was better to sail the trawlers from there so as to maintain the element of surprise. Greece closely watched traffic from the Turkish naval bases on the Aegean and the southern Mediterranean coast. Toprak had reasoned the three ships could slip out from Cyprus separately and join the main route for west-bound traffic, from the Suez Canal. Then they could regroup, to the south of Gavdos, without arousing Greek suspicions, and land in the harbour after nightfall.

The journey to Gavdos was the first time George had been at sea since crossing the Mediterranean in an inflatable raft, a few years earlier. He and Abdullah had been desperate to escape the clutches of the 'ISIL in Libya' militia leader, Abu Muhammed, and the only solution available was to infiltrate one of the migrant sea crossings from Libya, which Abdullah used to organise.

Whether it was a flashback to that time, or his general fear of deep water and rolling waves, it did not matter: anxiety struck George as soon as the ship cleared the dock. The knot in his stomach tightened, as the smell of the sea, diesel and fish began to creep over him. Combined with the persistent see-sawing and lolling of the boat, he was soon gagging over the side of the rails into the choppy waters.

Abdullah had spent the time busying himself around the trawler: ordering weapon checks, teaching his men to pronounce the complicated Turkish names they were to assume and distributing the fake Turkish identity cards and passports. There were fifty Libyan men involved and Abdullah and Toprak had decided to drop any pretence that they were real fishermen. The landing was meant to be symbolic, deliberately designed to provoke the Greeks. Whether Abdullah's militiamen knew how to fish or not was not relevant. They had brought with them amateur-looking, mocked-up banners, in Turkish, English and Greek, proclaiming their right to retake the island. Two 'fishermen' were to hang these around the port buildings, where foreign press attention was likely to be focused.

Carefully edited videoclips had also been prepared, against neutral backdrops, where seasoned Turkish actors, posing as the fishermen, articulately explained their rights and justified the reclaiming of this part of the Turkish homeland. These press packages would be released as news of the landings began to be picked up by the world's media.

Turkish drones had captured images that showed the Greeks were building a small base at Cape Tripiti, a sandy cove on the southernmost part of the island, only accessible by a rough ten-kilometre stretch of track from Karave, in the north west. The bulk of Abdullah's force would use RHIBs to leave the ships, before they arrived at Karave, in order to access this sandy cove and surprise the Greek soldiers in their slumbers. No one seriously expected a shot to be fired.

The significance of the base was that it supported Greek claims to sovereignty over the island and extended Greece's Exclusive Economic Zone further out into the Mediterranean, edging Greek territorial waters way beyond the area where MalTech Energy had acquired drilling concessions from the Turks.

By the third day at sea, there were no more preparations to be made. Weapons had been cleaned and oiled. Ammunition and foodstuffs were packed and ready for transportation and there had been several briefings. Abdullah was happy everyone knew their role and was prepared, but he was at a loss on how to alleviate the boredom of days at sea, on a smelly, noisy trawler plodding along at twelve knots.

It was George who had proposed a shooting competition and Abdullah had readily agreed, on proviso that every weapon fired had to be properly cleaned afterwards. George reckoned it would give the men a chance to get used to the weapons the Turks had supplied them with. The three ships slowed to a crawl and a RHIB was pushed down a trawl ramp, with some marker buoys to set up as targets. The buoys were over a metre tall and fixed with a length of chain, to ensure they remained upright in the water. The skipper complained about the cost, but Abdullah waved him away. The ships rafted up alongside each other and the men clambered between the vessels, until they were crowded around the port side of George's and Abdullah's ship.

Abdullah handed out the Turkish MPT rifles and George watched, as the men excitedly fired hundreds of rounds at the buoys, littering the decks with brass cartridge casings. After ten minutes of fun, he asked each ship to nominate one marksman and set up an inter-ship challenge. George had been secretly hoping that Abdullah would nominate him to represent their ship and was disappointed when he chose a popular boy, called Hamza.

He was in his early twenties, slightly built, with a mouthful of oversized teeth and energy to burn. He seemed to be everywhere on the ship, all at once. George never saw him without a smile on his face and he always seemed to be helping someone or doing something useful. In the three days they had been at sea, he had become the group's mascot.

The three designated contestants took pot shots at the buoy, from a distance of about seventy metres, as it rocked and tipped in the unpredictable swell. It was a tricky shot to make. Hamza had been a good pick as he hit the target with his second shot. It was an elimination shoot out and each of the three shooters had three chances. It did not take long for the other two contestants to rule themselves out of the competition and Hamza leaped around the deck, celebrating his victory, to loud cheers. It was then that Abdullah held up his hand and demanded silence.

"Hamza has proved himself worthy today of a mighty challenge… if he has the courage to accept it!"

A cheer went up from the deck.

"We have onboard with us the world's most deadly shot and Hamza has won the right to challenge him!"

There were more cheers, as Hamza was thrust forward by the

other men. George cringed, as Abdullah grabbed his hand and held it aloft, saying: "This is the world's best shot! I have seen it with these eyes. They do not lie. I will fight any man who disagrees!"

Silence fell as he glared at the assembled group, daring someone to challenge him.

"I have seen him kill an ISIL leader, from three thousand metres, with one shot. Yes, it is true."

There were cries of surprise from the men, followed by a burst of excited chatter. Only George knew how hard he had tried not to make that kill, but the wind speed and direction that day had delivered the flukiest shot that had ever been fired.

Then, not letting go of George's hand, Abdullah grabbed Hamza's wrist and held it up high.

"Who wants to see our boy in a challenge for the championship of the world?"

The fishermen erupted with excitement and started chanting: "Hamza! Hamza! Hamza!"

The kid grinned broadly, his large white teeth gleaming. He offered George his hand and they shook heartily. George had to laugh at Abdullah's showman's antics, but then set his mind to winning the shootout.

They tossed a coin for the first shot, which he won.

George took a rifle and felt its weight and balance. He checked the iron sights and positioned the stock against his shoulder. It felt good. He clipped in the magazine of bullets and settled against the rail. The men on deck fell silent as he moved with the sway of the vessel and tried to anticipate the pitching of the buoy. He aimed, took a breath, held it, fired – and missed.

Against the general background noise of the group, he repeated the process, but the buoy dipped as he squeezed the trigger. The last shot went the same way as the second. George was sure he would have hit the target had the wave not disturbed the buoy. He was bitterly disappointed.

It was made worse when Hamza smacked the buoy with his

first shot, giving rise to hysterical cheering and shouting. He was a gracious winner and commiserated with George, saying he had been unlucky with the waves. George smiled and clapped the young man on the back, receiving a round of applause for his sportsmanship.

As the others were climbing and jumping back between the ships, Abdullah came over to George and took him to one side.

"You are a wise man, George. You think I did not see what you did there?"

George was confused.

"Mela, what did I do?"

"You let the boy win and made the men happy. I know you could have easily hit that target. I have seen you take many harder shots. But I saw you miss, deliberately. I saw that with these eyes! Hah, you have to do better than that to fool me, my friend!"

He raised two fingers and pointed towards his eyes, nodding his head and smiling.

"So, now the men are happy, they like you because you are not surly in defeat and everybody is pleased. That is how a ship should be! Tomorrow, we become Turks!"

# CHAPTER 18
# NATASHA BONNICI
## CASTELLO BONNICI, MALTA

It was over a week after Luke's illuminating meeting with Matthäus Schober before he saw Natasha again. He was careful that his visits to Malta did not coincide with the *Samaritan's* arrivals; he did not want to create any hint of an association between them.

Meanwhile, Natasha had been busy, travelling to Milan, where she had been laying out plans to the Family's steering committee on their first venture into oil and gas exploration. They were both looking forward to a weekend at the castello, enjoying the summer sun and each other.

It had not taken her long to realise that Luke had arrived in Malta with an agenda, though he thought he was carefully rolling it out. Natasha entertained herself by deliberately ignoring his veiled suggestions and odd comments, leading him on to the point where he had no option but to tell her what was on his mind.

They were lying in wicker recliners, on the patio by Natasha's poolside bar. She had had it built using fifty-year-old redwood and hand-painted traditional Maltese tiles, in shades of yellow and blue. Her father would have been horrified, but by now

Natasha had accepted it was unlikely he would ever return to Malta, and therefore would never see it.

Luke continued with his attempts to soften her up, steering the conversation to subjects he thought would be of interest to her. He asked how Nick and Cristina were getting along after their ordeal in Jo'burg.

"I have no idea. And I don't care. I appreciate your help in organising that, but let's not talk about it anymore. OK?"

She raised her sunglasses and smiled at him.

Luke shrugged.

"I get it. Subject closed."

Natasha decided to try and push a little, see what was on his mind.

"I get the sense you're leading up to telling me something. Am I right?"

Luke laughed.

"Well, I could be, but I don't want to break our 'no business talk' rule." He paused, uncertain whether to go on. "But this is different. I wouldn't want to talk about it normally, but I think it's best you know."

"Interesting. OK, consider the 'no business talk' rule suspended, temporarily at least."

"I don't want *too* much, but I want something in return for what I'm going to tell you."

"Even more interesting."

He paused before asking: "What is 'the Family'?"

Natasha did not say a word. Instead, she raised herself from the recliner and went to the bar, to slip a brightly coloured coverall over her bikini. She slowly poured herself a glass of ice-cold, orange-coloured Spritz from a flask, mixing it with a shot of vodka and some ice. Taking a chair, she pulled it forward, towards Luke's recliner, so she could look down on him when she seated herself. Then, she said softly:

"Where on earth did you hear about that?"

"So, it exists?"

"Luke, I'm fond of you, but don't play games with me. Remember, it was you who wanted this to be a business talk. Where did you hear about the Family?"

There was a hardness in her face that told Luke he could be venturing onto very dangerous ground.

"I heard a whisper, that's all."

"Bullshit! Tell me."

"I had a dinner in Istanbul with this guy who was talking about it. He said it had links to Malta. I thought you might know something?"

"That's your first 'get-out-of-jail-free' card used up. Now tell me the truth."

Luke was growing uneasy. He tried to laugh off his mistake in raising the subject in the first place. Natasha was not laughing, not even smiling.

"OK, he was really drunk, it was probably nothing. If it doesn't mean anything to you, then that's fine."

"That's your second chance wasted. Tell me, I'm serious. Any more messing about and you pack, leave and it's over between us."

Luke sat up, on the edge of the recliner, and looked into Natasha's dispassionate face, that was calmly appraising him.

"He said the Family killed his father and that you were involved."

She considered what she had just heard. She bit her bottom lip and nodded her head.

"Quite possibly."

"Want to tell me about it?"

Natasha barked a short laugh.

"What a stupid question! I want the name of this well-informed drunk, who has most likely talked himself into an early grave."

Luke was shocked, not at the thought that his story could be responsible for causing someone's death, but that his distribution route through the *schloss* could be lost.

"No, no! He didn't say that much; I put two and two together. He didn't even remember your name. Just said a Maltese woman was involved."

Natasha stood and made ready to leave the deck.

"Is that all?" she asked. "You still haven't said what it is you want in return?"

Luke squirmed. This conversation was not going as planned.

"The most important thing he said was not that. He talked about getting revenge on the Family for killing his father."

"How?"

"He suggested... only a suggestion, mind... and he was very drunk, so I didn't really believe him... he suggested, that they were going to look for your father. They know he's in Serbia."

Natasha froze. She wondered who this could be. There were a few possibilities.

"And you're only telling me this now? When exactly did this conversation take place?"

Luke hung his head.

"Over a week ago."

She screamed at him: "Over a week ago? My father could be dead already, you unthinking idiot. You absolute fool. And you think telling me this now makes everything right, do you?"

She started pacing up and down the deck. Her mind was racing.

"You unbelievably stupid man. Name? His name, now!"

"Matthäus Schober."

She looked at Luke.

"Did you tell him you knew me?"

"No."

"I know Matthäus Schober."

She kneeled beside hm and put her face close to his, studying him for a moment. He could smell the coconut oil on her olive skin. Her mouth was slightly open, as if inviting a kiss; the faintest trace of alcohol tainting her breath. He noticed the faint hairs on her top lip. He had never seen them before. She turned her head to one side, so that her thick black hair fell over the left half of her face. She pushed it back. Her dark eyes were reading him and Luke had no idea what they had discovered. He was scared. He could not tell whether her expression was one of menace or insanity. She held her mouth even closer to his and began speaking, slowly and calmly, in a quiet voice that seemed to come from far away.

"I was in the next room when Matthäus's father was garrotted. I heard him kicking and scrabbling against the desk, as it happened. His father was an arrogant, misogynistic old man who had no respect for anybody. The son is an untrustworthy, useless alcoholic. The perfect person for a moron like you to be doing business with."

Luke was speechless. He had never seen Natasha like this before. He knew she was tough and the episode in Johannesburg had shown she had a cruel and ruthless streak, but had she really talked about a garrotting? He had not even reached the point he had been getting to, asking her how he could join the Family. At that moment, the prospect did not seem so inviting.

She stood up.

"I'm going for a shower, alone. I'll get dressed and be down in twenty minutes, and, then, we'll go through this, step by step. Afterwards, you can leave. I've got things to do."

She went to the bar and pressed a button under the counter.

Within seconds, Simon appeared and stood at the patio door, his chest and shoulder muscles bulging under a tight grey T-shirt. He looked impassive, but ready for action, arms folded in front of him.

"Everything OK, Miss Natasha?"

"Yes, fine. Can you fix Luke a drink, please? And make sure he doesn't leave the castello."

# CHAPTER 19

# ARTICLE IN MALTA TELEGRAPH

*Reporter: Amy Halliday*
*9 July 2021*

*MalTech Energy lease drillship for eastern Mediterranean exploration*

*MalTech Energy has announced its ambitions to become a player in the upstream energy market by taking a long lease on the drillship* Ocean Vantage. *The vessel, which has a crew of fifty, is valued at two hundred million US dollars and is operating from an initial position ten kilometres south of Gavdos, Greece's most southerly island.*

*The one hundred and seventy-four metre ship is equipped with the latest geological tools and will explore the seabed to the south of Crete, but within the area of the contentious Turkey/Libya maritime accord. If early reports of oil and gas are confirmed, the ship will proceed to drill, using anchors and its GPS positioning system to keep the ship in position.*

*The operation is a big step for the new Maltese company that has chosen to invest its earnings from importing Libyan gas into Europe, to trans-*

*form itself into a major player in the energy sector in the Mediter-
ranean. By implicitly acknowledging the legitimacy of the Turkey/Libya
maritime treaty, the Maltese government, which holds a minority share
in the company, is likely to make itself unpopular with many of its EU
partners and the US.*

# CHAPTER 20
# HAKAN TOPRAK
## TURKISH OIL AND GAS HEAD OFFICE, ANKARA

THE OFFICES of TOGO in Ankara, Turkey, were in turmoil. Executives were closeted in meeting rooms thick with cigarette smoke as accusation and counter-accusation flew back and forth. It had become apparent that a backup server, that was not password-protected, had had its entire contents exfiltrated onto an external server, outside the company's control. Messages had popped up on screens, telling those in the offices that all files were now encrypted and access was being denied until the senior management met the demands of the hacking group calling themselves the Prairie Dogs.

Management was in panic and there was uproar on the executive floor. Demands for money had been received, the amount known only to the Chief Executive and the government minister involved. The Chief Executive had fired the Director of IT, in a fit of temper, and the minister had called Hakan Toprak back from Libya, to take charge of the situation. Toprak had been a senior executive in TOGO before his recent appointment and the minister knew a cool head and nerves of steel were required to deal with this crisis.

On his return, he had immediately demanded the restoration of the Director of IT, who was sulking at home and had already refused the Chief Executive's offer of reinstatement. On learning this, Toprak personally went to the IT Director's house, in a desirable suburb of Ankara, and threatened him with arrest, on a charge of aiding the hackers, if he did not get back into his suit and return to the office immediately.

He also spoke to the Minister for Defence and explained the problem. He asked the minister for an introduction to someone in the Russian foreign intelligence agency, the SVR, who were famous for their understanding, and practice, of cyber warfare. Turkey had recently infuriated NATO by purchasing a Russian anti-aircraft system, an act that gave them contacts, and a reserve of goodwill, high up in the Russian Ministry of Defence.

When Hakan Toprak spoke to the senior technical officer at the SVR, he was not encouraged by what he heard. The Prairie Dogs were a professional outfit, widely respected in the Russian cyber world. They not only ran a ransomware business on their own account, but also, very profitably, licensed their software for use by other criminal gangs. His contact said they were formidable adversaries.

Rather than fight the attack in the ether, which the Russians said was nearly impossible, Hakan Toprak took their advice to go after the hackers personally. The officer at the SVR advised him to engage with the hackers, getting them to send as many messages as possible. Discuss how the money transfer would work, how they intended to fix the corrupted and encrypted data. Ask them to send a patch, to prove they could deliver what they promised. Seek details, anything, and send all their messages to a specialised counter-cyber warfare team of the SVR, at their headquarters, deep in a forest outside of Moscow. They would see if they could identify where the attack originated and who might be responsible.

They wouldn't find an address, with a postcode, but perhaps another sort of clue, something subtle – a hint or an echo of a known operator. Use of a characteristic phrase or piece of slang; a misspelling or linguistic trait in an email. A trail of virtual smoke drifting through digital space, a binary needle in a haystack of data, a dirty electronic footprint.

The Russian ordered: "Get us as much information as you can. Buy us time. We have many tools and we succeed more often than we fail."

# CHAPTER 21

# GEORGE ZAMMIT
### ISLAND OF GAVDOS,
### MEDITERRANEAN SEA

IT WAS a little over two weeks since Jamal had attacked Toprak's villa and the full moon was starting to wane. Low, heavy cloud blocked out the stars and thick humidity and sea-spray dampened the expeditionary party's clothing and their excitement. Sea and sky merged into one dark wash, the island only visible as a shaded, more solid mass, projecting up into a mid-black sky. Abdullah had a hand-held GPS. After consulting with the skipper, he stopped the vessels three kilometres to the south of the coast of Gavdos. Try as they might, they could not get used to calling it Gondoz.

The RHIBs were winched down the stern ramps and rope ladders were lowered over the side of the ships. The RHIBs were loaded with men and ammunition. The bulk of the cargo would be unloaded later, onto the Karave quayside. At midnight, the six RHIBs, with Abdullah and thirty of his most reliable men, nervously fingering their life jackets, set off across the waters to Tripiti, on the near-deserted south side of the island.

Reports from the Turkish surveillance drone had indicated that there were several large deployable army tents onsite and a small, partially constructed cinderblock building, that would eventually become the Greeks' permanent and most southern

Mediterranean base. The number of tents suggested they were also garaging vehicles or storing building materials under cover.

Abdullah had named George second-in-command and put him in charge of the aptly named lead ship, the *Güvenilir* – or *Trustworthy*. He was to be responsible for bringing the three vessels into the tiny harbour at Karave, unloading the SUVs and supplies, and then making a rendezvous with Abdullah's team at the base.

Several of the hard-bitten fighters had exchanged questioning glances at the suggestion that they would have to take orders from George. He himself had stammered and spluttered his objections, but Abdullah had addressed the men and quelled any dispute.

"I trust this man with my life. So, I trust him with yours, that I hold as equally dear as my own."

As Abdullah's RHIBs chugged off into the darkness, George peered into the gloom, hoping all would be well, whilst trying to ignore the churning of his stomach. It took another twenty minutes before he and the skipper could make out the green and red navigation lights marking the entrance to the small harbour. The *Trustworthy* cut her speed and edged forwards.

Immediately she had nosed past the breakwater, George could see there was a problem. Tied up alongside the jetty, where the Turkish skipper was planning to moor, was a long grey gunboat. The naval ship was as long as the *Trustworthy* and probably weighed over two hundred tonnes. Alarmingly, George noticed it had a three-inch gun on its bow and a Bofors anti-aircraft cannon mounted on its rear deck.

The skipper grabbed him by the wrist and whispered in his ear: "It's the 'blue and white', look."

"What's a 'blue and white'?"

"The flag of Greece. The Hellenic Navy is here!"

Sure enough, the blue-and-white flag of Greece hung limply from a pole on the gunboat's stern.

The skipper immediately became agitated and, with a backward glance, threw the throttle full-astern in his attempt to reverse out of the small harbour. George stood, speechless, peering out through the windscreen of the bridge. Despite Abdullah's orders for them to stay silent on the airwaves, the skipper grabbed the ship's radio, babbling excitedly in Turkish to the other two ships. It was obvious he had not signed up for a confrontation with the Hellenic Navy and was going to flee. George was coming to terms with the fact that the skipper might have the right idea, when young Hamza came onto the bridge and thrust an automatic rifle into his hands.

He took the weapon without thinking and turned to the skipper, swinging the gun barrel towards him. The skipper saw Hamza and George levelling weapons and his hands shot up in the air. He started to back slowly out of the bridge.

George looked over his shoulder and shouted: "Come back, the boat is reversing!"

Outside, on the deck, he heard raised voices and shouting. There were only seven or eight of Abdullah's fighters left on board the *Trustworthy*. The bulk of the men had left in the RHIBs and the remainder were spread between the other two ships, currently waiting outside the breakwater. What could they do against a bunch of armed and trained naval ratings?

The *Trustworthy* was now chugging backwards and rapidly gathering speed. Looking over his shoulder, George saw the starboard beam of the ship was close to the breakwater wall, about to collide with the curved harbour entrance. He heard a loud crunching sound, as one side of the *Trustworthy* crushed a small yacht that had moored up against the breakwater. Its fibre-glass hull disintegrating as the one hundred tonne fishing vessel steamed over it. George peered over the side of the bridge as the *Trustworthy* sailed on, backwards, leaving the flattened yacht sinking in its wake, its splintered mast and rigging strewn across the water. Shouting and yelling resounded from the main trawl deck as the men ran from one side of the ship to the other, pointing and panicking, unwilling passengers on the out-of-control ship.

George looked frantically around the bridge and saw the throttle lever the skipper had pulled backwards, to cause the ship to go astern. He reached this and pushed it as far forwards as he could, to apply the brakes. The engines went quiet for a second, then gathered momentum, as they started madly churning the harbour waters, creating a great mass of white foam in the pitch-black water. The *Trustworthy* slowed and lumbered to a halt, moments before disaster was due to strike. The momentum caused her to drift back until her stern very gently kissed the blocks forming the entrance to the breakwater, with a soft, dull clang.

The men cheered and George and Hamza left the bridge and made their way to find the skipper. George's plan was to coax him back onto the bridge and get him to manoeuvre the ship out of the harbour, then go back to collect Abdullah from the south of the island. He accepted the presence of the gunboat meant their occupation plan had failed and they were lucky to still have half a chance of escaping.

The skipper was being held on the trawl deck by two of Abdullah's fishermen, who were pushing guns into his stomach and shouting at him in an Arabic dialect a language George only partially understood. The skipper was remonstrating with them and jerking his head over his shoulder, at the gunboat. As George appeared on the companionway, everybody stopped and looked up at him. He realised they were waiting for instructions. Hamza was standing next to him, his toothy smile on display and his large, bright eyes gleaming with excitement.

"Well, what you say, Mr George, sir? What now?"

George tried to appear at his most commanding. He surveyed the tough, bearded, battle-hardened faces peering up at him from the deck. This was his moment, he had to be at his most decisive and assertive.

"OK, we're going back!"

Hamza looked at George, confused, glancing first to one side of the ship, then the other, then behind him, wondering what George meant. His puzzled expression changed, as a huge smile spread across his face. He leaped into the air with a shout, waving his gun. He screamed at the men on deck who all turned to look over the side of the ship.

George did not have much experience of sailing boats, let alone ocean-going, one hundred tonne ships, but, in applying the 'brakes', he had opened the throttle 'full ahead'. This had successfully stopped the backward movement of the *Trustworthy*, but the whirling propellors were now taking the trawler forward, at ever-increasing speed, straight towards the Greek gunboat.

George suddenly saw what had been apparent to Hamza. Fixed objects on the quayside were passing by, faster and faster. The gunboat was only fifty metres away from the *Trustworthy*, which was moving briskly towards it. George stood transfixed. He could have dashed back onto the bridge, pushed the throttle to the position marked 'Full Astern', even taken the wheel and tried to steer the bow away from the stern of the gunboat, but instead he stood stock-still in shock. They were 'going back' all right, but not in the way he had meant.

The men had fallen silent, as the *Trustworthy* inexorably ploughed her course direct for the gunboat. They could only wait for the inevitable collision. Some men hung onto the rails or parts of the superstructure. Two lay flat on the deck. Hamza was peering over the side, counting down the metres.

"Twenty, ten, five… *Ayyooh!*"

George threw himself to the deck, just as there was a massive, sickening crash, followed by a long screech of metal on metal. The impact smashed the rear of the gunboat away from its moorings and the two ships ground into each other, the momentum carrying both vessels forward until they approached the pontoons of the small marina at the base of the harbour.

One or two people had sleepily appeared on the decks of various yachts, wondering what all the commotion was about, and they were confronted with the sight of the combined ships, looming out of the darkness, heading straight for them, pushing a two-metre wave of foaming water ahead. The spectators dashed down the pontoons for the shore, but the displaced water from the approaching tangle of steel tipped them off their feet, spilling the fleeing yachtsmen and women into the chilly harbour water.

The *Trustworthy*'s engines continued to thrash, whipping up a huge lather, grinding it into the Greek gunboat, which finally became pinned to the harbour wall by the trawler's embedded bow. There was a four-metre tear down the gunboat's port side, that disappeared below the waterline. The Greek vessel was starting to list heavily to one side. The Turkish skipper was forced at gunpoint back onto the bridge and finally stopped the *Trustworthy*'s engines. An eerie calm descended over the harbour.

As the skipper pushed past and disappeared below deck, George watched as Hamza and four of the men jumped over the rails of the *Trustworthy*, onto the gunboat's deck, and confronted four confused Greek sailors who had cautiously appeared through a doorway. They stood on the sloping deck, hands in the air, dressed only in Navy-issue white boxer shorts. Hamza saw George looking out from the bridge and waved his gun in salute.

"George, he say, 'We go back!' Look, George, we go back! Have prisoners! Hey, George," he chanted, "we go back! We go back! We go back!" Hamza began to laugh, manically.

George exhaled deeply, as the skipper reappeared, fury written all over his face.

"Ship is finished. Under is all water. No more fish."

George looked at the man's twisted face.

"Oh, not good! I'm sorry."

It was then that he noticed two of their Toyota Land Cruisers, floating amidst the wreckage of the marina. The impact must have shaken them free from their shackles and they had somehow slid down the ramp into the troubled waters of the harbour.

# CHAPTER 22
# ARTICLE IN MALTA TELEGRAPH

Reporter: Amy Halliday
11 July 2021

*Turks serve US notice on Incirlik air base*

*The Turkish government shocked both the US and NATO yesterday, by following through on threats to serve notice on the US Air Force to vacate the Incirlik air base in Adana, eastern Turkey, before the end of the year. The base has been home to a significant contingent of USAF service personnel since 1954 and was initially set up to accommodate long-range bombers, within striking distance of the former Soviet Union.*

*The main strategic purpose of the base has shifted over the last twenty years, as the US conducted bombing campaigns in Iraq, Afghanistan, Syria and Libya. The five hundred US personnel supported a wide range of air operations on behalf of NATO and its allies.*

*The move is seen by Turkey as retaliation for US sanctions arising from Turkey's purchase of the Russian S-400 anti-aircraft system. The US Secretary of State had said the Russian system was incompatible with*

*NATO systems, gave the Russians access to existing NATO defence technology and provided much-needed funding to the Russian defence industry.*

*The US downplayed the expulsion, saying they had long been contemplating a move of their assets to their naval and airbase in Souda Bay, Crete, a move encouraged by the Greek government.*

*The riskiest part of the move will be the movement of the fifty light-weight, B61 nuclear bombs held at the Turkish base. The bombs are designed to be delivered by supersonic US strike aircraft but are said to be of low tactical importance. They have remained on the base due to fears that they could be damaged, attacked or stolen, while in transit.*

*A US Air Force spokesperson said plans for their deployment from the base were actioned immediately on receiving the notice to quit.*

# CHAPTER 23
# NATASHA BONNICI
## THE LATE SIGNOR BRUNO'S PALAZZO, MILAN

NATASHA WAS SITTING in what used to be Signor Bruno's book-lined study, in his *palazzo*, in Milan's fashionable old-town district of Brera. She swivelled in his revolving captain's chair, with its padded green leather seat, and looked across his large Tuscan desk. This was where he was sitting when her Uncle Sergio had appeared from the ante-room to one side of the study, and shot Signor Bruno dead.

It was also the room where, a few days later, Sergio had surprised Herr Wolfram Schober, Matthäus's father, and strangled him with a garotte – in part, to avenge himself for all the years that Wolfram Schober had treated him with contempt, for his rough Sicilian manners and for not being part of the northern European aristocracy.

Despite the circumstances of Signor Bruno's passing, his estate was happy to grant a lease of the *palazzo* to the Family, at an extortionate rent, so they could continue to use it as their base in Milan.

There had been no doubt in Sergio's mind that, as two of the four Wise Men of the Family, who governed its actions, Signor Bruno and Herr Schober would both have sanctioned the execution attempt made on him the day he had left Sant'Agata prison.

Sergio had sacrificed four years of his life in that prison, as part of a plea bargain to minimise any damage to the Family resulting from a failed Libyan oil-smuggling deal. Throughout his time behind bars, Sergio saw them disrespect every promise of support they had made him. Finally, when he was justifiably angry, they had sent two hitmen to kill him, as he had left confinement with his term served.

The two murders he had carried out in reprisal, along with that of a third Wise Man, Signor Lucca, had persuaded the one remaining Family high up that a life spent in premature retirement was preferable to eternity in a box. He had taken the money Natasha had offered him and fled. Her father too, had left the Family and arranged to retire to Serbia. Neither Marco nor Natasha Bonnici knew, at that point, that Sergio did not have long left to live

As the new head of the Family, Natasha had replaced the autocratic system administered by the organisation's Wise Men with a broader Committee, made up from the remaining senior members. She introduced some new blood, people on whom she hoped she could rely. With a mixture of charm, threats and bribery, she had convinced the Family that the best, long-term strategy for their organisation was to move away from some of the more troublesome areas of their business, such as waste disposal and construction, where it bumped up against the traditional organised crime groups. Her plan was to focus on capital-intensive, income-generating projects in infrastructure, finance, and, in particular, energy.

The Committee usually met early in the morning and then adjourned for lunch, taken in the *palazzo's* formal dining room. This left time for informal side meetings and conversations. Natasha had arranged to speak with one of the members whom she hoped would be able to throw light on her recent troubling conversation with Luke van der Westhuizen.

Bernd Kruder was a Committee member who lived in Vienna and had been a friend of Herr Schober, Matthäus's father. Kruder had been to the schloss on several occasions and had, many years ago, bought art from Herr Schober in one of his famous secret auctions, conducted in the castle's basement. The artworks they were bidding on had, in fact, been stolen by the Nazis during the Second World War. The Austrian government had appointed Herr Schober to recover the works and return them to their rightful owners – not sell them to his friends, and pocket the proceeds. The uncovering of his actions led to public disgrace and the end of Wolfram Schober's hitherto high-flying political career. It was then that he had channelled his many talents into the service of the Family.

Like all conversations with Natasha, she preferred to allow people to tell her what she wanted to know, without them realising they were doing so. She patiently listened to twenty minutes of Bernd telling her how Wolfram Schober's murder had caused resentment among the Austrian side of the Family, as he was one of only two members to be able to claim direct links to the once mighty Austro-Hungarian nobility.

Natasha had then intervened, to bring Kruder back to the point.

"Well, it's not quite true that he's the last link. He has a son, doesn't he? Matthäus?"

"Well, true, but that boy is nothing but trouble. Between you and me, Wolfram wanted me to introduce him around the Croce Bianca in Milan, but wiser counsel prevailed. He was never going to be one of us."

The Croce Bianca was the all-male, private members' club in Milan where northern Italy's hereditary aristocrats, industrialists, financiers and successful men of commerce all gathered. The eponymous Croce Bianca, or 'White Cross', was the family crest of the House of Savoy that had produced the last King of Italy, Umberto II. Natasha had understandably disapproved of the men's club's importance within the Family, but had realised this was one irritating tradition that she couldn't just sweep away.

Bernd continued: "Apparently Wolfram's... er, loss, hit his family hard, and their financial circumstances..."

"Bernd, don't dance around this. I treated them harshly, I know. But with good reason."

"Well, Matthäus has been struggling to make ends meet ever since. His mother and the rest of the family don't really understand the nature of their... change in circumstances. They believe life can carry on as before. Matthäus gets no thanks for his efforts, it's quite sad, really."

"If he's so useless, how has he managed to maintain the schloss and their entourage of hangers on?"

"Well, rumour has it – and I'm not certain about this, so don't call me out over it – that he has teamed up with some drugs ring and is sending wine bottles filled with heroin all over Europe. Online shopping for drugs! Can you believe it? Wolfram must be spinning in his grave."

Natasha sat blank-faced, while her mind started racing. This was all the proof she needed. Matthäus and Luke were in business together.

"Nobody from the Family is involved in this, are they?"

Bernd knew the organisation's strict prohibition on dealing drugs and realised he had spoken carelessly.

"Oh, no! Absolutely not! It's only a local thing, I'm sure."

"That better be true. Where's the supply coming from?"

"I heard, the Mediterranean somewhere. A new route through North Africa. The Turkey route is getting over-fished. The police and government there are becoming greedy. Paying for their protection is too expensive. That's all I know. It's none of my business, of course."

"Bernd, find out more. How long it's being going on, for one thing. But, most importantly, I want to know who the supplier is. I want a name. I also want to know his whereabouts – quickly! I don't care how you manage it, just do it. Spend whatever you need. I need to know, as a priority."

Natasha looked at Bernd, who did not seem too enthusiastic

about his new task. These bloody Austro-Hungarian relics, she thought, when will they wake up and realise it's all over?

"And, Bernd, I'm a liberal woman and we live in modern times. But if I think you're not doing your best on this, we'll see how your wife feels about that nice young waiter from Café Opera, you keep hidden away in Vienna, shall we?"

Bernd Kruder huffed angrily.

"There's no need for that! I'll do my best. I always do."

"This is important. Put local loyalties behind you. I don't care whether Matthäus Schober is the long-lost son of Franz Ferdinand himself. Get this done."

# CHAPTER 24

# SAVI AZZOPARDI

SAVI AZZOPARDI

SAVI WENT into the large room above Danka's gym. Below him, he could hear the heavy rock beats of her extreme cardio session belting out, and her loud, deep voice, urging on the sweating after-work crowd to greater efforts.

He did not mind the racket because as he went through the door, he immediately put a set of noise-cancelling headphones over his ears. The only sensation he felt was the vibration of the crowd bouncing on the floor below and the occasional shock wave from a twenty-kilo lump of cast iron hitting the deck.

After he had escaped from the cliff top chapel where Natasha had held him captive, she had sent a notorious local hitman, known as *Il-Barri*, or the Bull, to Danka's flat in Sliema, to dispose of Savi. By then, he knew too much about her business for his own good. What *Il-Barri* had not taken into account was the presence of Danka, who had managed to knock him senseless with a six-kilo kettle bell.

Simon had been horrified that Natasha had chosen to attack Savi and, indirectly, Simon's girlfriend. Once his anger had cooled, he had told Natasha that he had heard Savi had gone to England and enrolled in a northern university, to study computer science. Simon then told Savi to move out of the flat, find somewhere of his own and keep his head down. Natasha suspected that Simon might not be telling her the entire truth about Savi's whereabouts but, as time passed, she had lost interest in Savi Azzopardi. Until recently.

Hanging on the wall behind Savi's desk was a bank of six computer screens, all with programs running, dealing with various parts of the war he was currently waging on the Turkish Oil and Gas Organisation, in accordance with Mike Lloyd's instructions. He had bought a time-limited licence for Dragonfly 4.0 from a group he knew. He thought the Roaming Wolves were probably Russians, though they were careful to leave 'false flags', in the form of strings of code in French, Indian and Arabic, to make identifying their nationality difficult.

The program had worked like a dream. The employees of TOGO must have never heard of password protection or cyber security as it was all too easy to open multiple doors into their systems. Once in, Savi had had no trouble exfiltrating thousands of files of information. He had asked a group of his less-scrupulous hacker friends to comb through some of these, to find useful financial information which, if released, could cause embarrassment.

It had not taken long for them to uncover a thread of confidential emails, from the finance director to various board members, in which they conspired to hide a massive overstatement of the company's reserves of gas from their Black Sea fields. The overstatement of value was a sizable part of TOGO's market valuation and had been published in their yearly report and accounts. Savi had already sent this market-sensitive information to *Oil and Gas Monthly*, the *Financial Times*, *Wall Street Journal* and four of the Turkish dailies. He was waiting for the fall out, which he knew would have serious implications for the business, as well as the individuals concerned.

Savi held all TOGO's files on two stacks of servers that blinked and hummed against the back wall of the air-conditioned room. All the files were encrypted and his ransom demand for their restoration, of ten million euros in crypto-currency, had not yet been rejected.

Over the last four years, Savi had become a wealthy young man. Stuffed in a rolled, used football sock, in a zipped pocket of an old sports bag, slung in the corner of his bedroom at Danka's, was a 'cold wallet'. This was a bunch of data on a hard drive the size of a cigarette box. It was 'cold' because it was not connected to the internet, therefore unhackable. It was a 'wallet' because it allowed him access to nearly five million euros of crypto-currency. Not only did Savi hack for cash, both on his own account and on behalf of others, but he also mined and traded crypto, being smart enough to cash out profits into a US dollar account in Cyprus. He was happy to pay a negative interest rate on the cash, in exchange for security and privacy.

Savi did not care about the money. It allowed him to buy whatever trainers he wanted, and when Danka got pissed off with him and ordered him back to his own place, which happened a couple of times a year, he had enough money to make a big gesture that seemed to negate her threat. On one occasion, he had the gym fitted out with an expensive sound system. On another, he paid for Simon and Danka to take busi-ness-class flights back home to Poland. He had bought her a new Smart car and had it 'wrapped', with the gym's logo and straplines. The gifts, together with empty promises to keep her kitchen clean and pick up his stuff from the living-room floor, usually bought him another couple of months of sanctuary.

When he was not working or sleeping, Savi disappeared for hours into the world of online gaming or eSports. His handle, SnakeHead had become sufficiently well known for him to pick up sponsorship from a company specialising in online betting. There was not much money involved, though he received an assortment of branded clothing and free equipment. But, in the eSports world, the big rewards came from the prize money to be won in open competitions. These games took place in large arenas, attended by thousands of avid fans, who came to watch the 'athletes' battle it out in games such as *Call of Duty* and *FIFA*. In addition to the arena audience, thousands of others watched the competitions online and, of course, bet on the outcomes.

The truth was that Savi was borderline agoraphobic and suffered mainline anxiety, so he refused point blank to attend any competition away from the island, unless Danka or Simon went with him. As Simon was more often than not busy with Natasha, Savi's availability to compete depended upon his ability to persuade Danka to travel with him. He styled her as his 'security manager' and it was not unusual for the top eSports athletes to have a small entourage accompanying them. The organisers often paid travel and hotel expenses to have him and his 'team' present at events.

To Savi, cyber crime was another pleasant pastime, something outside of the present, where he could express himself without the stress and anxieties that flowed from real-world interactions. As an operator in the underground virtual world, he was recognised and respected by his peers and delighted in exposing the stupidity and naivety of the organisations he humbled.

As SnakeHead, he was an exciting eSports competitor; brave and courageous as any boxing contender and possessed of the same ruthless will to win as an F1 driver, and all with no exposure to physical harm and without the risk of humiliation or ridicule that followed him around in his non-virtual existence.

It was nearly midday and Savi was sitting on his favourite bench on Sliema promenade, the remnants of a kebab on the seat beside him, watching the tourists push and shove their way to the front of the queue for the ferry to Valletta. He was about to finish off his breakfast when the phone rang. It was Mike Lloyd.

"How's it going, Savi? Looks good from here."

"Yeah, they're in deep shit now. Two weeks and they're still trying to break the encryption. They're not going to do it without the key – and I'm the only one who knows that. They're idiots!"

"Yeah, good job, Savi, but leak more of that financial intelligence – I loved that! That must have them eating their livers!

Anyway, you've got a week to screw the ransom out of them, then it's game over."

Savi was disappointed; he was only getting started.

"But why? I haven't reached the operational stuff yet! I'm going to mess with the Black Sea pipeline this week."

"Good. Let's see what that does. But, when I say stop, you stop. Got it?"

"Well..."

"No, no 'wells'. The whole point here is to get the Turks back in line. When we think the shit is deep enough and they're desperate, we're going to come charging over the hill like the Seventh fuckin' Cavalry and I'm going to be General Custer. We'll tell them to get into line with UN Laws of the Sea, stop this stupid shit with the Libyan accord, hands off the Greek islands, and then we might – just might – give them their oil industry back."

"But what about me? I haven't been paid."

"Come on, Savi, you'll get something. Trust me."

He looked suspiciously at the phone and mustered such courage as he had.

"If you screw me over again, Mike, like you did last time, there'll be consequences."

He smiled at the handset and then pulled a mock-threatening expression.

"Consequences, huh? Such as?"

"You know what I'm saying. *Consequences*."

"Are you threatening *me*, Savi? Are you threatening the *US of A*? Really? Because think carefully about that, if you are."

"We can easily take down a bunch of stuff at the Pentagon, you know that, don't you? There are a bunch of guys waiting..."

"Stop right there, Savi! Say any more and I'll have to send a team to bring you in and take you somewhere nasty. Don't you ever talk to me like that again!"

There was real anger in Mike's voice and Savi's foot started to tap fast against the pavement.

"From now on, if anything happens in that building, one PC that doesn't boot-up, a printer that doesn't print, a file that gets lost... you'll find yourself hooded and on your knees in a basement. D'you hear me?"

Savi started trembling. Despite the midday sun beating down on him, he had suddenly gone cold.

"Yeah, I get it. OK, I was only joshing."

"Let's hope so, kid, 'cos you can forget skateboarding, when both your feet point backwards." Mike paused to let the threat sink in. He need not have bothered, Savi was quaking.

"OK, let's talk about good stuff. You know I said I had a 'tasty morsel' for you? A kinda bonus?"

"Yeah?"

"Well, you remember Natasha Bonnici, the pretty lady who never quite got round to throwing you off Dingli cliffs?"

"Yeah, I remember her."

"Well, you know she's a big deal in MalTech Energy?"

"So?"

"She's going oil exploring, with some boat called the *Ocean Vantage*, off the coast of Crete. And her friends in TOGO, who gave her the concession, have also given her full access to their exploration systems. You know about geoscientific analyses... mapping, exploration data, geotechnical testing... all that good stuff?"

"What's that got to do with me?"

"Well, she's leased a boat worth two hundred million US. She's insured it, obviously, but the policy says she's got to take – hang on, I'm going to read this shit to you, to get it right."

There was a brief pause.

"OK, she's got to take *'all reasonable steps to protect the vessel from others taking control of all or any part of the vessel, by whatever means'*.

"It's the normal anti-piracy thing. You know, you've got to keep out of Somali waters and, if you see the bandits coming, don't invite them on board for a beer or whatever."

"Mike, what the fuck are you talking about?"

"OK, here's the interesting bit. Our attorneys say if there was damage to the ship caused by hackers taking control of any critical system, and reasonable means of protection were not in place, then the ship would effectively be uninsured."

The penny slowly dropped and Savi sat back on the bench, smiling to himself.

"I get it. So, if there are no reasonable precautions, like passwords, firewalls and stuff, she cops for the expenses? Then, it's payback time for me!"

"There's a clever boy. I said you'd like it."

There was no love lost between Mike Lloyd and Natasha following her theft of the Libyan dinars from under his nose and he had waited a long time to strike back. But this was so elegant – using Savi as his Nemesis added a pleasing 'off the books' element to the master stroke.

"OK, Savi, you've got one week to extract some cash for yourself and the *Ocean Vantage* is all yours. But remember, no environmental disasters. We don't want those nice Cretan beaches covered in oil. The Greek Greenies wouldn't like it."

# CHAPTER 25
# ARTICLE IN MALTA TELEGRAPH

*Reporter: Amy Halliday*
*13 July 2021*

*Greek naval Vessel sunk by Turkish fishermen*

*The Greek Island of Gavdos, some fifty kilometres south of Crete, became the centre of a serious, but bizarre, international incident yesterday, when a Turkish trawler deliberately rammed and sank a Hellenic Navy vessel, moored in the island's tiny port.*

*The fishermen claim to be natives of Gavdos, which they call by its old Ottoman name of Gondoz. They say, in a video released to the press, that they are reclaiming sovereignty of the island on behalf of the Republic of Turkey.*

*There had been doubt about which country the island belonged to, but it was widely accepted that any claim Turkey may once have had, has long since lapsed.*

*Locals say the fishermen do not speak either Turkish or Greek, but seem to converse in Arabic. The fishing vessel is called Güvenilir (or Trust-*

worthy) *and is registered in Turkey, but there are questions about who these men really are and the validity of their claim.*

*The attack happened around midnight, local time, when the commercial trawler entered the small harbour and encountered the Greek gunboat. According to witness accounts, the trawler reversed to the harbour entrance and then charged full steam ahead, deliberately colliding with the gunboat and causing it to sink. The fishing vessel also sustained serious damage to its hull.*

*There were four crewmen asleep on the gunboat at the time. All of them escaped from the sinking vessel, without harm, and are now being held captive by the dozen or so Turkish fishermen. A contingent of thirty Greek Marines, who were brought to the island by the gunboat, are currently on exercises along with another dozen Greek soldiers who man a small garrison building at the southernmost tip of the island.*

*A statement from the Greek Minister of Foreign Affairs complained that this was an overt act of Turkish aggression, aimed at further escalating the ongoing disputes about Turkish access to Greek territorial waters and Economic Activity Zones. Athens demanded reparations for the damage to its naval vessel.*

*Turkey countered this by saying it had every right to protect the interests of its citizens and supported them in their actions to reclaim territory that had been illegally colonised by the Greeks, in an 'island-grabbing frenzy, aimed at gaining maritime advantage in the Aegean and the eastern Mediterranean'.*

*The UN has appealed for calm heads to be maintained and has asked for more information about the identity of the Turkish fishermen.*

# CHAPTER 26
# ABDULLAH BELKACEM
## SOUTH GAVDOS

ABDULLAH and his men landed on the pebble beach, heaving the inflatable boats up onto the shore and securing them with long anchor lines to an outcrop of rocks. It was pitch dark and Abdullah realised that, although these conditions favoured the surprise element of the attack, the inability to see a hand's width in front of them presented its own challenges.

It took fifteen minutes before they had all disembarked and were at the foot of a track leading up a narrow gully towards the interior of the island. Abdullah whispered frantic instructions to the dark shadows in front of him, while the wind and the rush of the sea carried the words away. His men were burdened with weapons and heavy military packs containing ammunition, food and water. They planned to use the supplies within the small barracks once they had taken it, but as a backup they had brought enough basic stores for three days.

Abdullah led them in single file up the narrow gully for a kilometre or so and then took a path branching off to the left, climbing steeply uphill. This turned out to be the wrong track and soon faded away to nothing. They were left in the dark, struggling on the loose, jagged limestone underfoot, while the sharp thorns of the scrub tore at their legs.

The men were falling and cursing and Abdullah's hissing and whispering became ever louder and more insistent. Eventually one of the men dropped to his knees, muttering, "There it is!" and the whole line paused. Abdullah strained his eyes against the darkness until he too saw the dense rectangular outline of a building, some two hundred yards away. The man nearest to him was called Ibrahim. Abdullah tapped him on the arm and gestured him forwards. Ibrahim was his second-in-command on the mission and had led many skirmishes in the past. The two trusted each other and worked well together.

Abdullah and Ibrahim crept towards the building, treading carefully on the unstable ground, to make sure they had located the right place. As they drew near, they saw it was a small hilltop observation post and the cinderblock, flat-roofed barracks itself lay a little below, on an open plateau. Beyond that were two large tents that looked like stores of some sort. Abdullah could make out at least six vehicles, two of them sizeable military trucks, randomly parked on the flat ground.

He had been led to believe they were facing a few Greek conscripts, but something about that intel did not seem to fit with what he was seeing below him. As they lay on their stomachs, overlooking the base, they heard voices, as three men appeared through the gloom, standing behind the vehicles and huddling together to light cigarettes. By the flames of their lighters, Abdullah could see they were carrying automatic rifles and were all dressed in combat gear, including tactical belts and light body armour. There was no way these guys were time-serving conscripts; they were professional soldiers and there were enough of them here to supply a three-man guard for the night watch. For the first time since agreeing to mount the invasion, Abdullah wondered what he had got himself into.

He lay on the ground, wondering what to do. He realised he could not trust the intelligence he had been given. To rush at an unknown and unquantified enemy would be foolish. Similarly, they could not just wait for daylight and reassess their position.

He had no idea where to hide thirty men and, even if he did, could never manage to locate such a place in this impenetrable darkness.

The problem was that George and the three ships would soon be mooring in the small harbour, and inevitably word of their arrival would get through to these regular Greek soldiers, who were sure to take a truck and investigate.

As it happened, the need for further deliberation was taken out of Abdullah's hands. At the back of the line, a hundred metres behind him, he heard their radio crackle into life and George's voice resonating across the limestone plateau.

"*Trustworthy* to Red Team, Trustworthy to Red Team, over?"

"Red Team to Trustworthy, radio silence, please. Over and out."

Abdullah cringed as he saw the three guards stop their conversation and look at one another, then cast wary glances around them and upwards, trying to work out what they had heard and which direction the strange noise had come from.

"*Trustworthy* to Red Team, come in, urgent, over."

There was an echoing silence after the operator belatedly turned the set off, but the damage had been done. Beneath them, cigarettes were extinguished and rifles unshouldered as the three guards made their way up the rise. They produced high-powered torches from their equipment belts and started to sweep the hillside. Abdullah and Ibrahim ducked down, as a beam swept over their heads. Abdullah remembered Hakan's orders. 'No dead Greeks', so turned to Ibrahim and put his fingers to his lips, making a chopping action with his hand. Ibrahim understood. The two of them slid out of their packs and gently put their weapons down on the rocks.

Abdullah then suddenly started talking very loudly in Arabic, putting his arm around Ibrahim's shoulders and addressing the line of men crouching in the shadows behind them.

"Do not move, stay where you are. We will disarm the

sentries. If we are taken, Wanis Ali will lead. Be warned, these are Greek Marines – not conscripts. They are many. But for now, stay still."

Then, to Ibrahim's horror, Abdullah started singing an old Agrawli folksong at the top of his voice. The Greek soldiers emerged out of the darkness, rifles held easily at their side, half smiles on their faces, watching Abdullah and Ibrahim swaying down the path towards them. One soldier hung back and two of them stepped forwards.

Abdullah flung up his hands in mock surprise and then started laughing. He stepped towards the soldiers and put his arms around one Marine, still singing and pretending to dance around him. He then danced around the second, bemused soldier, while Ibrahim, who now understood Abdullah's tactic, shimmied from one foot to the other, clapping along and moving ever closer to the first man.

Abdullah finished his song with a flourish, hitting a high note with the Arabic words: "Remember, no killing!"

He then struck the third Marine with a fast hard punch to the windpipe. The other two made the fatal mistake of hesitating to raise their weapons, allowing Abdullah to strike down the second man. He disabled the Marine's knee and then struck him hard on the back of the neck as he stumbled forward. Abdullah could not understand why Ibrahim had failed to disable the first man, but his friend lay in the dirt, with his hands over his face, as the first Marine slid down the hillside to the safety of the barracks, shouting as he went.

Abdullah screamed for the others to come forward and set up a line on the hillside overlooking the barracks. They lumbered over, dumping their equipment, as they covered the distance to the ridge. It didn't take them long to get a dozen guns trained on the carpark below. They had no line of sight to the barracks' entrance, but believed they could lay down fire and keep the soldiers bottled up inside until Abdullah worked out their next move.

Even before the fishermen were all in place, the carpark was swarming with Greek Marines, in various stages of undress, all tightening straps and banging magazines into weapons, flooding out of the two large tents. To Abdullah's horror, he realised these were not for storage at all, but housed a sizeable contingent of soldiers, a platoon of them at least. Abdullah's men let loose a volley of fire that immediately had the Marines running for cover into the block-built barracks, save for three or four, who took cover behind a jeep and started returning fire.

Abdullah stood back, clenched his fists and swore. The last thing he wanted was to get drawn into a firefight. If any of his men got injured, he had no means of helping them. They were exposed on a barren hillside and, when daylight came, their position would become even worse. All the Greeks had to do was summon some air support from Crete and they were finished. And, as for them being a group of fishermen – that cover was totally blown.

He told three of his men to work their way around behind the Marines at the jeep and try to force them back inside the barracks. Once they were out of the way, he had decided to get to the vehicles and make a run for it, to the port. If that served as a diversion, the rest of the men could make their way back to the beach and the RHIBs. But, Abdullah was worried the Marines would follow them and then the group could find itself trapped in the narrow gully or on the beach. He was furious with Hakan Toprak. He had been clear that the Turks did not want a pile of dead Greeks, for reasons Abdullah understood, but the lack of decent intelligence had put him in this impossible position.

As gunfire crackled around him, he grabbed the radio operator and retreated away from the action. He sent the call signal to the party in the harbour.

"Red Party to *Trustworthy*, over."

George replied almost immediately. His voice was shaky and it sounded as if he was speaking from inside a large tin can.

"Red Party, this is *Trustworthy*. Have you got them yet? We've had some problems here!"

"George, *you* have problems? You have twenty men, many guns, three ships… you're probably sitting around drinking tea!"

"Er – not quite. We have one ship and that's been holed and is sinking fast. There's eight of us and four prisoners. Oh, and a crowd of Greek villagers, plus angry yacht owners from the marina, who have surrounded us. We're trapped."

Abdullah tried to make sense of what he was hearing.

"George, I am not understanding. Where are the other ships?"

"They fled."

"Fled… ran away? From what? George, this is not making sense."

"There is a Greek gunboat in the harbour. In my vessel, the lead one, we could not retreat, but the others turned tail and left us."

"A battleship?"

"Yes! Well, a small one anyway. It was a Greek naval ship and it had guns on it."

"So where is it now? Are there sailors… Marines?"

"Yes, we took them prisoner."

"All of them?"

"Yes, four of them."

"Only four of them on such a ship? And the battleship?"

"It's not a battleship, but we rammed it and it sank."

Abdullah was speechless. He could not imagine how this had happened. The first signs of daylight were appearing in the east and it would not be long before the early-morning sun dispelled the cover of darkness. He was becoming seriously concerned. He knew they had to get moving.

"This navy ship is under the water? George, you are joking with me, yes? It is not much funny! Wait there, *bismillah*, we will be coming soon, perhaps an hour."

"Be quick, because it's filling up with water."

"Are you too prisoners?"

"No, we're staying on the boat. I don't know what else to do."

"Let me finish this here and I am coming, *inshallah*!"

# CHAPTER 27

# NATASHA BONNICI
### VIENNA, AUSTRIA

IT TAKES ten hours to go by train between Milan and Vienna, with one change at Innsbruck. Driving the eight hundred and fifty kilometres is marginally quicker, at only nine hours, but it took Natasha's Dassault Falcon jet just ninety minutes to reach Vienna from Milan's Linate airport.

She spent the time working on her laptop while Simon sat impassively behind her. The security man was worried. Danka had told him what Savi was getting himself into and he realised it could have serious repercussions for all three of them. He had not had time to get hold of Savi and wring his scrawny neck before he left, but had told Danka that, if the idiot was going to start meddling in MalTech Energy's business, she should take his laptop off him and lock him in his room until Simon got back.

Savi had only avoided meeting with a grisly end at Natasha's hands previously because Simon had risked his own neck, breaking the kid out of the remote clifftop chapel, where Natasha had been holding him, and secretly taking him to safety at Danka's place. If Savi thought he could get the better of Natasha, he was a naïve fool. Simon swore quietly and shook his head. No *if* about it. Savi *was* a naïve fool.

Simon noticed that Natasha had finished working and closed the lid of her laptop. She raised herself from the soft leather seat, smoothed her skirt and came to sit facing him across the narrow cabin table.

"Thirty minutes to Vienna. Are you driving or do we have a car?"

"We have a car waiting airside, Miss Natasha. Do you still plan to go straight to the restaurant?"

"Yes, I think so. When we arrive, get rid of the driver and you take me, please."

Simon nodded.

"Certainly."

She was studying him thoughtfully.

"You don't like Luke van der Westhuizen, do you?"

Simon smiled.

"He's none of my business but, for the record, as long as you like him, he's a friend of mine."

"Well, that's the point, you see. I'm not so sure I do like him much anymore."

Simon did not react in any way; not a twitch or a glimmer of surprise was visible.

"I want you to keep a very careful eye on him for me. I want to know what he's up to in Malta. He tried to unload an envelope of diamonds on Gerald Camilleri in the executive lounge of the airport, as a 'golden hello'. Gerald told him where to go, of course, and rang me straight away. Such a good friend."

"Is the Assistant Commissioner on Van der Westhuizen's case, too?"

"I've asked him to keep his eyes and ears open, he hasn't come back to me with anything yet. But you don't ply the Assistant Commissioner of the *Pulizija* with diamonds, unless you think you might need him on your side, do you? So, what exactly is Luke up to...

"And there's something else. Luke's involved with another

person, someone wholesaling heroin, who apparently wants to kill my father. That's who we're going to see now."

At this, Simon leaned forward in his seat, brow furrowed in concern. He not only respected his ex-employer, Marco Bonnici, but liked him. Not a common phenomenon amongst those working for rich people.

"Can I ask why someone would want to kill Signor Bonnici?"

"Revenge – to get at me. Sergio killed this man's father during the Milan upheaval. He knows I was involved."

"He's a Wise Man's son!"

Normally imperturbable, Simon was visibly alarmed.

"A former Wise Man's son, yes. Matthäus Schober, to be precise."

"This sounds more than a little dangerous, Natasha. Are you sure this is how you want to play it?"

"Oh, yes. Perfectly sure. I persuaded Bernd Kruder to set up a business meeting with Schober and he'll make sure our man shows. He thinks this is a meeting with an Italian drugs distributor, *mano a mano*. He's ours for the taking.

"What's the plan?"

Simon did not like this, it all sounded very sketchy.

"Nothing really. I'm going to whisper sweet nothings in his ear and hope he gets the message. And I want to know exactly what his relationship with Luke van der Westhuizen is. Luke, of course, assures me he has nothing to do with the drugs trade."

"Is that it?"

"Not quite. The Family's head of security, Bohdan, works with a Serbian team who are adept at hanging around in male toilets. They'll be waiting for Schober and know what to do with him."

Simon raised his eyebrows and sighed. He knew Bohdan, who was a ruthless, but very professional, ex-Ukrainian army officer. If he had to organise a take down, Simon knew it would be well thought through. He decided to ring and check the details with Bohdan as soon as the plane landed.

"If drugs are his business, our man's going to bring his own security. It doesn't matter if he's been told not to. I wish I'd been involved in these arrangements," Simon fretted.

"You'd only have tried to talk me out of it," Natasha soothed him.

"Now, this is what I want from you. Go in and help the injured, and no doubt bloodied, Matthäus Schober out to the car, so I can have a quiet word. Apparently, on the landing behind the gents, which is on the first floor, there's a fire escape leading down to the carpark, where you'll be standing by."

"Excuse me for putting it like this, but what if he doesn't want a piss?"

"He's been told to go there, for a security check before the meeting… guns, hidden wires, you know the routine."

"Clever. And if he won't come with me?"

"Well, he'll be handed over to you in no condition to refuse. I suspect he'll be compliant."

"OK." Simon saw there was little point in challenging the plan, so decided to lighten the mood.

"If he's in a mess, we could lose the deposit on the limo."

Natasha smiled sweetly.

"That's what I like: people who will go out of their way to save me money!" And she returned to her own seat.

The plane began its descent into Vienna and the co-pilot emerged to ask them politely to fasten their seat belts. Natasha was thinking about Luke van der Westhuizen and what a shame it it had been to spoil things by bringing business into their relationship. She knew he had something going on in Malta but could not work out what it was. He traded diamonds and that probably meant he smuggled diamonds, which did not bother her in the slightest. His clumsy approach to Camilleri was his first mistake. He probably thought she would not get to hear of it, which was sweet, because that showed her how stupid he really was.

His involvement with Matthäus Schober was even more

remarkable. Had Luke telephoned immediately following his dinner in Istanbul, to tell her of the threat to her father, she would have been grateful. But he had left it over a week. Why? He had an agenda in play, something he wanted from her. That could be the only reason he had held off telling her until they were together. And all the time, Marco was at risk.

She had phoned him, of course, and suggested he return to Malta, where she could keep him safe.

"Like you did Sergio?" was his reply.

Her father blamed her for the death of his best friend and cousin, at the hands of the Russian secret service. Natasha had stolen a billion Libyan dinars from them, and Mike Lloyd had told the Russians it was her, so payback in some form was inevitable. It was clear from the way the Russians had planted the car bomb in Marco's Range Rover that it had been intended for him. As luck would have it, Marco had told Sergio he could borrow the car that morning and so his oldest friend and associate died in his place.

Anyway, Marco had refused Natasha's invitation to seek safety with her and said he was leaving the estate in Serbia for a few weeks, for an extended trip to the Bernese Oberland, where he was researching a book on the Schynige Platte Alpine Garten. The historic garden, situated high in the Swiss mountains above Interlaken, boasted over five hundred species of Alpine plants it seemed.

Natasha was bitterly disappointed by her father's cold and dismissive attitude towards her. In fact, Marco missed his only daughter and thought about her daily; but that did not stop him from being fearful of what she had become.

Meanwhile, the fact that Luke had held back important information for over a week was only part of the reason Natasha felt uneasy about him. She also wanted to know what business he was doing with Matthäus Schober. Diamonds and drugs? She did not see the immediate connection. To her frustration, Bernd

Kruder had discovered very little about Matthäus's contacts or suppliers. Gerald Camilleri had made no progress in uncovering what Luke was involved with in Malta. Natasha was finding it all very frustrating. She would enjoy taking out that frustration on Matthäus Schober.

# CHAPTER 28
# GEORGE ZAMMIT
## KARAVE HARBOUR, GAVDOS

As GEORGE HANDED the radio back to one of Abdullah's men, he was conscious of all eyes on him again. The *Trustworthy*'s metal plates creaked ominously as the weight of water entering its hold caused the ship to settle onto one side. The shifting of the gunboat, which had been providing some support to the *Trustworthy*, caused the trawler to list still further to starboard and the rate at which they were shipping water increased. The men shouted and shrieked at every creak and groan of the stricken trawler, grabbing at rails and bulkheads for balance, as the angle of list became more acute.

The four prisoners were cowering in the darkness, in the far corner of the bridge. George knew, if the hold kept filling at the current rate, they would all soon be swimming in the dock, covered in the oil and filth leaking from the damaged ships. Well, some of them would be; not George, because he could not swim. They had no choice but to disembark and face the crowd on the quayside. They had weapons, after all, and he had the support of Abdullah's best men. He assured himself there was no reason to be frightened.

George took a deep breath and addressed the men, asking Hamza to translate for him.

"OK. We have to get off the ship. It's sinking. We need to get onto the quay and go into the town to wait there for Abdullah. He's coming soon, with the others. So, we'll find a building and wait. No shooting, except in the air, to frighten people into keeping back."

Hamza relayed this, then argued with the men, in an Arabic conversation that went back and forth for at least a minute.

George asked: "What're they saying?"

"They say, 'OK'," Hamza replied, managing to look past him, while apparently meeting his gaze.

"That's it? No, they didn't. What did they really say?"

"They ask, do you want to shoot the prisoners or should they do it?"

One of the Greek ratings understood English and immediately began to plead and remonstrate. George shut him up, saying nobody was getting shot, if they did what they were told.

They gathered together their rifles, the radio and a pack of ammunition and bottles of water, then pushed open the oval bulkhead door leading to the companionway from the back of the bridge to the trawl deck. They shuffled up this, while leaning against one wall, due to the crazy angle of the listing boat, and finally arrived on deck.

Like a group of pirates, they tumbled over the rails down onto the stricken gunboat that was jammed between the Trustworthy and the quayside, and made their way across its deck, to the gangway. There, a crowd of maybe a fifty people had gathered. Some were clearly from the marina and were dressed in yellow and orange sailing waterproofs, which they had pulled over pyjamas; others were locals who had driven down to the port to see for themselves what was happening. Some sat quietly on the ground, watching proceedings, resting their backs against the far wall of the breakwater.

The appearance on deck of George and his troop, lit by the first rays of the new day, brought the crowd to life. There were shouts and calls, many from the yachtsmen whose boats had been damaged, as the pontoons had shifted and the two ships had ploughed their way through the yachts' fibreglass hulls. George was trying to ignore the hostile crowd, while working his way down the acutely angled gangway, to get ashore. Looking up, he noticed a dozen small lights, scattered amongst the crowd, and realised people were filming them with their phones.

George was not carrying a weapon, but he shouted to Hamza to have the men shoot into the air, to frighten the onlookers away. The last thing he wanted was Marianna seeing him clambering around the side of a sunken gunboat. It also occurred to him that, ultimately, the judges, sitting in the courts in Athens, might also take a dim view of their antics. He could hardly claim he was in Gavdos on *Pulizija* business.

From behind him, a volley of gunfire whistled overhead and pinged onto the quayside, ricocheting against the harbour walls. It only took a couple of shots before the crowd went scurrying off down the breakwater. At that point, the whole of Karave was suddenly lit up by an intense red glare, coming from high in the dawn sky. One after another, bright red distress flares were being fired by the yachtsmen. They hung for a few moments at the top of their arc then gently fell, leaving a scarlet trail of sparkles in the deep blue, dawn sky.

George anxiously searched the small harbour for any sign of Abdullah, but he had yet to arrive. This was all turning out very badly indeed. They could not stand there on the quayside, so he waved the men forward, marching them towards the crowd standing around the few buildings that comprised the town.

As they reached the end of the breakwater, George noticed there was an elderly man and his wife standing defiantly in the middle of the path. It was clear they had no intention of moving aside. The man was well over sixty, short and plump, with a shock of white hair. He wore a voluminous white shirt over a pair of baggy blue shorts that hung past his knees. His wife was a grey sparrow of a woman who wore an oversize bright yellow wet-weather jacket from which, two stick thin, bare legs protruded. She kept tight hold of her husband's arm and crushed herself into him for protection.

Hamza was walking beside George. He idly raised his gun and swung it towards the couple.

"Put that down, now!" shouted the man, completely unintimidated.

Hamza immediately lowered the gun. This man had a way about him. He released his wife, set his hands on his hips and took an aggressive stance, legs sturdily planted a foot apart.

"Who's in charge here?"

A stand off had developed. The four young prisoners shuffled forward, their once-pristine boxers stained and wet and baggy, drooping from their hips. In their near-nakedness, they looked like spectres in the thin morning light. They tentatively edged past the couple, looking back over their shoulders at George and the fishermen. George let them go. He had no idea what to do with them, anyway.

"I said, who is in charge here?"

The old man was English. George recognised the type; he had grown up when there were still some old British ex-military sorts on Malta, bumptious and entitled, the lot of them.

George put himself in Abdullah's shoes. He spoke firmly and tried to inject some menace into his tone.

"Take your wife and leave! You'll not be hurt, if you go now."

"But you have damaged my boat! There are deep scratches all down the starboard side. They have gone through the gelcoat and I can see the fibreglass, by God! I want your name and your insurance details."

George took a couple of steps towards him and could see the man's face, probably florid in normal times, but now bright red with anger. George spoke softly into his ear.

"We are Turkish soldiers and your boat's is a casualty of war. Now unless you shut up and move, there'll be two more casualties! I suggest you contact the Turkish Embassy in London or wherever it is you're from. So, please, excuse us. As you can see, we've things to do."

With a furious glare at George, the man took his wife's arm and the pair of them stood aside.

George did not have anything to do until Abdullah arrived, but he did not want to be shown up by a pompous, elderly Englishman. Especially, if there were camera-phones involved.

The crowd seemed to melt away in front of them, as they slowly walked into what comprised the harbour. The people from the marina stood together in disgruntled groups, talking amongst themselves and muttering into their mobiles. George had a feeling that they would not be alone for very much longer and kept looking into the brightening sky for signs of aircraft or helicopters. News of the assault, if that was what he had commanded, must surely have reached the authorities on Crete, which was only fifty kilometres away.

They ended up sitting by the two petrol pumps that constituted the island's garage, which was where Abdullah eventually found them. George heard the high revving of the military truck and the grinding of the gears, long before it came into the harbour parking lot. Abdullah was by himself.

George came up to the driver's window. Abdullah was looking past him, at the carnage in the harbour.

"George... *Ya lahwi*! Oh my God! What have you done?"

He laughed out loud.

"You sank the battleship!"

Hamza jumped up alongside George on the step to the driver's side and started talking excitedly to Abdullah.

"*Wallah*, you won't believe it! George say, 'We go back, we go back!' And we go back, fast, and bang... *wallah*! Pooof! Ship it go down!"

Abdullah put his hand to his head.

"George, if I had not seen this with my own eyes, I would never have believed it. *Wallah* indeed! Well, Toprak will be pleased, the hornets are certainly angry now. We must go, while we can."

They all clambered into the back of the truck, except for George and Hamza, who sat with Abdullah. He was still laughing, in the front. He crashed the gears, clumsily turned the vehicle and set off up the hillside to find his way back south. He had told the rest of his group to make their way down the gulley back to the beach and make their escape. He only hoped his expeditionary force had managed to evade the Greek Marines so far.

He had told Ibrahim to leave one of the RHIB's in the next bay and secure it there, so that he and the others could make their escape later. Meanwhile the two remaining fishing vessels had retreated twelve nautical miles, to be outside Greek territorial waters and, unless they heard differently, they were to wait and collect the landing party. Abdullah was to take his group to the hidden RHIB and make his way out to the trawlers. It was a rough plan, but the best Abdullah could come up with, in the circumstances.

As they left Karave, they drove past the old couple, standing at the side of the road. The white-haired man stared after them, defiant and indignant. Feeling more secure, back with Abdullah and making their escape, George gave them a cheeky smile and a thumbs-up.

# CHAPTER 29

# SAVI AZZOPARDI
## SLIEMA, MALTA

SAVI HAD BEEN BUSY. Although lacking many social skills, he had a gift for formidable concentration. Had he applied these powers of focus and information retention to achieving more conventional goals, his life could have been very different. Unfortunately, the deeper Savi went down the rabbit hole of his latest obsession, the less attention he paid to the world around him.

To Danka, this meant the floor of his 'office' above the studio and, more importantly, her flat, became littered with uneaten slices of pizza, kebab wrappers and beer cans. The ashtrays overflowed with half-smoked joints and mangled cigarette stubs. The smell of stale tobacco, sweet rotting food and the presence of more flies than normal, meant Savi was engrossed in something. It also annoyed her that he demanded that the curtains remained permanently shut, to protect his red, sleepless eyes, as he peered into the backlighting of the screens that surrounded him.

Experience had shown her that these periods came and went. Rather than waste energy fighting him, she bit her tongue and hoped, whatever it was he was doing, would soon be over. Danka often wondered how she had got herself into this position. She had vowed never to lose her independence and level of fitness to motherhood. Simon and she often joked that looking after Savi was probably a better compromise than the pair of them becoming biological parents.

The hack into the Turkish Oil and Gas Organisation was still going well. Savi had noticed that a cyber-defence team had arrived and he could watch them, on his mirror system, doing a digital forensic search on huge volumes of data. When they had completed their initial review, he would strike again with a new suite of programs, sitting ready in the background, and prove to TOGO's management that paying the ransom was the only way to restore their systems. He had another few days to let them stew.

Meanwhile he had to see what he could do to disrupt drilling operations on the *Ocean Vantage*.

The oil and gas industry had been fighting cyber attacks for years. Their sprawling sites and distribution systems were filled with sensors and automated controls, all monitoring pressure and flow rates of oil and gas. These systems were linked to central controls by wireless technology, which made for a hacker's dream. Savi had been fascinated by a terrorist attack on a pipeline in Baku, Azerbaijan, where hackers had infiltrated the pipeline's surveillance systems and valve stations, super-pressurising the crude oil and causing a massive explosion. The dark web was full of such stories and Savi read them with a malicious smile on his face. He had to gain access to the drillship's onboard networks, then, he could attack their industrial control systems.

Most ships use one of the three big brands for their satellite communication and Savi was certain this was his route in. He started searching and found the *Ocean Vantage* was listed in the Inmarsat ships directory, on their website. This gave him the ship's satellite phone number. Savi was a big fan of the Shodan website, which is the world's first search engine for internet-connected devices. Most of his early research involved gathering information from such open-source intelligence.

From the Shogan search of the of logins to the *Ocean Vantage's* phone number, he could identify the wireless provider and type of comms-box the ship used. The comms-box gave the ship open-ocean connectivity, for both internet and phone. He idly applied the default password for that make of comms-box that had gleaned from his research: *admin/1234*. To his amazement, the comms-box home page opened. He was always shocked to see how many people never changed default passwords.

At the bottom of the page he saw a small tab that read '*Show Active Users*'. Hello! he thought. From this he would be able to see the names of all the crew of the Ocean *Vantage* currently logged-on to the ship's network. And that was how Savi met Estevan Vargas, a twenty-year-old cadet from the Philippines, who had been on the drillship for six months.

A simple trip to Google, then Facebook, and Savi knew everything there was to know about his mark. When the time was right, Estevan would be good for a 'phishing' trip. Savi would take control of his laptop, find a point of segregation onto the ship's network, and move into the control systems.

He had not decided whether to physically damage the ship or launch another ransom attack on MalTech Energy. He did not want to risk a spill, that was against his ecological principles. But, either way, he was going to enjoy having Natasha Bonnici begging at his feet. When he had first met Natasha, he knew that she was hot for him – she had contacted him on Tinder and offered to have sex with him. What further proof did he need?

Simon had laughed himself silly on hearing this and told Savi that Natasha was a dangerous, manipulative bitch, who had used the 'date' to lure him into a trap, so she could kidnap him and force him to help her steal the Libyan dinars. Savi was not so sure; he thought the uptight muscle-head did not get it. In his secret, soft romantic core, Savi believed there might still be something between him and Natasha. The thought of playing along the beautiful Bonnici woman, right throughout the hack, gave him delicious tingles of delight.

He had found photographs of her in the pages of a glossy European magazine, which he kept in a password-protected file.

Occasionally, he would look into those dark brown eyes, staring back at his, and imagine running his hands through the thick glossy hair that tumbled down over her shoulders – and more! Yeah, he knew she was into him, too. He could just tell!

Once he had the *Ocean Vantage* and MalTech Energy where he wanted them, he would contact her and own up to it. Natasha would have known it was him all along, of course. She could not fail to be impressed by the brilliance of what he had done. He would tell her he could fix the systems, and that, because it was her, he did not want any ransom money. She would be so relieved and appreciative... very much so. Maybe then they could start over, as equals, each at the top of their game.

He wondered if she was into *Call of Duty* or even *FIFA*. That would make everything perfect.

# CHAPTER 30
# ARTICLE MALTA TELEGRAPH

*Reporter: Amy Halliday*
*15 July 2020*

**Dispute on Gavdos escalates as Turkey pledges to defend fishermen**

*The Turkish Ministry of Defence has launched a scathing attack on the Greek government, accusing them of a full-scale military assault on a group of unarmed fishermen who had landed on the island of Gavdos twenty-four hours earlier, proclaiming its Turkish sovereignty.*

*Hamdi Ozan, the Turkish Foreign Minister, said the group had headed inland, to find shelter, when a platoon-sized detachment of Greek Marines ambushed them in a ravine, firing live rounds at them. It is unknown whether there are any casualties. The rest of the fishermen fled the island, frightened for their lives.*

*The Turkish trawler that was sunk in the capital's harbour, Karave, had a crew of eight, who have also fled inland, but have yet to be captured. Given the small size of the island and its open terrain, the Greek authorities say this will only take a matter of hours.*

*Foreign Minister Ozan has pledged the full might of the Turkish Navy will be deployed to rescue the crew of the fishing vessel. The Greek and Turkish naval forces are evenly matched and traditionally avoid confrontations with each other. In this case, it seems this might prove difficult.*

*A Greek spokesperson said that any injured fishermen would be flown to the University Hospital of Heraklion, Crete, for treatment, while those taken prisoner would be taken to a military prison on the mainland. The spokesperson for the Greek military authorities said they were no nearer identifying the fishermen, but sources say they are Arab mercenaries, paid by the Turkish government, who are believed to be behind the entire operation.*

*Foreign Minister Ozan said that the Greeks' assault on its citizens amounted to an act of war and was being viewed very seriously by Ankara.*

# CHAPTER 31
# GEORGE ZAMMIT
## ISLAND OF GAVDOS, GREECE

GEORGE AND ABDULLAH were both conscious that night was now giving way to day and the search for them would soon start in earnest. Abdullah was staring intently up the road, through the windscreen of the military truck. The low growl of the engine was so loud it must have been audible across the whole thirty square kilometres of the island. George was pushing Abdullah for details of his encounter with the Greek military.

"Mela, how many Marines were there?"

"It was dark and I could not count them."

"Well, what do you think? Ten, twenty... a hundred?"

"Many."

George sighed.

"That is not helpful."

"Allah will find a way. Have faith."

"Oh, so it's Allah we follow now, not your plan?"

Abdullah banged the steering wheel in frustration.

"I have no plan – I have no time to think! This place is small – too small. This lorry, you hear the engine? Boom! Boom! Boom! Maybe the noise will make the Marines deaf and then we can creep past on our bellies. But now, they come towards us and we go towards them. It is no good; we will be prisoners by tonight, I know it."

George thought for a moment and said:

"OK, I have a plan. We have to turn back. You're right, we're heading the wrong way. I think this might work... but it's only good enough to get the three of us off the island."

Abdullah and Hamza looked at him askance. George jerked his thumb over his shoulder towards the eight men sitting behind him and silently shook his head.

"Not them," he mouthed.

Abdullah said, irritably:

"Why with the whispers, my friend? There is only Hamza and me who have the English!"

George glanced behind him at the fighters and said quietly to Abdullah:

"Tell them the truck isn't a good idea and we've got to split up. Tell them to go ahead on foot, find the inflatable, wait till midnight, then go to meet the trawler coming into Tripiti beach. Say we're going back to the harbour to try and make our escape from there."

Abdullah furrowed his brow and was about to start arguing when George hissed:

"Do it, now, or we'll all end up spending the next ten years in a Greek jail."

Abdullah abruptly stopped the truck and got the men out and into a semicircle, to explain the plan. They seemed to agree it was the best idea and there was much nodding of heads and clasping of shoulders. Eventually, the eight fighters disappeared up the road in the dim morning light.

The three of them got back into the truck and Abdullah smashed the gears together in an excruciating three-point turn, and set off back to Karave. There was silence in the cab, until Abdullah suddenly stopped and wound down the window, sticking his head out. He looked back, in the direction they had come from and heard the unmistakable crackle of small-arms fire. Their fighters had run into the Marines. Abdullah looked at George, shaking his head.

"So, my friend, this plan of yours, it is a good plan?"

"Keep driving, we'll find out soon enough."

Abdullah drove back down the road for a few minutes and the port came into view. When he arrived at the filling station, he stopped the truck and turned to George.

"Time for the plan. *Inshallah!*"

The three of them left the truck, shouldered their weapons and walked past the small convenience store, towards the marina. George scoured the groups of people still milling about and caught sight of the shock of white hair belonging to the man who had accosted them on the breakwater.

They walked onto the pontoon, between the moored vessels, towards the place where the Englishman was standing with a small group of fellow yachtsmen. Soon, all heads turned in their direction.

George stood a little way back from the group and beckoned the white-haired man towards him. He lumbered down the pontoon, with his tiny wife scurrying behind.

George moved his head close to the other man's and spoke conspiratorially.

"I've been having a word with my senior officer," he nodded at Abdullah, "and it turns out he's authorised to make reparations to civilians for damage arising from our operation."

"Ha! And I should think so, too!"

"Yes, but first he needs to inspect the damage and agree a sum. We don't want everybody here getting involved because, if they all start mobbing him, he'll lose patience and that'll be that. I know what he's like."

"Absolutely! Mum's the word!"

George continued: "Sorry, I don't know your name?"

"Thompson McCauley."

His mouse of a wife emerged from behind the billowing

white shirt to join in with the introductions, saying, "But he likes to be called Tompy. And I'm his wife, Margery."

George was momentarily confused. Then he remembered that Englishmen of a certain class often called each other by strange names.

"OK, Tompy and Margery it is. Can we see the boat and inspect those scratches?"

The group headed towards an impressive sixteen-metre yacht, moored at the end of a pontoon. It had a dark blue hull and a towering mast. George knew little about boats, but this was clearly an expensive one. Tompy made everybody take off their shoes: "Grit on the soles scratches the decks, you know."

As soon as they were on board, George said to him: "Have you got a pen and some paper down there?" pointing at the companionway down into the cabin.

"Yes, got plenty on the chart table."

"Let's go down and take a few details, before we look at the damage."

Tompy took the seat at the small chart table, that had all the navigation and communication equipment around it, and swivelled round to face them.

"Well, I'm sorry, Tompy, but I'm going to disappoint you," George said, straight out. "We need you to take us home before we pay you. Then, when we arrive there safely, this man will give you five thousand US dollars, won't you, Abdullah?"

Tompy sprang to his feet, outraged. Hamza casually but roughly prodded his temple with the barrel of a rifle. He sank back into his chair, rubbing the side of his head.

"Ow! Bloody hurt, that did."

George looked at him with a sympathetic expression.

"Well, I've been around these men for some time and I've seen them do much worse things than that." He looked at Margery, who was cowering, with one fist pressed to her mouth. "They can also be very cruel to women." He instantly regretted the open threat. "I'm sorry, Margery, I'm sure it won't come to that."

Tompy made to jump up again, but received another rap on his head from Hamza.

Then Tompy became authoritative.

"Alright, stop the thuggery. Where do you want to be taken?"

George calmly said: "Western Libya."

"Libya! You must be bloody joking? Do you know how far that is? It's a thousand kilometres away... about five hundred and something nautical miles... no, more. It will take four or five days!"

George remained calm. "OK, what do you need to make a journey like that? "

"Diesel, water, food – well, we have got plenty of food in the freezer, so fuel and water. We can top up the water here, we're connected to the supply, and can get fuel as soon as Yannis shows up..."

Abdullah had hung back for the moment. Now he opened the small bag he had slung over his shoulder and produced a grenade.

He smiled, malevolently.

"Now, my friend, this is a nice boat, yes? And very expensive?"

Tompy said nothing, but his expression showed he understood where Abdullah was going with this conversational gambit.

"It looks to me like a new boat, very shining. And you, and your fine wife, Margery, are making nice holidays in your nice new boat, no?

"So, simple thing. You like to sail boat and you want money to fix small scratches, yes? We want to sail home and we want you to take us and we pay you very much money. You have my promise, and I am Berber, not Arab. A Berber never makes a promise he will not keep.

"So, all is good, no? If there is trouble, before we leave, I throw you in the water and then this will explode and all dreams are finished. No nice boat. If we go sailing and I see navy ship or coastguard, you and Lady Margery go swimming. No questions, I promise – you swim. So, no radios, telephones, flares or anythings. Or else you die and nice boat sink. OK?"

Tompy sat and stared back defiantly at Abdullah, until, in one lithe movement Abdullah sprang at him, threw him to the floor of the cabin and, taking Hamza's gun, pushed it into his mouth. Margery whimpered.

"I said, 'OK'! Is it OK, fat Tompy?"

"It is OK," he mumbled, with the metallic shaft of rifle between his teeth. "No need to be beastly!"

"Good. Now we make ready for nice time. All friends again!"

An hour later, the boat fuelled up and ready, Abdullah, Hamza and George watched from the cabin as Tompy started the engine, took the helm and started barking instructions to Margery.

"Prepare to cast off. Loose bow lines."

Margery made her way nimbly to the bow of the boat and pulled in the slimy ropes that had been attached to the harbour's fixed moorings.

"Raise anchor. Watch out for debris, Marge!"

Tompy stood behind the large wheel, but had a direct line of sight down the companionway, into the cabin, and was proudly talking George and Abdullah through the casting-off procedure.

"We usually use an automatic winch for the anchor, but it is buggered at the moment. So poor Marge has to do it by hand. Weighs a ton, you know. Got to remember to get it fixed.

"Come on, old girl, put your back into it! Now, quickly, loose rear lines."

Through the portlights they saw Margery's feet flitter past as she made her way to the rear of the boat, behind Tompy, to untie and gather the final lines.

"Fenders in, Marge, on the double, we are under way. And neatly stowed, please!" He looked down at George and Abdullah. "Would love to help her, of course, but dicky hip. No balance, you see."

Once they had left the harbour and cleared the breakwater, they were in the open sea. Tompy cut the engine and started shouting for his wife again.

"Marge, we are ready for the mainsail."

Margery, meanwhile, had been below, starting to prepare breakfast, and emerged with an apron tied around her waist, to stand precariously on the roof of the cabin and start removing the mainsail cover. Once the ties were loose, she attached a stainless-steel handle to one of the winches in the cockpit and began labouring through the clockwise turns. The enormous sail started unfurling, as her strenuous efforts slowly pulled it up the mast.

"Good girl, Marge, nearly halfway… keep it coming."

George looked at the tiny struggling, woman as she heaved the winch handle round.

"Shall I help her?" he offered.

"Certainly not! She knows what she's doing. Don't you, Marge? Come on, keep it going. This sail won't raise itself!"

Margery glanced around at them, the effort visible on her face. She managed a thin smile, then bowed her head to continue with her laboured two-handed rotations of the winch handle.

Abdullah looked at George as the boat started to tilt alarmingly, the wind catching the unfurling sail, and said: "Is this how all Englishmen treat their wives? I must tell Rania she is lucky to marry a Berber!"

# CHAPTER 32

# NATASHA BONNICI
### VIENNA, AUSTRIA

SIMON EDGED the large Mercedes into the rear car park of the block that housed Die Blau Osteria, a five-star restaurant that, according to its website, specialised in Austrian tapas. It was late evening and the light had almost gone. Two or three sodium lamps cast a yellowish hue across the rain-soaked carpark.

"What on earth is Austrian tapas?" asked Natasha, as she studied the menu on her phone. She continued, as if speaking to herself: "I speak three languages fluently and know a little Spanish, from my time at Stanford, but the German language has never appealed to me. Don't know why."

Simon was always amazed by how calm she was, even before an operation like this, where violence was not just possible, but an integral part of the plan. He looked around the poorly lit carpark. There were some service vehicles and vans, three skips for bottles and waste and what looked like six or seven staff cars. The problem with carparks behind retail parades, such as this one, was that the staff from the bars and restaurants invariably used them as places to hang out and smoke, when on their breaks. Simon was pleased to see there was nobody visible on the ground or on the fire escape leading from the first floor of Die Blau Osteria.

He checked his watch and said to Natasha: "We're a little early, so I'll go and have a walk around the place. That's the fire escape, I'll bring him down over there."

She glanced up from her phone, distractedly.

"Got it."

Ten minutes later Simon returned and opened the rear door.

"Natasha, you sit in the front passenger seat and I'll sit with our boy in the back. This is just a 'talking-to', yeah?"

"At the moment, that's how I see it. But be prepared to be flexible."

"OK, I should be down in three or four minutes, if Bohdan's men have done their thing."

With that Simon adjusted his jacket and left. It was exactly four minutes later when Natasha saw a block of light appear at the top of the fire escape and two silhouetted figures emerged onto the steel platform that formed the landing. One was broad-shouldered, erect and upright, the other slumped and being supported by the first. Natasha smiled and put her phone back into her handbag, removing a pack of tissues, which she held in her hand. She got out of the car and took up position in the front passenger seat. Simon dragged Matthäus down the second flight of steps. He was making feeble attempts to resist, hanging onto the banister.

Eventually, they appeared at the rear doors of the car and she heard her bodyguard say gruffly: "Inside."

Simon pushed Matthäus's head down roughly and propelled him into the car, releasing the arm he had been twisting behind his back. Matthäus was breathing heavily, taking in great gulps of air. Natasha watched him in the rear view mirror, altering the angle to get a better view of his condition. There was the inevitable bleeding mouth and nose and a pronounced swelling around one eye socket that spoke of a possible fracture. She heard Simon open the other rear door and slide in, closing it behind him.

They sat in silence, punctuated by Matthäus's gulps and

exhalations. Natasha took the tissues and handed them back over her shoulder to Simon, who opened them, pulled out a handful and pushed them into Matthäus's hand. Gingerly, he dabbed his mouth and nose. Then, he sat back and tilted his head back against the headrest.

"Why am I here?"

Natasha said: "Good question. But, before we get into that, I need to make one thing very clear. There're only two possible outcomes here. One, co-operation will be rewarded. Two, non-cooperation will mean a short trip to an industrial estate and a bullet. Understood? Because I don't think I can put it any more clearly."

There was a further silence as Matthäus let the words sink in.

"Who're you?"

"I'm the person who killed your father."

Matthäus said nothing, but Simon sensed him stiffen slightly. Natasha reached across the driver's seat and pressed the child-lock button. There was a firm clunk.

"Just in case." She smiled and Matthäus saw her face for the first time.

"You're Natasha Bonnici? You're not what I imagined."

Natasha shuffled round in her seat, so she could get a clear view of Matthäus's face and study his reactions.

"You're exactly what I imagined," she told him

She studied his thin, angular face and foppish straight, light brown hair, brushed to one side, with a strong left-hand parting. His herringbone tweed jacket had an ample cut and a good clean drape, not fashionably tight or skimpy. It told her he was a traditionalist whose clothes came from a bespoke tailor, probably somewhere in Vienna. Someone who had served generations of Schobers before him. His open-necked, British-styled shirt looked like a blend of cotton and linen. Had the circumstances been different, she would have asked him where it came from. What looked like a hand-stitched silk crepe handkerchief peeked out of his top pocket. She smiled, noting that

Matthäus had not used it to staunch the flow of blood from his nose.

"So, shall we begin? First, I have nothing against you personally. If you were part of the Family and were caught wholesaling heroin, we'd kill you. It's a 'no-no' for us. But you're not, so that's not the problem.

"Secondly, it's natural a son wants to avenge the death of his father. Obviously, that *is* a problem for me.

"Thirdly, I need to know about your supplier. That'll involve a breach of confidence on your part, hence this element of coercion. Understand? So, let's make this quick and easy. Can you help me or shall I drive us to the industrial estate now?"

There was a brief pause, but the answer was never really in doubt.

"I'll help you. But I need the supplier, I need the money. You killed Father, took his money and left Mother and me penniless. I've got a family who depend on me."

"I know all about your family. I've had a chat with Bernd Kruder who's told me all about the estate and the grasping relatives, the domineering mother. Really, Matthäus, you're going to have to grow a pair."

"Huh, Bernd? Never liked him."

Matthäus shifted position and let out a low moan.

"My arm hurts."

"Listen, how much do you make from this precarious heroin trade? You know, of course, it could easily stop tomorrow or lead to you spending the next twenty years in prison?"

"I make enough to keep the estate going and support the family."

"So, how much does a schloss in the wine country, filled with non-productive, parasitic relatives, cost you?

"I need about one hundred thousand euros a month to keep things going as they are."

She laughed out loud.

"Wow! You must have some great parties. And you can cover that from the heroin business?"

"I think so. It's early days, but yeah, I have to."

"OK, so here's the deal. Say, I let you have fifty thousand a month, from the money due to your father. On that, can you stop the heroin business, shed some relatives, tell your mother the facts of life, and find a way to get by? Incidentally, that's six hundred thousand euros a year, tax-free."

Matthäus looked at her, not believing what he was hearing.

Natasha continued: "You see, the thing is, I feel I was wrong to cut you off, after your father's death. It went down badly with the rest of the Family. Attacking a man's inheritance was seen as a low trick and I'd like to put that right. It'll make my business partners feel that little bit more secure... more trusting of me.

"So, I'm prepared to make a gesture. Fifty thousand a month, for life, paid direct to you. You needed cash, you've tried something and you're earning money – I can see that, well done. Long-term, though, I don't think you're cut out for the drugs business; you're not tough enough. Someone's going to come along and chew you up, sooner rather than later. Then Mutti and the other leeches will be back in shit street again. So, what do you think?"

"What d'you want from me?"

"As I said, I want there to be no bad blood between us. It's over, done. I want to know exactly how your supplier operates and who he is. And don't say you want time to think about it!"

"No, no, I'll do what you want."

"And your idea of taking revenge for your father's death, the bad blood with the Family?"

"Over with, done."

She smiled at Simon, who looked on impassively, not knowing whether to believe in this offer or not.

"There we are, that wasn't so hard, was it?" Natasha said sweetly. "Where can we drop you, Matthäus? You can tell me the rest as we drive.

Simon had got out of the back of the car. He drove them to the address of an apartment block where Matthäus said he had a friend. On the way, Natasha pressed him for details of the heroin supplier.

"Look, I don't know many details, it's not the sort of thing that gets shared around, you understand? The heroin is from Afghanistan. It comes into Turkey, where the police and the government have been taking a slice for decades. Then, it crosses the Med to Libya in containers. A local middleman in Tripoli repacks it and takes it out to sea, where it's collected and makes its way to Malta."

"How often?"

"Monthly, mostly. It depends."

"OK, so it arrives on a ship. Whereabouts does it land – the Freeport, the Grand Harbour? What kind of ship? Fishing vessel, cargo ship, yacht?"

"I don't know, that's his business."

"Ahhh! Now we come to it. *Whose* business, is it?"

Natasha could feel the hesitation, as Matthäus got ready to take the final step. Once he had taken it, there was no going back. He was pledged to her.

He swallowed and dabbed his mouth with the tissues.

"A South African called Luke van der Westhuizen. He's behind it. He picks up the stuff in Turkey and pays for it with diamonds he smuggles in from South Africa. He brings it in through Malta, via Libya, then gets it delivered to me in drums of isinglass – you know, the wine-clarification agent we use in the trade. Seems to work well."

"So, the packing into the drums is done in Malta?"

"Yes, somewhere in the docks."

"Interesting. This Luke, how did you meet him?"

"I was in Istanbul, meeting with diamond dealers. I needed cash, as always, so I had to sell some of Mother's jewellery. Heirloom stuff, very valuable. Large South African gems. It was too much money for most of my usual people, so a broker set up a meeting and van der Westhuizen showed up. He liked the pieces and offered me a decent price. He paid it quickly, with no fuss.

"He must've realised we were broke and started to speak to me about how we operated the distribution side of our wine business. A few weeks later, he called and we met again. He suggested a way of increasing the value of what we distributed. I had no choice but to say yes. It was as simple as that."

"There! What an interesting chat."

"You'll protect me from Luke, right?"

"I never said that, but there's something you can do for me, that'll turn the tables on Mr van der Westhuizen. Just continue with business as usual, for the next month or so, and I'll tell you when I want to step in.

"And, to be absolutely clear: in the meantime, never go drinking with Luke again. And, if he gets wind of our conversation, or you don't do exactly what I ask, not only will I hunt you down, but I'll enjoy making sure Mutti and the rest of the parasites know what it's like to be out on the street."

# CHAPTER 33
# HAKAN TOPRAK
## TURKISH MINISTRY OF FOREIGN
## AFFAIRS, ANKARA, TURKEY

ANKARA SITS FIRMLY in the middle of the Anatolian Plain, on the Asian side of the Bosphorus. After the defeat of the Ottomans in 1918, the Allies were going to parcel up Turkey between themselves. But the Turks began a War of Independence and, in 1923, defeated the Allies and won the right to form a republic. The city of Angora changed its name to Ankara and became Kemal Atatürk's proud new capital. Modern Turkey was born. Hakan liked the city with its cold snowy winters and hot dry summers. Its elevation, at one thousand metres gave the air a freshness that was absent from stuffy, humid, more commercially driven Istanbul.

Istanbul had swallowed its pride at the loss of its capital city status, but continued to prosper, becoming one of the wealthiest cities in the world. Its position between Europe, Asia and the Middle East placed it at the centre of trade, culture and politics. Turkey borders Bulgaria and Greece to the west; Armenia, Azerbaijan and Iran to the east; Georgia to the north east; and Syria and Iraq to the south. To the north, through the narrow Bosphorus Straits and across the Black Sea, are Russia and the Ukraine.

As an officer in the Millî İstihbarat Teşkilatı (MIT), the

National Intelligence Organisation, there was much to keep Hakan Toprak occupied. He liked to think he sat high above it all, the eyes and ears of the state, watching and listening while the business of the world went on beneath him. Money, people, ideas, beliefs and enmities, all flowed from east to west, north to south, and back again. He could not remember when he had acquired the sobriquet 'The Hawk' but did not dislike it. In fact, that was how he saw himself: the hawk at the crossroads. Sitting on a crag, patiently watching the human traffic bustle through the geopolitical intersection that was Turkey, ready to swoop down on any person or organisation whose behaviour threatened to disturb the delicate political balance of the region.

Hakam Toprak prided himself on being one of the few honest men in Turkey. He did not seek power or popularity but, in a ruthless political landscape, riven with conflict, he had been described by a British Ambassador as the 'the man who held the coats', while others fought it out. Being inscrutable made him few friends, but that was how he wanted it to be. When an informed view was sought, or an important message was to be delivered between the permanently conspiring political and military factions, he was summoned into the smoky backrooms of power around Ankara and Istanbul.

Ostensibly, he worked for the MIT, but he had had long secondments within the Turkish energy, banking and finance sectors that underpinned the economic engine creating Turkey's wealth. He watched the money and stayed close to the conspiracies and cabals. He became known as someone who knew how to fix things, and had been called upon to act in a whole range of strange capacities.

At that moment, he was seated in a comfortable leather chair at a large conference table, high up in the white tower of the Ministry of Foreign Affairs, awaiting the arrival of the Foreign Minister, Hamdi Ozan. There was one subject on the agenda, the shambles at Gavdos, or rather Gondoz.

The minister eventually entered the room, followed by three

male assistants. All wore smart suits and all, except for the minister, carried bundles of papers. Hamdi Ozan nodded at Hakan and lowered his bulk into the chair at the head of the table. No other introductions were made, but Hakan recognised the assistants and acknowledged them with a nod.

The minister looked weary. The large, bruised-looking bags under his eyes drooped onto his cheeks. Heavy jowls overhung his shirt collar. It was as if the flesh of his face was detaching itself from his skull. His grey moustache was nicotine-stained and the smell of forty Camel Yellows a day clung to his clothes. Hakan had caught the familiar odour within seconds of Ozan's arrival. He thought, if this was what high office did to a man, they could keep it. Hamdi Ozan was in his mid-sixties and had survived many years of turbulent Turkish politics. He was a supporter of political Islam, which had served him well in the current regime. Hakan knew Hamdi liked and respected him, but the politician had long-since accepted that nobody was indispensable and sacrificing friends and allies was a perfectly legitimate strategy, when things got tough. No hard feelings.

Ozan addressed Hakan in the deep, gravelly voice of a committed smoker.

"So Hakan, Gavdos or Gondoz, whichever it is – success or failure?"

Hakan smiled. There could be only one answer.

"Well, I would say success! We landed the Libyans, released the PR and scared the shit out of the Greeks. We got our claims to sovereignty out there and we have the MalTech Energy drillship heading towards our new two-hundred-mile Exclusive Economic Zone, ready to get to work. However, there were some Greek fatalities, which is not so good, and a fifty-year-old Hellenic Navy gunboat went to the bottom, sunk by a trawler. Makes the Greek Navy look pretty stupid, do you not think?

"Also, there were no prisoners taken, so our story cannot be contradicted. Our heroic, unarmed fishermen fled the ruthless and disproportionate attack on them and were driven from their homeland by force. It is a disgrace that the Greeks turned their guns on honest Turks, who were only seeking to return to their homeland, and were compelled to return fire in self-defence."

He paused and shifted in his chair.

"On the other hand, there was a complete failure of military intelligence and our fishermen walked straight into a hornet's nest that resulted in a nasty gunfight with some injuries to our brave fishermen. We are lucky they all made it to the boats and none of our people were killed. That could have become a huge embarrassment for us. We should have been informed that a Greek gunboat was sitting in the harbour and that forty or fifty Greek Marines were waiting for us. But, I am not going to air that view in front of the Generals."

"Very wise," said Ozan. "The idea that there was a failure of intelligence never even crossed my mind."

"Quite so. We will run the narrative I have just described. People will not believe it, but so what? We made our claim for another two hundred miles of coastal waters. We have put down another marker, shown we are determined to defend 'the Blue Homeland' *and* given the Greeks a bloody nose. So, back to your question, success or failure?" Hakan banged the tabletop with the palm of his hand. "Success, Ozan, total success!"

The minister allowed himself a short chortle and the assistants felt they were on safe enough territory to smile.

The Blue Homeland was an important doctrine for the Turkish government. The essence of it was that the continental shelf and the coastal waters were as important to the state as the land itself. When explaining Turkish belligerence in maritime matters to non-Turks, Hakan Toprak often said: "Our policy is not to cede a drop of our homeland's water to others, as we will never cede a handful of our land."

Ozan lit a Camel Yellow and the pungent, clove-scented smoke floated across the table.

"So, we managed to collect all these fishermen, did we?"

"Yes, we got all but three. The main party made their retreat to the inflatable boats they had landed in. Luckily, they were found bobbing around ten miles offshore by our trawlers, before the Greeks could get to them. The Marines chased the main party down to the beach, shots were exchanged, but only minor casualties on our side. Once they were off the beach, they were safe. The others left the same evening and were picked up five miles offshore. The Greeks had no gunboat left to follow them out to sea!"

Ozan wheezed out a laugh that deteriorated into a fit of coughing. After dabbing his mouth with a soiled handkerchief, he said, "There is a funny side to all this. It is so ridiculous!"

"True. But, unfortunately, two of those missing are the party leader and his Maltese special adviser."

Ozan looked serious again.

"Hmm. Let's hope they make their escape. It would undermine our story if the Greeks managed to capture any of our valiant Turkish fishermen and paraded Libyan mercenaries!"

Ozan burst into another fit of chesty coughing. He quickly took another drag of the cigarette, to calm the irritation in his throat.

"Any idea where the missing men have got to?"

"No, but they are a resourceful pair. If they had stayed on the island, they would have been picked up by now and we would have heard about it. Gavdos is not a big place. My guess is they have stolen a boat and are trying to make it to Crete. We will hear from them shortly."

"Let's hope so."

Then, with a flick of his wrist, Ozan dismissed his assistants, who hastily gathered their papers and made for the door. There was a moment's silence, while the two remaining men waited to be sure the room was empty and the door shut.

Ozan was looking down at the tabletop, his pudgy fingers interlocked in front of him.

"Hakan, be careful of your fellow Generals. You are Intelligence, not the military. Do not think they see you as one of them, because they do not. There is a hard time ahead for us all. Lines are being drawn at present. Do not put yourself on the wrong side. I speak to you as a friend."

Not many knew that Hakan Toprak had risen to the highest rank in the intelligence services and, as such, often sat with the General Staff, whose chief was the commander of Turkey's armed forces. Politics here had become a struggle between the secularists, who traditionally had the backing of the officer corps, and the new wave of Islamic politicians, supporters of the Muslim Brotherhood, which Ozan and the current leadership favoured.

The country had, until now, trodden a precarious middle path, keeping as close as it could to Europe and NATO, but that was changing. Since the formation of the new republic in the 1920s, the Turkish Constitution had removed Islam as the state religion and Sharia from the legal code. Amendments to the constitution to reverse this were now being enacted. Political Islam was emerging as the direction in which the country was heading.

"Hamdi, you know me. I sit to one side. It is my way."

"That is no longer good enough. I need to know you are with us. You can see which way the wind blows, so do not get caught in the storm. We are going to leave the NATO alliance. You know we have already asked the Americans to quit the base at Incirlik. We need to stand together. We must look to the East, forget the West."

The American base was in Adana, on the very far east of Turkey, and housed a full complement of five hundred US military personnel. It was less than two hundred kilometres from Aleppo in Syria and, from the base, a US F-15 Strike Eagle could reach Tehran in less than thirty minutes. The defeat of ISIL in Syria was partly the result of missions flown from Incirlik. The base was also home to over fifty nuclear warheads.

Ozan waited for a reaction. Hakan remained impassive. So, he went on.

"It is known you are against such a move," he was told. "Also, be careful at TOGO. You are negotiating the payment of a multi-million-dollar ransom, to an unknown person. I have heard it said, maliciously, that this could be the perfect crime and you could be the perfect criminal. It is nasty talk, but it is better you should know about it. Integrity is not always enough to protect you, my friend."

Hakan sat silent and looked into Hamdi Ozan's lugubrious face. His own remained expressionless, his dark brown eyes revealing nothing. Ozan tutted, took a deep breath and hauled himself up from the chair.

"I didn't have to warn you, Hakan."

He sighed with the effort of raising himself from the seat.

"One last thing. We never belonged in the West. The Christian West never wanted a country of Muslims. The republicans have wasted one hundred years playing their game, but now we can see the way forward more clearly and we will become an Islamic country again. I am working to make that happen. Today I am your friend, but you know how fast that will change, if you stand in our way."

As he left the building Hakan worked through this disturbing conversation with Ozan when he suddenly heard the email tone on his phone. Pausing to one side of the main door, he checked the sender. It was his Russian contact in the SVR.

*Some notes attached to coding suggest they are written in Maltese shorthand and some emails read back to Maltese servers. Our systems suggest large data packages received from Maltese servers. You should investigate active Maltese cyber criminals. We believe SnakeHead to be Maltese national and is associated with Prairie Dogs.*

*We have no information on the identity of SnakeHead but we have a contact who might help with ID. Will follow up and get back.*

Turning his attention to the cyber attack on TOGO, Hakan nodded his head. Yes, this was definitely interesting. Lately, all roads seemed to lead to Malta.

SAVI HAD BOUGHT four litres of Dr Pepper, sixty Marlboro Light and three multipacks of Walker's crisps. He settled himself down in the office above Danka's gym and put on his headphones. It was time to go phishing for Estevan Vargas. Savi had learned from Estevan's Facebook page that he had been a deck cadet for over two years and a quick look at Google had told him his mark had all the necessary qualifications to move on up and become a third officer. Savi knew the best way to drag someone into a phishing scam was to select the right bait. Vanity, greed or simple curiosity were all parts of human nature that could be used to elicit a reaction.

In this case, Savi decided the best way to bait the hook was to exploit another part of the human character: ambition. He crafted an email with a corporate logo, purportedly from an agency, saying a colleague had recommended Estevan for a Third Officer's post with a reputable shipping line. If he was interested, he could open the attachment to get full details of the job, the ship and the salary.

Savi could tell from the comms-box logins when Estevan went onto the system and was not surprised, three minutes later, to see the attachment opened, allowing the malware programmes to flood onto his target's laptop and beyond. Savi was not interested in Estevan's laptop; he only needed the compromised device so he could work his way through to the *Ocean Vantage's* servers. It was there he could start to have some real fun.

The best protection against cyber attacks is to divide the various parts of a computer system, to tightly control the access between the various segments and minimise the damage an attack might cause. Savi was amused to note there was very little segmentation across the *Ocean Vantage's* network. He installed a 'backdoor', which identified him as an authorised user, enabling him to gain high-level access to all the ship's computer systems, networks and software applications, whenever he chose.

Savi had some thinking to do, but for starters he decided to let the *Ocean Vantage* know it had a problem. The best jokes take time to reveal themselves. So, he started with the ship's autopilot system, programming a series of course adjustments into the course selector. The compass would then compare the actual course of the vessel with the course selected and make the necessary adjustments to the steering gear. Savi had arranged that every hour the *Ocean Vantage* would change its course, make a sweeping turn and start circling. This would no doubt be spotted by those on the bridge and corrected, but the programme repeated the sequence every two hours. One by one, he planned to attack the ship's key systems.

Savi waited for the officers on the bridge to either stop the *Ocean Vantage* so they correct the software problem with the autopilot, or until they disabled it entirely. Then, he would attack the technology that held the ship in place, while it worked the drill bit, thousands of metres beneath the seabed. Drillships had a complex series of thrusters under the hull, like the individual jets of a spa bath. These jets operated independently and could keep a vessel stable on a five-metre radius, even in stormy seas, which enabled the ship to keep its position directly above the wellhead. The technology included a combination of high-tech navigation systems such as GPS, ultrasonic beacons and lasers. All fair game!

Once this software was engaged, Savi had programmed the launch of a piece of malware that would operate the ship's thrusters, causing it to rotate on its axis! His fingers danced over the keyboard as the multiple screens rolled files, programs and a reflection of his malicious grin.

This was fun and the ship had not even reached the exploration area yet! A flicker on a screen on the upper bank, to his left-hand side, caught his attention. It notified him that an email had been received. It was from the Turkish Oil and Gas Organisation. offering to pay a ransom of two hundred and fifty thousand US dollars. Savi promptly replied asking when they proposed to pay the other nine and three quarter million US dollars. He knew, once they started quibbling about price, he had got them! It was only a matter of time before a more serious offer would come through.

For a moment, he imagined telling Natasha what he had done. It was super-cool; she was bound to get it. Then, he thought about the insurance bit. He bit his bottom lip, a thing he always did when he was concentrating. Maybe not. If he damaged the ship, she would lose a shit load of money and she definitely would not be happy with him . And that was what he wanted, wasn't it? There was no point going to all that trouble just to send a ship around in circles.

Mike had put him on to it, so as to get revenge on Natasha for how she treated him after the heist but, by now Savi was feeling confused about his own motivation. According to Simon, Natasha had wanted him dead all along. He had to remember that. She had messed with him and that was unacceptable. Yeah. Even if they were hot, no one messed with SnakeHead.

Back in TOGO's offices in Ankara, Hakan Toprak opened Savi's reply and shrugged his shoulders. It told him nothing, but he forwarded the response to his contact at the SVR, in the woods outside Moscow. They responded immediately, asking if

Hakan had any connections with a man called Valentin Petrov of the Russian oil and gas company, Euromasio. They thought he might be able to help identify SnakeHead.

Hakan racked his brains. Yes, he knew of Petrov. He had been behind the Russian acquisition of the VertWay pipeline, from Libya to Sicily. If his memory was correct, Petrov had initially been in partnership with Natasha Bonnici and MalTech, until Natasha had received a better offer from the Americans and ditched the Russians. He recalled it had all turned sour between them. Rumour had it, Petrov was so angry, he had tried to kill Natasha's father, but succeeded in murdering Sergio Rossi, instead. There it was: Malta again!

He decided he reach out speak to Petrov.

# CHAPTER 35

# GEORGE ZAMMIT
## MEDITERRANEAN SEA

AFTER TWO DAYS AT SEA, the vomiting had stopped and George slumped, weak and aching, against one of the cockpit's white, padded faux-leather benches. No sooner had he relaxed and held his face up to the warmth of the sun, than Marge brought him a plastic bucket with a short rope attached and a sponge. She pointed to flecks of puke, drying on the starboard side of the boat.

Tompy stood at the wheel, face glowing from the wind and sun. He wore a white peaked naval cap. It turned out he was an ex-Royal Navy officer. Of course, he was.

"Come on, George, you know the routine. A clean boat is a happy boat!" he called over.

Wearily, George dipped the bucket into the sea, using the rope, and hauled it back up, to rub off the baked-on relics of his suffering. Abdullah was skulking in the cabin, where he spent most of his time. Life at sea suited neither man. George hated the ocean, with its dormant power and restless motion, while Abdullah hated Tompy with an equal intensity.

"I swear by Allah, as He is my witness, I must stay inside, away from that man, or I will kill him. Two days we have been on this boat and you have been doing the puking and he has been doing the shouting! There is no peace for me here."

George had tolerated Abdullah's temper tantrums, realising he was desperate to know what was happening back in Tripoli. The mission had not been a success and Abdullah was worried Toprak might not keep his promise of leniency for Jamal. The uncertainty made him impatient and moody.

Hamza, on the other hand, was thoroughly enjoying himself. He had cleaned the paintwork from bow to stern; learned how to coil and stow the lines and to polish the stainless-steel winches. He and Marge now trimmed the sails, working as a team, and Hamza would sit at Tompy's side, while the old sailor taught him the weird sailing terms. Ropes were lines and sheets; portholes were portlights; sails were jibs and genoas; there were goosenecks and kickers, clews and shrouds. On and on it went but, after the third day, much to Tompy's delight, Hamza could recite it all.

Abdullah commented snidely to George: "He can hardly speak the English, why is he learning the sailing?"

Right on cue, Tompy's booming voice echoed down the companionway.

"Hey, Marge, Hamza! Come on, crew! Sun's over the yardarm! It must be pink gin time!"

Marge emerged from the front cabin with an armful of clothes, which she dumped on the sofa before she dived into the chest fridge for a bottle of gin. Abdullah put his hands over his face, as Marge rattled a fistful of icecubes into a large plastic glass.

"Margery, does he ever stop drinking the alcohol? And does he ever use his own legs for anything?"

"It's hot up there, he needs to drink. And he can't run around the boat, it's his gammy hip, you see. His balance has gone."

Abdullah was not convinced. Once she had sliced some lemon for the gin, and disappeared to give Tompy his midday drink, George whispered to him: "I think that's the first time I've heard her speak, since we set off!"

The *Solent Pride* was a big yacht, but the cabins, lounge and cockpit all started to feel very small, after three days' sailing. The five adults lived on top of each other and the cramped conditions tried the scant reserves of patience that Abdullah had left. Margery seemed to spend the entire voyage smiling grimly, with teeth clenched, as she bustled around, Hamza tagging along, on an endless series of tasks. For the first two days, George was preoccupied with his seasickness. The only person who seemed to be oblivious to the suffering of others and having a thoroughly good time, was Tompy.

The hours dragged. There was little to remark upon, other than changes to the windspeed, the movements of the clouds and the chop of sea. The north-westerly wind blew constantly at around ten knots and, allowing for the current, the course was a straight line, nearly due west. The sails were set for a beam reach, so there was no need to gybe or tack. They crossed the main shipping lanes, which ran from the Suez Canal to the Atlantic, beyond the Straits of Gibraltar, but never came close to any other vessels. In the distance, they saw the silhouettes of tankers and container ships, but these gradually fell away as their courses diverged or their respective speeds separated them. Tompy informed them they were averaging a very respectable seven knots and, at that speed, should reach Marsabar in four days.

Abdullah had been smoking, standing by the helm, on the first night at sea, wistfully examining the night sky, when Tompy appeared, in his blue-striped pyjamas, to wish them good night.

"You go to bed? To sleep?"

"Yes, that's what I usually do when I go to bed."

"What about this?" Abdullah pointed at the wheel.

"Ah, no need to worry. Autopilot. Anyway, nothing to hit for miles around, eh?"

Abdullah had looked at George, not believing what he was hearing.

"But, what about other boats?" George asked. "There are a few of those around. You said some of the tankers weigh half a million tonnes! It's all right for them, it's us who'd be flattened!"

"Relax, you have to be very unlucky for that sort of thing to happen! Has been known, mind you. Anyway, have got a collision-avoidance alarm, part of the radar rig. Gives me a shout, if things get sticky."

"What if you don't hear it?"

"Yes, deep sleeper, especially after a few gins!" Tompy laughed heartily. "But Marge will get me up, no problem. Very light sleeper, our Marge. It's my snoring, she says. Cannot be helped. But, if you want to keep watch, be my guest. Good night."

Hamza, like all young men, could sleep anywhere. He curled up like a cat on the sofa behind the cabin's table. So, George and Abdullah took it in turns to sit in the damp, cold cockpit throughout the night. The wheel spun as the autopilot corrected their bearing and the *Solent Pride's* sails rippled and cracked in the wind. The bow ducked and surged through the white-topped waves, as they relentlessly sailed on at a stately seven nautical miles per hour. Meanwhile, from the double cabin at the bow of the boat, came the harsh snorts and stertorous, un-musical sounds of Tompy's breathing.

In all the sleepless hours they spent huddled in their heavy waterproof jackets, they did not see so much as a light on the horizon. Abdullah and George were comfortable in each other's company and there was little chat. The only thing that seemed to be increasingly on Abdullah's mind was whether they had done enough to secure a better future for Jamal. The nearer they got to Marsabar, the greater Abdullah's anxiety became.

They had agreed not to make any contact with Hakan Toprak or anyone in Marsabar until they were almost in the harbour. Abdullah would then arrange for a substantial group of men to meet them, to provide security for the expensive yacht, as well as Tompy and Marge.

The Libyan coastguards were an unpredictable, lawless bunch and, although Abdullah was well known, it was better to avoid any confrontation with their larger, well-armed gunboats. Abdullah explained all this to Tompy, who seemed to understand. On the fourth afternoon, the *Solent Pride* circled around outside Libya's territorial waters, waiting for dusk to fall. Abdullah told them it would arouse less interest if they could bring the boat into the port, once it became dark. Abdullah would then secure the vessel, replenish its food, fuel and water, and get hold of the sum agreed for their passage. Hopefully, Tompy and Marge could be under way, and out of Libyan waters, before morning.

At 21:00 hours on the fourth day of their trip, the *Solent Pride* majestically sailed into the rough, commercial port of Marsabar. Marge had gathered in the sails and tied the cover, then dropped the fenders. She and Hamza ensured everything was ship-shape and tidy for their arrival. Tompy brought them neatly alongside the wharf, using the engine. Marge and Hamza stood by to climb the slimy iron ladder up onto the quayside, lines at the ready, to moor the boat.

Abdullah was shouting instructions and threats into the VHF radio, to the port authorities, while simultaneously conducting a tense conversation with Rania on his mobile phone.

When he paused for a moment, George could see he had a face like thunder.

"Well? What news of Jamal?"

Abdullah stared at the deck, his shoulders slumped and his chin tucked against his chest.

"He is back in Abu Salim. My friend, your bravery on the island – it was all for nothing."

# CHAPTER 36

# MIKE LLOYD

SLIEMA PROMENADE, MALTA

"GOD, you stink, Savi, and you look like shit!"

Mike Lloyd wrinkled his nose. Savi was a mess. He had not slept for a couple of days and had not washed for longer. His breath stank of cigarettes and coffee. His olive-green T-shirt, with the death's head symbol on the front, had chilli sauce all over it, slopped from the kebab he had eaten on his way to meet Mike.

"Hey! I've been working, doing what you asked me to!"

"So you say. Where're you at with TOGO?"

"They're so fucked! But listen, enough of the IT systems. They've been staring at blank screens for two weeks now and, yesterday I sent out all their financial projections for next year, together with an email from the chief accountant guy to the Finance Director, saying the numbers are a complete load of bollocks! I don't know shit about this stuff, but I've got this guy in Prairie Dogs who is super-smart! Anyway, he says, together with the way they've been blagging about their oil and gas reserves, no bank will go near them, once everyone knows their numbers are just fairy dust!"

Mike nodded appreciatively.

"Good work."

But Savi was still on a roll. One Converse baseball boot was drumming a tattoo on the pavement and his wired brain was telling his arms to jump around in the air as he spoke.

"But, listen, this is the most exciting bit. I'm ready to move in on the operational systems. You remember the hack in Baku in 2008? The Kurds attacked a pipeline; super-pressurised the oil by jamming the valves in a pumping station... and boom! Big fire! Very cool!"

Mike had heard enough.

"OK, Savi, cool it. You already told me about that. When we started, remember? I said a time would come I'd tell you to back off? That time has arrived. Just for a bit. A pause, a truce. Can you do that? No booms! No big fires. An orderly return to business as usual. OK?"

"What for? Things are beginning to bite."

"Because I say so! That was the deal. What's the current ransom offer?"

"Quarter of a mil."

"Take it."

"No way! This is a payday. I'm going to double it."

"Don't be stupid, Savi."

"I'm not stupid!"

"Anyway, what you going to do with the money?"

Savi shrugged.

"Might get a Merc."

"Can you drive?"

"I can learn."

"For Christ's sake, you're such a dipstick. Listen, this is the new deal. Take the two hundred and fifty thousand dollars. Jesus, I can't believe I'm saying this – you and two hundred and fifty Gs? If you must, try and chisel whatever else you can but, by tomorrow evening, it's all over. Business as usual for our Turkish friends. Unless my little chats with them don't go the way I want them to. Then, you're back in business and we'll blow their frigging pipelines sky high."

Savi's face brightened.

"All right! Yeah! Anyway, I've already skimmed some more money from their payment systems. So two hundred and fifty thousand pounds is fine."

"How so?"

"Well, easy peasy. I'm into their emails, so I picked one or two suppliers who were asking for payment. I changed the supplier bank details and TOGO sent the cash to me, instead! I use the money to buy digital currency, close the account, end of story."

Mike shook his head.

"Are there no honest people in this world? OK, second piece of business. What's happening with the *Ocean Vantage*?"

Savi laughed.

"Well, it's got steering problems and the dynamic positioning system seems to be sending it round and round in circles. But no real damage, so far."

"Couldn't happen to nicer people. Do they know about you yet?"

"I don't even think they know they've been done over."

"Can you kill the engines?"

"Kill the engines?"

"Yeah, kill 'em."

"Well, I can access the main switchboard that controls all the electrical systems. That shuts down the engines, in case of fire and stuff, so yeah, I suppose I can kill them. They have a backup generator for emergencies, but they won't want to operate on that for long."

"OK, so do that and let the boat drift. Then, that's it for the *Ocean Vantage*."

"What? No way! I haven't twisted the knife deep enough, yet. I know how to engineer a blowout, once they start drilling!"

"I've told you before: no blowouts, no birds covered in oil, no catastrophes on the beaches, absolutely zero environmental disasters! Just the threat of it will have people's heads spinning. Shut her down, let her drift. Be ready to bring her back to life when I tell you.

"And listen, word to the wise. Be careful and keep your head down for a while. Think about covering your tracks. This is major-league stuff. If you can, take a holiday. And stay offline for a while, for your own sake."

"Yeah, I'm not stupid. Anyway, it's cool. I know what I'm doing."

Mike looked at him, doubtfully.

"I'm warning you, Savi. Stay low. Don't do anything to attract attention to yourself. That Bonnici woman's deadly. She'll chew you up."

"Yeah, sure. Don't stress, I've got it all covered."

# CHAPTER 37
# LUKE VAN DER WESTHUIZEN
## ÇERKEZKÖY, THRACE, WESTERN ISTANBUL

LUKE HAD BEEN TAKEN three weeks ago, in the late evening, as he stepped out of his car to climb the steps to his own front door. The blunt-ended, cold steel of a gun barrel was pushed, hard against his temple, as two men pinned his arms and slipped plastic restraints around his wrists. He smelled warm coffee breath, as a voice said calmly in his ear: "If you ever want to walk through that door again, be quiet and come with us."

He was taken in a large SUV, parked across the road from his house, and pushed into the rear. A thin, cloth hood was put over his head. The car drove for maybe an hour and a half and his instincts told him they were heading west. They had not crossed any of the bridges over the Bosphorus, and the smell of the sea, to which he was attuned, had vanished.

He did not bother to ask questions or resist; these were professionals and he knew it would soon become clear what they wanted from him. Eventually they arrived at a residence where the only thing Luke registered was the smell of bougainvillaea and the barking of dogs. There, they had taken him downstairs where, behind a steel door, there was a windowless basement room. It was painted white with a comfortable bed, a small bathroom with a shower, and an easy chair. There were some books, a bottle of water and a TV, with a dozen or so DVDs. It smelled faintly of damp.

The restraints were removed so he was able to shower and lay on the bed. He tried the TV, but there was no channel, other than that for the DVD player. He lay on the bed that night, not sleeping, wondering who had taken him and why. He could find no answers to either question.

The next morning, he was woken by two bearded Turks, in their early thirties, wearing T-shirts, jogging bottoms and clear, full-length plastic aprons. Luke immediately started to panic, but submitted to the fitting of the plastic ties around his wrists. They dragged him out of the room in his underwear, down a short corridor, to a second steel door. His dignity left him, his breathing fast and erratic as he started to plead and beg.

His struggles had all three of them panting, as they thrust him into the room. There were two pale yellow bulkhead lights and, in the middle of the floor, a long workbench from which restraints dangled. Luke's panicked glance took in a kitchen sink and a side table on which lay several gleaming surgical implements. The floor was tiled and badly stained. The place had a strange smell; he recognised it as piss and fear.

The taller of the two men released his grip on Luke, but only to thump him hard in the face. The shock caused him to reel and the pair of Turks took the opportunity to cut the wrist ties, push him back and swing his legs onto the bench. Limb by limb, they secured him.

Opium production had increased during the US presence in Afghanistan and the Balkans route to Europe had flourished. It was estimated that between four to six tonnes of heroin a month passed through Turkey. Luke's fortunes were tied to that traffic.

None of it happened without the active participation of the Turkish police and government officials. They protected the trafficking business from the Syrian border to Bulgaria and beyond, using state agencies to smooth the path. The commissions paid to those in authority were said to amount to tens of millions of euros annually.

Luke knew this because he paid them. He also helped launder their commissions, trading their bundles of cash for diamonds. The cash he had, in turn, given to Natasha Bonnici's BetHi, who, for a hefty commission, laundered it on his behalf. He tried to think who might be doing this to him. He was a source of riches for several senior policemen, justice officials and of course, the Anti-Smuggling & Organised Crime Department. But, despite his better judgement, he had recently started doing business with the PKK, the Kurdistan Workers' Party, a Kurdish militant political and armed guerrilla movement, fighting for a free state. The money he paid for their heroin would go towards fighting the Turks. It was probably enough to have brought him to this torture chamber.

His thoughts were quickly brought back to the present, when he saw one of the men approach him with two heavy duty electrical wires, large crocodile grips on each end. One aggressively pulled down his undershorts, while the other clipped the wires to his genitals. The sharp grip of the clips was enough to draw a cry of pain from him. He bucked on the bench, but the restraints bit into him

One of the men smiled and said: "You think that hurts? We wait for one hour; we go to eat. You think. Then we come back and we start, for real."

Luke lay on the bench, oblivious to the physical pain in his genitals and the bite of the straps into his wrists. His eyes never left the door. Occasionally, he heard people moving about and his dread soared. He thought of what he had heard about Turkish cruelty. The worst of it was he had nothing to give them, to make them stop. He could spit out one or two connections to the PKK, but nothing important. How could he ever make it stop?

After an age, he heard men's laughter and the noise of footsteps coming down the corridor. He started shaking, as the key was turned in the lock. The laughter stopped and the two men entered the room again, their game faces dispassionate and unyielding. With them was another man, a shorter light-haired figure, whose pale skin contrasted with the swarthy Turks. It was Matthäus Schober.

He was dressed in an impeccable grey suit with a contrasting navy waistcoat and white pocket square. His hair had been gelled back, accentuating his high cheekbones and angular jaw. The only thing that spoiled the effect was the tight, distressed expression on his face.

Matthäus was not comfortable with this situation and, for a moment, Luke thought he too was being held captive. Luke did not know what to say, but was painfully conscious of lying on the bench, stripped from the waist down. As if reading his thoughts, Matthäus's expression showed his distaste. He turned to one of Luke's tormentors and said: "Get those off him and pull his shorts up. I can't talk to him like that."

Matthäus went across to the stainless-steel side table and for a terrible moment Luke thought he was going to select one of the implements. Instead, he took something from his pocket and returned to the bench. To his relief, Luke saw it was a digital recording device,

"OK, Luke. Sorry about this, but it looks as if you're in a bit of trouble. Tell me everything about your smuggling operation, in detail. How it works, places and names, who is involved, how long you've known them, what it costs. All the way, from the moment you take delivery, to when the heroin arrives at the schloss. If what I hear is acceptable to those I'm working with, we'll keep you here for a couple of weeks, then let you go. That's the deal. If you don't tell us – well, you can see what's going to happen and they won't let you go afterwards, either."

Luke started talking. Matthäus sat on the bench by his feet and listened, almost disinterested. From time to time, Luke would break off and check with him.

"Is this what you want, yeah? Is this OK?"

"Yeah, yeah. It's is fine. Fine. Keep going."

After an hour, Luke had finished. His head fell back onto the bench and he closed his eyes. Matthäus had come to stand beside him.

"Are you sure that's all? If something's missing, there won't be a second chance to put it right. Do you understand?"

Luke nodded. A moment later, he heard the door close. When he opened his eyes, Matthäus had gone.

Later, in the indeterminate period for which he was detained, Luke would watch repeats of the collection of DVDs in the white room, going over and over the conversation with Matthäus in his head. Luke was sure the Austrian was not there on his own account; he had come on behalf of someone else. He had said as much. Matthäus did not care about the smuggling arrangements; all he wanted was to record Luke speaking and pass on the digital record to whoever was pulling his strings.

Luke thought about who Matthäus might be in business with. He also wondered how such a mummy's boy could have stitched up a better deal for himself than the one he had enjoyed with Luke. He was certain Matthäus was never going to become a player higher up the chain; he was not the type and was aware of his own limitations. None of this made any sense.

The one thing that did worry Luke was that he had told Natasha that Matthäus had threatened to kill her father. She had taken that news badly. What if she had struck back at Matthäus? The way they had left things that day in the castello, it seemed quite possible she would act against any threat, however drink-fuelled. He had never seen her that angry. Not an outburst of temper, but a white-hot fury, intense enough to burn for a very long time.

If she had caught up with Matthäus, she would have killed him. She had that look about her. And as for Luke, he began to wonder if he would ever get out of that room. If Matthäus had disappeared, Luke could not see the two Turks letting him walk free. As the days went by, his anxiety mounted. Each time he heard footsteps coming down the corridor, his throat would go dry and, as the key turned in the locked steel door, he would cower in his chair, trying not to show his fear. One day followed another, and he felt the odds of Matthäus returning slipping away.

His confinement in Çerkezköy finally came to an end when one morning the two Turks appeared in the cell and, without a word, tied and hooded him. Luke began to shake as they led him from the basement room to the driveway outside. He immediately became aware of the heat, and sunlight, which pierced the black cotton hood, warming his face and drying his tears of fear. The car journey was interminable but eventually, Luke heard the sound of taxiing aircraft and recognised the smell of aviation fuel. He guessed they were airside, at the private terminal of Istanbul International airport.

The hood was removed, but his arms remained bound. A black jacket was slipped over his shoulders, to conceal his restraints from prying eyes. He was confused and frightened as he was led up the short flight of steps, onto the Dassault jet, for the flight back to Malta. Once on the plane Luke saw there was a seated man, who appeared to be waiting for him. He was small and thin, with a shining, hairless domed head, poking out of a black polo necked sweater. When he spoke, his wide, smiling mouth was crowded with large oversized, brilliant white teeth.

"Hello, my name is Bohdan and we're going for a trip."

# CHAPTER 38
# NATASHA BONNICI
## CASTELLO BONNICI

IT WAS a weekend in August and Malta was unbearably busy with tourists. They crowded the few small sandy beaches and their hire cars blocked the roads. In St Julian's and St Paul's, the pavements were strewn with fast food cartons, bin bags, piled high, awaiting collection and discarded flyers for boat trips to the Blue Lagoon and other destinations. Sliema's stylish promenade had become a racetrack, as excited youngsters who descended on the island to attend the dozens of language schools, flew around on rented electric scooters.

Natasha preferred the quiet of the castello and only left her residence to visit MalTech Energy. They had recently moved out of Valletta and opened their new corporate head office on the top three floors of a skyscraper in the new Central Business District, in Mriehel. She was in a contemplative mood as she considered the demise of her relationship with Luke. There was no doubt he had taken advantage of her, but he would not realise that she knew that.

Natasha had never nurtured any long-term plans for the relationship, but she had enjoyed his natural, almost childlike, enthusiasm for everything, be it swimming, drinking or sex. Until recently, he had been so at ease with her. Unlike most men she met, Luke really did not know her, or her background, so was not overawed. He also had a natural animal need for her that she found both flattering and exciting. These days, she was so well known, potential suitors tiptoed around her, trying to impress her with ill-judged displays of wealth, macho prowess or false charm, embarrassing both themselves and her.

She felt certain that Matthäus Schober would keep his mouth shut and not mention to Luke the conversation in the restaurant carpark. The Family's Committee had convened by phone and unanimously agreed to pay the Schobers a monthly allowance. Bernd Kruder had asked Natasha why she had changed her mind.

She had replied that, over time, she had grown to feel it was the right thing to do, but she hoped it would not be seen as a sign of weakness that she was able to acknowledge her mistakes. There was a surprised silence on the conference call line before Bernd had said: "I think you'll find that change of heart will earn you the respect of all the Committee." There were murmurs of approval.

She felt the money was a price worth paying to unmask the duplicitous Luke van der Westhuizen. Who did he think he was, to worm his way into her life, her bed, and then use her island as a base for his drug dealing? It was one thing to be naïve, but he had blatantly taken advantage of her. How could he believe she would not find out about it? Particularly since he put her onto Matthäus Schober in the first place. He had seriously misjudged her and now he would pay the price. Men! So disappointing, so stupid; all of them.

Her thoughts, inevitably, led her back to Nick Walker. He knew her better than anyone did. True, he knew the bad, as well as the good. But that was what a relationship was supposed to be about – through thick and thin, in sickness and in health and all that stuff. He'd left her, dumped the job she had brought him back from Gibraltar to do; given up the money, the car and the white villa. Then he had fallen for that stupid simpering little blonde bitch. He had rejected Natasha and let her down. Walked out on her. That was more reprehensible than anything Luke had done! True, they had never really been an item since Nick's return; in fact, they had agreed that could never happen again, but all the same! God, what hold did that woman have over him? She thought: 'What does she have, that I don't?'

The trick at Oliver Tambo Airport seemed a long time ago, although it had only been a few weeks, and the satisfaction Natasha had felt at pulling it off had all but dissipated. She jumped out of her chair in frustration. The sudden movement rocked the small wrought-iron table beside her, toppling a glass onto the flagged terrace in the process.

'Damn!'

Katia, the housekeeper, magically appeared a minute later, dustpan and brush in hand, to sweep up the debris. Natasha apologised and they spoke a few words to each other. Then, as Katia left the terrace, it occurred to Natasha what was wrong; why she felt bored and empty. She was lonely. It was a Sunday afternoon and she was by herself. There was literally no one she could ring or talk to. For the first time in her life, she had discovered she had the capacity for loneliness.

Fortunately, this negative train of thought was interrupted by the ringing of her phone. She looked at the screen and was surprised to see it was Hakan Toprak calling her.

"Natasha, I am sorry to disturb you on a Sunday, but I need to see you urgently. What is best for you?"

"How urgently is urgently?"

"Now would probably be best. I landed thirty minutes ago and I am in the queue for a taxi at Malta International."

"Oh! It's like that, is it?"

"Yes. And before we meet, why not surprise your head of operations at home and ask him how things are going with the *Ocean Vantage*. Say you have had a tip off that they are not going so well."

"OK, Hakan. Give me an hour. Athina Hotel, St George's Bay.

Check in there, it's not too bad. Oh, and avoid the cocktails – they haven't got a clue!"

Natasha immediately rang grumpy Joe Wojtek, the Texan they had hired to lead the offshore development operation. Joe picked up after a dozen rings. In the background, Natasha could hear the sound of children splashing around in a pool.

"Joe, what are the problems with the drillship? I hear there are issues."

"Natasha, it's Sunday! Can't this wait? I've got a thing on here."

"Joe, we don't pay you to play with your kids in the pool when there's shit going down. Find out what's happening on the *Ocean Vantage* and ring me back in fifteen minutes. Got it?"

She slammed the phone down.

It did not take long for Joe Wojtek to ring back.

"It's true, there are problems. It seems the ship lost power four hours ago. Before that it had been hacked and was just circling."

"Hacked? Circling? Circling what?"

"Going around in circles. The owners flew out some specialist electricians and IT guys yesterday and they reckon there'd been a hack. The ship's not under the crew's control."

"Jesus Christ! And you didn't know? What the hell have you been doing?"

"Listen, sorry, but we've had this thing for Shelley's birthday and I said to the guys I'd be kinda busy, so…"

"We'll talk about this later. Full status report in thirty minutes, sent to my phone."

"OK. Just so you know, *Ocean Vantage* has asked the Turkish coastguards for help. Apparently, we suggested them rather than the Greeks…"

Natasha cut the call and screamed a high banshee yell.

By the time she had changed and had Simon drive her to St George's Bay, she was outwardly calmer but burning with repressed anger. Hakan Toprak was sitting in the hotel's airy reception, looking comfortable in an elaborate wicker armchair, with a drink in front of him. He wore a white open-necked shirt and grey trousers. He looked up from his phone, face expressionless, when Natasha approached. She sat down and plonked her hands in her lap.

"Hello," said Hakan. "I would offer you a drink, but you were right about the cocktails. They are truly dreadful."

"I'll take water. Something to douse my temper."

"Yes, frustrating, isn't it? We are on the point of paying a quarter of a million US to some hacker to reinstate our systems at TOGO. That will not even buy a safety guarantee for our future operations. I would happily kill them, if we only knew who they were! They originally wanted ten million out of us. Ten million! Where do they get their ideas from?"

He took a sip of the drink, winced, and pushed it to one side.

"Have you heard of the Prairie Dogs? A nasty bunch of cyber criminals who create all sorts of mayhem. They were behind the attack on us, so I suspect they are the same people who have captured the *Ocean Vantage* systems. Have you had any contact yet?"

"None."

"You know you cannot start drilling until you've regained control of the systems? The environmental risks are far too great."

"Hakan, please, I'm not stupid. How do we go about finding these bastards and getting them out of our lives?"

"Well, that is one of the reasons I am here. We have got friends in the SVR, the Russian cyber people, and they've been looking into the TOGO hack. They believe… wait for it… the trail leads back to Malta."

Natasha sat there, open mouthed.

"No? That can't be. Malta? Why not China or Ukraine or somewhere?"

"I do not pretend to know and it is only a suggestion, you understand. But the fact that MalTech Energy has now been dragged into it as well, rather supports the view it could be someone here, do you not think? I won't be so gauche as to ask if you have any enemies, but you see where I am coming from?"

He leaned forward and poured himself a glass of water. He looked at Natasha, protuberant dark brown eyes betraying nothing, nursing the glass on his knee.

She returned the look.

"Prairie Dogs, you say?"

He nodded, noticing she had started to fiddle with her sunglasses, obviously distracted and thinking hard. She shook her head, almost in disbelief.

"I might know something. I stress, *might*. But, if my hunch is right,, I'd still hardly believe it."

She snorted.

"If I'm proved right, you'd better stand back because you've never seen me really angry! I'm sorry, but be warned, I don't behave well when I'm furious!"

Hakan smiled.

"Oh dear, then let us hope you are wrong. For all our sakes! Will you keep me in the loop if things become any clearer? It is important to us. I am trusting you on this one."

He abandoned the water, reached over and took another drink of his cocktail, and grimaced again.

"Remember, Natasha, annoying though this may be, we cannot afford to become distracted by it. The bigger game is still in play. The stakes are high."

"Sure, I understand that. But listen, there's someone on the island who'd certainly be worth talking to. There's got to only be a small community of hackers on Malta. They must all know each other or *of* each other. He helped us once before and was impressive. I mean, not personally, he was a grungy kid, but very capable. I'll look into it. But I might not be his favourite person. There was some arm twisting involved last time we did business."

"Sounds like I should leave that one with you. But it does

sound promising. What is the latest with the drillship, by the way?"

She sat on the edge of her seat. Saviour Azzopardi could wait for later.

"Well, as of fifteen minutes ago, it stopped revolving on its own axis and is, apparently, dead in the water. Just as I wish my useless head of operations was! It's costing us tens of thousands a day, I might add. The ship only has access to auxiliary power. It's waiting for the Turkish coastguards. What they're going to do, I've got no idea. Also, it seems the Greeks have taken an interest, and are sending some naval vessels from Crete. It's a total cluster fuck and, now, to cap it all, the press is onto it. I can already imagine the headlines tomorrow."

Hakan sighed.

"It is not quite what we all wanted, is it? Find the hackers, pay them, then kill them if you want to. That is really all we can do. Different subject – I need a favour from you. Your Libyan and his friend the Maltese policemen."

"Batman and bloody Robin?"

Hakan had to smile.

"They certainly stirred up a hornet's nest on Gavdos. Which is fine; it is what we wanted. Raises the issue of sovereignty of Gavdos, then Crete. But anyway, I need them for another couple of weeks."

"Well, it's not really my call, is it?"

"No, but I can guarantee the Libyan will say yes to whatever I ask, for as long as his son remains in that hellhole prison, and his Maltese policeman friend will go along with him. We need Abdullah Belkacem on the next project. I have got some plans for him, which are crucial to our success, and it seems that your policeman is the id to his ego, the yin to Abdullah's yang, the passive to the active." Hakan smiled to himself. "Excuse the clumsy analogies!

"I'd like you to square the policeman's absence with his superiors. Can you use your contact? Stress his importance to us over the next few months. I am sure you have enough influence to do that?"

Natasha raised an eyebrow.

"I can let them know you asked, but that's about it." She took a sip of her drink and then fixed Hakan with her eyes enquiringly and asked:

"Has it happened yet?"

"Oh, yes. We took the big step on Friday. I am here to open discussions this afternoon. I do not want to appear rude, but it is really best if I do not say anything more, right now. But I have to be seen by our American friends to be doing something about it, so I need the services of..."

"Batman and Robin?"

Hakan's expression gave nothing away. He promptly changed the subject.

"What do you know about Mike Lloyd?"

Natasha's face hardened. She sat back in her chair.

"Agency. I have him down as being indirectly responsible for the murder of my uncle, in a bomb attack that was meant for my father. He set the Russians onto us. I hate the bastard."

"So, he is a man of action. Does he play by the rules? Can you do business with him? Can you trust him?"

"He's rude, bad tempered, got a chip on his shoulder because everybody hates the CIA. Boo hoo! He's a born maverick, effective enough in the field, but I'd guess terrible at office politics. What's that got to do with anything?"

"Well, he and I have to look into our little problem. Full disclosure on both sides."

"And that's why you're really here – to meet up with Mike Lloyd? And I assumed it was for the pleasure of my company."

"I would not patronise you by saying it was."

"That's a shame. I recently became available."

She briefly considered the inscrutable Turk. He was an oddly attractive man, with extraordinary self-possession. He conducted himself with a dignity she had rarely encountered, but she knew he also possessed ambition, determination and calculating ruthlessness. She wondered where the cool exterior finished and the instinctive human landscape began. Natasha ventured a personal question.

"So, if we've finished with the subject of Mike Lloyd, tell me, how close did Abdullah Belkacem's son come to killing you? Were you scared?"

He took a moment to consider his response.

"It is the bullets you do not see that you have to be scared of. These days, in Ankara, it is having the wrong friend, using the wrong phrase or believing in the wrong god – or even worshipping the right God, in the wrong way! That is more frightening than facing some teenagers with a grenade launcher and automatic weapons, because you never know when the attack is coming."

"So that's what drove your decision to act first?"

"Well, as they say, attack is the best form of defence. Apparently, that expression dates from the American Revolution. Don't you think Mike Lloyd might appreciate the irony of that?

"Anyway, can you drop me off at Manoel Island? And what is that, by the way? Do I need a boat?"

Natasha smiled.

"No boat required. It's a small island, reached by a bridge, with some wrecked World War II submarine pens and a restored eighteenth-century fort. Nothing there really, but great views. Is that where you're meeting Mike Lloyd?"

# CHAPTER 39

# MIKE LLOYD

MANOEL ISLAND, MALTA

THE URBAN SPRAWL of Malta's Central Eastern district boasts one of the highest population densities in Europe. Further development is now impossible, since every inch of available land has already been exploited. A wide promenade follows the line of the rocky limestone foreshore that stretches from St Julian's, past Sliema, to the outskirts of Valletta, some eight kilometres to the south.

From Sliema, the promenade cuts inland to form a circuit around the edges of Marsamxett harbour, affording striking views, across Manoel Island, to Valletta's mighty fortifications. The capital is a walled city, built on a peninsular, in the sixteenth century, dividing Marsamxett from the larger, parallel Grand Harbour.

Mike Lloyd had walked across the short bridge, away from the bustle of the mainland, and wandered along the overgrown service roads of Manoel Island. He went past the derelict old buildings that had been used by the British Navy, as a base for their submarine squadrons, in WWII. Beneath his feet, a maze of tunnels once housed an underground military hospital. The eighteenth-century Fort Manoel, on the northern tip of the small island, had been known by the British Navy as HMS Phoenicia for a period of one hundred and sixty years. Reminders of its historical significance lay all around, though weeds and shrubs were rapidly reclaiming the landscape and gradually smothering those relics of the past.

Mike had arrived early to look around the location. It was quiet, little chance of any interruptions there. There were good lines of sight, useful for spotting any approaching strangers. A stiff north-westerly breeze blew straight into the large natural harbour, rustling the grass and low shrubs, creating background noise that would defeat any electronic listening device. It was good enough.

Fifteen minutes later, he watched, as Hakan Toprak approached, walking up the long asphalt road. Hakan stopped and did a full three hundred and sixty degree rotation, making the same security evaluation as Mike.

The two men saw each other. They had never met before, but each had been told it was imperative they work together and be cooperative. They both knew the importance of what they had been asked to do. It would not be over-dramatic to say that failure to achieve it could be catastrophic.

Hakan had slung his jacket over his shoulder, to give him some respite from the afternoon heat. Since it was Sunday, Mike wore a sky-blue polo shirt and deep blue cotton shorts. His mid-calf white socks and trainers made him look as if he had stepped off a golf course. Hakan held his dark woollen jacket out to one side as he made his way over, to show he was not hiding anything.

The two men nodded to one another and Mike said: "So, what do we do now? Frisk each other?"

Hakan nodded and raised his arms away from his sides.

"That would be a start."

Mike Lloyd dismissed the idea.

"Oh, fuck it. If we can't trust each other, we might as well go home now."

Hakan dropped his arms and stood waiting for him to continue.

"OK," said Mike, "I'll start. You got any update yet on who stole the container? Any thoughts?"

"No. We have the camp commander, his four deputies, the guys on the gates, the inventory checkers, the team on watch, all in the military wing at Diyarbakır Prison. They are being held in solitary confinement and will stay there until this episode is behind us. They will have no contact with anyone, other than their interrogators. The interrogators report to me, daily, and I report to Hamdi Ozan, the Foreign Minister. He reports to the President. No leaks from our side and no one has any idea how this has happened. So far, the interrogators believe the stories they are hearing."

"Gee! I wish we could do things like that. Let's say at our end, the President, the Joint Chiefs and the Director of the CIA are all in the loop."

Hakan shook his head in disbelief.

"Really? So, all of Washington knows!"

"Not entirely fair, but yeah, we gotta move quickly! Any guesses how the hell this happened?

"Well, there are over five hundred of your air force personnel on the base and you can double that number, if you count Turkish civilians who work there. Your relocation from Incirlik has created a lot of activity and we had to open two additional gates to cater for the increased traffic, in and out. We think it was an opportunistic theft and that whoever took it, does not know what they have got. Or, if they do, they do not know what to do with it."

"Yeah, great, but that won't last forever!"

"So, they will either dump it, or move it on to someone who might be able to make use of it. Tell me, why did you plan to move a nuclear bomb in an unprotected, commercial container?"

Mike stared at Hakan, who remained calm awaiting his answer.

"Isn't that the million-dollar question, Mr Toprak! The argument for doing it like that is easily made: stealth. A big convoy attracts attention and there's any number of people who might want to hit it. Take your pick: the Kurds, ISIL, Iran, Al-Qaeda, the Russians, Chechnyans. There's a lot of pissed off people in your neighbourhood. There's the chance of drone attack, ambush, missile strike, roadside IED. The risk assessment ran to three volumes! Incirlik is practically on the Syrian border. In our book, it's a war zone and you're the ones throwing us out. We didn't wanna move the warheads, precisely because we were worried this exact damn thing might happen!

"So, we sneaked them out, one by one, or a few at a time, in containers, with the rest of the stuff, to Souda Bay, in Crete. Genius, yeah?"

Hakan sneered at him.

"It would have been, if one hadn't gone missing."

Mike was stressed and, when that happened, his temper got the better of him.

"Listen, you want recriminations? Someone walked into an airbase on your territory and stole a nuclear warhead. They drove it through the gates, passed through your city, Adana, population two million, then travelled the thirty-five kilometres to Mersin, population one million, where it was then loaded onto a ship, on course for Benghazi. Where were your guys at the gate? Where was your national security when this got called in? I'll tell you: nowhere! We put this on you Turks!"

Hakan ignored the accusation. The Americans had, of course, had their own security at the base, but it was convenient for them to forget that now. He focused on the destination of the warhead.

"I had heard that – Benghazi, Libya – you probably could not pick a less friendly place for a Turk and an American. I assume the B61 had a tracker on it?"

"Yep. But it's gone dark now."

"So, someone has found it?"

Mike stared over the waters towards the huge bastions of Valletta and nodded. Hakan looked shocked.

"Why did someone not stop them?"

Mike stamped his foot in frustration.

"Fuckin' politics, Hakan, politics! Don't you think we could've had assets all over that thing? It was already in the docks at Mersin, when we realised it had gone. But your president wouldn't green light the strike. Too busy rounding up witnesses. Looked bad, kicking us out, then the very thing we'd been warning against, happens. What the hell d'yer think the Saudis, the Israelis or the Iranians would say when they heard there was a rogue warhead drifting around the neighbourhood?

"We couldn't get an answer out of Ankara! To charge in, by ourselves, not knowing exactly what was going on, would've created chaos amongst civilians, possibly alerted terrorists and provoked a reaction, all with a nuclear warhead astray in the middle of it."

Mike paused for a moment. He stared out over the gentian waters of the harbour, studying the sunlit, biscuit-coloured limestone walls of Valletta's bastions.

"By the time we got there, the trail had gone cold."

They both remained silent for some seconds, gathering their thoughts.

Hakan asked: "What does this thing look like?"

"A B61 is four metres in length, weighs under four hundred kilos, and is long and thin, shaped like any missile, with fins and all that stuff. It's a rocket, ready to be strapped under an F-15. It's anchored to a trolley and the trolley is encased in a wooden crate. We didn't expect someone to walk in and haul the container onto a low loader."

"What else was in the container?"

"Nothing exciting. Technical stuff: pumps, mechanical spares, anything big enough and uninteresting enough to stop someone from looking into the crate buried at the back of the load."

"Is the missile stable?"

"Well, until it's fused and armed, it isn't going to go bang! But it's stuffed with uranium and high explosives. This particular one is a strategic, rather than tactical, weapon, which is bad. Meaning, just our luck, it's big. It's gotta yield of around three hundred kilo-tonnes; that's equivalent to three hundred thousand tonnes of TNT – get it? I remember from my schooldays that the Hiroshima bomb was only eighteen kilo-tonnes. So, there you go! We lost one and now we need it back."

Hakan paced around the ancient parade ground. There were a couple of boys crossing it, fifty metres away, fishing rods in hand. Mike and Hakan remained silent, until the youths were out of sight.

"So, if this container is going to Benghazi, why do you not take the ship while it is at sea? You have the resources on Crete, they would sail right past you."

Mike shook his head with frustration.

"Do you not get it? It's seven hundred and fifty nautical miles from Mersin to Benghazi. It'd take a container ship less than forty hours to make the trip. My guess? It's nearly there by now."

They both looked at each other.

Hakan said: "So, you're happy with my idea of sending Abdullah Belkacem and the Maltese policeman to Benghazi, to have a look around?"

"I've got no better ones. We've got every resource focused on Benghazi: satellites, drones, subs, and a strike group of ships has left Souda Bay. But you're right, we've got no one on the ground and eastern Libya is a no-go for us at the moment. So, yeah, I'll let you know when we can get hold of them. It'll be a day or so, before they're ready to travel."

Mike had not finished. He smiled at Hakan and said:

"And by the way, as a gesture of goodwill – your TOGO systems will be back up if you pay the little shit of a hacker two hundred and fifty grand. He wants more, but he'll do what he's told. I'll make sure of that!"

Mike Lloyd turned his back to walk off.

Hakan Toprak regularly practised Sayokan, a Turkish martial arts program developed from central Asian principles, in combination with Ottoman-style strikes and the Turks' love of wrestling. For a moment, he nearly lost the sense of calm for which he was famous. The arrogant little American, in his stupid clothes, never realised how close he came to being smashed to the floor and choked to within an inch of his life.

Hakan shouted loudly at Mike's receding back.

"Stay!"

Mike was so surprised, he instantly obeyed.

Hakan closed on him. Mike glanced around. He had chosen the meeting place well. There was no escape or help within sight. For all his big talk, Mike was not a fighter and he had underestimated the Turk. He could see fury burning behind his dark eyes.

Hakan yelled at him: "Why?"

"Why what?"

If Hakan wanted to talk, not fight, Mike felt he was on firmer ground.

"All the usual stuff. You guys need to know, you can't make up your own rules with this Blue Homeland stuff. And we were pissed about Incirlik. Anyway, it's small change, compared to what's on the table now, yeah? It's over, case closed. I might even say sorry."

"You people make me sick. We will find your little hacker and I will personally cut his balls off. Now I'm going to forget this disagreement between us. There is work to be done and, unfortunately, I have to do it with you. Fuck me about again, though, and I will show you what it means to disrespect a Turk."

# ARTICLE IN MALTA TELEGRAPH

*Reporter: Amy Halliday*
*26 July 2021*

***MalTech Energy exploration of Turkish continental shelf ends in failure due to computer hack***

*MalTech Energy today confirmed that a systems failure aboard its drill-ship,* Ocean Vantage, *has resulted in the ship returning to Malta for repairs.*

*The costly project was supposed to be the company's first step towards becoming an integrated energy provider with significant upstream and downstream operations. The delay to the project is likely to be significant and the systems failure is said to be due to an unauthorised intrusion into the vessel's computer network. All expenses arising, estimated at several million euros, are said to be due to a lack of cyber security aboard the vessel and, as such, are not believed to be covered by the vessel's insurers.*

*The* Ocean Vantage *was approaching the controversial maritime area south of Crete, which is claimed by both the Turkish and Greek govern-*

ments. *The drill site is close to the Greek island of Gavdos, which recently saw an armed encounter between Greek Marines and alleged Turkish fishermen. The fishermen sank a Greek naval vessel, destroyed several luxury yachts, terrorised residents and kidnapped a British couple, to make their escape from the Greek military. The couple and their three captors are still missing.*

*MalTech Energy has close relations with Tripoli's Government of National Accord, which is in turn highly reliant on Turkish arms and support. The endorsement by Malta of the contentious Libyan-Turkish maritime treaty is further evidence of the growing links between Malta and Turkey. It was telling that the* Ocean Vantage, *while drifting in open waters without power, chose to wait twenty-four hours for help from the Turkish coastguards rather than seek Greek assistance, which was readily to hand in Souda Bay, Crete.*

*MalTech Energy has said it is disappointed about the minor delay to its plans and hopes the* Ocean Vantage *will be back on station within a few weeks.*

GEORGE COULD NOT EXPRESS how good it was to feel the warm concrete of the quayside under his feet. It took time to get used to its stability and, like all sailors newly ashore, he swayed from side to side, compensating for the rolling of an imaginary boat. Abdullah had radioed ahead and one of his men had collected Rania from the farmhouse. He had asked her to bring some food-stuffs for the boat and a case of US dollars from his strong room, hewn from the limestone, beneath the kitchen.

The reunion between Abdullah and Rania was not joyful, as the purpose of the trip to Gavdos had been to secure better conditions for Jamal. They were both heartbroken to discover he was back inside Abu Salim. Rania wailed and beat her fists against her husband's chest in frustration. He felt ashamed for failing them both and tried to hold her close and calm her. George sat quietly, letting the pair of them vent their anger and despair. He was however, confused, and could not see why Jamal had been returned to prison, unless Hakan Toprak had being lying to them all along. He felt he was missing some piece of the story.

Back on the boat, Tompy and Marge peered into the shopping bags Rania had handed down to them and pulled out packets of pulses, spices, tins of palm hearts and all manner of other food with colourful labels, covered in Arabic script. Hamza did his best to explain what the contents were but looking at Tompy and Marge, he realised something was wrong. Eventually, Tompy heaved himself up the ladder and onto the quayside, where George was sitting on a large cast-iron bollard.

He said, dejectedly: "Sorry, old boy, been looking at the provisions and it's a no-go. Can't eat half that stuff and the other half … no idea what it is! The old girl likes plain food. Cannot digest the spicy whatnot. Dicky tummy, you know how it is. Also, there is no gin and we are nearly out. Won't do, I'm afraid. Have to make another run to the supermarket."

George looked up at Tompy, his round, expectant, red-tinged face.

"Mela, it's too late, Tompy, the markets are shut. This is Libya and you've got Libyan food. Also, Muslims don't drink alcohol. It's *haram*, forbidden. So, you're going to have to do without your gin for a while, until you reach the next port. I'm sorry"

As Tompy's face started to crumple in disappointment, George was distracted by a cavalcade of security vehicles streaming in through the entrance to the docks, on the other side of the harbour. Four police cars and two army trucks raced down the wharf and pulled up, blocking the exit from the quayside. Their blue lights revolved and darkly clad, armed figures piled out of the back of the trucks.

Abdullah had about a dozen men with him and shouted for weapons. Someone threw him a rifle and they scattered to take positions behind such cover as was available. George ushered Tompy and Rania behind a nearby skip and shouted to Hamza to take Marge into the cabin. He peeked over the top of the skip to see what was happening. An uneasy standoff developed, with the two groups facing each other. There were about fifty metres between them.

After a minute, two men emerged from one of the cars and started to walk confidently towards Abdullah's position. When they got twenty paces away an American voice said: "Drop the weapons, Abdullah, it's me, Mike Lloyd. I'll be really pissed if you shoot me!"

Abdullah shouted back to him.

"Move to your left, into the light."

A pale orange lamp cast a lozenge of light onto the quayside. The two men shuffled sideways into it.

"*Ya salaam!* Well, look who this is, Rania! Shall I kill him now? It's the dog Hakan Toprak!"

Rania suddenly emerged from the deep shadow of the skip and marched up to Toprak. He stood impassively, with his arms by his sides, as she swiped her hand viciously across his face.

"Where is my son?" she screamed. "You promised you would take care of him – you lied!" She sobbed and held her head in her hands. Abdullah ran to put his arms around her and led her away back towards George.

"Take her." He pushed her into George's arms, where she continued weeping into his shoulder.

Mike Lloyd was bemused.

"Whoa! What's going on here! This is some reunion!"

Toprak wiped his face with his hand and checked his mouth for any trace of blood. Satisfied he was not bleeding, he said to Mike: "I told you I knew Abdullah Belkacem and Inspector Zammit. But, until now, I've never had the pleasure of meeting Mrs Belkacem."

Hakan Toprak calmly turned to address Rania, who lifted her head from George's shoulder.

"Mrs Belkacem, *I* asked the authorities to move your son from the military base back to Abu Salim, so it would be easier for you to visit him and assure yourselves I have kept my part of the bargain. He is safe. If you can travel first thing the day after tomorrow, you can meet Jamal in the gardens of Tripoli Zoo, for one hour. Then, he must return to Abu Salim. There will be guards present during your visit," he looked pointedly at Abdullah, "and please do not do anything foolish. If your husband does as we ask, I will forget Jamal tried to kill me, accept his apology and, when the time is right, I will consider his release. I can do no more than that, can I, Abdullah *bey*?"

Rania grasped her headscarf tightly and dabbed her face dry. She looked at her husband whose dark eyes blazed. His jaw was clenched. He nodded at her and jerked his head to one side, signalling to her that she should leave them. Rania put a hand on his arm, squeezing it tightly. Toprak turned and beckoned a policeman to take her over to the cars, whose flashing blue lights were playing over the whitewashed walls of the quayside.

George accompanied her towards the oncoming policeman. It felt like handing over a hostage. He watched Rania walk down the quayside, away from them, without looking back. He returned to stand by Abdullah's side.

Mike Lloyd smiled at George.

"Families – don't ya just love them? Hey, George. How's it goin'? Helluva stunt you pulled in Gavdos. Remind me never to let you anywhere near Pearl Harbour!"

Mike looked disappointed when nobody laughed.

"Look at us all, who'd have thought it? The gang, together again."

George had a question.

"*Mela*, how did you know we were here? No one knew we were on that yacht. There's been no radio contact. We even turned our phones off."

Mike threw back his head and laughed.

"Come on, George, this is the twenty-first century! There've been satellites above you for the last four days. Cost us over a million dollars to watch you throw up! The only boat to leave Gavdos and set a course, straight as an arrow, for Libya? Please, give us some credit.

"Now, to fill you in a bit more: Hakan and I got have a little problem in common. Actually, it's not so little. Anyway, we were tossing a few names in the air about who might help us – and, guess what? We thought of you two. How about that?"

Mike Lloyd clapped his hands in faux-delight.

"Play your cards right, George, and there might be another medal in it for you! And, tell you what, we'll persuade the Greeks not to send you a bill for their gunboat! It's win, win."

Mike paused, his expression serious again.

"I think Mr Belkacem has already agreed to our terms. And, George, Camilleri agreed we can ask you to help, but he can't order you to agree, this time. Apparently, you look after pedestrian crossings now, or some shit like that? Must be real important work."

Abdullah was watching George carefully. He could see the policeman was not happy and he had already been coerced into helping with the trip to Gavdos. If Toprak and Mike Lloyd were working together, whatever they were going to ask for, it would not be easy.

George replied, "Mela, before I agree to anything, I need to know what it is you want us to do."

Abdullah became more hopeful. At least George had not refused outright.

Hakan Toprak said: "We cannot talk about it here." He glanced to one side, where Hamza's head was visible, peeping over the quay. He was standing on the ladder from the boat to the wharf, openly listening to their conversation. "But we want you to find something."

George glanced at Abdullah, who raised his eyebrows questioningly.

"No, Abdullah, don't look at me like that. One day our luck's going to run out. I've done enough for you already. You can't ask me again. Whatever it is they want, I'll have no part in it. Why me? And don't give me any more of that Goose nonsense, it won't work."

Hakan looked at Mike and pulled a confused face, mouthing: "Did he say a goose, like the bird?"

Mike shrugged.

At that moment Tompy emerged from behind the skip and nervously approached Mike Lloyd, one hand extended.

"How do you do? Tompy McCauley, ex-RN, Lieutenant Commander."

"Hey, Lieutenant," said Mike.

Tompy cast a glance down the quayside at the large group of soldiers, now standing easy, chatting amongst themselves.

"Err.. need a favour from you. No chance of asking one of your boys to tootle off for a bottle of gin, is there? Happy to pay. Need to be on our way shortly, is all."

Mike looked at Tompy's wide eyed, smiling face in disbelief.

"D'ya know where you are, Lieutenant? This ain't the Royal Yacht Club."

Tompy pointed towards the policemen.

"Well, they look a likely bunch – somebody must have it in them to help the Senior Service and all that?"

Mike looked around the empty dockside, lit by the occasional pool of pale, lemon-coloured light. He had no idea where to find a bottle of gin. On the other hand, the old guy had just stepped ashore, after a four-day trip, as a hostage, and all he wanted for his trouble was a darn' bottle.

He whistled over the most senior of the policemen, who put his cigarette out with the heel of his boot, and slouched down the quay towards them. Mike emptied his wallet of Libyan dinars and aggressively pushed the cash into the policeman's top pocket.

"You wanna do something useful? You got an international hotel in this place?"

Abdullah stepped in and, glaring at Tompy, started rattling off instructions to the policeman in Arabic. Once the man had left, Abdullah said to Mike, "If you are serious, to give this man more alcohol, then there is an oil man, Adel Abu Khader, who runs the Marsabar Oil and Gas terminal. He lives twenty minutes away. He has cupboards full of the alcohol for European businessmen. I will text him, then Tompy can leave and drink till the sun comes up! *Inshallah!*

Mike looked around the group.

"Hear that, Lieutenant? You're in luck. OK, are we done here?"

A small voice from the edge of the dock piped up: "No! One more thing. Hamza is coming with us."

Abdullah spun on his heel to face Marge. He glowered down at the little woman.

"Hamza? That is not for you to decide! He is with me!"

Marge took a few short, feisty steps towards him and fronted up to Abdullah, who towered above her. She threw her head back and stared up into his face.

"Hamza has decided for himself! I need help, I am getting too old to manage the boat alone. Tompy is no use, it's his bad hip, you see. No balance. Hamza wants to work with boats. I'll teach him. Then he can get work in a marina or on the big yachts. We've decided together." She glared at Tompy. "Haven't we?"

He looked at Marge, confused.

"Well, yes, 'course. First I have heard of it... but I suppose so."

George stepped up to them.

"Well, Marge, that's all well and good, but does the boy have any papers – a passport, for example?"

At that moment Hamza emerged from behind her, his trademark wide, toothy smile in place.

"Oh, yes. Nice Turkish guy gave me good Turkish passport. I am now Kemal Küçükbay from Istanbul! Good name, no?

Hakan Toprak tapped Mike on the shoulder and said: "We are definitely done here!"

# CHAPTER 42
# ARTICLE IN MALTA TELEGRAPH

*Reporter: Amy Halliday*
*27 July 2021*

*Malta to host Knife Edge Games' first southern Europe eSports event at Malta Fairs and Convention Centre*

*Never heard of eSports? Don't worry, you soon will. Malta is rapidly becoming southern Europe's centre for computer-based gaming tournaments, attended by thousands of screaming fans. The game developers, Knife Edge Games, are organising the KoC Malta tournament, featuring their real-time strategy game, Kings of Conflict. Two teams of five compete against each other, trying to take each other's base. Sound simple? It's really not. It takes years of practice and lightning reflexes to become an elite player. In the US, top players have amassed earnings and sponsorship of over one hundred million US dollars.*

*The tournament is being held at Malta Fairs and Convention Centre, where a theatre-style arena will seat over three thousand fans and the tournament will be streamed live to hundreds of thousands more, worldwide.*

*A group of five top Maltese players have teamed up to form SnakeByte, with the intention of taking on the best teams in southern Europe. We wish them luck!*

*This is no flash in the pan, with bedroom heroes acting out on their PlayStations. The eSports business is projected to become a billion-dollar global industry in the next two years and is amongst the fastest-growing sectors on the planet. Hosting this event is seen as part of Malta's commitment to its vibrant online gambling and video gaming industries.*

*And, yes, punters do bet on the outcome of eSports events!*

SAVI HAD LEFT Mike on the promenade, after the warning to keep his head down for a couple of days. Savi had agreed, then gone back to Danka's and slept for twenty hours straight. When he woke, it felt like it could be the middle of the night, but he did not bother opening the blackout blinds to find out. He got up, had a piss, lit a cigarette, put on his headphones, sat at his PC, palmed his mouse, tilted his keyboard and made ready for battle.

The tournament at Malta's MFFC was happening soon, it could even be today – Danka would tell him. He had to get some hours of practice in. He knew the others practised up to ten hours a day, and some of the Italians longer than that. Gaming had moved from being the pursuit of lonely teenagers stuck in their bedrooms to an online community activity. *Kings of Conflict* was Savi's and Danka's favourite and they regularly teamed up with other online friends to play the game. Savi was a Master, meaning he captained the team, while Danka usually played a defensive role, protecting the home base from attack.

Once games got to the elite level, Savi was in his element. He seemed to sense targets before they appeared on the screen. His fingers never stopped clicking the mouse and working the keyboard. In the arenas, players wore noise-cancelling headphones so they could not hear 'call outs' from the hysterical audience, warning players of approaching enemies or oncoming perils. Once the game began, it required utter concentration. Savi, or SnakeHead, was one of its foremost practitioners. Danka was good, in a limited role, but if she did not have Savi organising things ahead of her, she would be mediocre at best.

As Simon drove them to the MFFC arena, he could feel the tension in the car mounting. It was mid-morning and they could see groups of youths, in team colours, making their way from the bus stops, through the parkland surrounding the MFFC, past the National Stadium, to the entrance gates. Excited crowds of young teens were milling around, buying drinks and snacks and large foam hands to wave in the air. As a competitor, Savi had a VIP parking pass. As soon as Simon pulled into the carpark, Savi started with his usual crisis of confidence.

"Sorry, guys, I'm not feeling great today. I'm not going to be on my game. It's a waste of time. Can we go?"

Danka tried to encourage him.

"Come on, you're always like this before a tournament. Remember Milan? I had to drag you out of the taxi! That Carabiniere thought I was mugging you! As soon as you sat down, you were awesome."

"No, this is different, it's something I ate. I've got the shits. Can we go back, please?"

He forlornly rested his head against the glass of the window, refusing to make a move. Simon parked the car and walked around to open the passenger door.

"Come on, superstar, get out, stop whining and get on with it."

Savi was pale and wide eyed. For a moment, Simon wondered whether he was telling the truth. But, no, Savi always looked like that. Simon reached inside, one beefy hand circling Savi's skinny bicep, and firmly pulled him out of the car.

"Hey, get offa me! You can't push me around like that!"

Danka moved quickly, linking Savi's other arm. Much in the

style of two prisoner officers bringing a reluctant charge to the dock, they led him into the tournament.

As they approached the VIP and Press entrance, she stopped and said to Savi: "Remember this moment, Simon and me dragging you in. Because you're going to say thank you to us when you've kicked the shit out of them! Now, let's go and get down to business."

Savi's team SnakeByte had to play three forty-minute games to qualify for the evening finals. There was a ten thousand euro prize for the winning team, which the five players had agreed to split equally between them, if they won. Savi was not interested in the money. On Mike's instructions, he had taken a quarter of a million euros from the Turks the previous week, so his cold wallet was looking even fatter.

The stadium was full and the noise deafening. Savi and the Maltese home team were first on and appeared from the back to parade through the cheering crowd and take to the stage, like champion boxers. Danka felt a wave of vicarious pride, as the team received the adulation of the home supporters. The players held their hands up for high fives, waved their clenched fists in the air and smiled at friends and family. As Master, Savi led them down the centre aisle, eyes fixed firmly on the path ahead and his hands thrust deep into the pockets of his dirty, baggy jeans.

Two more rounds and Savi and the boys were in the final. It was a long and exhausting day. Danka followed every heat, applauding the big hits and groaning at missed shots. The tournament commentator screamed himself hoarse, celebrating manoeuvres and good shooting. Simon was exhausted, but Danka had energy to burn, jumping on her seat and yelling her support. The auditorium was chaotic, as Savi's team returned to the stage. It took thirty-five minutes for SnakeByte to finish off Israel's MVP. Simon and Danka hung around, like proud parents, to watch the presentation of the cheque and trophies. When all the hullaballoo was over, Savi came down from the stage, hands in pockets, a silver trophy under his arm, a slight smile on his face.

"We kicked ass!'

Danka ran at him, arms outstretched, but hit him with such force, she knocked him off his feet and the pair of them rolled back onto the floor of the arena, laughing hysterically. Simon sat down in a chair next to them, as they lay on their backs, holding hands, waving their legs in the air, enjoying the moment. That was the image that a press photographer captured and sold that night to the picture editor of the *Malta Telegraph*. It accompanied the front page article on how a home team had won the first KoC Malta eSports tournament, in front of three thousand fans at the MFFC.

That was the picture Natasha Bonnici saw the next day, when she sat drinking her pre-lunch aperitivo, on the terrace of the castello.

Mike Lloyd also saw it, in the press reports that arrived on his laptop every morning. He was shocked.

"Jesus H. Christ! I told him to keep his head down for the next few weeks. Little shit-for-brains!"

IT WAS the early hours of the morning when they all returned to Abdullah's secure farmhouse on the outskirts of Marsabar. The house had been built with materials brought into Libya by the Americans, in thanks for services rendered. It featured Italian tiling and bathrooms, German kitchen appliances and a small swimming pool, which Jamal and the local children had loved when they were young. It also had a fortified four-metre-high wall, with twenty-four-hour guards and an expensive rising bollard system, to prevent any evil bursting through the gate.

Abdullah was a wealthy and important man in western Libya. But tonight, none of that mattered. He was primarily a father, seeking assurances of the release of his son from the horrors of Abu Salim. Rania had prepared a light supper for them all and Mike Lloyd, Hakan Toprak and George had all agreed to accept her hospitality and get some sleep, before resuming their planning in the morning.

As they lay in bed, Abdullah held his sobbing wife close and tried to comfort her.

"Do not cry woman! I promise you; I will do what the American asks. We will get him back. I am certain of it. He will be here with us and it will be as it was before."

"What now, Abdullah? What do they want now? Nothing is ever enough. How can you say we will get him back? Do you know the future? We will never get him back, I know it. They ask you to go to Greece, and you go. What if you had not come back, eh? Then, I would have no husband and no son! Where would I be, I ask you?"

"Hush woman, hush." He rocked her gently.

"You are too old for this life Abdullah. All I want is for us all to be together and, like other people, for us to get old peacefully. Is that too much to ask?"

Abdullah had no answer to her questions. She eventually wept herself to sleep, leaving Abdullah watching shadows from the slowly turning ceiling fan dance around the room.

The next morning, Rania rose early to set out a table of freshly baked breads, yoghurt, honey, dates and *shakshuka*: eggs poached in a rich tomato sauce. She encouraged George to pile his plate, commenting on how he had filled out since returning to Malta.

Fearing she might have insulted him, she put her hand on his shoulder and said: "It shows a man is happy and being cared for by his wife. When you have a skinny husband, like Abdullah, I know they say I do not feed him and am no good as a cook!" She did her best to raise a smile.

Feeling guilty about his failure to contact Marianna, George gobbled down his breakfast. He then went around the side of the house to ring his wife, after borrowing Abdullah's satellite phone.

He was surprised when Marianna answered after two rings, in a cheerful mood.

"Oh, George, you're back! Everything OK? Well, I know it is, because Gerald's been round, saying what a good job you've been doing. He's been ever so nice about what we've had to put up with... what with you being gone for so long. Anyway, I asked him about you being promoted back up to superintendent and he said he was sure something would come along soon! So that's good news, isn't it?"

George gasped in frustration.

"Marianna, I've told you before, please don't interfere with my work. Especially not with Gerald Camilleri. You know not to trust a word he says."

"*Mela*, he and I've always got along very well. I think you've got Gerald all wrong. He's a gentleman, and a gentleman never goes back on his word, does he? And... wait for it... he's looking into paying you a hardship allowance! That's good, isn't it? It'll pay for the Spanish holiday!"

"Oh, Marianna, please! I'll sort things out when I get back. But that's going to take a little longer than I thought."

"Oh, that's OK. Listen, Gina and I were thinking. When Gerald makes those hardship payments, can we go back to that nice hotel in Nerja again? We all had a lovely time, didn't we? And Giorgio can come too?"

Unwilling to spoil her good mood, George promised to press Camilleri for special hardship payments and agreed, if the money allowed, they would all go on holiday back to Spain, including Giorgio, Gina's fiancé. With a loud exhalation of relief, he rang off.

Abdullah came up to him in the garden and asked tentatively: "So, my friend, how was the volcanic Lady Wife? Very happy to hear from you?"

"Yes, she was surprisingly friendly. It looks like all I've got to do is promise to take them on holiday to Spain and everything's all right."

Abdullah squatted on his haunches and said wistfully: "If only everything here could be arranged so easily, eh?"

He lit a cigarette and stared down at the short rough grass beneath his feet.

"You know they will ask you to come with me on whatever this trip might be? And Jamal's life will depend on your answer. You know that?"

George looked away. He knew what was at stake. But he was not going to commit himself to anything at this point.

Abdullah raised himself to his full height of just under two metres. He was a tall man, but George noticed the stiffness in his movements and the beginnings of grey in his oiled beard. He no longer appeared as invincible as he had when George first met him, all those years ago, in the dusty carpark of the Vai Vai Café.

Abdullah flicked his cigarette away into the dust and turned to George: "Let's go and see what suicide mission they have in mind for us next."

Then, Abdullah suddenly stiffened and looked at the western horizon. After a few seconds, George could hear it too. A low-flying helicopter was approaching. It grew from a distant black spot, until it hovered a few hundred metres outside the farmhouse's perimeter wall, before descending, throwing a cloud of dust and grit high into the air.

George looked at Abdullah, who seemed unsurprised by its arrival. He asked: "What's this?"

"Mike Lloyd warned me it was coming, so my men would not shoot it out of the sky."

George peered at the helicopter, shielding his eyes from the glare.

"There's nobody getting out?"

Abdullah looked at him.

"No, it is for us. To take us where we have to go."

George looked horrified.

"What? Where to? Now? What's happening?"

"I do not know. Shall we go and find out?"

They met in the formal lounge that was rarely used save for special occasions and family celebrations. Several of the chairs still had thick plastic covers over the seat pads and the best rugs were partly covered with older mats, on which guests were expected to place their feet.

Mike Lloyd was pacing around like a tiger in a cage, while Hakan Toprak sat perfectly still in a high-backed chair, his legs crossed. Rania was sitting on a couch, nervously twisting a loose headscarf in her hands. Abdullah and George entered and

Abdullah waved his hand towards the door, gesturing for her to leave and let the men begin.

George noticed she made no move to get up, but seemed to brace herself before she spoke.

"No, husband, I have decided I will stay. This is about my son and I am entitled to hear what is said."

Mike Lloyd shook his head.

"Mrs Belkacem... Rania, please, this is confidential stuff. I feel bad enough having to talk about it at all, but it's best if you leave us."

"Well, perhaps your Turkish friend should have stuck by his promises and then you would not have needed to have this conversation in my house!"

Abdullah erupted: "Woman, I swear by Allah, if you do not leave this room, I will make you leave and you will disgrace this family. Go!"

Rania looked to be on the point of tears, but there was no doubt she intended to stay where she was.

"No, I will not. I will stay and hear the fate of my son. You men will not decide this alone. I am his mother and you will answer to me!"

Hakan Toprak spoke quietly, from the corner of the room.

"Let her stay. Do not fear for your son, Mrs Belkacem. No harm will come to him. I told you, I had him brought back to Abu Salim so it was easier for you to visit him, while your husband is away. You will see him tomorrow and Jamal will tell you he is being well treated.

"Now, if I can forgive the boy who tried to kill me in my sleep, and his mother who struck me, you can put your fears aside and listen in silence. But you need to understand that what you hear will distress you and we will ask your husband to put himself in quite some danger. If you stay, you must vow never to speak of anything you hear inside this room."

Rania glanced at Abdullah, who glared at her. She nodded and remained silent.

Mike Lloyd left his window seat and walked into the middle of the room, hands clasped behind his back.

"OK, now we've got the housekeeping out of the way, maybe we can start. How are we gonna do this? Let's see…"

Mike went to a file on the main table and handed Abdullah and George a picture of a long slender missile, sitting on a trolley, hitched to a small truck.

"Gentlemen, and lady, allow me to Introduce the B61 nuclear bomb. This little baby is a pretty average-sized strategic nuclear weapon. Nothing to worry about, yeah? The warhead has an explosive power of three hundred kilo-tonnes.

"If this thing were ever to go pop, in a millionth of a second, it would release three hundred trillion calories of intense light. The surrounding air would instantly become a fireball, creating a blast wave of incredible power. This fireball would be a mile across and reach two hundred million degrees centigrade. About four to five times the temperature of the sun. All this, in a millionth of a second.

"So, within *half* a second the heat would melt the roads, burn paint off walls, and melt metal surfaces. The interior of vehicles would explode into flames. And people? Well, they'd turn to vapour.

"About one second later – one second, people, ticktock – the blast wave and seven-hundred-and-fifty-mile-per-hour winds would rip through a city ten kilometres away and throw everything up in the air. It would be in flames. So, look, that's what happens *one second* after this little sweetie goes bang! D'yer want me to go on? Because there's more, a helluva lot more. This B61 is a real bad boy."

There was total silence. Rania sat with the end of her headscarf in her mouth.

"The worst of it is that, in the real long term, just think of the sickness. All the land for hundreds of miles around, contaminated by the fallout. Everything poisoned. The deaths would continue for centuries: from cancer, leukaemia, all those freaky babies. Much of the land contaminated by the fallout would be uninhabitable for decades. People within hundreds of kilometres would be screwed, for generations."

He walked back to the window and looked out, beyond the security wall, over the rough fields and scrub towards the flues and stacks of the Marsabar refinery, some ten kilometres away on the coast.

"Scary shit, don't ya think? And guess what? We've lost one."

# CHAPTER 45

# SIMON MICHALLIK

MSIDA MARINA, MALTA

WHEN SIMON COLLECTED the post from the letterbox fixed to the wall outside the castello's secure main gates, the *Malta Telegraph* had already been delivered. His routine was to take the post and sort the bills and junk mail, giving them to Katia to deal with. Personal mail and magazines were left on a small table in the main hall and the *Telegraph* went to the kitchen to be placed on the breakfast tray. As only Miss Natasha was staying at the castello, Katia no longer prepared a full breakfast buffet, just a serving tray with fruit, a croissant and a flask of coffee, set alongside the *Malta Telegraph*.

As Simon walked down the drive, he was idly scanning the headlines, when he saw the photograph in the bottom left-hand corner of the front page. He froze. He lowered the paper, then raised it to check again and realised his time at the castello was over.

He sat on the stone bench opposite the main door to the castello and tried to think clearly about his situation. He could not bear the thought of staying there in uncertainty, wondering if Natasha had discovered the truth and, if she had, what retribution she would be planning. He could see himself nervously trying to read her expressions, looking for a sign that her trust in him had disappeared. Waiting for the summons; the arrival of Bohdan from Milan; waiting for the point when it was all too late.

Then, Simon realised Savi and Danka were also at risk, particularly Savi. Danka had told him the kid had been busy on one of his 'jobs' and had met the important American. Savi had also been bragging about the cyber attack on the MalTech ship, going around in circles somewhere off Crete, and even asked Danka if she thought Natasha would see the funny side of it. It was beyond naïve. Simon had told Danka to lock the kid in his room, if that was what he was up to. But it was certainly too late for that now.

He folded the paper and went through the back door into the kitchen. Since Marco had left, Simon and Katia were the only full time, live-in staff. The cleaning teams came and went, the gardeners attended, but only on a contract basis. The agricultural estate had been leased out to the former tenants, who were rarely seen about the castello. On the rare occasions there were events or business dinners, Katia would hire caterers, but Natasha mainly entertained in the private dining rooms of the island's large hotels.

In the kitchen, the digital radio was tuned to a Polish station that was churning out upbeat pop, while Katia was preparing the fruit. Simon came in and helped himself to a slice of mango from the glass platter.

"Hey! Get your big paws out of it, you."

He took the knife from her and said: "Come, sit down for a minute."

Katia wiped her hands on a cloth and they sat on stools at the worktop. Simon took another piece of mango and popped it into his mouth. This time, Katia said nothing but looked at him uneasily.

"Listen, I've screwed up, big time, and I've got to go. Nothing serious to most people's way of thinking, but I've been hiding someone Miss Natasha had on her list. He's only a kid... been staying at Danka's for the past two years or so. You understand? She'll go ape-shit when she finds out and I can't be around then. She won't trust me anymore. You know I've been here a long time. I've seen and heard a load of stuff, believe me, she knows how much. So that's it. I've got to get out, while I can. Today."

"Oh, no! Simon, you can't leave me here by myself! Not with that crazy woman!"

He glanced quickly behind him and put his finger to his lips. Then, he shrugged and raised his hands in the air.

"I've no choice, Katia. I'll get my stuff, then I'll take a car to the MalTech office and leave it there. I'm putting my gun on my bed, the phone and the keys on the hall table. That's me done."

"But what will I tell her when she asks where you are?"

"Tell her I left a note, saying I was going out to do some errands but I never came back. Play it straight. Say you found my keys and phone in the hall, which was strange. I'll scribble something and you can dig it out of the bin when someone asks for it, because they will."

"What about Danka?"

"I'm not sure how much Miss Natasha knows about Danka; I've never said anything. But she knows of her, so they are bound to question her. I'll ask her to come with me and start again somewhere new. But I don't know if she'll agree."

"I'm not even going to ask where you're going."

Simon laughed and said: "You can, because I don't know myself yet! But it will be somewhere back east. Take care of yourself and just play it cool. Natasha relies on you, keep doing what you're doing. You'll be fine. Think how much you're banking every month! One last thing. Say the paper was late arriving this morning. Don't give it to her before 11:30. I need a bit of time."

"Why, what's in it?"

"Nothing much, just a photograph of me with Danka, with somebody we shouldn't have been seen with."

He kissed her cheek and gave her a final wave from the doorway. Katia stood against the kitchen island, arms folded. She looked pale and was pressing her lips together. He noticed her eyes had filled with tears.

Simon took the Mercedes and drove to the new MalTech Energy offices, parking the car in Natasha's basement space, thinking ruefully that he probably would not sit in an S-Class Merc for some time to come. He left the ignition fob with the reception desk and said someone would be along to collect the car later in the day. Leaving the keys and returning company items would count for nothing in the scheme of things, but he liked to feel he had acted decently and tidily. That was his nature.

He went to the rack of hire bicycles that were supposed to tempt the business types working in the Central Business District to venture out onto Malta's ring road, in thirty degrees of heat. He planned to take a bike the few miles downhill to the coast, to Danka's studio. Then he realised he had left his phone in the hall of the castello, so he couldn't unlock it.

At that moment, a young girl in shorts, with a large green box strapped to her back, arrived on an electric bike. She was obviously delivering food to one of the offices in the tower block. She leant the bike against the hire-bike racking and went into the building. Simon duly appreciated the irony of him carefully doing the decent thing for the billionaire Bonnici family, while he had no alternative but to steal this poor girl's bike and set off back into town.

He caught Danka between classes at the studio, mopping the sweat off the resin floors. She smiled at him and said: "You look all warmed up! I can only give you twenty minutes so, if you've come for some fun, you'd better be quick."

She saw immediately from his expression that sex was not the purpose of his visit.

"It's that photo in the newspaper, isn't it? A guy in the first session showed me. Is there trouble?"

"There will be. I'm running and I want you to come with me."

Danka screwed up her face.

"Simon, no. Really? Just like that! You can't walk in here and lob that at me!" She leaned against the mop and looked around her. "Look at what I've built here." She waved her arm. "This is my life. No. There has to be another way?"

He shook his head.

"I don't think there is. Not for me, anyway."

"You and me… I mean, we're good together, but we've never even really lived with each other. We see each other a few times a month. How do you know this is it? You can't expect me to drop everything and come with you, when you don't know for sure there'll be trouble."

"This isn't a game, Danka. If I run, and I've got no choice, I can't protect you and Savi."

"Oh, so we're taking him too? Nice little threesome? I didn't realise he was part of the deal."

"Come on, you know what'll happen to him now Natasha knows he's on the island. She can be an evil bitch. You don't know her like I do. Let's all go now and we'll work it out properly when we're safe. Yeah?"

"No, Simon. I get it, but you have to go on your own. But, I'm staying. You get sorted and tell me where you are. Then we'll see. I can't say 'yes', just like that, today, here, now. My God, my head's spinning!"

"You're making things difficult, Danka."

"Well, it's not me who makes a living being a bodyguard for a female gangster, is it? You've brought all this on our heads."

"Out of order. It was you becoming best friends with that boy that's really done this. I would've cut him loose, after getting him out of the chapel. It was you who treated him like a spoiled stray cat. He's the bloody problem."

Danka glared at him.

"Savi's as much your friend as mine and you know it."

"*Do diabla ztym!* Anyway, I need to speak to him. She'll come for him. One hundred per cent. He fucked her over with that stunt on the drillship. He won't get away with it. That was stupid. I mean, really stupid."

"He had no choice. The American guy threatened to tell the *Pulizija* about his ransom attacks. And, besides that, Savi still has a thing for her. He calls her 'that woman I used to know', thinks he was in some kind of relationship with her. It would be funny…"

"It's not funny. Far from it. He's a dead man – seriously. She sent that guy before; she'll do it again."

Danka remembered the visit from *il-Barri* and nodded her head.

"Savi's asleep in the flat."

"I need your help. If you won't go, he won't. Savi trusts you."

"Looks like he's going to have to lay low and take his chances then." Danka set her jaw and tilted her head to look up at Simon. She had made up her mind and he did not have the time to press her further.

Danka put a note on the door and sent a message to her WhatsApp groups, cancelling her two morning classes and, after that, left with Simon to wake Savi up. When they got to her flat, a hundred metres down the street, she put her hand on Simon's chest and said: "You stay here. I'll go speak to him. I don't want you coming on all heavy with him. He'll get scared. I'll come and get you when he's had time to get used to the idea."

"Scared? *Kurwa!* I *want* him to be scared! Scared out of his wits. I am, and you should you be too! And the days of me hanging around street corners, out in the open, are over. Ring me when… shit, I haven't even got a phone!

"You go talk to him, I'll get some cash and a burner. I'll ring you when it's safe for us to meet up."

NATASHA WAS SITTING in the cool library, surrounded by the thousands of priceless books that her ancestors had collected since the castello first became the Bonnici home, back in the eighteenth century. The room smelled of leather, and smoke from the wood fire that always burned there in the chilly winter months. A ghostly remnant of tobacco fumes, from the thousands of cigars, pipes and cigarettes once smoked here, had cured the leather of the armchairs, the bindings of the books and penetrated the grain of the wooden shelves. It smelled of history; it signalled family, continuity.

Natasha was conscious she was approaching her forties, unmarried, childless and alone. She would be, in all probability, the last Bonnici to live here. Her father had said legacy was important to old men. She was starting to understand what he meant. She had no close friends and those who gathered round her did so through duty, obligation or fear.

That was why Simon's email hit her particularly hard. She had liked and depended on him for nearly twelve years. He had worked for her father originally, but had often taken her back and forth to the airport, to work, shopping – everywhere, in fact. He had always been respectful, calling her Miss Natasha, and had never, ever made her feel uncomfortable. When she sunbathed, he would arrive unbidden, with a drink and a smile, but his eyes never lingered.

He knew when she needed levity and when she did not. Whenever he needed to put himself in danger for her sake, she knew he would do so. When there was strongarm work to be done, he did not flinch, and if a mess needed cleaning up, he did not need to be asked twice. He had been faithful and loyal – up until now.

She had seen the newspaper, of course, and had not failed to notice Simon sitting, looking on, laughing, while Savi Azzopardi and some squat woman in a yellow vest, with heavily tattooed arms and shoulders, rolled around on the floor. Simon had been out with the little hacker shit, the same person who had most likely hijacked the controls of the *Ocean Vantage*. Why had Savi done that? There had been no ransom request, so the only motive she could think of was revenge. It had been some years since she and Simon had held the hacker captive in the family chapel on the cliffs. Savi was a child, that was how she thought of him. Children have ungovernable tempers. They flare up, lash out – then subside. They do not wait three years to act, their brains are not that developed. But she could think of no other motive. It had to be him, taking his revenge. But after this long, it could not have been his idea. Yet, there he was! With her head of security, laughing along and having a good old time at some bloody gaming competition. It made her blood boil.

But she could not decide what to do about it. Was firing Simon enough? Had it been anyone else who had committed such treachery, she would have summoned *il-Barri*, the mute hitman from St Paul's, who combined small-scale, coastal fishing with breaking limbs, lacerating flesh and, sometimes, ending lives. Weighted corpses were disposed of miles offshore, over the side of his jolly, brightly painted, traditional fishing boat.

But with Simon, she was inclined to be more tolerant. He should have disposed of Savi in the first place, when she asked him to. She had suspected he had been involved in the escape; the boy was too stupid to have worked out how to leave, via a tiled roof by himself. But, again, she had been soft and let it go. Not followed through. And, now, it had come to this!

She read the email again.

*Miss Natasha,*

*You will have seen today's* Malta Telegraph. *I'm sorry, but yes, I've let you down. You won't be surprised to learn that, by the time you have read this email, I will have left Malta. Don't waste money on il-Barri or Bohdan's team. I put plans in place some years ago and have made sure even the best tracker will not be able to find me.*

*It seems such a stupid thing over which to leave, but you rightly expect total loyalty and I have not given you that. Yet I have always been proud to work for the Bonnici family and hope I have made a small contribution to your family's continued success.*

*I felt I had to help Savi escape from the chapel, he was only a kid and I would not have been able to dispose of him in the way you suggested. So, I don't regret it.*

*Just so you know, Savi did the hack on the* Ocean Vantage *and the Turkish energy company, but it was organised by Mike Lloyd, who blackmailed him into it. Savi is an innocent in all of this, as is Danka. I have their interests at heart, so I made Savi prepare a data dump of everything I know about the family/Family that will be released to the press etc unless there is a weekly refresh of a code. There wasn't time to get down everything I know, but it's enough!*

*So, please, forgive my crude attempt at taking out insurance and let things be. I wish you the best in recruiting my replacement, and if it is not too much to ask, will you pass on my best wishes to your father? I always had the highest regard for him.*

*Simon*

Suddenly she did not feel so mellow and her screech of anger brought Katia hurrying into the library, to check everything was alright. Natasha wondered if the housekeeper knew any more about Simon's disappearance. Her tone was sharp and accusatory when she addressed Katia.

"So, you know Simon has gone, I expect? Not much gets past you."

Katia looked at the floor.

"I guessed."

"When?"

"He was here this morning, but left a note saying he had gone to do some errands on your behalf and wouldn't be back until evening. Which was odd."

"What was odd about that?"

"Simon never leaves notes. He always texts. Then, I saw he'd left his phone and keys in the hall."

"And you didn't think to say anything to me?"

"I'm a housekeeper, Miss Natasha, not security."

Natasha flashed her a threatening look.

"Get out. And bring me that note!"

Natasha picked up her phone and rang Bohdan, head of the Family's security in Milan. She told him she needed some immediate assistance and to find her a short list of candidates to replace Simon. She told him to vet them all personally and that she wanted brains, not brawn.

Bohdan asked: "What's the problem with Simon? Has he gone?"

"Yes, he has, and he understands far too much to think he can disappear with no comebacks. I know where to start looking and that involves bringing a couple of people in for a word, which may not be just a friendly chat."

"That sounds like something I should do personally."

"You're probably right. Bring some help. One of the people I have in mind can handle herself. Let me know when you can get here. The sooner, the better."

"Herself?"

"I'm not kidding! Don't underestimate her. How's the operation in Turkey going?"

"Things are moving. Everything is where it should be."

"And our guest? How is he enjoying his stay?"

"The boys tell me he's climbing the walls."

Natasha thought for a second.

"For the time being, bring him here, please. He might be useful. Don't lose him on the way. Take the plane."

She was determined not to make the same mistake twice. If she could be bettered by a pair of jerks like Savi and Simon, she did not deserve to be the head of the Family.

# CHAPTER 47
# ABDULLAH BELKACEM
## DUÉSA, NEAR BENGHAZI, LIBYA

ABDULLAH HAD ASKED Mike Lloyd what he expected of them and Mike had bluntly said: "I want our nuke back. I don't care whether we send in a team and take it by force, whether we buy it, whether you and George carry it back on your shoulders. I want it back."

Hakan Toprak was scrutinising them. He sat forward in his chair, arms resting on his knees. Both Abdullah and George were wearing long *djellaba* robes and, as usual, Abdullah had bound his head with a blue-chequered cloth turban. Abdullah had Rania cut his hair and always oiled and trimmed his beard. Since leaving Malta, George had let his stubble grow and, with skin darkened from his time at sea, could easily pass for a North African.

Abdullah was not impressed by the instructions.

"You want this bomb back? That is fine and understood. But the question is, how is this to be done? Shall I go to the docks in Benghazi and say, 'I have an American friend and he wants his bomb back?'

"Or maybe I should say, 'Someone here has a nuclear bomb and can you all help me look for it?' Is this the way?"

Hakan Toprak stood up and walked to the window. It was

plain to see that Mike Lloyd had no plan for how they should approach their mission.

He turned to Abdullah.

"Listen, you know all the militia leaders around Benghazi?"

"Oh, yes. And most of them would happily kill me on sight!"

"Do you know any of Boutros's men in the Libyan National Army?"

"One or two, but they would definitely kill me."

"Well, you have to take that chance."

"OK for you to say – I am the one who's going to be killed!"

"Which militia has control of Benghazi and the docks?"

"I do not know, but in Benghazi, the most feared militia are the il-Bibi brothers. They have houses to the south of the city, in a village called Duésa. The locals call it *Jahannam*, hell, a place filled with the terrors of the fire."

Mike shrugged.

"Sounds like a good place to start!"

Abdullah looked at him long and hard, dark eyes fixed on the American, who held up his hands and shrugged.

"What did I say?"

"You talk like a fool who knows nothing."

Hakan Toprak stepped in.

"Maybe it is the best place to start. Tell them you are looking for a special weapon and will pay a lot of money to secure and neutralise it. Make them as scared of it as you are. Tell them you have to protect it from falling into the hands of ISIL or Boutros or any other lunatics. Say you are talking to them, because you know they are wise, and they will be rewarded."

Abdullah looked sceptical.

"You think these men are ready to do the right thing? You do not know them."

Toprak ignored Abdullah's objection.

"Whoever took that bomb, most likely did not plan to do so and will want to sell it on as soon as possible. I have asked our military to contact arms dealers working in Africa and see if anyone has anything 'special' on their lists.

"Tell them, if they are found with this weapon, the rules change and the American attacks of three years ago will look like a flea bite. Barter arms, money, anything. You know, everybody has a price. That's what we want, is it not, Mike?"

But Mike Lloyd was sulking.

"I want it back, don't care what it costs. The thought of it in the hands of some local militia leader, who might set it off to settle a score, not understanding what hell he'll unleash... That makes me feel physically ill."

Abdullah looked at him and screwed up his eyes.

"Now that, my friend, is something that could easily happen in this broken country.

———

The helicopter was to take them to Duésa, eighty kilometres south of Benghazi. Abdullah was leaning over the seat to direct the pilot, pointing to a field of red clay, a few kilometres outside the small town. As the helicopter started its descent, George was puzzled to see an array of oblong holes had been dug in a grid, possibly twenty holes across and ten wide. There were small mounds of earth by each excavation. It looked like an archaeological site, with lengths of yellow plastic tape being blown everywhere by the chopper's downdraft.

There was a small group of locals looking up, watching the helicopter land. Some were wearing rubber boots and some wore plastic protective clothing, despite the summer heat.

Abdullah and George got out of the chopper, while the rotors were still turning. The pilot quickly increased the revs and the machine lifted off, leaving them alone and exposed on the edge of the rough ground. Abdullah looked wistful, as the helicopter became a speck in the pale blue sky.

"There goes someone who has heard of the il-Bibi brothers."

Quiet descended over the field and those labouring on the excavations resumed their work, realising the strange visitors were nobody they knew or were expecting.

Abdullah squatted and took a handful of the red soil, which he rubbed between his fingers.

"Good earth." He lit a cigarette and blew smoke high into the air.

George was puzzled.

"OK, why are we here and not outside the il-Bibis' compound?"

"Because I wanted to see this."

Abdullah pointed to the excavations.

"What are these? Ancient burial sites or something?"

"Unfortunately, not so ancient. These graves are where the il-Bibi brothers put their victims. The secret is out, but nobody dare point the finger."

George began to get a sinking feeling.

"Who are these brothers?"

"There were originally six of them, although some may be dead by now. They are ignorant peasants, gangsters, guns for hire. Together with their gang, they fought for Gaddaffi, then when he died, they fought for themselves against both sides in the civil war. Now they probably fight for Boutros. They are murderers and thieves, but they are the most feared militia in Benghazi."

"What about the bodies? Aren't the police involved?"

"These people do not care about the police, George. The police won't do anything to them. The victims buried in that field? They are not just the people who crossed the brothers, but their wives, children, parents. Entire families were taken in reprisal and ended up in that field. I told you, they do not care about anything."

"*Mela*, and you want us to meet them?" George was terrified. The field was a graveyard.

"They will have heard the helicopter and they will be interested. They will come to us. You will see."

Ten minutes later, Abdullah spotted two technicals speeding down the track from the village towards them, trailing a cloud of dust. At the rear of the small convoy was a black SUV.

"I said they would be interested."

George looked desperately at the crowd working on the site. Their backs were turned. They did not want to see or hear anything.

The first technical drove straight for them, at speed, swerving at the last second before coming to rest a matter of centimetres from George's toes. He stood back, as a slightly built man in a white shirt and clean pressed denims got out to face them. Several others also stepped out of the vehicles, but hung back from the confrontation.

The man in the white shirt spotted Abdullah and, slowly, a smile of recognition spread across his face.

"Well, *as-salaam 'alykum*, Abdullah Belkacem. Dropped in for a chat, I see. Where are my manners? Come with us and we'll have tea."

Abdullah nodded his head and said: "And peace be upon you. Tea is always welcome. You are Walid il-Bibi, no? It is hard to remember which ones of you are dead and which remain alive."

"Don't worry, Abdullah Belkacem, there are still enough of us alive to cause you very much trouble."

They drove the short distance to the village, which was built in grids of newer-style single-storey cinderblock housing around a central square. Abdullah noticed the small mosque, a collection of shops and, as with all Arab villages, groups of toothless, older men squatting on the kerbside, watching the world go by. He saw how they all lowered their eyes to study the ground beneath their feet, as the convoy passed through. He wondered how many of them had lost brothers, sons, cousins, to the murderous il-Bibi family.

For a militia so infamous throughout Libya, Abdullah was

surprised that their compound sat behind nothing more than a high brick wall, topped with barbed wire. There was a steel gate for access. There were bars on the windows and grilles in front of the doors, but it was the same for many Libyan houses. With other groups, he would have questioned their thinking, relying on such minimal security. But these were the il-Bibis. They were not normal people. They relied on their reputation to protect them.

They got out of the vehicles and Walid il-Bibi set off walking around the back of the house, followed by the other militia guard. It resembled a rubbish tip. A large patio was littered with rotting old car parts, discarded gas cylinders, stacks of wooden pallets and a collection of odd chairs. The loose stone paving was covered with cigarette butts and beer cans. A skinny Alsatian barked madly, mouth foaming and its hairless neck red raw from straining against a thick wire collar. It was a double plot and at the bottom were a series of low block-built buildings.

Walid il-Bibi smiled and said: "This is our guest accommodation. Would you like to see?"

"I did not come for a demonstration of your cruelty," Abdullah said. "You already have a fine reputation for that. I came to do business."

"But you must come and see. It is important you know what we do to people who cross us. It is compulsory for all visitors who wish to ask something of us."

They started to walk down the dusty plot towards the buildings.

George whispered to Abdullah: "What are these – kennels for dogs?"

"No, for men. Do not show any fear or disgust. It is important. And stand tall."

They walked down a narrow corridor, where George detected the lingering smell of wood smoke. To George's horror, he saw that each pen was about one metre square and roughly one and a half metres high. They were designed to be neither tall enough for a man to stand, nor long enough for one to sit. Not every pen was occupied but there were at least a dozen men here being tortured by confinement. George could not bring himself to look at the wracked bodies inside the pens and Abdullah forced himself to stare straight ahead, avoiding any eye contact.

Walid il-Bibi said: "We use these blocks for punishment... say, three days; to loosen tongues, perhaps four days. To rid ourselves of enemies, the top of the pen is made of concrete so we can light a fire there. It soon becomes like an oven – we can bake bread if we need to! It is not a quick death and, of course, the heat brings extra suffering to the others."

He smiled broadly, then turned to return to the house.

"So, you like what you see? And you still want to talk business with us? We are honoured. We will go inside and you can meet my brother, Abdulsalim."

Abdulsalim was the eldest in the family. He sat on grubby cushions, on a plastic garden chair, in the house's stiflingly hot kitchen. On the Formica-topped table in front of him lay a pack of cigarettes and an overflowing ashtray. He wore a stained white undervest, strained tight against his enormous breasts and gut. His grey hair was curly and hung in loose strands onto his shoulders. The body hair on his shoulders, chest and arms was the same washed-out grey colour and grew thickly over the many moles and growths than erupted from his torso. He had dark brown, Basset-hound bags under his eyes and plump, lascivious lips. George thought it unlikely he ever moved from the kitchen chair.

His hooded eyes rolled lazily towards Abdullah and a casual glance directed at George obviously rated him as being of no consequence. Abdulsalim did not get up but took a drag of his cigarette and pointed to the chair opposite his. George made to sit down, but Abdulsalim rapped the table with his knuckles, causing everyone to jump.

"Him," he pointed at Abdullah, "not you! You stand over there."

George didn't need to be told twice. He leaped away from the chair and backed across to the side of the room.

"We don't get many visitors, Abdullah Belkacem. Those who do come are never from the west. You arrive from the sky without our promise of safe keeping and put your trust in us. Not many would do that."

Abdullah remained silent, maintaining a neutral expression.

"So? What is it that brings you to the east, and to us?"

"There is a weapon I'm interested in purchasing. Maybe you've heard about it, maybe not yet, but you soon will. This weapon was stolen and it is very dangerous. I want your help in getting it back."

"Why would I help you? A friend of the GNC in Tripoli? An Islamist?"

"Because you know that the power I have in the west is a match for yours in the east. You know neither of us is an Islamist and we both hate the ISIL scum. If this weapon falls into their hands, this country is finished. There will be the same outcome if some ignorant peasant finds it, uses it to settle a grudge. They will not know what they unleash and will destroy our country; our land will be blighted for generations to come. Our sons will die of cancer, and their wives' children will be malformed, and their children after them.

"This weapon has arrived in Benghazi. I need your help, to find it and pass it on to me. I will send it back where it belongs, where no one can touch it. We will both be paid well for our work."

"And who is our paymaster? In whose service do we work?"

Abdulsalim lit another cigarette and peered across the table through the rising spiral of smoke.

"The weapon belongs to the Americans."

"The Americans? They killed one of my brothers when they bombed Boutros's airfields. Why should I help them? Allah has given us this gift and you say we should return it? That shows us to be weak. Not able to help ourselves."

"We should do it, because to help them is the least evil option. If Tripoli gets hold of this weapon, they will threaten Benghazi. If Boutros gets it, he will threaten Tripoli. Allah created the heavens and the earth and all that is between them, and if there is one place that this 'gift' does not belong, it is here. This weapon can only bring pain and destruction to our country. And we have had enough of that."

Abdullah smiled then continued.

"I too thought about what I would do with such power. But remember, the Prophet, may peace be upon Him, said Paradise is surrounded by hardships, and hell fire is surrounded by temptations. And the Prophet, is never wrong. Just because it is there, does not make it right to use it, or even keep it.

"We will stay in Benghazi for one week. Will you consider what I have said? You will be the first to know if this weapon comes up for sale, or when talk about it begins."

Abdulsalim crushed out his cigarette and sat for a moment. Finally, he nodded.

"You come here to teach me the Quran, I see."

He ran his hand over his sweaty top lip and scowled, heavy jowls swaying slightly.

"I will think about what you have said. Few would have had the courage to come here and yet you ask nothing for yourself. For that you have my respect. So, I will put out the word for information.

"How will you get to Benghazi? Your bird has flown."

"Allah will provide."

"Sometimes waiting for Allah can try a man's patience. Walid will arrange something. And you have one week in Benghazi. After that, you no longer enjoy my protection. Walid will take you to a guest house – one with high ceilings and beds, do not worry! Stay there. If anything happens, we will come for you. You have seen, there is space in my other guest house for those who cross me. And those fools in the fields, digging holes? They are saving me the trouble."

# CHAPTER 48
# NATASHA BONNICI
## CASTELLO BONNICI, MALTA

NATASHA SAT on the castello's terrace with Gerald Camilleri, feeling the sea breeze cut through the summer heat. A broad canvas sunshade protected them from the afternoon sun, while they ate a lunch of a seafood risotto and red prawns. Natasha roughly peeled the long prawns and delicately separated the shell from the soft meat in the tail. Then, she took the head and crunched it between her back teeth, sucking out the juices.

Camilleri looked on with distaste. This lunch was his worst nightmare. Impossible to eat without making a mess and he dreaded his sticky fingers staining his tropical-weight pale grey suit. He hated the way the resinous oils covered his fingers and stuck to his lips. He spent more time using the finger bowl and wiping his mouth than he did eating.

Natasha saw him watching her. She could not help but smile at his expression.

"Sorry, it's a disgusting Sicilian habit. Sergio taught me how to do it. He used to say the heads are the best part and he was right. I'm sorry, Gerald, I can see this is not working for you."

Camilleri gave his mouth one last wipe, lowered his knife and fork and sipped his water.

"The risotto was perfect, I shall thank Katia, but I am afraid prawns are not for me."

Natasha pushed her plate away.

"You know Simon's gone? Disappeared, actually."

"Oh! That's unfortunate. May I ask why?"

"Yes. You remember Savi, the little hacker guy who worked with Mike Lloyd?"

"And yourself, as I recall."

"Hmm, well, Savi's been behind the trouble at Turkey Oil and Gas and also hacked into the controls of the drillship we leased. He's generally made quite a nuisance of himself. Well, apparently, Simon is a good friend of his. I suspect he knew what was happening all along and did nothing to help us."

She reached under the table and pulled out the newspaper. Camilleri looked at the photograph and then at her.

"Careless of him. I can see why he left. Shame, I always thought he was highly competent."

"Yes, it leaves rather a gap here. Anyway, Luke van der Westhuizen is returning."

"No offence to Mr van der Westhuizen, but is this within his skillset?"

"Mr van der Westhuizen's a diamond and drug smuggler. He's using Malta as a gateway to bring Afghan heroin into Europe. So, no, he's not coming to take Simon's place."

Camilleri looked down his long thin nose at her.

"Drugs? I thought this was one area on which we had an understanding?"

"It is, which is why you haven't seen Luke around for a while. I've been holding him in Vienna. He thought he could go behind my back and I wouldn't find out."

"Very silly of him. So, why is he coming back?"

"I need him for a project we have underway. It's sort of a punishment, but he's important to us. And I need your help, too."

Natasha reached into her bag and pulled out a pair of blue

latex gloves and some tweezers. She smiled knowingly at Camilleri and put on the gloves. Using the tweezers, she extracted a transparent plastic wallet containing a piece of paper. She slid it across the table to Camilleri, as he fished around in his pocket for a pair of reading glasses.

To add to the drama, Natasha calmly said: "Right at this moment, what you have in front of you is possibly the most valuable piece of paper in the world."

Camilleri glanced at her to see if she was kidding him. She did not appear to be. He opened it and studied the typewritten text. There were five separate strings of letters and numbers.

He folded the paper and made a big show of reaching for his black leather briefcase, opening it and placing the paper inside.

"Are you going to tell me what it all means?"

"No. Not yet. The source of this sheet of paper must always, always remain confidential. I'll leave you to make up a cover story about how you came to have it. Maybe it appeared in your letterbox or something. But be aware, this paper will be subject to intense forensic scrutiny. So, if you say you found it in a letter box, make sure it spends some time there, OK?"

————

It was early evening when Bohdan and his companion pulled Luke out of the car onto the castello's gravel turning circle. Luke was cowed and frightened. He was worried Natasha had brought him here for the satisfaction of watching him be shot. During his time in the basement, in Istanbul he had put the pieces together and saw her hand behind his imprisonment. She must have found Matthäus and threatened or blackmailed him into revealing his part in the smuggling. Then, she must have forced Matthäus to reveal all the details of how he transported the goods from Turkey, to Malta and beyond. What he did not understand was, why? How he regretted overplaying his hand with her. He desperately searched for a way out of his situation, but always came up with the same answer. There wasn't one.

On arriving at the castello, instead of going under the portico, up the steps and through the ancient, wooden double doors, Bohdan took him towards a garage at the side of the house, which Luke had never noticed before. Inside was a room within a room, constructed from interlocking hygienic white panelling. Luke felt a sickness in his stomach, as he took in the chair and bed, bolted to the bare concrete floor. In one corner of the room was a prison-style, stainless-steel lavatory and sink unit.

After twenty minutes spent sitting nervously on the edge of the bed, twisting his hands together, Natasha breezed in through the door. She looked radiant. She spun around, gesturing to the surroundings, long wavy hair loose on her shoulders and her skirt rising to show her slim tanned legs.

"Luke! How do you like our new guest accommodation? You'll have to sign the visitors' book! Umm, no, maybe that's not such a good idea. You're not going to be here for long."

Natasha was shocked to see how much the brash, muscular, super-confident South African had been diminished. He seemed a broken man: pale, slouching, fearful to meet her gaze. She could not believe this was the man who would wrestle her down and nearly force her to submit to sex. His appetite for her had amazed her. No sooner had they finished one session and she had showered, changed and rejoined him than he had wanted her again, taking her no less vigorously than before. She studied him closely. There was not an ounce of juice left in the man.

She sat down next to him on the bed, making sure their thighs were touching.

"Well, Luke, I have something I want you to do for me. And, if you agree, I'll forget that you went behind my back and set yourself up as a drugs dealer on my island. Oh, yes, and in partnership with someone who wanted to kill my father. I'll forget you put him in danger, because you didn't think the threat was important enough to tell me, and I'll forget you tried to bribe a good friend of mine, behind my back. One little thing and all of that's forgotten!"

Luke looked at her with hope in his eyes.

"What do you want me to do?"

"I want you to take your ship on its usual run to Benghazi, bribing the police and harbour officials as usual, collect a cargo and bring it back to me in Malta. A normal day at the office."

"What's the cargo?"

"Ah, well, that would be telling! For the manifest, let's say – machine parts. It comes in a crate about four metres long and weighs less than four hundred kilos. But I advise you to leave it well alone. It's rigged with sensors and, if you open it, I'll know. Best way is to fly to Tunis then to Benghazi. I want you there in advance of the boat. And make sure security is watertight. The load is waiting with your usual shipper. Will you need money?"

"A little."

"So that sounds like a yes – you're going to do it? Good!"

# CHAPTER 49

# SIMON MICHALLIK
## MSIDA MARINA, MALTA

SAVI HAD PROVED MORE stubborn than Danka on the question of going into hiding and had point blank refused to leave her flat, let alone Malta. Simon and she were arguing over the phone; she was taking a break from a class and Simon was sitting in the Munchy Moose outdoor café in Gzira Park, next to the yacht marina.

"Danka, you and Savi have to come with me. I can't leave you by yourselves. We've been through this."

"Look, ordinary people have to get on with their ordinary lives. We can't go around as if there are hitmen hiding round every corner; it doesn't make sense. Anyway, Savi refuses. He doesn't believe that Natasha is mad at him."

"For Christ's sake, how stupid…"

"Maybe you've spent too long hanging around with paranoid international criminals. It's getting to you. In real life, people just can't drop everything and run off. It doesn't work like that."

"You might think you're ordinary, but Savi certainly isn't. He goes around extorting hundreds of thousands of euros out of people, for the sheer fun of it! And now he's been dumb enough to interfere with one of Natasha Bonnici's multi-million euro projects. Jesus! He humiliated her, pissing around with that ship. She'll kill him on principle. She's furious with him!"

"OK, but we aren't going anywhere, Simon. I'll be careful and I'll keep Savi indoors for a couple of days. He's got to practise for the next *Kings of Conflict* tournament anyway. It's in Madrid." She paused for a moment. "Will you come to that?"

Simon let this sink in then said softly: "Danka, given that newspaper photograph, if somebody's looking for us, where's the first place they'll go?"

There was a pause, as she thought about it.

"The next tournament."

"Exactly. So, no, I won't be there. Neither will you or Savi. I'm sorry. Listen, we'll talk again, but I need to go. I'm meeting someone."

Her face dropped. Simon was leaving.

"You'll see me again though? Before you do whatever you're going to do."

"Of course, I will.'

Simon checked his watch and left the café. He walked across the bridge onto Manoel Island and down the road that ran alongside the marina. In that part, the water had a good depth and some of the larger boats were moored stern up, against the dock. He found the *Just Reward* with no trouble and stood back to admire her. She was even bigger than he had imagined.

A 1960s, one hundred foot twin-masted sloop, with beautiful low lines and a teak deck, it was obvious she had been refitted several times since her original build date. Simon could see the white-leather-upholstered furniture through the tinted glass double doors leading into the saloon. The hull was painted navy blue, and everything above that was a brilliant white. The sloop's aluminium masts towered above the smaller boats around her. His friend, who organised security for all the boats in the marina, had told Simon the *Just Reward* could motor for five thousand nautical miles, but to do that you would need to fill the fourteen thousand litre fuel tanks. Simon thought if anyone was worried about the cost of the diesel, they shouldn't be buying a boat like that.

The owners were some Dutch people, who also owned an Argentinian vineyard and were not due back in Malta for several months. His friend was happy for him to stay for a few weeks, in exchange for Simon doing his night time rounds at the marina. The good thing about the *Just Reward* was that it was only a kilometre from Danka's studio and apartment so, if there was trouble, he could use the electric scooter that came with the boat and be there in minutes.

———

Over the next couple of days, Simon sat before his laptop, at the highly polished dining table in the yacht's salon, putting together a series of notes on his time at the castello working with Marco and Natasha. He had told Natasha in the email he had sent her, that he had already done it, but that had been a lie. Once he started, however, the recollections kept flowing. He not only described the events in which he was directly involved, but also all the phone conversations he had overheard, while driving Natasha, Sergio, Marco and even Camilleri. All the times he had delivered drinks to tables where members of the Family sat in discussion about matters he only later came to understand. He had spent hours standing at the back of rooms, as a security presence, while Natasha or Marco had been fully involved.

At first, he shied away from implicating Assistant Commissioner Gerald Camilleri or the politicians and government figures who had been involved in the various corrupt schemes he had witnessed, but eventually thought, he had no reason to care about any of them. They had zero interest in the lives and preoccupations of the little people, so stuff them!

He went through the Libyan oil-smuggling deal; the money laundering at BetSlick, now the giant online betting company,

BetHi; the goings-on in the Albanian basement, where the fraudulent accounts were created, and then Natasha's murder of the chief fraudster, Elbasan in the carpark of the National Aquarium. He detailed the bribery of government officials, which had led to the establishment of MalTech Energy; then, the murders of the Wise Men in Milan, when Natasha seized control of the organised crime group, the Family. He went on to explain the inner workings of the Family and the people closely involved in it, as well as some of their high-profile activities, moving on to relatively minor offences such as abducting and beating up Matthäus Schober, and incarcerating Luke van der Westhuizen in the basement in Istanbul.

And there was more, much more, but he finished with a paragraph about how Natasha had organised the kidnap and unlawful detention of Cristina Cassar, as she tried to board an airplane at Oliver Tambo Airport, for no other reason than jealous spite. He thought that was a nice finishing touch.

Simon's fingers ached and he stretched his stiff back. The document was a damning indictment of corruption on the island over the decade he had been involved with the Bonnicis. He was not surprised when he noticed the word count had ticked over ten thousand.

When he had finished writing, he copied the document onto two flash drives and deleted it from his laptop. After a short period of reflection, he picked up the phone and, following an awkward conversation, put on his full-face helmet and rode out of the marina.

He took the scooter up the Coast Road to a small kiosk on the seafront, in the tacky resort town of Qwara. Between the back of the kiosk and the rocky foreshore, amidst some low thorny shrubs and the deep crimson flowers of several bougainvillaea trees, were a few dusty metal tables and chairs. Simon sat at the table furthest away from the entrance and waited for Nick Walker.

It did not take long for the Englishman to arrive. He

cautiously poked his head around the side of the kiosk, noticing Simon at his table. There were one or two other occupied tables, but Simon had chosen well and there was little risk of them being overheard.

Nick had let his blond hair grow, so it was just over his collar and had recently acquired a close-trimmed beard. His light blue Oxford shirt and pale flannel trousers were slim fitting. He looked cool and fresh, every inch the Englishman abroad, with whom Natasha Bonnici had been obsessed. And still was, perhaps. He approached the table, pausing to dust off a seat with his hand, before sitting down.

"So, what's all this about, Simon?"

"I wanted a friendly chat."

"We've never been friends and, as I seem to remember, the last time I saw you, you tried to shoot me in Gammarth Marina before chasing me halfway across Tunis?"

Simon smiled. It was true, but only up to a point.

"Yeah, I suppose it's reasonable to hold that against me! But I'll have you know, I shot to miss. The last thing I wanted was a corpse on my hands in a public place. Remember, you were stealing Marco's million-euro yacht at the time, and we did all think you'd tried to kill Miss Natasha."

"God, you still call her that, do you? Miss Natasha. So, anyway, what's up?"

"I have fallen out with our mutual acquaintance and now find myself high on her list of people who have offended her."

Nick snorted a laugh.

"Oh, really? How inconvenient for you. So, the worm's finally turned, has he?"

Simon ignored the sarcasm and reached into his pocket for a flash drive, placing it on the table in front of Nick.

"Here's a document detailing the many bad things the Bonnicis have been up to over the past ten years. It's my insurance."

Nick screwed up his face in puzzlement.

"What the hell do I want with it?"

"I would've thought, after what happened to you at Oliver Tambo, you wouldn't be averse to a little extra protection yourself?"

Nick scrutinised Simon, searching for any reason why he shouldn't accept this at face value.

"So, I guessed she had arranged it all? I mean, I knew that, but obviously I had no proof."

"Yes, her new boyfriend... well, her ex-boyfriend now... is South African and I think he wanted to impress her. But she paid for it all. You know her better than anyone. She can be pretty spiteful. You know she can't stand rejection and is insanely jealous of other people's happiness. I'd say that puts you well in the shit."

"What do you want from me?"

Simon glanced around, making sure nobody was showing any interest in their conversation.

"You're friends with Amy Halliday, the journalist at the *Telegraph*. Natasha knows that. Amy would kill for this file! I'll tell Natasha straight to hands off us both, and our loved ones, or this goes to Halliday. Mutual protection. Anything happens to me, you release it; anything happens to you, I will. Make no mistake, releasing it is a nuclear option. You and I would probably go down with Natasha, because we've been personally implicated in some of the stuff I'm accusing her of."

Nick shuffled in his seat, crossed and uncrossed his legs.

"I don't know... are you sure it's a good idea, threatening Natasha?" He laughed hollowly. "I'm not sure I've got the appetite for that."

"Yeah, well, it's not my first choice either, but you know how she thinks. She'll go for those close to us. Look what happened to Cristina. I'm not going to sit still and let her do that to the people in my life. If you think she's going to sit back and let you and

Cristina Cassar play happy families for the rest of your lives, while she sits and broods alone in the castello, you don't know her as well as I thought you did."

Nick reached across the table and accepted the small white flash drive.

# CHAPTER 50
# GEORGE ZAMMIT
## BENGHAZI, LIBYA

THEY HAD BEEN in Benghazi for two days and Abdullah insisted they should do nothing but sit and wait for word from Abdulsalim il-Bibi.

"It is his city, he knows the people here. If we go sticking our noses where they are not welcome, nobody will tell us anything and he will likely cut them off."

George was only too happy not to do anything to annoy the il-Bibi brothers. In the last few years, he had been to some terrible places, but the town of Duésa was perhaps the most depressing and frightening he had ever visited. Abdullah was right – the image of the cells at the 'guest house', filled with writhing, agonised bodies and the roasting fires above them, was something straight out of hell itself.

So, for two days they wandered around Benghazi. They strolled down the Italian-constructed Lungomare promenade, took a watery Nescafe in the medina and tried to show some interest in the Arab, Ottoman and Italian architecture. They spent an afternoon sitting on a small, dirty beach to the south of the city, but, even there, they could not pretend that they were not bored and fed up. It was with a mixture of fear and some relief that, when they got out of the ramshackle taxi at their hotel, they saw Walid il-Bibi and two of his henchmen sitting on their haunches against the wall of the hotel.

Walid came over and challenged them aggressively.

"So, you take holidays, eh? We wait hours, wasting our day!"

Abdullah pulled his mobile from his pocket.

"You see this magic thing? It is a message machine. Learn how to use one and then there is no need to sit on pavement, making hole with arse!"

"If Abdulsalim say wait in hotel, he doesn't mean go to beach."

Abdullah waved the complaint away with a flick of his wrist.

"So, what news do you bring? Or, is this just checking that we sit in hotel all day doing nothing?"

"There's news. There's a man, South African. He has appeared at Rasif Juliana Wharf, checking out pontoon. He make *baksheesh* payment to customs and there is cargo that he will move in two days, into transit shed seven. We've seen the manifest. It says machine parts. Is one crate, long and thin and under five hundred kilos. It'll be shipped out on a migrant rescue vessel, *Samaritan*. The *Samaritan* has permission to load, for one hour only, then she goes. Abdulsalim has been told this is not usual. The cargo is a protected load and the police are already in transit shed seven, waiting by it and clearing out all other people. Abdulsalim asks, what you want to do?"

Abdullah was nodding his head enthusiastically.

"Right, so Abdulsalim thinks this is the cargo we seek? Well, this is news, indeed, but I do not wish to stand on the street talking about it. We go inside."

Walid followed Abdullah and George into Abdullah's single bedroom. It was a squash, but they weren't there for long.

"*Samaritan*'s owner is some NGO 'do-good' business," Walid said. "I always say, these charities a sham. The boat arrives at nine hundred hours in two days, loads and goes. There will be many policemen standing guard, but Abdulsalim say he has men and can attack and steal cargo for one million US."

Abdullah narrowed his eyes and pursed his lips. He had been expecting something like this.

"Tell him, we thank him for his help, but the cargo must leave Libya, for the sake of our wives, mothers and children. He knows this. Tell him he has earned a hundred thousand for his assistance and has shown great wisdom. I respect him for it."

The pair eyeballed each other for several seconds, then Walid sneered at Abdullah and said: "You're a coward, like my brother. But you've got his word; you take it and leave. I would not be so generous."

With that, he opened the door and left. Abdullah sat on the bed and waited for a minute, listening to the sound of feet retreating down the corridor. He kept his finger to his lips while he peered out of the door.

"Yes, they have gone."

Now was the time to speak to Mike Lloyd and tell him what they knew. George rang and Mike picked up immediately.

"Where the frig have you two been? Bangin' Benghazi's best?"

George had little patience for the American's leaden attempts at humour.

"We've got some information, do you want it or not?"

Lloyd listened and was elated at what he heard.

"Sounds good, sounds good! Right dimensions and right place. And a South African, you say? Major players in the arms trade. Big police presence also? So, it's a valuable load. I'll make some enquiries about the *Samaritan*, but it sure is odd, an NGO ship sneaking in and out of a Libyan port to collect a mysterious, heavily guarded box of machine parts."

George saw Abdullah gesturing at him, rubbing his thumb and first finger together. He scribbled a note on a menu on the dresser and held it under George's nose.

He frowned and waved his friend away.

"Oh, yeah, Abdullah has reminded me... we need one hundred thousand dollars in cash to pay off the il-Bibi militia leader and…" Abdullah was scribbling and pointing frantically "… another one hundred thou' for expenses."

"How much! What did he tell you for that? Who shot Kennedy?"

"It's a bribe, to stop him muscling in and taking the crate for himself. He's really interested in why we're making so much fuss about it. I mean, on the other hand, we could save the cash and give him the box?"

"OK, George, don't play dumb with me. Tell him he'll get his money."

Abdullah put his hand over his mouth to stifle laughter.

"Photos, George, we want photos of the people involved, the crate being loaded, the ship. As many as you can get. Send them, then call me immediately."

After they'd hung up, George thought for a moment and said to Abdullah: "I never heard you agree to pay anything to the il-Bibis for expenses?"

"No, I did not. But is it right he works for nothing, eh? And if that is not right, then it must be right that I too should be paid. So, the expenses? They are for my suffering. The Prophet said, peace and blessings be upon Him, 'Give to the worker his wages before his sweat dries.' Yes! He is never wrong! They blackmail me, keeping Jamal in prison, is that right? No! Allah will not judge if we take a small profit for ourselves."

George gave him a sceptical look. "*Our*selves?"

Abdullah considered the problem.

"Well, no! You being a policeman, that would be an illegal thing. The Prophet could not approve of that! So maybe it is best that I take all the money."

It was an elegant solution.

After another day wasted, walking around Benghazi, George and Abdullah packed their bags and, before dawn on the day of the *Samaritan's* arrival, headed for the docks. Abdullah bribed a lax security guard with a substantial roll of Libyan dinars and they went into the port to find the Rasif Juliana Wharf. Jutting off at right angles into the oily waters of the harbour were some substantial floating docks, poking out like three long fingers, all empty of shipping.

Where the docks met the wharf, there was a large static generator, the size of a small van, pushed up against the sea wall. Abdullah and George eased themselves behind the oily engine and stood with their backs to the wall, giving them a perfect view down the three pontoons.

George felt a sharp edge of the machine digging into his protruding belly. The smell of oil and spilled diesel was already filling his nostrils and stinging his eyes.

"How long are we here for? It's uncomfortable."

"Until the sun comes up, until the boat arrives, until the boat leaves, until we take the picture snaps. Then we can go."

George groaned.

"Would you rather be resting in the il-Bibi's 'guest house'? Be quiet."

George shut up.

The sun came up and the heat seemed to stir the fumes and flies. George screwed up his eyes to fight off the headache that was beginning to tighten across his forehead. To his surprise, he found himself dozing off, dreaming he was sitting on a limestone cliff, looking out over the rural landscape of north-west Malta, while Marianna unpacked a picnic.

He was shaken roughly awake by Abdullah, who pointed to a crowd of around a dozen armed police coming down the wharf.

George became nervous.

"What do we do?"

"We go and introduce ourselves perhaps, is that a good idea? Shush! We hide!"

The police took up position all around the central pontoon and, to George's horror, one man stood directly in front of the generator, cradling his submachine gun.

Abdullah poked George in the ribs and gestured down the wharf. A squat, athletic-looking man, dressed in a safari-style jacket and pale cargo pants, was walking towards them, with three more men. Abdullah was making gestures George did not understand, until he made a square with a finger and thumb of each hand.

Photographs!

George slid his iPhone out of his pocket and selected the camera function. All he could see on the screen was the back of the policeman standing three metres in front of them. He waited until the man he assumed to be the South African was in his sights, then took a picture. The phone made the faint whirring and clicking sound effect of an old-style camera. They both ducked their heads down and held their breath. Abdullah glared at George, eyes blazing. He looked back helplessly, then fumbled with the phone, removing the sound function from its settings.

Abdullah risked a look over the top of the generator. The policeman had wandered off a little further down the wharf. All the police were looking out into the mouth of the harbour, where a gaudy-looking forty-metre ship was coming in to berth.

The South African had a hand-held VHF radio and directed the ship towards the pontoon. As the vessel turned to make its approach, a small convoy left one of the large transit sheds at the foot of the wharf. At the head of it, was a police car with its blue light turning, followed by a flatbed truck on which stood a long crate. Behind that, an open truck with a few more armed police in the back.

All the police on the wharf tensed and readied their weapons. Abdullah exhaled softly.

"So many police means many dinars in bribes!"

George set about taking as many photos as he could. The *Samaritan* arrived at the dock, its thrusters bringing it gently alongside the central pontoon. Ropes were hastily thrown ashore and secured to mooring bollards, as the convoy pulled up parallel to the *Samaritan*. At the rear of the ship, George saw two of the crew preparing a small deck crane, its hydraulic jib slowly extending to drop the line down to the load on the truck.

The crate already had four, evenly spaced woven-nylon slings wrapped around it, which were attached to a three-metre spreader beam to ensure a stable lift. The beam was attached to the line and George watched, as the deck crane slowly hoisted the load aboard, into the steadying hands of the crew and onto the deck of the *Samaritan*.

Within ten minutes, it was all over. The South African had stepped aboard the *Samaritan*, the crane was stowed and the crew had strapped the new load to the deck and securely wrapped it with a large blue nylon sheet. A line handler had cast off the mooring lines and the *Samaritan* was moving gently astern, away from the dock. The police were back in their trucks and George was still crouched behind the generator, discovering how long it would take to send Mike Lloyd fifty photographs across the Libyan mobile network.

# CHAPTER 51

# BOHDAN BONDARENKO
## SLIEMA, MALTA

NATASHA WAS RIGHT. Simon was right. Savi should have run, while he had the chance. The fact that he stayed where he was and kept doing what he always did, made him the easiest person in Malta to find. His win at the *Kings of Conflict* tournament had earned him plenty of street cred and turned him into an overnight celebrity. Almost every youth, between the ages of fourteen and twenty-four, knew who SnakeHead was, and more to the point, where he hung out.

Bohdan started with the other members of the SnakeHead team who had actually given their real names to reporters and featured heavily in online articles and eSports websites. Savi's attempt at privacy had only spurred on speculation about his identity and a long thread on the Maltese Gamers' website featured a post from a SnakeByte member, revealing Savi had a place in Sliema and ate a Turkish kebab every morning for breakfast!

Bohdan found that there were ten Turkish takeaways in Sliema. A brief round of visits, posing as an eSports agent who wanted to sign Savi for an up-and-coming tournament, gave him confirmation that the hacker made a daily visit to Cairo Zak's on Sliema's Strand. Natasha could not believe Savi would be so stupid but, then again, it should not have come as much of a surprise.

She told Bohdan to bring him in and put him in the guest accommodation, but not to be too rough with him. She had made Katia clean the room after Luke had left, and the housekeeper had been shocked to discover that the old garage was now what looked like a detention cell. She knew that the Bonnicis were not your regular employers, the size of her salary alone told her that, but seeing the darker side of their operations manifest itself in the castello frightened her.

Katia had felt deeply uncomfortable after Simon had left and had hated the slimy Bohdan on sight. She did not like small men and his stick-like frame and bulbous bald head repelled her. His teeth were oversized for his mouth and the line of veneers were an unnaturally radiant white, accentuated by his deep walnut tan. He also had a strange chemical smell about him. It was not a scented aftershave, more like he regularly dabbed his face and pate with nail varnish remover or an antiseptic. He later told her, with the smile of a hungry hyena, that he soaked his hands in mentholated spirits every night, to harden the skin on his knuckles.

Once Natasha had retired to her rooms to work or watch TV, Bohdan would follow Katia around the castello, pretending to chat or help clear things from the dinner table or the terrace, but she had no doubt what he was really interested in. She had asked Natasha how long Mr Bondarenko might be staying, but had received only the curt reply: "For as long as I need him."

Natasha told Katia that there was going to be a resident in the guest accommodation and, when he arrived, she was to deliver meals to the door. Bohdan would then take them in. She felt like she had graduated from her role as housekeeper to becoming a gaoler and did not like it. She wished Simon were there and cursed him for leaving her exposed in that way. She had been at the castello for years and, like Simon, had enjoyed the times when Marco ran the house and Natasha was younger. Now, she did not like the person her employer had become.

She wondered if Danka was still in touch with Simon. She knew of the relationship. Katia had a day off on a Wednesday and resolved to pay Danka a visit then. She needed to speak to *someone*.

Bohdan had watched Savi arrive for his breakfast at Cairo Zak's at 3.30 in the afternoon. Savi emerged from the shop, face buried in a kebab, and Bohdan followed him to the front door of a narrow block of apartments, off the Strand. Bohdan waited until his mark had unlocked the door and stepped inside, before bursting in behind him.

"Savi Azzopardi! Hey, what's going on?"

Savi spun around, causing some onion and salad to fly out of his kebab. With his mouth full, he took a step back

"Hey yourself, who're you?" he mumbled.

"Miles Mercherson, saw you in action at KoC, you were awesome! Listen, you gotta minute? Can we go and sit somewhere? I want to talk to you about a big-time sponsorship opportunity with a US gaming company. Forget the small-time deal you've got now – you've moved so far past that!"

"Er, yeah. OK, we can talk. Sounds cool."

And that was how Savi ended up walking out to Bohdan's car and finding himself in the passenger seat, with the doors locked and Bohdan holding a gun to his crotch.

It was twenty-four hours before Natasha paid Savi a visit in the guest accommodation. She had decided to ditch the temptress look and had scraped her hair back tight against her head, applying only the minimum of makeup. She wore black jeans, flat black pumps and a plain black crewneck top. She and Bohdan went down to the garage together. Savi was relieved and delighted to see her. He leaped off the bed, a broad expectant smile on his face.

"Natasha, what's going on? I've been here for days."

She looked around the room. There was so little in it, she was surprised that Savi had still managed to make it look a mess. She wrinkled her nose at the smell of a confined adolescent, making a mental note that he must be at least thirty years old by now and not a kid anymore.

"You're in deep shit, Savi. You fucked me around and cost me serious money. Maybe you don't understand who I am and what I do, but I can't let you get away with that."

Savi raised his arms and let them flop down to his sides.

"Oh, come on! Look, I'm sorry, I shouldn't have, I know, but Mike Lloyd said to do it. He said you had no insurance and stuff and it would be good payback for me."

She snapped back at him.

"So that's it – payback? You wanted payback? Well, Savi, you're going to get your payback. See my man here?" Bohdan smiled, raising his fine plucked eyebrows and showing his perfect veneers. "There are things he's going to do to you that will change your appearance forever. He's going to change how you walk, how you piss..."

"Natasha, don't mess around, this is me you're talking to." It had finally dawned on Savi that maybe Simon had been right all along and this woman was not what he had believed her to be.

"You're a fly, an ant. It's hardly worth my while stamping on you. You don't know what you've done. Your biggest mistake was not taking me seriously. Now we're going to change that. First, we're going to tie you down. Then I'll be back with a doctor in an hour, to help repair some of the damage this gentleman is going to do to you."

She turned to Bohdan.

"Have you got the restraints?"

Savi was starting to panic.

"No! It was supposed to be a joke. I thought you'd get it."

"Oh, I get it all right. I certainly got your little joke. You stupid, immature little prick!"

Bohdan pulled a bunch of plastic ties out of his pocket and

approached Savi, who leaped off the bed and scuttled across the room.

Natasha looked at him with a faint smile on her face.

"Where're you going? You're in a locked room. D'you think you can run away?"

Savi huddled pitifully in the farthest corner.

"Please don't hurt me." A sob burst out of him, as he grabbed his knees and buried his head in them.

Natasha squatted in front of him.

"Ah, now you're starting to understand. Yes! You've realised you're in big shit. Hurting shit! Life-changing shit! You understand that now, don't you?"

"Yeah, yeah, I get it, I do!" His face was pressed to his knees and he had started sobbing. He didn't see Natasha and Bohdan leave the room. He only realised they had gone when he heard the door click behind them.

Then, the terror of waiting for their return set in.

# CHAPTER 52

# MIKE LLOYD
## SOUDA NAVAL BASE, CRETE

GIVEN the seriousness of the theft of the B61, Mike had based himself in the operations room in Souda Bay, officially known as the Ronald W. Reagan Conference Room. The bunker was a concrete box below the base's main administration block, equipped with the latest secure communications systems and panelled out in mahogany, to conceal a variety of audio, video and other systems. Sensors in the ceiling alerted security of any visitor who had failed to leave their phone, or any other item of electronic equipment, in the lead-lined box at the room's reception.

Souda Bay was a deepwater port on the north coast of Crete and home to the Hellenic, US and NATO allies' navies. Wharf K-14 was the only place in the entire Mediterranean where the massive, nuclear-powered, US Nimitz-class aircraft carriers could berth. It was also an important NATO checkpoint for vessels entering and leaving the Black Sea, the Russian navy's only route into the Mediterranean.

It was from Souda Bay that the US Navy's operations team had assembled a Surface Action Group, made up of a missile cruiser, a missile destroyer, and a high-speed littoral combat ship, the USS *Buckingham*, capable of speeds of up to forty-seven knots per hour. The Action Group had taken up position fifty nautical miles off the Libyan coast, north of Benghazi, and was awaiting further orders.

Mike Lloyd was exhausted. He understood that losing a nuclear warhead was a big deal. Leading the operation to get it back was also a big deal. But why was everybody behaving as if it was his friggin' fault? The video screens were never empty. Blurry figures in all manner of uniform presented themselves constantly, demanding hourly updates, risk assessments and recovery strategies. Meteorologists gave him weather predictions, statisticians updated him with projected casualty numbers, should the missile detonate, PR experts outlined media plans should news of the theft get out, scientists advised him on handling procedures and safety protocols, and from time to time the President's Chief of Staff came on, to shout at him about why he had not yet got their nuke back.

Mike complained to the Director of the CIA about the number of people continually hassling him. The Director told him the operation was being run strictly on a 'need-to-know' basis, with only essential personnel involved. Mike said that was 'good to know'. Another problem was that Crete was seven hours ahead of Washington, which meant when Washington came to life at 14:00 Eastern European Summer Time, Mike had already been working for eight hours, and when Washington logged off after its usual twelve-hour day, it was 2 a.m. in Crete. There was only so long Mike could survive on three hours' sleep in twenty-four and his worsening temper proved it.

When he saw the pictures from George, the adrenaline started to flow. It was mid morning by the time he had assembled a full portfolio of them and had the crate confirmed as being similar to the one that had housed the B61 missile at Incirlik. It was a sweet moment when he ordered Langley to get the President's Chief of Staff and all the Joint Chiefs out of their beds, in the early hours, and gather them in their secure conference room, to confirm Operation Rescue Harry had begun. After all, they were the ones who had insisted on being updated *immediately* there was any change in the status of the operation.

The *Samaritan* was doing twelve knots and making good progress when the first F-15s from Incirlik screamed over the masthead, their downdraft flattening the water. The crew gathered on the front deck, looking up and trying to track the low, ominous rumble of the jets, as they circled around the ship, hidden in the low cloud. Then, as the reverberations seemed to fade away to nothing, someone spotted them coming in from the west, only metres above the water. The high-pitched wail turned into a roar, as sound waves bent and twisted while the jets swept overhead. The crowd on the deck instinctively ducked, the sweet smell of exhaust flooding their nostrils. At that point, the skipper cut the engines and the *Samaritan* stopped dead in the water.

Luke ran up the short companionway to the bridge, to find out what was happening. He saw the shocked expressions of the skipper and first officer. The skipper had the handset of the radio telephone in his hands.

"That was the US Navy. We've been told to hold position, otherwise the planes have orders to open fire on us. They say, if we interfere with the load, they'll strike us anyway. We are under satellite surveillance." They all peered out of the bridge windscreen up into the sky.

"What the fuck is in that crate?" said the skipper.

Luke did not have time to answer before the planes made their third pass. The first officer grabbed some binoculars and fixed on a point off the starboard bow.

"Look," he said, pointing, "there's a naval ship approaching at two o'clock, and it's moving very, very fast."

Luke replied in answer to his question: "Yeah, what the fuck *is* in that crate?"

At that moment, another two aircraft appeared in the skies above the *Samaritan*. The first was a Sikorsky Seahawk helicopter that operated from the large cruiser attached to the Action Group. It closed to within one hundred metres, letting the shocked crew get a good look at the racks of Hellfire missiles hanging from the sides of its fuselage, then shot upwards several hundred metres astern of them.

The crew did not know it, but, for some unknown reason the skippers of the planes and ships had been prohibited from firing on the *Samaritan*, in any circumstance, including in self defence. It was a primary objective that the crate be recovered intact, with its contents remaining confidential.

The second aircraft was a small unarmed drone from the *Buckingham*, which by now was sitting a nautical mile off the *Samaritan*'s starboard bow. The drone caried a Geiger counter and was assessing the risk of radioactive contamination. It approached and hovered within five metres of the crate. Finally, satisfied its mission was complete, it soared up into the air, with an intense, whining noise and made its way back to the ship. Only then did the *Buckingham* drop its RHIBs off the stern of the ship and give a 'go' to its team of ten Navy Seals and two air force technical officers from Incirlik, to board the *Samaritan*.

An hour later, the vessel was underway again, with its skipper at the helm, acting on the orders of two of the Seals. The skipper had set a course to Souda Bay and the *Samaritan* was being closely shadowed by the three ships of the Action Group. Luke and the rest of the *Samaritan*'s crew had been ferried back to the cruiser and were locked up in the custody suite, pending interrogation on arrival at the base. The two technicians sat on the crate, removing their protective clothing and stowing their kit. They laughed and cracked jokes at the stupidity of it all.

Mike Lloyd sat in a cubicle in the well-appointed gent's toilet of the Ronald W. Reagan Conference Room. He held his head in his hands, feeling exhausted, tearful and humiliated. There had been some low points in his career, particularly the heist of the shipping container that was supposed to hold one billion Libyan dinars, but was filled with men's black puffa jackets. But, this latest failure was of a different order of magnitude. To add to the chaos, Hakan Toprak had disappeared and was nowhere to be found, leaving Mike to face the music alone.

On board the captured boat, the technical officers had carefully prised open the crate and, to their surprise, had found it was practically empty. How could the damn' crate be empty? Or, not entirely empty. It weighed exactly four hundred kilos, but that was due to the presence of a generous quantity of cheap Libyan grain, and not a B61 nuclear missile! The crate itself was genuine, but the original contents had disappeared.

"Fuck it!" Mike Lloyd screamed as he kicked the toilet door with all his might.

Just then there was a gentle tap on the other side and a tentative voice said: "Sir... Mr Lloyd? The President's Chief of Staff is waiting for the video conference with the Joint Chiefs. I've said you're on your way in. Er... you should probably know, sir, I think the President's joining them to offer you his congratulations."

# CHAPTER 53

# DANKA BIJAK

### BELLS TO BULGES STUDIO,
### SLIEMA, MALTA

IT WAS eight in the evening and Danka had finished another hard afternoon. Her hair was wet and the whole of her short, muscular body shone with sweat, after the post-work sessions. She wore a tight yellow singlet that showed the result of five years of continuous hard exercise and the thousands of euros she had spent at the tattooist. She ran her hand through her short blonde hair, spiked now with sweat, revealing the full extent of her dark brown roots.

The studio, like all gyms, smelled of sour feet, but Danka had long since ceased to notice except in the mornings, when she opened up for the lunch-time sessions. Then, it seemed familiar and comforting almost; it smelled to her like home.

Danka did not know what to expect of Katia's visit. They were country girls from around Lodz in central Poland but, apart from both knowing Simon, they had had little to do with each other. Danka was suspicious of anything connected to the castello and, from what Simon had said, she felt that anyone who had anything to do with Natasha Bonnici was definitely best avoided.

So far, Simon had been gone a week and she had heard nothing from him, apart from a phone number to use in case of emergency. Savi had also disappeared for the last few days. That, in itself, wasn't unusual, but these were difficult times and she was suspicious of anything out of the ordinary. Danka and Savi had argued about the forthcoming *Kings of Conflict* tournament in Madrid. Savi had told her there was no way he was not going, and, if Simon had got himself into shit with Natasha, that was his look out. Danka had said it was he who had got Simon into shit with Natasha, by hacking her damn' ship, and he had better think carefully before ever saying another bad word about the man who had saved him.

Savi had then accused Danka of letting him down and being jealous of his success in the tournaments. She couldn't take it that he was a far better player. He told her she knew he could not travel alone because of his 'sensitivities' and, in refusing to go with him, she was being selfish. She could happily have punched him, but instead said a few cruel words to him that she later regretted. She had not seen him since.

Danka was sitting on a bench with a bottle of water in her hand when she heard the studio door swing open. Katia was standing on the threshold. She was still in her working clothes of black polo-necked top and high-waisted black trousers. Her bottle-blonde hair was pulled back into a short ponytail. She was a tall, slim, pale-faced woman, into her forties, with high cheek-bones and a tight mouth that rarely smiled. She saw Danka looking at her and knocked on the swing doors before entering.

"Come in, come in, it's not the castello, you don't have to knock!"

Katia looked around the empty gym.

"Are we alone?"

Danka swung an arm around to indicate they were.

"Just us!" She shuffled along the bench and said, "Grab some water and take a seat."

Katia sat down and nervously glanced at Danka, who stared back, waiting for her to speak.

"You know Simon's gone?"

Danka nodded and sat forward, forearms resting on her thighs.

"Yeah, he told me he'd had a falling out with Natasha and felt it best to go."

"He did the right thing. I don't know how much you know about what goes on up there but since Natasha's father left, it has got a lot worse. That woman is out of control. She terrifies me."

"Listen, Katia, I don't know anything about what happens in the castello or with Natasha Bonnici and I want to keep it like that. I'd like to know that Simon's OK, but I'm giving him some time to get clear and set himself up somewhere else. Where? I really don't know. When he wants to contact me, *if* he wants to contact me, he will. I mean, we were close but, as you know better than anyone, service to the castello comes before personal relationships. Simon and I accepted that several years ago."

It had occurred to Danka that Katia might have been sent by Natasha Bonnici to glean information about Simon's whereabouts and so she was playing it safe. Katia seemed to sense her suspicion.

"I'm not here to pry or to find out anything. I understand what you're saying – the less you know about what goes on, the better it is for you. I keep a good house, good food, do what I'm asked. I try to avoid all the business stuff as much as possible. But one thing, lately, has freaked me out.

"Natasha has built an 'accommodation suite', as she calls it, but anyone can see it's a cell. She asked me to clean it. It's freaky and it's too much. This is stepping over the line for me. Something I can't deny knowing about. Anyway, there was this South African guy, one of her former boyfriends, locked in there."

"A boyfriend? She has boyfriends, then imprisons them? That woman!"

"She doesn't often have men round, but he's gone now, God knows where. Then there's this evil little Ukrainian who came from Milan and is filling in for Simon – Bohdan. He seems capable of anything, believe me. He gives me the creeps. But now, there is this kid, a skateboarder type. It's pathetic. He cries at night and is terrified of Natasha. Bohdan winds him up and pretends he's going to do things to him and the kid dissolves into tears – but, the thing is, I think he's a friend of Simon's and that you might know him? That photo in the *Telegraph*…"

The blood drained from Danka's face and she felt faint. She dug her nails into the palms of her hands.

"Savi," she said. "Yes, that's our friend Savi."

Once Katia had gone, there was nothing else Danka could do. She rang Simon on the burner phone. She was hysterical, crying and punching anything within arm's reach. It was her fault, if only she hadn't…

Then he picked up.

"She's got him," Danka gulped between sobs. "She's installed a cell… God knows what they're doing to him in there. It's all my fault." She wept and sobbed. "I don't know what to do. Simon, where are you? I need you back here."

"Calm down, stop it." She sobbed some more. "STOP IT! It doesn't help. Go outside, walk through Gizra Park to the marina. Look towards Valletta and count nine boats after the café. Find the one called *Just Reward*. Wait there."

Danka stopped crying immediately. The news that he was still nearby shocked her out of her tears.

"What? Really? Is that where you are?"

"Yes, I knew this would happen. I told you… I won't say it on the phone. Just come."

She ran along the promenade and into the park, her feet slapping the paving stones, as she picked up the pace. It was what she needed to clear her head and help her shake off the trauma of what Katia had told her. There were one or two hard types who came training in the gym and Danka reckoned, if she was careful, she could probably ask them to get her a firearm of some sort. She would have no trouble shooting this Ukrainian, or Natasha, if it came to that. They were not going to get away with kidnapping Savi and torturing him! The angrier she got, the faster she ran, until she arrived at the gangway of the *Just Reward* like a rugby centre, on a charge. She stopped, putting her hands on her knees and her head down, blowing hard.

Simon appeared between the white mock-leather and chrome sofas on the rear sun deck. He looked up and down the marina service road, then beckoned her aboard with a smile, saying: "Shoes off. Wait on deck, I'll get you a towel."

# CHAPTER 54
# GEORGE ZAMMIT
## ABDULLAH'S FARM, MARSABAR, LIBYA

AFTER THE *SAMARITAN* left the Port of Benghazi, George and Abdullah went to the airport. They waited six hours for the next plane to Tunis, where they transferred to a short flight to Tripoli and from there made the journey back to Abdullah's farm in Marsabar. The convoluted journey was due to the state of near civil war that had split the country into two. This meant travel between the east and west was dangerous and time consuming, hence George and Abdullah's arduous journey from Benghazi in the east of the country, to Marsabar, in the far west. As soon as they landed in Tunis, Abdullah had tried to ring Hakan Toprak. His calls all failed to connect. The line was dead. Abdullah rang the offices of the Libyan Resources Corporation in Tripoli and they told him Toprak *bey* had finished his assignment and returned to Turkey.

Abdullah stood in the middle of the arrivals hall and shouted: "*Ya allah!* God help me, I will kill this man with my own hands! Does he not know I need to speak to him?"

"Calm down, I'll speak to Mike and I'm sure we'll find him. Anyway," mused George, "at least we can sleep easy. That evil thing will be back with the Americans by now."

Abdullah glanced at him uneasily.

George wandered to the other side of the arrivals hall to find some privacy and rang Mike Lloyd. He was puzzled not to get through. Mike's phone was never switched off. George didn't realise that it was currently locked in a lead-lined box at Souda Naval base in Crete. He rang the office number that Mike had given him, to allow people to contact him twenty-four seven. A recorded message said that he was engaged in a project and non-contactable, but asked George to leave his name and number, saying a message would be passed on to Mike in due course. Abdullah was apocalyptic.

There was nothing to be done but continue their journey to Marsabar. George looked wistfully at the departures board, seeing a flight for Malta later that evening, but knew he couldn't leave until Abdullah was certain of Jamal's release.

On the plane the pair of them sat in silence, busy with their own thoughts. After several hours more travelling, it was with relief that George recognised they were on the road to Abdullah's farmstead. As they walked through the door Rania's beaming face soon became crestfallen when she saw their expressions. She sat on the sofa next to Abdullah and took his hand between both of hers.

"I was with Jamal last week and he was very thin. He is not eating properly. They only give him soft vegetables and a little bread …"

"Quiet, Rania! Enough of your gossip. I am not interested in the food. It is not holidays. He is alive, yes?"

"Yes."

"He has not been tortured, no?"

"No, but he says …"

"He is not in a grave cell, no?"

"No."

"He is not injured or ill?

"No, he is well and …"

"Good, then there is hope. Let us try to speak to these sons of dogs and make them honour their promise to us. If not, I know what I will do. I will make their promise to us happen."

Rania had seen this look in Abdullah's blazing eyes before. It was that of a man bent on action, rash and reckless. It was the madness of men who would charge the guns head on or stand and fight against the odds, men who do not care if they cross the line between valour and frenzy.

Abdullah seemed to sense her fear and pulled his hand from her clasp, crossing the room to stand by the window. Rania looked at George for help, but he knew there was little he could do while Abdullah was in this mood. The day dragged on and George could hear his friend constantly on his phone, voice rising and falling, shouting and occasionally insistent, often threatening. He made calls all through the afternoon and into the early evening.

George asked him: "What's going on, Abdullah? Who are you talking to?"

Abdullah tapped the side of his nose.

"You don't understand the Arabic! Hah, all in good time, my friend. Hakan Toprak will learn not to make false promises. Yes, he will learn. But for now, you rest. There will be a time for action later."

"Action? What action? I don't want any action."

Abdullah looked at him grimly.

"I know you are eager for revenge, my friend, like me, but we wait until the time is right. It will come soon."

"Revenge?"

George was spared from further evasion when his phone started to ring. Finally, Mike Lloyd. George showed Abdullah the caller ID, put the phone on the table and pressed speaker.

"George, you're back. All OK? And you rang me?"

"Well, yes. We're back and have done what was asked of us. Now we need to find Hakan Toprak so he can deliver on his side of the bargain and get Jamal Belkacem out of Abu Salim. That's what has to happen next, yes?"

Abdullah hunched over the phone, listening, his face grim.

"Well, you know, George, along with all the other shit things that are going on here, Hakan Toprak seems to have disappeared without a trace. It's not just me that's looking for him. Some big cheese Turks are on the hunt as well."

"Well, we can't find him either! How are we supposed to get Abdullah's son out of prison – as promised, by you and Toprak?"

"Listen, George, I've got a lot on my plate at the moment and I can't deal with this right now. When things calm down a bit, we'll talk again."

Abdullah had had enough. He pushed his face against the phone.

"You listen to me, Mr Big American. We went into the bad militia camp, we found your bomb, you know that ..."

"Shut up, guys, this is an open line!"

"... no, you will not shut me up! We tell you when and how to get it back. We did that, risking our lives. We make you look good and save your neck. Now you help us like you said you would!"

"Well, Abdullah, here's the thing: you and me were double-crossed. There was nothing in that friggin' crate. Zilch! You were set up, and you helped whoever did that, to set me up too. Made me look pretty darn' stupid, in fact. So I don't owe you anything, except a 'thanks for trying'. And now it seems Toprak has ridden off into the sunset, with half the Turkish spooks he used to work with after him! So, nobody involved in this is looking good right now."

"It's George again," he said, gesturing to Abdullah to let him speak. "So, where is the thing we can't talk about?"

"Who the hell knows, George? But what about these middle-men, the il-Bibis? Did they take it, do you think?"

Abdullah leaned forwards to speak.

"It is possible. Abdulsalim il-Bibi, the oldest brother, was asking questions. He is man who likes power and he likes to make people frightened. He is a very bad man."

"You told him what it was?"

"How is he supposed to find it, unless he knows what it is? And I told him what you told me, how this thing is no good in this country. He believed me, I am sure of it!"

"For Christ's sake! So, these guys are the il-Bibi brothers and they operate out of which village?"

" Duésa."

"Huh. How many of them?"

Abdullah saw where Mike was going with this.

"Not so many as to frighten thirty American Marines."

"Got it. I'll ring you tomorrow. Stay cool and don't do anything stupid. Leave it to the grownups!"

"And don't *you* forget my son Jamal – because that is all that concerns me now, *inshallah*. Getting him back. A man is only as good as his promise, Mr American, remember that."

"I try and bear it in mind always. Sorry, busy, gotta go."

Abdullah cut the call and spat noisily on the tiled floor.

"So not even my expenses, eh? They say those who trust in Allah, never lose hope. But right now, He is testing me!"

———

A little later that evening Abdullah found George sitting on the terrace, drinking tea and swatting the mosquitoes that buzzed around him. Abdullah seemed to be in a much better mood.

"So, my friend, it is all arranged. Tomorrow we go and collect Jamal from Abu Salim. I have spoken to the people who run the prison and they are happy he can go free. That is good news, eh?"

For a moment George felt a wave of euphoria flow through him.

"Really? That is good! Have you told Rania? She was very upset."

"No." Abdullah shook his head, as though deep in thought. "I think we will make it a nice surprise. It is better that way."

"Oh, come on! You can't keep such news to yourself. You must tell her."

Abdullah's demeanour clouded over and George's euphoria changed to suspicion.

"No! She must not know. It is not quite so easy. She will only worry."

George watched Abdullah's eyes turn shifty as he shuffled in his chair.

"Go on."

"Well, we must pay, of course. That is all. They want the money before they release Jamal. That is right and proper, I understand." Abdullah nodded to himself at the reasonableness of the arrangement. Then added quickly: "But a neutral person, not a family member or one of my militia, must take it to the commander of the prison."

George sat back in his chair, immediately realising the implications.

"You want me to go into that hell hole, to see a corrupt prison governor, carrying a stack of dinars? I might never come out. No! They kill people there, make them disappear, torture them!"

"That is why we must get Jamal back! Do you not see? Toprak could use his influence to protect my son. With the Turk gone, now there is nobody! I already owe you my life. Now I must beg you to do this one last thing for me."

"It's always 'one last thing'! *George, please do this. George please do that. Please, George, one more little thing* ... Well, no, I won't! It's too bloody dangerous!"

"Is it more dangerous that going into the desert to kill Abu Muhammed? Is it more dangerous than the gunfight at the Vai Vai Café, or fighting the ISIL at the airfield at Ubari? Sinking a battleship and arresting all the crew? Crossing the sea in a migrant boat? All of that was dangerous and you did not say: 'I am sacred, I cannot do it.' All I ask is that you walk into an office, say 'Good morning', hand over a briefcase and leave. *That* is not dangerous."

Abdullah glared at him.

"Say you will do it."

"You can't bully me like this!"

Abdullah played his trump card.

"Rania!" he shouted loudly.

"Don't bring your wife into this. That's blackmail."

"No, my friend. If her son is to spend his life in Abu Salim, what remains of it, the fault is not mine and she should know that."

George heard the sound of Rania walking across the tiled floor towards the terrace.

"OK, OK, I'll do it." He was furious. "But you are no friend of mine. You trick me constantly and are deceitful."

Abdullah pulled a mock sad face.

"I know, that is true. Rania will tell you: I am a terrible man."

She stepped out onto the terrace and looked at him enquiringly.

Abdullah raised his arms in the air with a show of outrage.

"Woman, what sort of house is this you keep? George's tea has gone cold! We need more tea!"

Rania looked at them both, studying their expressions, her arms folded over her bosom. She sensed something important had happened, but couldn't guess what.

"Be careful with your tongue, husband, or you will find the cat's food in your dinner tonight!"

# CHAPTER 55
# ARTICLE IN MALTA TELEGRAPH

*Reporter: Amy Halliday*
*6 August 2022*

*US forces involved in ground operation and airstrike near Benghazi*

*Last night a squad of US Special Forces, from the US aircraft carrier USS George W. Bush, launched a helicopter raid on an unnamed militant camp, situated to the south west of Benghazi, Libya.*

*The purpose of the mission was to extract the leader of the militia currently aligned with General Boutros's Libyan National Army forces. A US Navy spokesperson said the Special Forces completed their mission, without sustaining casualties, although a number of militia personnel were believed to have been killed or wounded.*

*The militia compound, incorporating several properties, was destroyed by a Hellfire missile fired from a US Reaper drone. The spokesperson added that the troops found certain disturbing factors that warranted the destruction of the entire facility.*

*Local sources confirmed the militia in question is run by the il-Bibi brothers from the village of Duésa, where officials have recently begun work in a field, discovering over a hundred buried bodies, killed in execution-style shootings. The il-Bibi brothers and their fighters had control of much of Benghazi and eliminated several competing militias in their struggle for power. The bodies are suspected to be those of their rivals.*

*This is the first time in several years that US forces have had 'feet on the ground' in Libya and the mission was described as 'exceptional and unlikely to be repeated'.*

# CHAPTER 56

# SAVI AZZOPARDI
## CASTELLO BONNICI, MALTA

ON SAVI's third day at the castello, everything changed. Bohdan woke him at some point. It was hard for Savi to know what time it was in the windowless room, but it must have been morning, as the Ukrainian carried in a tray of orange juice and pastries. He pulled a pair of swimming shorts from his pocket and threw them at Savi, who stared at him, half awake and confused.

Bohdan said: "Eat, drink and put on the shorts. I'm back in twenty minutes. You're going for a shower and a swim, then Miss Natasha wants to talk to you."

Savi rolled over in his bed, as the day's first wave of misery crashed over him. Sleep was the escape, the only place where fear could not follow him. Now, Bohdan had dragged him back into the harsh, brilliant light of the box, with its white plastic panelling and cold stainless-steel bathroom.

Savi raised himself on one elbow. He was still alive. They had not hurt him, yet. He had been frightened, but nothing really bad had happened – yet. They must want something from him. They would not keep him like this if that was not the case. The questions rolled round and round, as they had done for the last three days. He wondered who would miss him, who would search for him, who would even notice he was missing. Simon had gone and Savi realised he had been pretty harsh with Danka. In turn, she'd been angry with him and what she had warned him against had happened, exactly as she said it would. He cursed himself for not listening to her.

He supposed if he did not turn up in Madrid, his friends on the SnakeByte team would wonder where he was, but they would be so pissed off with him, they would not care whether he was alive or dead. They were a dangerous team in the alleys and ruins of the *Kings of Conflict* game, but he could not see them taking down the real-life Bohdan, or Natasha for that matter. The answer was always the same. Savi was on his own.

Twenty minutes later, he was ready, one hand holding up the oversized swimming shorts. It was a remarkable fact that his skinny white body had never seen the sun. Savi had noticed people sunbathing, tanned and ripped, but he had never so much as taken his shirt off in public and did not even own a pair of shorts. His skinny, tripe-coloured legs disappeared into the red shorts, giving no indication they would ever meet at the top. His dark brown nipples lay perfectly flat on his ribs, in the absence of any intervening fat or muscle, separated by a small tuft of downy hair. He looked down and saw his dirty feet with their long discoloured toenails. He promised himself that, when he got back to his flat, he would take the bike out of the shower cubicle and wash more frequently.

The lock turned and Bohdan was standing there, flashing his teeth malevolently, a towel slung over one arm.

"Come on, Tarzan. Shower time."

Savi hopped and tiptoed across the sharp stones of the gravel drive, shielding his eyes from the bright sunlight. Bohdan marched him down a stone-flagged path to the rear of the house. The castello's ornamental gardens, lovingly tended by Marco for years, stretched ahead of them, while in the distance the high ground of the Marfa ridge marked the end of the island and the beginning of the five-kilometre-wide channel that separates Malta from its neighbouring island of Gozo.

Not that Savi noticed any of the surroundings, his focus was on keeping up with the wiry Ukrainian who marched ahead, towards the sparkling waters of the ten-metre infinity pool. This hung on the edge of the castello's gardens before they started stepping down in terraces to the valley floor below. The sound of trickling water, recirculating though the pool, promised relief from the heat that was already building. To one side was an enclosure of blue mosaic tiling with two outdoor showers. Bohdan commanded: "Wash, then swim."

Savi stood in his shorts under the warm water from the shower, shampooed and rinsed his shoulder-length greasy hair. He poured shampoo down onto his scruffy feet and rubbed one against the other. He lathered his body and realised this was the best he had felt in days. Once he had towelled down, he noticed he was totally alone. Bohdan had gone and Natasha was nowhere to be seen. He contemplated the pool. Bohdan had said to swim.

Savi could not swim. He had never seen the point of learning, so he sat on the steps in the shallow end, with the tepid water up to his waist, which was where Natasha found him. She was wearing brightly patterned blue leggings and a matching athletics top. Her hair was gathered on top of her head and she had the rosy complexion of someone who had recently finished exercising.

She sat down at a white wrought-iron table and took a sip from the bottle of water she was holding.

Savi hunched sulkily in the pool, ignoring her presence, feeling the breeze and watching the light dancing on the ripples.

"So, have I made my point about how upset I was by your interference with my oil exploration project?" she asked.

Savi looked at her, with the surly expression of a ten-year-old.

"I guess."

"I don't like having to be a bitch, you know. I always thought you and I got along, that's why it upset me so much when you let me down like that. I mean, it was purely about being nasty;

you didn't even ask me for money. The only reason you did it was to hurt me." She furrowed her brow and looked pained. "Well, you succeeded. I was upset. And when that happens, let's just say, I'm not the best at hiding it."

Savi looked down into the water. He felt ashamed of himself. It was true, Mike Lloyd had said 'payback' and he had gone and done it, to spite her. He had upset her.

He risked a glance at Natasha.

"Are you still angry?"

"Well, yes and no. I realise the American put you up to it and I'm still angry with him, but I suppose I'm not angry with you anymore, so much as disappointed. You see, people like me, we don't have many friends. When you've got what I've got, everybody always wants something from you. It's hard to make a real connection. You were different. I don't get a chance to meet many people like you. You're honest. What you see is what you get."

"Really?"

Savi had started to feel a little better.

"Yeah, it's true."

"You haven't been very nice to me since I got here. I was scared."

"Yeah, I know, I've got some anger issues. But that only happens when the people I like let me down. Really, it's a compliment; it shows I care. But you can make it up to me."

"Yeah?"

"Do this one thing for me and we'll be fine. Quits. You can go back to the flat in Sliema and get on with your life. Hey, I'll even pay you for the work."

"Well, that's fine, but I never got paid for the last job I did."

"That's because you broke out through the roof of the chapel and ran off with Simon! If you'd hung around, like we'd agreed, you would've got your cash. No problem. You see, you let me down again!"

"Simon said you were going to throw me off the cliffs at Dingli. Is that true?"

"I said that, sure, I was fuming! You'd run off. But would I do it? Come on. It's me you're talking to here." She gave him her winning smile, then pouted her lower lip in disappointment that he should think so badly of her.

"I like you," she told him.

He smiled back at her. Things suddenly seemed much better.

"So, what's this little job then?"

NICK AND CRISTINA sat in the conference room at the *Malta Telegraph,* while Amy poured them all water. The room was hot and stuffy, blinds rucked and hanging lopsidedly, letting sun flood the bottom half of the room. There was a film of dust and a collection of dead flies on the windowsills. Stacks of yellowing newspapers lay in piles, a metre tall, in one corner of the room. Cristina turned up her nose in disapproval at what seemed to be the faint smell of stale cigarette smoke.

Amy settled herself and began the conversation.

"I'll start by saying, thanks for the call, Nick, but I've no appetite for taking on the Bonnicis again, in any of their manifestations. Three years ago, they nearly got me fired, threatened to kill me and nearly bankrupted me. There are still half a dozen legal actions against me in the courts that they have stayed: defamation, libel, injury to reputation and the like. MalTech Energy, BetHi, Natasha Bonnici, can resurrect them any time they choose. You don't take on the Bonnicis, unless you're prepared to wage war and you can afford a fortune in lawyer's fees. Even the newspaper bottled out of the fight, eventually."

Nick was nodding along as she spoke.

"You know Natasha but, from what I can tell, she is even

more crazy now than she was before. I'm not stupid, we aren't here to wage war, we're purely seeking to protect ourselves. I mean, she had some police thugs ambush us in Johannesburg and framed Cristina with planted diamonds. It was terrifying, and we can't live with the threat hanging over us that she can do it again, anytime she pleases."

Cristina looked at Amy, face creased with fear and trauma.

"I spent three days and nights in the women's prison in Jo'burg. It was horrible. She did that to me, for no better reason than getting at Nick."

"I know," Amy sympathised. "Natasha made me ill, bringing legal case after legal case, tying me up in court for weeks on end, freezing my bank accounts, putting me at odds with the paper, scaring the shit out of me with fake bombs. Just because I was doing my job and threatening to call out her illegal behaviour. I know all about her bullying, believe me."

Nick reached into his pocket, took out a white flash drive and put it in front of him on the table.

"This could change everything. It contains one file of ten thousand words, describing what the Bonnicis have been up to, over the last few years. It's the background to the oil-smuggling deal, the money laundering, everything. Written by someone who was there at the time."

"Wow! Who?"

"Simon Michallik, Natasha's head of security."

"Does he know you have it?"

"Sure."

"And he'll verify in court that he wrote it and it's a true account?"

"No, I don't think he'd do that."

"So, he doesn't know you're bringing it to me?"

"Sort of. He gave it to me, so I could pass it to you if anything happened to him. He said it would be reciprocal. We each hold a copy and he's told Natasha he's written notes. I thought you'd be interested in taking a look? Deep background. A place to start."

"And you can verify all this?

"I could, some of it at least, but I'd rather not. For the same reasons as you've just said. Also, I was working for the Bonnicis for several years, so my hands are not entirely clean. You understand what I'm saying?"

Amy sat back in her chair and shook her head.

"Well, I'm sure it's all very interesting, but if nobody will confirm it's true, I'm not sure what you expect me to do."

Nick said: "Can't you at least use this to start some sort of in-depth investigation? Find proper proof. This tells you where the bodies are buried."

"I can't do that, Nick. Natasha Bonnici is off limits – the paper would fire me, if I brought down another load of legal trouble on their heads. I'm sorry."

"OK, but I want you to keep this drive and then, if there's any future trouble or anything untoward happens to either Simon or me, if anything at all makes your life difficult, you can use this information."

"So, Natasha knows about the existence of this file and that's going to deter her from making any further moves against you two? That's the idea?"

Nick nodded.

"Yeah, that's about right."

"But you're not going to tell her that I've got a copy, are you? That's a no-no!"

"I'll tell her it's held somewhere safe."

Amy held the small USB drive in her hands, flicking the cover open and shut.

"OK," she said, "have you ever thought about letting sleeping dogs lie?"

Amy thought it was stupid to try and blackmail Natasha Bonnici, possibly one of the most ruthless women she had ever come across. But she could tell that Nick had to be seen to be doing something to protect his new lady from future harm. She thought she would try and give him a way out.

"Listen, I don't want to be sitting here with what is basically a series of unsubstantiated stories that neither you nor Mr Michallik is prepared to swear to. This paper hasn't got the appetite to investigate Natasha Bonnici further. That's proved to be a bad idea in the past. But leave the file with me. If anything happens, God forbid, I'll have a close look at it then. Maybe – who knows? – something will come of it. In the meantime, Natasha's made her point and my bet is she'll leave you alone now. If she doesn't, we can always talk again."

Amy shrugged her shoulders.

"Best I can do. Sorry."

Nick looked at her and then at his girlfriend. Cristina was angry, the sort of anger that brought tears to her eyes and venom to her voice when she said: "Natasha wins. She always wins, the bitch! I don't know how you people can sit and take it. You're spineless, both of you."

———

Late the next night, Cristina lay on the sofa in the lounge, exhausted, but unable to sleep. When something got under her skin, she would obsessively and destructively pursue it. She hassled and harangued Nick again and again. Said he had a duty to protect her and he chose not to. She blamed him for her time in Sun City; said he secretly still loved Natasha, which was the reason he would not act against her; she called him weak and cowardly for not standing up for her. The tirade lasted throughout the late afternoon and into the evening.

When rational argument failed, Nick tried to disengage, but Cristina would not allow that. She followed him around, pumping up the emotional intensity, to the point where she was nearly hysterical. Every time the quarrel seemed to be losing momentum, she would manage to reignite it with some twist or turn that would trigger another outpouring of anger, grief and recrimination. Eventually, long after midnight, Nick retreated to bed and left Cristina on the sofa, exhausted and empty, apart from the contents of half a bottle of vodka.

She lay with her legs curled up and her arms cradling the cushion under her head, face and eyes swollen from the hours of raging and crying. After a while, her focus sharpened and she registered that she was looking at the side table opposite the sofa. On it stood an oriental-design ceramic lamp with a maroon silk shade, and a small pile of glossy travel books. On top of the books, lying innocently, screen up, was Nick's phone. She was drunk and gazed abstractedly at the table. Suddenly, she realised why the phone had held her attention for so long. The answer she needed was there, right in front of her.

She unfolded herself from the sofa and unsteadily went across the room. Nick's security code for everything was the date of his birthday, so she soon had the screen lit and functional. She scrolled through the contacts directory and there it was: 'Natasha'. If he would not protect her, she would do it herself, Cristina decided.

She composed the message, cracked a weary smile and pressed send. She took a final swig from the bottle and retreated to the sofa, where she curled up in a ball and fell into a deep and trouble-free sleep.

# CHAPTER 58
# ASSISTANT COMMISSIONER GERALD CAMILLERI

## MADLIENA, MALTA

ASSISTANT COMMISSIONER GERALD CAMILLERI stood in the large bay window of his house, looking out into the nothingness of the moonless night. He knew some two hundred metres below him and three kilometres to the north west of his boundary wall, lay the shifting blue and green Mediterranean. His recently constructed, white-painted bungalow occupied a plot on one of the high points of the island. The landscaping had yet to mature but, when it did, the trees and shrubs would provide the privacy he sought. Meanwhile, he spent the majority of his time on the rear terrace, where the hillside fell away steeply, ensuring his neighbours were beneath him and not overlooking him.

During the summer, he could watch the armada of yachts and motorboats heading north, to the beaches and coves, trailing behind them white plumes of wake, like giant feathers. As evening came, as sure as the tide turned, the boats would come flooding back, towards the marinas of Marsamxett and Msida.

He checked his watch. Camilleri was a punctual man. He lived alone, enjoying a rigorously ordered private life that allowed him to enjoy Italian opera, online chess and his cats, named after the Barbary pirates, Dragut and Barbarossa. He glanced at his open laptop, which showed the feed from the half-dozen security cameras around the house.

A change in the lighting on the front drive caught his attention. He checked his watch again. The main gate was closed, but between the rails he could see the shape of a powerful motorcycle. Yellow light from the headlamp bounced off the stone gate post and reflected back onto a man, who appeared to be dressed head-to-toe in dark clothing, plus a full face helmet.

The rider approached the letter box incorporated into the stone pillar supporting the gate. He put something inside. He glanced momentarily towards the house, then remounted the bike, turned it to face the road and rode away. It took a matter of seconds.

Earlier that day, Natasha had phoned Camilleri and told him she needed to talk to him about the three lines of numbers she had previously given him. First, she had asked: "You've still got them, haven't you?"

"I recall you said they were particularly valuable. So I have taken precautions to keep them safe."

"Good. Now I'd like you to pretend they came into your possession via an anonymous source, with instructions to send them on to Mike Lloyd, care of the American Embassy. If you copy the numbers or email them, make absolutely certain they are correct. And make sure nothing, I mean *nothing*, can suggest the information originated with me. You're just an innocent, unwitting messenger into whose hands this intelligence has fallen."

"I understand. Are you going to tell me what this is all about? I do like to know what I'm getting involved in."

"I'm sorry, Gerald, on this occasion, I'm afraid I can't say any more. I've got to ask you to trust me and do me this favour."

The idea of trusting Natasha Bonnici did not sit well with Camilleri, but nevertheless... He grimaced into the phone and, in his most obsequious tone, said: "Of course, Natasha."

An hour after the call, he went to a local stationer's and

bought a ream of A4 paper, some A3 and A4 envelopes, some paper files and a cheap biro. He picked up the phone and called a young officer from the Immigration team, Denzel Zammit, George's son, and asked him to come to the office, as soon as he could. Camilleri had marked Denzel out as a bright, ambitious officer, more so than his father, and crucially he owned a large motorbike. On his arrival, Camilleri asked him to slip on a pair of gloves he had taken from the workbox of scene of crime officer, take a biro and write down the series of numbers he dictated onto a sheet of A4. They read them back to each other, checking they were correct. Camilleri then told Denzel to put the sheet of folded paper into an envelope and dictated an address.

"'For the Attention of Mike Lloyd, c/o American Embassy'."

Still wearing the gloves, Denzel put the envelope inside a larger one and wrote on the larger envelope: 'For the Attention of AC Gerald Camilleri, 3 The Rise, Madliena'.

"Denzel, I would like you to bring this envelope to me, by motorcycle, at twenty-one hundred hours tonight – no earlier, as it will not be completely dark. Stop as you enter the estate and cover your number plates with bin liners and tape. Wear dark, non-descript clothing, a plain helmet – no personalisation like stickers, for example. Then, put this into my letter box in the pillar, but make sure the end of it remains visible, so that I would notice it if I stepped out of the house. Wear a full face helmet, visor down. Remember, you will appear on my security system, so make sure there is nothing by which you can be identified. Most importantly, wear your biking gloves and do not touch the envelope with your bare hands. I will put the envelope inside this file so you can handle it without leaving prints. Take the file back home with you and put it in the recycling immediately. Once you have put the letter in the box, press the button on the security panel and leave. Do you understand? Repeat these instructions back to me."

Denzel had done exactly as asked. Upon hearing the bell, Camilleri activated the speaker and asked who was there, conscious that his system recorded the calls from the gate. When he received no reply, he went outside to check. He then went through the motions of glancing at the letter box, having a second, more careful look, then exiting the gate and retrieving the envelope that protruded from the slit in the box. He looked up and down the road, so the security camera could record his curiosity.

When all that was done, Gerald Camilleri breathed deeply and called Mike Lloyd. To his relief the call diverted to the American's messaging service, so he left a request to talk and waited for Mike to call him back. It took less than an hour.

"Gerald, you rang? What's up?"

"Well, a very strange thing has happened…"

Mike Lloyd was silent for a while, listening to the tale, and then he said to Camilleri: "Open it. This is too weird to ignore and I'm miles away. It'll take time to reach me."

"Are you sure?"

"Yeah, you've probably looked inside anyway."

"Mike, I resent the implication."

"We're professionals. In your shoes, I would've. Go on, your eyes only and all that."

Camilleri made a fuss out of getting a paperknife and slitting open the envelopes.

"Hmm. Sorry," he said, as if he had only just thought of it. "I suppose I should have worn gloves. Apologies."

"Get on with it! What does it say?"

"Wait a minute… reading glasses… hmmm, it's separate lines of letters and numbers, no words. That's all."

"That's it? Is it a code?"

"I have no idea."

"Read them to me."

He did.

"Well, I'll get someone onto this. Meanwhile, keep the envelopes and paper, I'll send someone to collect them tomorrow. Do you have CCTV?"

"Yes, a full system."

"Can you copy or save the last forty-eight hours?"

"I would imagine so."

"Great, I'll get the boys to have a look at the footage and see if they can find out who's been creeping around your house."

"I'd appreciate that, I don't like the look of this at all."

"Yeah, it's interesting. I'll get back to you."

# CHAPTER 59

# GEORGE ZAMMIT

GEORGE ZAMMIT

IF WALLS COULD SPEAK, Abu Salim's would scream. Systematic mental and physical abuse of those confined within was a daily reality. The intolerable conditions and violence, by both guards and inmates, had led to the charity Médecins Sans Frontières being forced to withdraw medical support, leaving the sick and injured in the prison to look after themselves.

Worse, an historic mass grave within the walls, containing the bodies of one thousand two hundred and seventy-one detainees, massacred by Gaddaffi's security forces, served as a reminder to those within that death was always close. The ultimate insult to those who had died was that the corrupt guards of Abu Salim had continued to encourage relatives, unaware of the massacre, to bring boxes of food, medicines and clothing for thirteen years after their loved ones were killed.

The site was surrounded by five-metre-high block walls, coated with peeling white paint, on which the names of long-suffering prisoners and those who had died within were graffi-tied on the outside. The walls were breached by numerous gates of green-painted steel and guarded by watch towers, festooned with razor wire. The prison building was surrounded by an open area used as a car park. It was under this asphalt surface that the bodies of Gaddaffi's victims lay.

The prison site itself was five kilometres south of Tripoli's city centre and accessed from the main Airport Highway. Inside, the regime running the prison was appointed from, or associated with, the Tripoli Defence Force, an amalgamation of four militias that had operated within Tripoli. The TDF was led by Motasem al-Beshari, who had strong links to the Government of National Accord. His guards brutalised the inmates, who were not only political opponents of the UN-backed GNA but, increasingly, migrants forced back from their maritime crossings by the Libyan coastguards, awaiting deportation or sale into forced labour or slavery.

The prison was split into twelve blocks, each containing two hundred prisoners; double the number for which it had been built. Inside the blocks there was little sunlight or air ever circulated. The atmosphere was stiflingly hot and the overcrowding and hopelessness of the forgotten, brutalised prisoners made for a febrile atmosphere, which erupted at the slightest provocation.

Abdullah woke George before daylight and they sat in the kitchen while Rania served them bread and eggs, with sweet thick coffee. She said to George: "Eat, George. Abdullah has told me his plan. Today you do Allah's work and return my son to me."

Abdullah said: *"Inshallah!* God willing."

George did not feel like eating; he had a strong presentiment there was something Abdullah was not telling him and, if he was right, this would not be good.

Abdullah kept looking at his watch and then at Rania. She bowed her head and kept her eyes lowered, until they all heard the sound of vehicles arriving in the compound. George looked at them both. Only Abdullah's fierce dark brown eyes were staring at him.

"It is time."

Rania came to the table where George was sitting and took his hand.

"*Aallah yarhamuk.* May God go with you."

He gave her a thin smile. Abdullah nodded to his wife and said to George: "Come."

Outside, he saw a formidable convoy of at least ten vehicles. Some of them were technicals mounted with canons and machine guns, while others were minibuses, capable of carrying a dozen fighters. The vehicles emptied, until there were about fifty armed men standing around chatting and smoking.

The local imam appeared from the crowd and turned to face north east, to lead the group in prayer. There was the clatter of weapons being unshouldered. Then, silence descended over the farmstead, with only the imam's shrill voice, and the reverberations of the men's responses, breaking the silence of the morning. When the prayers had finished, Abdullah fired a shot into the air and the men cheered, as they returned to their vehicles.

Abdullah appeared at George's side, carrying two automatic weapons over his shoulder and pushing a blue sports bag at his friend. It was heavy from the weight of the currency it contained. George took it without a word. Abdullah slid one of his matched Turkish battle rifles down his arm and handed it to him.

"You can never have too many armed men. Inside, beware. The prisoners are more dangerous than the guards. Come, my friend, and bear witness to the good thing we do."

George did not really understand what the 'good thing' was, but he knew it was not going to be as simple as handing over the sports bag and then leaving. His fears were compounded when they drove into Tripoli and found that the roads were strangely empty.

Abdullah was barking instructions into the VHF radio and using the vehicle's wifi hotspot. He had a live visual image of the prison on his laptop, the feed coming from a small drone that circled overhead. Looking at the screen, George saw that the major roads around to the south east of Tripoli's centre were filled with queues of cars, but their route, down the Airport Highway, was wide open and empty.

Abdullah smiled grimly at him.

"There are many roadblocks this morning. It is fortunate, no?"

He had made a financial arrangement with Motasem al-Beshari, whose Tripoli Defence Force had blocked the traffic around the prison to allow him access and, more importantly, to prevent any outside interference while they were inside. He had told Abdullah the break-in would have to look authentic. Although Motasem al-Beshari would provide the means of access, Abdullah should expect a token resistance from those who remained.

The convoy roared into the district of Abu Salim and came to a halt in the side streets around the prison. Abdullah saw a low-loader, parked alongside other construction vehicles, opposite the prison entrance. On the trailer sat an old rusted bulldozer. With a burst of purple diesel smoke belching from the bulldozer's exhaust, it started reversing down the lowered ramps.

The bulldozer slowly, and noisily, rattled across the street, its tracks swivelling, tearing into the thin coat of asphalt, while proceeding down the short drive to the prison's main gate. Two men ran alongside the prison wall and set satchel charges, on magnetic fixings, against the gates. They scampered back and detonated the breaching charges, using a car remote. The two explosions ripped the gates off their lower hinges and left them hanging across the entrance. The bulldozer then casually pushed them aside and the entrance was wide open.

Abdullah was screaming "Wait!" into the radio, as the bulldozer approached the inner gate made of steel mesh and razor wire. It was at this point that the men in the waiting vehicles heard the first signs of resistance from within. Several cracks rang out from the watch towers and the wall, but the shots were too little, too late. The bulldozer ripped the wire gates from their concrete base and pulled a huge tangled train of wire with them.

It then turned left, into the inner courtyard of the prison, yanking the jumble of fencing and barbed wire to one side, leaving their access completely unobstructed.

It was now that Abdullah shouted: "Go!" Five technicals pulled up in front of the entrance and the crews quickly mounted the cannons and heavy machine guns. They blasted the entrance and watchtowers with a hail of fire for several seconds. All fell quiet within. Any resistance had faded away. The bulk of the invading force then stormed through the space where the main gate had been, into the prison.

When Abdullah and George entered, there were twenty or thirty staff members lying face down in the dirt yard, while behind them, in the cell blocks, there was a cacophony of noise as prisoners shouted, whistled and banged against the steel doors of their cells. Abdullah strode towards one of the guards and grabbed his collar, lifting him to his feet. The man was wide eyed with terror and visibly trembling.

Abdullah said, "Take me to the Commandant, Juma bin-Saud." The guard shook his head. "You take me or I will kill you. I have no time to waste."

To prove his point, Abdullah swung his battle rifle low to the ground and aimed a series of shots between the guard's feet.

SAVI SPENT the rest of the morning with Natasha, lounging around the pool and chatting. He sat in the pool on the steps, smoking while she worked on her laptop, occasionally breaking off to answer his questions and give him a potted history of the castello. He tried to persuade her to come in for a swim, as the sun was hot and the air heavy with humidity. The idea of being that close to her, in their swimsuits, made him hot and bothered. Natasha, however, smiled knowingly at him and coolly declined the offer.

During their conversation, she had asked him about the best way to establish a one hundred percent secure auction site on the dark web. This was meat and drink to Savi, who had hacked dozens of databases and then ransomed their return or on-sold them to others in marketplace forums.

Natasha said: "Hypothetically, out of interest, if I wanted to sell something… say, the most valuable thing in the world, which only a few hundred people could afford… and I wanted to remain absolutely untraceable, how would I do it?"

Savi thought for a moment.

"Well, to start with, you've to let people know you've got

something to sell that they want. I assume this thing isn't suited to eBay?"

"Let's assume that."

"So, you know who your top buyers might be?"

"I could make an educated guess."

"Then, you need to let them see something that proves you've the goods, you know?"

"Yeah, I'm with you so far."

"And, if this really is the most valuable thing in the world, I suppose those who have been contacted will be wetting themselves with excitement and shit scared one of the others will get the jump on them?"

"Yep."

"So, we build an auction site on the dark web, show them the goods and make them wait for the auction functionality to go live. We'll protect the site, so only accredited bidders can enter and, even then, only if they've got special digital keys. I can close most back doors and there'll be next to no traffic until the bidding window starts.

"We let them know the site is going live and they've to provide proof of funds available for their bids, using special encrypted email, with a double key or signal or something. Then, we sit for a while, making them wait… it increases tension and buyer nerves. After you've got them all revved up, we give them a narrow window to bid, an hour at most. The winning bidder pays the full price in Bitcoin into an escrow account, say within twelve hours, and then you have to organise delivery or collection. I've no idea how you're going to do that, 'cos you won't tell me what this thing is.

"Then the site disappears, gone. Keep it simple. We don't want any traffic flowing between us and them. The bidders will want to know there's super-cool security. Once delivery is complete and the buyer agrees he's got what he wants, the payment is transferred to your wallet.

"We take it in Bitcoin. It's not quite as secure as Monaro and some of the others, but the transaction volumes are higher, and you'll need that if you don't want to blow the deal out of the water. When we get the Bitcoin, we'll split it up and spread it across several platforms."

Natasha was impressed.

"OK, the only problem I can see is, who's going to hold the money in this escrow account? There is going to be a large sum involved."

"The most trusted escrow managers are some Russian dudes, I know. Russians, yeah, OK, you may say, 'no thanks!'. But, they take two point five percent of the winning bid, so it's in their interests to be straight up. From what I've heard, they've done all sorts of arms sales, oil from embargoed countries... super-big league. Ever wonder how Iran pays for things when nobody'll touch their banks, 'cos of sanctions? Getting these escrow runners involved is a sign you're a real player."

"You trust them?"

"Well, yeah. You have to, otherwise there's no way to do the deal."

Natasha suddenly saw it all starting to happen. She was pretty sure that the morning by the pool had won Savi over; he seemed relaxed and cheerful. She now had to keep him that way, at least until he had built the site and helped her go through the process of setting up the auction.

She had no intention of using the site, but establishing an auction process and dangling it amongst the few players who might be interested, would not go unnoticed. That would suit her purposes. She called for Katia, using the call button on the pool bar, and asked her for two burgers, with all the extras, and some French fries.

Katia looked at her askance and said: "I'm sorry, but I'm not sure we've got burger buns and I don't think I can make stringy chips. Can I get you anything else?"

Natasha smiled at her.

"You're not understanding me, Katia. Please drive to St

Paul's, to the McDonald's there. Oh, and bring a couple of shakes."

She looked at Savi for approval and raised an eyebrow at Katia. Savi was impressed.

"Yeah, cool."

Katia looked bemused, but nodded her agreement and left.

Savi lit another cigarette and said to Natasha: "If you're going to ask me to do this, I've got terms."

Natasha closed the screen of the laptop and turned towards him, to give Savi her full attention.

"Oh, this is interesting! And there I was, thinking that if I forgave you for screwing up a multi-million-euro oil exploration project, that might just be enough! But for the sake of argument, go for it, tell me."

"OK, I need the proper gear. I need full wifi. I want decent food – kebabs and stuff. Cigarettes, beer and weed. I want half a percent of the winning bid, into my digital wallet, as soon as the auction closes, otherwise the escrow will never get the instruction that the deal's been done and the coin can be transferred. Oh, and I want to sleep in the house, not the garage or whatever you call that place."

"Done, but you've got the decimal points wrong. I'll pay you nought, point nought, nought five percent of the bid and you'll stay in the guest accommodation. I can't stand the smell of weed and I don't like the idea of you padding around the castello all night. Bohdan would probably end up shooting you, or something.

"Oh, and all this is subject to complete confidentiality. If I even suspect you're messing me around, Bohdan will be very upset and I'm afraid our newfound friendship would be over. So, no messaging friends or anything silly. Do the job and keep your head down. OK?"

Savi thought for a minute.

"OK. So, what're you selling?"

She went to her bag and took out a sheet of paper, laying it on the table. He got out of the pool, one hand holding up his baggy shorts, the other towelling the long brown hair that was plastered over his rounded shoulders. Natasha suppressed a smile at the sight of his prepubescent, skinny, grey-white body. For a moment, she compared him to what she remembered of Luke van der Westhuizen. His hard muscle, the breadth of his shoulders, the strength in his upper body, as he pinned her firmly to the bed, while his knees forced hers apart...

Savi dried his hands on the towel and stared at the paper. On it were three lines of numbers and text. Each line was in the form of a three-letter prefix, followed by a five- to seven-digit number. After thirty seconds he looked up.

"And?"

Natasha pushed the image of Luke from her mind and smiled knowingly.

"And nothing, that's it."

Savi understood more than Natasha realised. He wasn't impressed by her nonchalance.

"OK, the buyers will know what this is?"

"I'm banking on it."

"When do you want all this for?"

"Start now. Sooner you're done, sooner you can get back to your life, playing computer games."

Savi thought hard.

"Yeah, I need to be in Madrid next weekend, but my bit should be done by then."

That afternoon Bohdan arrived with a stack of boxes from a list that Savi had specified. Bohdan dumped them onto the floor of the guest suite and said malevolently, "There's nearly ten thousand euros' worth of hardware there. You'd better be worth it."

Savi was feeling cocky.

"Tell it to the boss!"

Bohdan walked towards him and, as Savi was looking at the

box containing the new laptop, swiped him across the face with a vicious backhand.

"Don't get cheeky with me, you greasy little shit, I'd still happily kill you."

Savi nursed his bruised cheek and his good mood evaporated, as he set about the task of building his system. He was not unhappy to see Bohdan leave and lock the door behind him.

After a few hours, he began to think about the sheet of paper Natasha had given him and the alpha-numeric codes. His depression lifted, as he focused on the strings of characters in front of him. Savi loved a puzzle and this would do to help pass the time and make him forget about that bastard Bohdan.

The strings did not look sufficiently random to be some sort of code or encryption and there was a comforting familiarity about the set-up of the numbers. Savi knew, in the commercial world, that most numeric references were generally between five and seven digits long. This avoided the risk of the number being mis-keyed on transposition, say into a purchase order. So, if the numbers were reference numbers for, say, a component or an account, what did the prefix refer to? Savi's starting point was to discover whether the three-letter prefixes were acronyms, abbreviations or even backronyms, acronyms spelled backwards. He started searching the three-letter configurations. The numbers stared out at him. So simple, yet quite baffling. It was a big digital world now where everything was referenced or categorised. Somewhere in this morass of identifiers were three groups of data that would tell him what he was getting himself into.

CNS485739
BeN2398765
LKM968485

Savi knew there were thousands of three-letter acronyms. He looked randomly at various financial institutions, law- enforcement agencies, intellectual property references, pharmaceutical companies, tried combining the three prefixes, but in his heart, he knew this was not the right approach. The 'BeN' was different from the other two prefixes, the lowercase 'e' suggesting it and the 'B' were connected. Perhaps the prefixes related to a producer of some sort.

He then started to prioritise those areas in which he knew Natasha already had interests. Energy, oil, banking, online gambling, Libya, crime, criminals – but found nothing. Then he thought of what she was planning to do. To sell something, of great value, to the international criminal underworld. That was why he had been asked to build the auction site on the dark web. So, he searched again: drugs, smuggling, crypto, heroin – nothing. He asked himself what else was worth a load of money sold illegally? He searched people trafficking, stolen art, weapons.

After three hours of digging, he found something of interest. An entry for 'CNS' led him to the Consolidated Nuclear Security Corporation. Savi had heard of this outfit, since it was mentioned on the numerous conspiracy theory sites he visited. A few clicks told him the company was part of the giant conglomerate that operated the sprawling Y-12 nuclear weapons complex in Oak Ridge, Tennessee. He checked the names of the other members of the partnership; they were all at the heart of America's nuclear weapons program: Boeing, Lockheed Martin, Bechtel National, Sandia National Laboratory and Orbital ATK being just a few.

Then, it suddenly clicked. Consolidated Nuclear Security Corp., Bechtel National and Lockheed Martin! CNS, BeN, LKM! They were all there. They made the parts for the US Department of Energy's Pantex plant, which was the primary nuclear weapons assembly facility at Amarillo, in the Texas panhandle.

The numbers following the prefix must relate to key components made by each of these companies, for a nuclear warhead, or missile, assembled in Amarillo. Anyone who knew anything about these things must be able to tell what sort of weapon they went into. It all started to make a horrible kind of sense.

"Shit!"

He kept looking, using all the search engines, his eyes flying across the screen, speed-reading the text, as he flicked through page after page until his vision blurred. Finally, he thought he understood what it was Natasha had to sell.

CNS produced the bomb-grade uranium jackets at the heart of the warhead, Bechtel National developed the missile technology that delivered the bomb, while Lockheed Martin were working with Boeing on a significant upgrade of the B61 warhead and missile, to make the world's first 'smart bomb'. Savi wondered how exactly you made a 'smart' nuclear bomb; they seemed pretty dumb to him. If he was right, though, Natasha had an American B61 nuclear missile and she was asking him to help her sell it.

He went to the bed and lay down. He did not know whether to laugh or cry. It gradually dawned on him that this was not cool, and he was in big trouble. There was no way Natasha was going to let him go, if she knew what he had found out. But he was being stupid, Natasha wouldn't let him go anyway. This was way too big. His heart sank. She was playing him and he had thought it had all been going so well. Had hoped there was finally something happening between them. Shit, how could he have been so stupid? Twice over. He wished Danka and Simon were with him; it seemed ages since the three of them had been together. Savi felt very alone.

He quickly downloaded an email program, set up an account and sent a message to Danka. Then, he immediately uninstalled the program, a moment before Bohdan opened the door to bring in a tasty-looking kebab, twenty cigarettes and a four-pack of beer.

Bohdan put down the food and picked up the laptop.

"OK, you've finished, I'm taking this away now. Let's hope when I have a look at it, you haven't done anything silly. Because if you have, I'm coming straight back here and you won't like what happens next."

He left, turning when he was halfway out of the door to see Savi inspecting the kebab.

"I hope it chokes you."

Bohdan immediately made his way to the library with Savi's laptop and Natasha sat and watched as he got to work. Savi had underestimated Bohdan, whom he took for an ignorant bully. Cyber crime and cyber defence were two of Bohdan's many competencies. It took him two minutes to find the PST file on Savi's disk drive that held the email to Simon and Danka. With a smile, he pushed the laptop across to Natasha.

She read the email and smiled grimly.

"They'll be coming for him. You'd better be ready. When will the help be here?"

"Tomorrow. Should be soon enough. I'll cover tonight myself."

"Simon's threatened me. He's a security risk. There's only one outcome for both of them, you understand? Keep hold of the laptop until we've got rid of these two, then it's supervised access only. Well done! You were right. The boy was stupid enough to lead them right to us."

# CHAPTER 61

# ABDULLAH BELKACEM
### ABU SALIM PRISON, TRIPOLI, LIBYA

THE GUARD LED ABDULLAH, George and a group of a dozen of Abdullah's men into the administration building and started unlocking the steel-barred gates along the deserted corridors. The hot, sour air hung heavily and their footsteps echoed down the airless passages. When they got to a point where the corridor turned a ninety-degree corner, the guard cowered back and pushed against them.

"They'll be waiting around there. That's how they defend the offices." He pointed round the corner. "It's an ambush; it's death to go further."

Abdullah flung the man around the corner and watched as he fell to his knees. Immediately there was the crack of a rifle, a bullet ricocheting off chipped plaster. The guard started shouting and calling out, and eventually crawled back to where Abdullah waited. Abdullah then strode forward, going around the corner into the line of fire, holding his rifle above his head with both hands.

"I have brought someone to see Juma bin-Saud, the warden, he knows we are coming."

George poked his head around the corner and saw Abdullah had hoisted the guard to his feet and now held him in front as a human shield. Facing them was a wall of men at the top of the narrow corridor, all pointing guns. Abdullah glanced behind him, smiling, and beckoned George to walk down the corridor towards the bristling guns. Abdullah and his men came after him.

Gradually, the gunmen pulled back and let George push his way between them. He could smell sweat and cigarettes, and something else – the acrid smell of their fear. George then realised what Abdullah knew. These men were more frightened than they were. Bolstered by this knowledge, he brushed past them, holding their gaze.

At the end of the corridor was a control centre, protected by floor-to-ceiling steel mesh with a locked wicket gate. Inside cowered six or seven armed men. Eventually a short, fat, unshaven one emerged from the back of the group. He had large sweat patches across the chest of his white shirt and under his arms. His thin hair was plastered against his head.

"Do you have Abdullah Belkacem's money?" he asked.

"Yes, I have it for you." George showed him the sports bag of cash, swinging it up onto his raised knee and unzipping it, to reveal the wads of notes.

Abdullah shouted down the corridor at Juma bin-Saud, as he stood there, sweating and twitching.

"You have been paid. Now I want my son."

"I need to count the money, first."

Abdullah came close with his men behind him.

"Open the gate, take your money, then take me to my son. Or I will open all the cells myself and let the animals loose."

Juma bin-Saud looked shifty and unsure what to do. His greed was matched by his fear of Abdullah and his small army. He was also afraid of the thousand or so prisoners in the blocks, whose shouts and screams echoed eerily across the yard and down the corridors. He hesitated a moment too long.

Abdullah pushed George to one side, put the muzzle of a rifle to the lock of the steel-mesh door and rapidly fired three shots.

The door flew open. Abdullah was through like a flash and, holding the barrel against the chin of the warden, screamed at Juma bin-Saud, who screamed back. Everybody else pointed guns at each other.

A tall shaven-headed man in a stained blue military-style shirt quickly stepped forward. He held a bunch of keys high above his head.

"There's no need for trouble – everybody'll get what they want. Warden, trust Motasem al-Beshari. I have keys, Abdullah Belkacem. Follow me."

The man in blue pointed to several companions and waved them forward. He turned back to Juma bin-Saud.

"You can stay here; it is safer if you do as I say."

Blue-shirt looked at Abdullah.

"We need weapons. It is dangerous in the blocks when the cells are open."

Abdullah was curious.

"You're opening the cells?"

"Yes." Blue-shirt had a crooked smile on his face. "Motasem al-Beshari wants it to look like a mass breakout. It's better for your son's escape and we can blame the warden, say he was bribed to do it by a faction in the Nawasi Brigade."

Juma bin-Saud's head swivelled between Blue-shirt and Abdullah. He started to protest and moved towards the tall man in blue, making a grab for the keys.

"No, don't you dare do this!" the warden protested. "This is not your business. Al-Beshari will hear of it!"

A guard standing behind Blue-shirt casually slipped him a handgun. In one smooth movement, Blue-shirt raised the gun and shot the warden in the head. The noise was deafening and temporarily stunned everybody into a shocked silence. Blue-shirt watched dispassionately as the man crumpled and collapsed to the floor, his brains and shards of bone, splattering the wall behind his. Blue Shirt needlessly poked the body with his foot.

"Bin-Saud was a greedy *chelb* and Motasem al-Beshari is glad to be rid of him. I will take the money, al-Beshari gives you his thanks. We'll leave this body in the corridors and blame it on the escaping prisoners, or else the Nawasi Brigade... whoever. In Tripoli nobody knows who the killers are. Yes?"

He looked threateningly around the control room. Blue-shirt's confederates nodded. Those who were more taken by surprise kept their heads down, avoiding eye contact.

"OK, Abdullah Belkacem, follow me. Bring your men. Keep your gun barrels high. Don't hesitate to shoot the animals. They are desperate and stupid; they'll attack us and each other."

He looked meaningfully at Abdullah.

"We've work to do in the high-security wing, where we hold important Nawasi Brigade prisoners. Al-Beshari thanks you, he says this is a perfect opportunity to be rid of them. You take your boy and go."

Blue-shirt led them back out into the yard, where the noise coming from the blocks was deafening by now. He looked at Abdullah's technicals, lined up, engines running, facing the blocks, their guns pointing forwards and the main gate behind them.

Blue-shirt grabbed George, pointed at the trucks and said: "Pull them back or they will be rushed when we open the blocks. There'll be many killed, if they start firing machine guns at prisoners."

George went and gave the order, stepping onto the running board of a rust-red Toyota. The trucks started their engines, turned, and George led them out of the yard, back into the side streets. He had jogged up the road, rifle banging against his spine, and back into the prison yard, just as the first dishevelled, disorientated inmates emerged, blinking in the sunlight.

Many were shirtless and some barefoot. They had roughly chopped hair and untrimmed beards. All looked unnaturally thin. As they came out of the blocks, most held up their over-sized pants with one hand. George noticed that several had red sores and wounds on their bodies. Even in the yard, the smell from the three-storey, flat-roofed blocks was terrible. A deep, foul stench of human rot and ammonia, from the urine that had soaked the floors for decades.

Two of the prisoners were looking at George, who stood slack-jawed, uncertain what to do next. One wild-eyed inmate approached him with an air of menace and started heckling him in Arabic, saliva spraying from his lips. His shouting attracted the attention of others gathering in the yard, frightened and confused, wondering what to do next. George realised he had to act quickly, otherwise he was at risk of becoming a target of the mob. He quickly seized the arm of the man who was accosting him, putting the other arm around him and turning him to face the gate.

"*Alhamdulillah!* Thank God, you're free!" He smiled as broadly as he could and pointed to the gate. "Motasem al-Beshari says, run! *Auhrub! Auhrub!* Run away! *Taqdim alshukr!* Give thanks to Motasem al-Beshari! *Auhrub!* Run!"

The man started to move towards the gate, then began shouting to the others, urging them to follow him out. Before long there was a steady stream of inmates, some hobbling, some supporting others, but most of them running, willing to take their chances outside these cursed walls.

George edged around the sides of the yard, trying to find which block Abdullah and Blue-shirt had gone into. He was moving against the tide of men emerging into the sunlight. Off to his right, he noticed a prisoner lying on the ground, clutching his stomach. Two others were standing over him, plunging what could only be homemade knives into him. He could see the man rolling on the ground; the shouting and calling in the yard making it impossible to hear his screams. Horrified, he watched the hellish drama unfold. More horrific still was that it was totally ignored by those rushing past to reach the gate.

George's instinct as a policeman was to intervene, but he knew it was hopeless to imagine he could bring order to what was happening in front of him. At that moment, he heard shots coming from the third block of twelve. There was a moment's silence in the yard and then pandemonium broke out, as what seemed like hundreds of men started running towards the main gate and out into the city. George stood cowering against the wall, as far away from the entrance to the blocks as he could get. He was hoping he was invisible to the desperate rabble in the yard. He held his rifle behind him, in case any of the prisoners should see it and try to take it from him. He knew he could use it to bring down one or two assailants, but it was useless against so many.

He shut his eyes, as another assault broke out only twenty metres away from him. Four men had grabbed a youth and were dragging him through the yard, punching him as they went. The youth was bleeding from the mouth and nose and limping from an earlier injury. He seemed to be wearing only pyjama bottoms. His head hung low and the injured foot trailed in the dust. At that moment, one of the men punched the boy hard in the midriff and he doubled up in pain. He turned his bloodied face towards George who, to his horror, he recognised Jamal.

George had known this boy since he was twelve years old and had met him many times while he was staying with Abdullah and Rania. His hair was longer and ragged and he had a faint teenager's moustache, but it was definitely Jamal. George instinctively unslung his rifle and aimed it at the attackers, shouting: "Stop, put the boy down! Orders from Motasem al-Beshari!"

The men turned to him angrily. One came across and roughly pushed George, saying: "Who are you? We don't care anyway. This boy's a hostage. He's the son of Abdullah Belkacem of Marsabar and he's ours, so go!"

George had no choice. He fired a burst from the automatic battle rifle into the ground, directly in front of the man. Unfortunately, two of the shots ricocheted up from the hard earth into the man's groin. He fell, screaming and rolling on the ground.

George stepped out of his way and levelled the rifle at the three others.

As the man lay screaming in the dirt and clutching his bleeding abdomen, summoned all the authority he could muster and said to them: "Put that boy down, collect your friend and go, before I shoot you all."

Reluctant to lose their prize, the three men exchanged glances with each other, dropped Jamal and rushed George. He fired another burst of shots, before he was knocked off his feet by the two who had charged at him. The second assailant was hit in the shoulder and chest, and he too fell to the ground. George had involuntarily retained his grip on the ageing Heckler & Koch G3, which had a rate of fire of five hundred rounds a minute, so when he rolled over and inadvertently put pressure on the trigger, a spray of bullets took out the third assailant. The last man, seeing his friends lying bleeding and helpless in the dirt, turned, and hastily jogged off, glancing over his shoulder, to join the stream of prisoners exiting through the gates.

George had a superficial graze on his face and blood ran down his cheek. He was on one knee, picking himself up, when he noticed the rangy figure of Abdullah and two of his men jogging across the yard, weapons at the ready.

"George, I saw from the door they were attacking you. You did well!"

Cursing in Arabic, Abdullah gratuitously walloped the head of one of George's injured assailants, who was trying to get to his feet, with the butt of a gun.

George frantically, grabbed Abdullah to get his attention. He turned him to face the youth, sitting on the ground, head hanging low, feeling the wounds on his face. Abdullah stopped in his tracks,

"Jamal?"

Hearing his father's voice, the boy looked at him for a moment, almost in disbelief.

He spoke faintly, his voice coming through a mist of pain and hopelessness.

"Father! Is it you? And George, my God! George, it *was* you! Father, George saved me!"

"I saw it, my son. I saw it all, with these eyes! Alhamdulillah, Praise be to Allah!"

Abdullah squatted down on his haunches next to his boy. He put a hand on Jamal's head and ran his fingers across his cheek.

"Yes, it is me and George. George saved you, I saw it all." He looked up at George and pointed to his eyes with the first two fingers of his right hand, repeating: "I saw it with these very eyes!" Then to his son, "I am sorry it has taken so long."

"It's not your fault. It wasn't you who went to Tripoli and tried to kill the Turk. My friends died. It was all my fault, *baba*. Knowing that is my prison now."

Abdullah helped him to his feet.

"Come, your mother waits for news." Abdullah grabbed George by the arm. "My brother, I am more in your debt than ever. How can I ever repay you!"

George looked around him at the chaos of the prison yard and heard the prolonged sound of automatic fire from the end block. Again, and again. Abdullah heard the continuous firing and looked up grimly.

"The man in the blue shirt has found those he was looking for. They are shooting them in their cells. The Tripoli Defence Force are taking revenge on the Nawasi Brigade. In Tripoli the fighting never stops."

George shook his head.

"It's all madness. You can repay me by getting us out of this terrible place."

# CHAPTER 62
# MIKE LLOYD
### GEORGE BUSH CENTRE FOR INTELLIGENCE, VIRGINIA, UNITED STATES

MIKE LLOYD DIDN'T LIKE BEING KEPT waiting. Especially when he was certain he was the subject of the discussion going on behind the glossy, walnut double doors leading to the conference room in CIA headquarters. The six-storey complex had a floor area of nearly two hundred and fifty thousand square metres and stood in the semi-rural setting of Langley, a twenty-minute drive down the George Washington Highway from the White House.

Finally, an immaculately presented young naval officer in full dress uniform emerged and asked Mike to join them. Inside he was surprised to see only five people huddled at the top end of the conference table, instead of the usual twenty or thirty who routinely turned up at Langley meetings.

He knew Harry Muller, the President's Chief of Staff, who had been shouting at him down the telephone for the past two weeks. Sitting next to him was Nick Cole, Director of Central Intelligence, Mike's ultimate boss. Alongside them were two scientific types, packing up a stack of lever-arch files. They wore ill-fitting suits, no doubt donned especially for the meeting, and both had untidy hair that hung over their collars. Mike knew Nick Coles could not abide long hair, which he saw as a sign of moral degeneration.

The fifth man also wore full uniform, his left breast covered with more badges than a troop of boy scouts. Mike guessed this was Staff Army General Howard H. Howard, chairman of the Joint Chiefs of Staff, the nation's highest-ranking military officer and principal military adviser to the President. Mike knew him to be a blustering redneck from Texas, with a reputation for warmongering at every opportunity and a publicly stated preference for independence for the Lone Star state.

Looking at the assembly and their expressions, Mike guessed he had not been summoned to receive a vote of thanks. Nick Cole made the introductions and started the discussion.

"So, this paper from the police guy in Malta tells us someone has our nuke. My guess is this is the opening gambit for a round of blackmail, or worse." He looked around the table, inviting comment or challenge. "OK, so we are agreed on that. The numbers and prefixes are component parts from the B61 missile stolen from Incirlik. We should take this for proof they have the goods." He paused again, to see if the others were with him. "We've looked at every atom of the letter and the envelopes and spent nearly two hundred hours looking at the CCTV of the delivery and any other camera footage that was available in the area, which was not a lot. And what have we got? Nothing. Absolutely nothing.

"We've checked out the Maltese police guy, Camilleri ... that his name? He's a character with fingers in every pie, but this is not in his league. He's a player on the island, but our instinct is he was picked as the messenger because he knew you, Mike. I believe you two tied up during the murder of our Chargé d' Affaires in Malta, a couple of years back?" Mike nodded. "Now we need a complete list of all parties who might be aware of your link to Camilleri."

"Sure. You've got it."

Harry Muller, the Chief of Staff, then addressed Mike.

"Why Malta? You've spent a lot of time there. I had to look for it on Google Maps, I'd no idea where it was. Thought it was off Cyprus! We've got the delivery of the message on Malta; the NGO rescue ship was headed there; you met this Camilleri on the island … so there is definitely something going on there."

Mike Lloyd was thoughtful.

"I've got nothing concrete yet. We took the owner of the *Samaritan*, a South African, Luke van der Westhuizen, to Souda Bay and interrogated him. Remember, all we had was an empty box. The ship was clean.

"His story was, some guy rang him and said he could pick up a crate of life-jackets that a charity had bought. His ship does the humanitarian thing, picking up maritime migrants who get into trouble."

The General muttered: "Should let them face the consequences."

Mike Lloyd ignored this comment.

"He got a second message on the ship's radio to say that the cargo was ready – we've verified that with the skipper. He was an hour out of Benghazi, in their normal search sector, so he sailed in and picked them up. He says he didn't look at the crate, the deck crew lashed it down and covered it in a tarp. He thought no more about it. It's all a load of hooey, but that's what we were told. We have to let him go."

General Howard slapped the table with his fat hand.

"The hell we let him go! What about that crowd of armed police? The South African personally supervised the loading. This was his first trip on a 'routine' patrol. He was one hundred percent up to something!"

The General threw a stack of George's photographs down on the table.

"You're right General. I put it to him and he said he was surprised by the police presence, but didn't really think about it as he was only there for fifteen minutes and busy supervising the loading. He said he'd spoken to the port police and paid for some protection for the vessel. It's a normal thing in Benghazi."

"It's horseshit!" said the General. "Why was there no paperwork? Why didn't he see the yellow triangle radiation warnings on the crate? Why didn't he see the 'US Air Force' stencils?"

"He said it was early morning and the light was poor."

"What a load of bull!"

Harry Muller looked at Mike.

"This guy is a South African diamond trader, right?"

Mike answered.

"Yep. Possibly a diamond smuggler as well. But South African Intelligence can't confirm that."

"What the hell is he doing buying an ocean-going ship and shuttling about in the Gulf of Sirte, looking for drowning refugees? You're telling me he's suddenly developed a conscience? I don't buy it. Can't we send him to Guantanamo?"

Mike looked at the General.

"He's a South African national who has committed no offence I can think of, other than taking an empty box out of Libya. We propose to let him go and track every step he takes subsequently."

Mike was keen to wrap up the meeting and get out of the room as soon as he could, before the group started sniping at him. The game in Langley, as well as Washington, was always to make sure the other guy was in the firing line.

"So, we let him go and track him: eyes, ears, satellites, the lot. And we wait. My team has a list of possible buyers and we're working on what we know about each one. We're also combing all digital messaging and online activity for a trace of any relevant conversation.

"The only other interesting thing is our Turkish contact, Hakan Toprak, who is now officially a person of interest in Turkey. I have a hunch that his disappearance is related to the missing nuke. We are working with Turkish Intelligence, but Toprak *is* Turkish Intelligence and has extensive connections, particularly in the east, namely the 'Stans. If he doesn't want to be found, he won't be."

The General sat back in his chair and scratched his paunch.

"Fucken' 'Stans. We can hit them from any number of places. Thin population densities, large geographical land masses and very little emotional blowback. Most Americans have never heard of these countries. If we hit them hard, it will send a nice message to the Chinese and the Russians. My money is that one of them is in the game, somewhere."

The Chief of Staff looked at him sceptically.

"Slow down, Howard, we're nowhere near that point yet."

Mike stood up and made to leave.

"OK, I think that's it. We done?"

Before he could turn his back and start the walk to the door, his ultimate boss had one more comment.

"Oh, Mike. Remember: teamwork. Use the resources we have here. This is not a 'one man in the field' operation. There is a feeling we've been on the back foot since this show began. You're running too far ahead of the pack. That's got to change. You understand me?"

Mike could only nod. He understood perfectly. The finger was pointing firmly at him.

# CHAPTER 63

# SIMON MICHALLIK
## CASTELLO BONNICI, MALTA

"YOU'RE NOT COMING! How many times do I have to say it? You stay here, so if anything happens you can go and tell Nick Walker what's going on. You're my insurance!"

"I'm better insurance if I'm right behind you, watching your back! You can't stop me coming. I'm responsible for this and I'm going to get him out. Savi's been there two days now – God knows what they've done to him."

"It's been thirty-six hours. It's Savi who's responsible for this whole bloody mess and he doesn't know how lucky he is to have a friend like you. But getting him out is down to me."

"Go then! Go on, do it! I'll follow you."

Danka stood rock-solid in the middle of the saloon of the *Just Reward*, hands on hips, legs splayed. Her neck muscles bulged and her lower jaw was set, like a boxer waiting for the bell.

"I'm coming!"

"If you come, you stay in the car and you only get out if I say I need you."

"No! I'm coming with you."

"*Kurwa.* If you don't listen to me, I won't go. I'll pack and be off, leave him to it. Do you understand me?"

Danka stood in silence. She watched Simon push a Glock

handgun into his shoulder holster and strap a knife sheath to his lower leg. He wore a tactical belt, with pepper spray, lock picks, a torch, handcuffs, a bundle of plastic restraints, a roll of gaffer-tape and a short extendible baton.

She looked him up and down.

"So, you're all tooled up and expecting trouble, yet you won't take me?"

"Danka, you're a pitbull, but I can't be responsible for the two of you."

"Give me the baton and a spare gun; you're not responsible for me."

———

Two hours later they were slowly working their way through the olive groves on the south-east approach to the *castello*. The night was thick with the chatter of cicadas, which conveniently hid the sound of their approach. The moon was in its third quarter and cast a pale metallic light on the narrowly terraced hillside, that rose from the valley floor to the rear gardens of the *castello*. A rough farmer's track climbed in a series of hairpin bends, from terrace to terrace, until it reached the huddle of outbuildings that was the *castello's* farm. Simon, of course, knew the security layout better than anyone and this was the best way to covertly approach the rear of the site.

At a certain point they left the track and climbed the hillside vertically, to avoid a point that was covered by CCTV camera. Dirty, sweaty and scratched by bramble thickets, they reached Marco's ornamental gardens twenty minutes later. They edged round the paths and beds until the *castello's* main building came into view. It seemed to be in complete darkness and its ominous, brooding, crenellated towers loomed over them.

Simon looked at his watch.

"Give it fifteen minutes. Let's see if they've got a patrol on the go."

They sat quietly in the garden, backs against a wall, legs outstretched, catching their breath, waiting and watching the path, twenty metres in front of them. Almost immediately after they had made themselves comfortable, a dark figure emerged from the narrow pathway that ran around the side of the *castello* to the front drive and garage complex, containing the new security accommodation. The figure walked slowly around the back of the house, pausing to light a cigarette. The lighter flared briefly, to silhouette the back of his head. He then disappeared into the shadows of the building, to begin another circuit.

Simon looked at his watch and waited. Seven minutes later the figure appeared again from lower down the track and disappeared around the far side of the building. Simon shook his head.

"Not enough time to do the extraction. Wait here."

He jumped to his feet and made his way towards the shadows of the main building. Danka waited nervously until she saw the guard approach for the third time. He had no idea who it was that chopped him so viciously on the back of the neck and rapidly gagged him with roll of silver adhesive tape. His arms were tied behind his back with restraints and his legs likewise bound together. Simon dragged him along the path and bundled him over a stone wall into an adjacent field, where he fell heavily.

Danka rushed out of cover to join Simon in the shadows. They edged their way over the unlit ground towards the front of the house. On reaching the corner of the main building, they saw the entrance portico, with the dimly lit turning circle, before them. The garage, that was the exterior of the new detention room, was made from white-painted limestone blocks, with a traditional flat stone roof. A second guard leaned against the wall, next to the heavy wooden door, the reflected light of a phone illuminating his face.

"Shit!" whispered Simon. "It's another contractor. He'll see me way before I can take him."

Before he could turn around to Danka, she had pushed past

him and was comfortably padding across the gravel, hands in pockets, toward the guard. He immediately jumped up and put his hand to his hip where a black holster was attached to his thick belt.

Danka held up her hand.

"Chill, man, I'm early kitchen staff. Do you guys want coffee and have you eaten?"

The guard visibly relaxed. His hand fell to his side.

"Yeah, coffee, that'd be great."

"So, just the two of you?"

"And the boss."

"OK, where do you ..." She punched him as hard as she could on the point of his jaw, so hard, Simon thought, that from the way his head snapped back, she must have broken the man's neck. Somehow, he stayed on his feet, only for Danka to spread her arms and bring her fists crashing onto both sides of his head, stunning him like a felled ox and making him drop to his knees. She pushed him onto his front, face down in the gravel. Simon ran forwards and, with Danka kneeling on the guard's spine, bound and gagged him. They dragged the semi-conscious man deep into the shrubs by the main gate and left him there.

Simon looked at the garage door and its formidable lock. He scratched his head and had begun unpacking his tools when Danka tapped his shoulder and waved a key ring at him, with several large security keys attached.

"Try these. From his pocket!"

He glared at her smiling expression and, with a turn of the second key, found the door opened into a small foyer. Simon held his ear against the inner door for several minutes, then hearing no movement from inside, slowly tried the most likely-looking key in the lock. It clicked and clunked as the bit pushed against stubborn tumblers. He tried the next one and similarly worked the key in the lock.

From inside the room, on the other side of the door, they heard a small voice say: "Who's there?"

Simon and Danka looked at each other, sharing a quick smile.

Simon said softly: "It's Simon and Danka. We've come to get you. Are you alone?"

"Yeah, sure! Simon and Danka! Wow, you came for me!"

The third key turned smoothly in the lock and the door opened. A dishevelled Savi rushed over to Danka and embraced her tightly.

"I've been so shit-scared!"

Danka sounded tearful when she told him, "Well, it's OK now. We've got you."

Simon ruffled Savi's hair and looked him up and down.

"OK, put on some pants and shoes and let's go, we're not home and dry yet."

"That madwoman has a fuckin' bomb, a nuclear thing! She's going to sell it to Al-Qaeda or someone. She's ... I swear!"

Simon looked at Danka, who pulled a face and shrugged. He turned back to Savi.

"Yeah, sure, we'll talk later. Now we've got to get going."

It took Savi thirty seconds to get ready. Simon peered out into the darkness and, on his command, they stepped outside the guest house and onto the gravel of the turning circle. They had taken three paces when the floodlights came on.

Two more guards stood facing them, five metres away, with handguns raised. Under the light of the portico, some ten metres further back, stood Bohdan. He shook his head in reproof.

"You must really think I'm stupid. Or rather, I didn't believe *you* could be so stupid. Did it never occur to you to wonder how a prisoner like Savi suddenly got access to an email account?

"And you, my troublesome and naïve little friend, you insult me, assuming I couldn't do a search for messages on your hard drive. Errors for which you will now all have to pay."

Simon had enough training to realise this was the time to act. In the next minute he would be disarmed and restrained. He threw himself to his left and rolled, taking the handgun from his holster and diving while at the same time firing two shots towards the guards as he slid across the gravel.

"Run!" he yelled to the others.

And out of the corner of his eye, he saw Danka pull Savi towards the path down the side of the *castello*. Lying on his stomach, on the ground, Simon had enough time to shoot and disable a guard whose attention was focused on the fleeing figures. The second guard had crouched to fire and his shot hit Simon in the back of the thigh. The impact ripped deep into the flesh and splintered the bone. The intense pain made him twist and his hand grabbed the wound. His gun spun away onto the ground beside him.

In the salon of the *Just Reward*, Simon had given Danka a second handgun, with basic instructions on how to use it. On reaching the corner of the *castello*, steeped in murky shadow, she turned, pushed Savi ahead of her down the path and took the Glock from a bum-bag slung diagonally across her shoulder. She held the gun in two hands, as Simon had showed her, and aimed at the second guard, who was moving away from her towards the prostrate Simon. She firmly pulled the trigger, together with the safety trigger. The crack of the weapon surprised her, as did the way the guard threw his hands into the air and collapsed to the ground.

Before she could react further, two rapid shots whistled past her and a third and a fourth smacked into the stonework of the *castello*, centimetres from her head. Bohdan had drawn his gun and was firing while crouching behind some large stone vases on plinths beside the entrance steps. She stayed flat against the wall, breathing heavily. There was silence for a few moments and then she heard the substantial bolts in the *castello's* front door slide open and the creak of the huge wrought-iron hinges.

A moment later Bohdan shouted: "Stay where you are, Miss! It's under control."

Danka risked a glance around the corner. A woman who had to be Natasha, dressed in what looked like steel-grey silk pyjamas, was standing in the doorway. It was the first time Danka had ever seen this figure who had imprinted itself so deeply onto her mind. This was the woman who had sent *il-Barri* to kill Danka and Savi. She had kidnapped, plotted murder, and so much more. Danka was fascinated to see her standing only twenty metres away.

The fabric of her pyjamas caught the beam from the portico's spotlights and she seemed to glow with a luminous radiance. Her face was not visible in the shadow, but a fiery corona had formed around her hair, radiating light. Danka was so captivated by the moment she didn't immediately notice that Bohdan had risen from behind a vase and was moving swiftly towards Simon.

With a glance towards where she was standing, Bohdan calmly placed a shot into the side of Simon's head. There was no noise other than the whip crack of the cartridge pushing the lead down the barrel. In his pain, Simon probably didn't even see Bohdan walk over to him. He didn't call out or make a sound. As the shot entered him, his body instantly relaxed, went limp and he ceased to be.

Danka was stunned, couldn't believe what she had seen. A second later she screamed, raised her gun and fired a shot, not caring where the bullet went. Natasha ducked back inside the door and Bohdan fired another two rounds back at Danka, forcing her to retreat around the corner again.

Bohdan kneeled down to examine Simon's body and gave Danka the chance she needed to make her escape. For a second she felt strangely emotionless, but held the thought that if she and Savi didn't make it away from the *castello*, then this would all have been for nothing. Simon would have died for nothing. That was not something she could live with. It was not something Simon would have wanted.

She tried to grab Savi's hand and urge him on but he had stuck his head around the corner and realised what had happened.

"No!" he screamed. "No! Simon, get up! You leave him alone!"

Bohdan was still kneeling by Simon's body, only now registering that his bullet had killed him. Savi's voice caused him to turn his head. He saw the boy was frantic, trying to break free from the woman's grasp. Although this was not the first shooting Bohdan had been involved with, he had never killed a colleague before and was momentarily stunned.

Savi's hysterics broke Danka's calm and her emotions started to spill over. She gasped for breath and squeezed her eyes tight shut, refusing to believe what was in front of her. She let out a sound somewhere between a sob and a wail. She knew they had no time for this and used every bit of strength she had to take another deep breath, so she could say, fighting back her sobs: "Please, Savi. Please! We have to go."

Seeing Bohdan get to his feet and turn towards them, Savi let Danka drag him along the side of the building and then the pair of them started running; back through Marco's ornamental garden and plunging down the terraces, through the olive groves and vineyards, to where they had left their vehicle.

Bohdan stood at the top of the hillside and heard them crashing through the hedges and sliding down the rough scree between terraces. He watched them as they dashed between the olive trees, disappearing and reappearing, in and out of the shadows and the black, midnight canopy of the trees. Natasha had told him she'd had what she wanted from the boy and Simon was the one who had to be dealt with. That had been accomplished. Bohdan wasn't going to risk a chase where, in the darkness, he might easily run headlong into the mad Pole who had proved she was competent with a firearm and perfectly capable of executing an ambush.

He let them go. It would be easy enough to find them later if he needed to.

# CHAPTER 64

# NATASHA BONNICI
## CASTELLO BONNICI, MALTA

Natasha watched, as Bohdan swiftly followed Danka and Savi and disappeared from sight. Her attention turned to the body that lay in the centre of the drive. She approached it slowly, feeling the sharp gravel press through the soles of her soft leather slippers. The night was warm and the breeze that blew in from the coast rustled the large jacaranda tree that stood guard by the entrance to the castello. Simon lay on his side, as if peacefully asleep. The only thing spoiling the image was the gaping wound in his skull and the dark stain that covered one side of his face and soaked into the gravel drive. She kneeled down beside him, turning her head to one side to look into his face and saw that his eyes and mouth were open, as if he had been caught in the act of speaking. What was it he wanted to say? She smiled to herself and thought: *Well, Simon, we'll never know now, will we?*

She was really disappointed in him. He had understood her and she had thought they worked well together. There had been no need for him to threaten her. She knew him well enough to trust him with her secrets. She surprised herself with the depth of the faith she had in him. Even after he had left her, the knowledge he carried with him did not cause her concern. True professionals were hard to find. It was a shame it had ended like this; so unnecessary.

Nick Walker and that wimpish woman, on the other hand, were a different matter. She had been perplexed when the text had arrived in the early hours of the morning. Natasha had been sleeping lightly and the alert from the phone had woken her. To her surprise, she saw Nick's name and smiling face appear on the screen. After a first read of the message, she lay still for a few seconds to digest what she had seen then sat bolt upright in bed. After fumbling for the bedside light, she re-read the words carefully. She knew immediately this was not Nick's style. He did not have it in him, the raw anger that jumped out at her from this text. It must be her, that pathetic little bitch, taking Nick's phone and threatening Natasha. How dare she!

It had been over two months since the pantomime at Oliver Tambo International Airport and, although at the time it had satisfied an urge she had to inflict some pain on the couple, Natasha had more or less forgotten about it now. But, if they had Simon's notes, as Cristina claimed, the threat they now posed was real. If Cristina was stupid enough to come at her like this, then Natasha had to respond.

Sadly, what was also apparent was that Cristina felt confident enough to put Nick in the firing line, and that could mean she had the upper hand in the relationship. Acting solely against Cristina would only provoke Nick into using the information Simon had stupidly given him. There was no other way; they had to be dealt with together, and Natasha knew who to call on. While he was about it, he could help her out with another problem, too.

Natasha arranged to meet *il-Barri* at a kiosk in a layby on the Coast Road. She saw him immediately she drew up. The fisherman sat in a white plastic chair, his back to the road, staring ahead of him at the cobalt-blue ocean, beyond the white stone wall. She pressed her horn. He carefully lifted his bulk out of the chair and approached her car with his usual rolling gait.

*Il-Barri* did not speak, although it was not known whether this was through choice or affliction. He had an aversion to the company of others, which was also a matter for conjecture. Some said he was a farmer's son who had spent his childhood locked in a barn. Others were adamant he had been traumatised by the cruelty of the Carmelites at the Saint Ġorg orphanage. Nobody knew for certain. What was certain was that the strange, solitary fisherman, whose skin glistened with the scales of the *orata*, *spigola and tonno* he illegally scooped from the nets of the fish farms, was to be feared and, most certainly, avoided.

Natasha reached out of the car window and passed him a large envelope of fifty-euro notes, a hand-drawn plan, showing him where on the castello's estate he could find Simon's body, and a photograph of Nick and Cristina, with Nick's work address on the rear.

Looking slightly to one side, so he didn't have to take his eyes off from the rolling waves, breaking on the limestone platform beneath the highway's retaining wall, he took the envelope. Weighing it in his scarred, meaty hands, his knuckles deformed through many acts of violence, he judged the value of its contents. Without a word being spoken, the weight of the envelope told him exactly what it was Natasha needed him to do. He turned his back on her and returned to his chair, slowly placing the envelope on the small side table, to return to his can of cheap beer and his endless vigil over the rushing waves.

# ARTICLE IN MALTA TELEGRAPH

*Reporter: Amy Halliday*
*28 August 2020*

*Turkish armed forces seize control of bridges and television station in signs of an attempted military coup*

*First reports are coming in of a military coup against the hardline Turkish Islamist government of Bilal Kırmızı. The Turkish Parliament, the Presidential Palace and the Asian side of the Bosphorus Bridge have all fallen to the rebel military, who have organised themselves under the banner of 'Peace at Home Movement', a name taken from the motto of Turkey, 'Peace at Home, Peace in the World'.*

*The first government casualty appears to be the Foreign Minister, Hamdi Ozan, who was shot by rebel soldiers in the act of seizing the Ministry of Foreign Affairs in central Ankara.*

*From the 1920s Turkey was a Western-leaning, secular state that steadily industrialised and became a major, non-aligned power in the region. Over the past ten years, however, the government of Kirmizi* dismissed the country's dream of joining the EU and he became the embodiment of political Islam and neo-Ottomanisim.

In Istanbul, Ankara and across Anatolia, the rebel troops have released thousands of dissidents, imprisoned by Bilal Kirmizi following the failed coup attempt in 2016. Those held included journalists, judges, military officers and university lecturers. Troops loyal to the government are still involved in skirmishes with the rebels, but reports suggest the rebels are rapidly gaining popular support, and territory, in Istanbul and Ankara.

For many years the armed forces believed they had a constitutional duty to uphold the founding principles of the Republic including, 'secularism, social equality, equality before the law'. Under Kirmizi, many thought those principles had been blatantly sidelined. A spokesperson for the Generals leading the coup said: 'The military is bound to protect the Constitution and the Rule of Law. The regime of Bilal Kırmızı resulted in an erosion of secularism, the elimination of democratic rule, a disregard for human rights and Turkey's loss of credibility in the international arena.'

Kirmizi had recently served notice on US to close their air base at Incirlik, angering many in the Turkish Armed Forces, who saw the presence of the US as a deterrent to potential rivals in the eastern Mediterranean.

The situation is being closely monitored by regional rivals in Greece, Israel and Iran. Moscow is also interested in the outcome of the situation as its access to the Mediterranean is through the Bosphorus. A new regime, that attached more importance to its membership of NATO, would be a setback to Russian ambitions to become a power broker in the southern and eastern Mediterranean area.

This political turmoil could spell trouble for Malta-based energy giant

*MalTech Energy that has invested heavily in exploration for gas and oil under the contested seabed lying between Libya and Turkey. If the regime of Bilal Kırmızı is ousted, it could lead to uncertain times for the business Malta depends upon to meet its energy needs.*

# CHAPTER 66

# GEORGE ZAMMIT
BIRKIRKARA, MALTA

FOLLOWING the dramatic rescue of Jamal from Abu Salim, Abdullah's convoy had sped out through the traffic south of Tripoli and looped around the city, to join the coastal road that headed west, back to Abdullah's home in Marsabar. The local militias had kept their word and the convoy's exit from the city was trouble free. At George's insistence, he had been dropped at a house near the airport that belonged to Abdullah's cousin. The cousin had been cajoled into getting him onto a commercial flight back home, to Malta.

Abdullah and Jamal were reluctant to let George leave and Abdullah even said it was unfair of him to depart before Rania could properly thank him for what he had done for the family. But George had had enough of Abdullah's use of that particular tactic and, with more embraces and protestations of eternal brotherhood, he sent Abdullah and Jamal on their way, back to an anxious Rania.

On arriving back into Malta International Airport, he changed a handful of Abdullah's Libyan dinars into euros and took the short taxi ride from the airport to his home. It had been nearly two months since he had left Malta and he was unsure how his return would be met. He had phoned when he could, but his whereabouts and wellbeing seemed to be of little interest to Marianna, who now seemed to consider George's prolonged absences and dramatic exploits as part of a normal day's work to him.

George's taxi pulled up outside the three-storey apartment block where his family lived on the ground floor. After glancing up and down the street, to take in the familiarity of his surroundings, he knocked hesitantly. He had bathed before leaving Tripoli and was wearing baggy white cotton trousers and a loose collarless cotton shirt, given to him by Abdullah's cousin.

As usual when he went to Libya for any time, he had let his beard grow so, with his southern Mediterranean colouring, appropriate facial hair and clothing, he could easily be taken as a local Libyan.

Gina opened the door and, after a screech of delight, threw her appreciable bulk at him, nearly knocking him down the three front steps. Marianna appeared next. After a perfunctory hug, she looked him up and down.

"Well, I can see someone who needs a shave and a haircut. What on earth are you wearing? Gina, get him inside and go and run the bath, I can't even begin to guess where you've been, George…"

A wave of pleasure swept over him at the sound of their familiar voices and the predictable fussing and chiding. Marianna turned away from the front step to re-enter the house and George called after her retreating back: "You want to know where I've been? You know something? Even if I told you, you wouldn't believe it."

She stopped in the hall and, over her shoulder, replied: "It's that Abdullah. I don't know why you go along with him. He's no good – I've always said so! Everybody I tell agrees with me. That sort is nothing but trouble!"

George shrugged and smiled. It was pointless arguing.

Gina took him by the hand and led him inside the cool hallway, which was almost overwhelmed by the dark mahogany furniture George had inherited from his parents. The familiar smell of polish hung in the air, to be overpowered by the aroma of fried onion and garlic as they neared the kitchen. He would recognise those smells anywhere; they told him he was home.

After George had cleaned himself up and changed into his casual clothes, which hung a little loose on him, Gina forced him into a kitchen chair and set about trimming and grooming his beard and hair. She prattled on about her wedding plans to Giorgio, who worked in Mifsud's butcher's shop. George was exhausted and started to doze, as his daughter went about her work. He muttered his agreement to whatever she said, oblivious to the cost implications of his inattention. Sensing her father's guard was lowered, she enthusiastically listed all the items she considered essential to make her big day the happiest ever! George had relaxed totally and his light nap had become a deep sleep. His chin had slumped down onto his chest, so Gina moved behind him, to trim the back of his head and complete the most expensive haircut of his life.

As he relaxed, Marianna worked on preparing a late lunch, chipping into the conversation, making observations and comments, to George's sleeping form. Gina chattered on. George was oblivious. All thoughts of missing nuclear missiles, the zombie-like waifs who had wandered out into the daylight of Abu Salim prison yard, the tortured bodies in concrete boxes, being slowly baked by fire, in the squalid town of Duésa, were gone. They would return in the early hours of every morning, to bathe him in sweat and set his heart pounding but, for now he was at peace.

George's son Denzel (Marianna had insisted on the name) had got the message his father was back and immediately cut short his shift, to dash home. He was a tall, dark-haired, good-looking boy who suited the island's light blue *Pulizija* uniform. As he entered the kitchen, smiling broadly, George woke in his chair and looked at his son, suffused with a warm feeling of pride. Denzel was working in the Immigration section, George's old team and, by all accounts was a competent officer and well thought of.

It was true that Camilleri had used his influence to get Denzel into the force, a thing that should have been impossible after the boy's ill-advised association with some small-time drug dealers. But Denzel had grasped the opportunity and seemed to be thriving there. Of course, George knew that any help from Camilleri came at a price and bound him even closer to the manipulative Assistant Commissioner.

Lunch was pasta, with a simple tomato sauce, followed by breaded chicken, beaten thin and fried in breadcrumbs. George allowed his son to open a bottle of cheap local wine and felt the warmth of the food and alcohol soak into him. He said very little. Chatter flowed back and forth across the table and George gradually became more and more sleepy.

He was about to announce he was going for a nap, when Denzel pulled him to one side and suggested they take their coffee in the chairs in the back yard, outside the kitchen. The yard was surrounded by the other apartments in the block, but only George's had access to this shady space, where a square block of blue sky cast light and heat onto Marianna's washing and a variety of herbs and shrubs, planted in large red clay pots. It was a haven George made the most of. Even the chatter of televisions from the neighbours' windows would not interrupt his afternoon naps in the old wicker chairs.

George settled into his seat, stretching his legs out in front of him. Denzel conspiratorially pulled his chair closer.

"Listen, Dad, sorry to talk shop, I can see you're tired, but I need your help."

"OK, as long as I don't have to go back to Libya."

"No, no, that's not going to happen. But listen, I've been down documenting a new batch of migrants today, from the *Samaritan* on Boiler Quay. I met a Malian who said he knew you. Do you remember a Moussa Bangoura? You helped him, you and Father Joseph. Got him a place in a hostel in Marsa. He says you once gave him twenty euros; saved his life when he had nothing."

"I'm not sure I do, you know. So many faces."

"Well, he remembers you and he knows you're my father. Anyway, he's working with Father Joseph's team now, helping new arrivals and he's got a strange story concerning the *Samaritan.*"

"The *Samaritan*, you say?"

"Yeah, the ship is now owned by a South African charity and the crew are a real rough bunch, not your typical bleeding-heart types. I've seen them and it all seems a bit strange. Anyway, Moussa says he knows a guy who's on the cleaning crew and every time the ship docks, they throw away six or seven life jackets."

George was tired and confused and did not understand why Denzel was getting himself so excited.

"So?

"Well, this guy happened to see some other blokes scavenging through the bin bags, which get left alongside the rubbish skip. These guys took the jackets away. He thought nothing of it at the time. The jackets all looked OK and he wasn't surprised somebody thought they were worth having.

"But then he saw the same thing happen again, the next time the *Samaritan* docked. He reckons it could be a smuggling thing."

"Smuggling what?"

"It's got to be drugs, hasn't it?"

George thought for a moment. It was a possibility.

"So, what are you going to do?"

"Well, this guy, Moussa's friend, won't talk to me, but Moussa's told him about you and persuaded him to tell you what he knows. Moussa says they'll both be in the Tiger Bar in Marsa, this afternoon at five o'clock."

"Why me? I don't even know this fellow."

"Moussa's told him you're the only honest cop in Malta and

he can trust you. You know what they're like. The immigrants never talk to the *Pulizija*."

"Huh! You're kidding? You've only just found that out?"

"Come on, Dad! I don't want to go up the line in case I end up looking foolish – asking for a raid on a humanitarian aid ship, which turns out to be clean. I'd look a real prat. I need you to talk to Moussa and his friend and tell me what you think. It'd be a real help. This could be big!"

"Well, OK, but does it have to be now?" George looked at his watch.

Denzel smiled at him, hopefully.

"It's three-thirty. If we're going, it's got to be today."

"Oh, I suppose so. You tell your mother I'm doing you a favour. Don't mention it's police business. Things are going well with her – so far!"

Denzel smiled, jumped out of the chair and rushed into the kitchen.

IT HAD BEEN NEARLY five weeks since Mike Lloyd had met Hakan Toprak on Manoel Island and just under two weeks since the military coup in Turkey. The bunch of know alls in the Situation Room had been driving him up the wall ever since and news of the coup had made things ten times worse.

There was a feeling that the timing of the coup and the theft of the warhead had to be related. The Chair of the Joint Chiefs was adamant that whoever had the nuke would find a way to strike at Tehran and ignite a major conflagration in the Middle East, while the Chief of Staff, Harry Muller, was certain the new regime had taken the missile and would use it to blackmail the White House for concessions or some other form of support. It was all guesswork and starting to sound a little desperate.

So, it came as a relief when Mike Lloyd received a call from Camilleri, saying he had received another message, in identical circumstances to the first. Mike didn't hesitate.

"Open it and read it to me."

He listened, as Camilleri shuffled about, putting on his spectacles and opening the envelopes.

"Well, how mysterious. It is another long sequence of numbers. Do you have a pen?"

"Shoot."

"35.90306853372747, 14.505561846455091, 14091400 + x."

"That's all?"

"That's all."

Mike Lloyd looked at it, put the phone to his ear and tapped his laptop.

"OK, got it."

"What does it mean?"

"Assistant Commissioner, that's for me to know and for you to mind your own business about! Listen, I'm coming back to Malta and I'll need a car, a driver and an office. Can you do that for me?"

Camilleri was put out by his tone.

"Well, I suppose so, but I would appreciate a little more courtesy in our discussions."

Mike Lloyd had already put the phone down.

He convened the team in the Situation Room in Langley and briefed them on the new message. He let them look at the numbers and took a moment to luxuriate in the confusion on their faces.

Howard H. Howard, Chair of the Joint Chiefs, was first to comment.

"Well, the long numbers are obviously a grid reference."

Mike nodded. He ought to know, being a General and all that.

"Correct. It is a place called Manoel Island on Malta."

The General frowned.

"Any significance?"

"Yeah actually. It's the exact same location, to the metre, where I met Hakan Toprak, back in July."

Nick Cole whistled through his teeth

"Well, I'll be... Toprak! Makes total sense. What does the rest of it mean?"

Mike looked at their excited expressions. To save time, he explained: "Well, 14091400 has to be fourteen hundred hours, 14 September. And '+ X'? If you remember your algebra, 'x' is the figure that stands alone. He means, I guess, come by yourself."

Cole looked sceptical.

"I cannot abide a wise guy. Why didn't he say that? I'm tempted to grab him. There's too much going on and too much we don't know. We gotta get control here."

Harry Muller was unconvinced.

"Let this play out, Nick. Remember, it probably means this guy has our missile. That makes it a delicate situation. He is not going to have it on him, is he?"

Mike cleared his throat.

"If I may, sir? I know Toprak, he's straight up. I'm thinking, I'll go and meet him, alone. You can keep some surveillance satellite above us, so at least you'll see what is going on. I've got to go into this blind, no back up, no wires. Just me and him. We need to know what he wants."

Nobody around the table was happy. Control was what they liked; that made them feel comfortable. Handing over the rendezvous to someone like Mike Lloyd, someone who was only barely still trusted, made them nervous. After fifteen minutes, and then another twenty, when Mike was asked to leave the room, they agreed that there was no other suitable option.

———

So it was, that a matter of twenty-four hours later, a US Navy Gulfstream jet deposited him at the VIP Terminal at Malta International Airport. Assistant Commissioner Camilleri and a senior customs official welcomed him and Mike was transported to a suite that took up an entire floor of a five-star Athina hotel, thirty minutes away, at St George's Bay. As Camilleri had said, "An American at Pulizija HQ would only set tongues wagging."

Gerald Camilleri had unexpectedly received a call from the Prime Minister no less, saying that the CIA man was to be extended every hospitality and the entire resources of the Armed

Forces and the *Pulizija* were to be at his disposal. Camilleri was surprised and miffed, to say the least, that things were afoot on *his* island that he did not know about. The fact that some 'here today, gone tomorrow' politician might know more than Mike Lloyd was prepared to tell him, was irksome to the Assistant Commissioner. Knowledge was power, and the thing with power was that you could always have more of it.

As they sat in the back of Camilleri's police BMW, negotiating the congestion of Malta's Central Belt, Gerald Camilleri casually ventured a question.

"So, Mike, are you going to tell me who you are meeting on Manoel Island on the fourteenth of this month? Or do I have to have you followed?"

Mike Lloyd shifted in his seat to look directly into Camilleri's long thin face. It was starting to show the wrinkles and liver spots that come from living sixty years.

"Well, Gerald, you are a clever boy, working that one out. Not so difficult really, was it? And, no, I'm not saying another word about it, except to remind you that you've been instructed by your big boss to do what I say. Haven't you? So, what I'm telling you is – don't pry! Because, believe me, this is above both our paygrades. Help me move it along and I'll make sure your contribution is recognised, but I can't tell you jack shit. No offence."

"Oh, none taken," said Camilleri through gritted teeth.

---

In 2018 the North American Aerospace Defence Command (NORAD) told the world it had just suffered its most expensive failed mission ever. The three and a half billion US dollar surveillance satellite Zuma III had failed to separate from its upper-stage payload and entered an orbit so low it was ultimately pulled into the earth's gravitational field and destroyed on re-entry.

This claim was hotly disputed by amateur astronomers who over the years, produced evidence of a geostationary satellite the shape and size of Zuma III orbiting over two hundred miles above the earth's surface. They claimed NORAD's reports were disinformation, to discourage further enquiries into the satellite's capabilities and purpose.

In fact, they were right to do so, as on the 14 September, Zuma III had mysteriously moved its location to be in geosynchronous orbit with its secret, enormous lens, continually monitoring the site at the coordinates given in the mysterious message received via Assistant Commissioner Camilleri. Zuma III's digital camera was so powerful it had an imaging resolution of five inches, which meant it could see anything that size, or larger, on the earth's surface.

The remarkable digital camera fed the group in the Situation Room in Langley video images of a black-suited Hakan Toprak walking across the expanse of parade ground at Fort Manoel. Mike Lloyd stood right in the centre of the square, hands on hips, jaw jutting, in a conspicuous lemon-coloured short-sleeved shirt and white chinos, awaiting Toprak's arrival.

General Howard H. Howard commented to Nick Cole, "Your man looks like a fuckin' popsicle!"

He replied to the General: "Leading-edge tech, pictures taken from hundreds of miles in space, costing billions – and your first observation is about our agent's shirt? I told him to wear something that would stand out: I didn't realise how darn good those cameras would be."

The General smiled.

"He certainly got the message!"

"This is the guy who's going to get our missile back! Who cares about the colour of his shirt?"

Hakan Toprak came level with Lloyd. The pair of them stood looking at each other, unsmiling. September was the month when high, fluffy cumulus clouds usually formed over Malta, marking the end of summer and the return of the children to school. They were late this year and the clear skies allowed for good satellite imagery of the stream of perspiration that ran down Mike Lloyd's torso, darkening his yellow shirt. He was wearing mirrored sunglasses and Toprak could not see his eyes. It did not matter, he could hold the standoff for as long as he had to and not flinch; he knew the American was the impatient type. He was right. Mike kicked off.

"So, what the fuck? Hakan Toprak, international man of mystery, man of the moment. What's all this about?"

"Peace between nations. Peace and cooperation between our nations. Support for our regime; a new, free, Western-leaning, secular Turkey. A loyal and willing member of NATO, ally of the US, architect of peace in the Middle East."

"Funny way to start, by stealing our nuke."

"On the contrary, we wanted your undivided attention. We think we have it."

"OK, great, then we can all be friends. I'll pass it up the line. When do we get it back?"

"Oh, Mike! You disappoint me. Not so fast. You didn't think it was going to be that easy, did you?"

"And?"

"Well, how would you like us to rescind the notice on Incirlik? How about a naval base in the Sea of Marmara, at the mouth of the Bosphorus, bottling up the Russians in the Black Sea? How about you equip our armed forces with fully US-compatible weapons systems and build a buffer state between the Middle East and the West? What about buying some goodwill with the Europeans and funding us to build refugee cities in some scrubland in Anatolia? There is plenty of space there. I mean, there could be no end to the depth of our friendship."

"Sounds great! When do you get to fuck me in the ass?"

"Very soon, actually. We want your enthusiastic and unequivocal support for our new government, and military help if we request it. We want you to publicly champion our regime. Also, we need to protect ourselves. The immediate threat is from the

Iranians. They will take steps to protect the old Turkish Islamists. You must lift your opposition to the Israelis' all out strike on the Iranians, at Natanz and Fordo uranium-enrichment plants in the mountains.

"You know the Israelis have been sniping at them for years and would have hit them hard, a long time ago, had you not vetoed it. Now, the time has come. We want their minds on other things, while we consolidate our position. In fact, you should vigorously encourage the Israelis to act, now."

"You want us to green light a hit on the Iranians? Start a war between Iran and Israel, so you can settle it? Are you totally nuts?"

"Not at all. Not just green light it: urge them on. Make it happen. Assist them. Do whatever it takes."

"Jesus, this shit has gone to your head. You're talking batshit crazy."

"Iran is full of crazy people, Mike. I need you to get rid of a few of their centrifuges and scientists."

"Is that it?"

"One more small thing. We need you to accept the validity of our maritime treaty with Libya."

Mike looked at him, trying to work out the implications.

Hakan continued, "And, in so doing, accept our argument that the continental shelf is the determining factor in deciding exploration and exploitation rights. Not territorial waters around an island."

"Won't that piss off the Greeks?"

"Oh, yes. Hugely! At a stroke, it will transfer power over most of what they consider to be *their* seabed, to us. There is nothing they can do about it, though, as the US will have entered into a mutual support treaty with us, in the event of any conflict."

Mike was aghast.

"You've got to be kidding? This turns the Law of the Sea stuff on its head, it's got global consequences."

"Not really. You can argue a 'carve out' to resolve the unique circumstances that exist in the eastern Mediterranean. Hand it over to the lawyers, but you know what we want."

Mike stood back to look up at Hakan, who was by far the taller man. Behind his sunglasses, Mike Lloyd was blinking furiously.

"You're in no position to dictate to us. You'd never use that nuke and you know it. At a stroke, all your bargaining power would be gone, you'd be global pariahs and we'd come at you so hard, you wouldn't know what hit you."

Toprak treated Mike Lloyd to one of his rare smiles, showing large even white teeth.

"You have us all wrong, Mike. We have no intention of using it. No need. First, we would let it be known that one of your tactical B61s has been stolen. We'd describe the size of this particular missile and say the US had deceived its allies and those at home, by covering up the loss. I can only imagine the immediate political consequences, the international loss of face and the implications for getting future spending on weapons through Congress. Plus, I suspect there would be an impact on the careers of all those involved in the failed attempts to manage the cover up. It would destroy your argument that you can safely maintain a nuclear arsenal.

"Then, we would covertly auction the bomb on a site on the dark web. The site has already been built; it needs a password to go live. It is non-attributable to us. A teaser has been sent to possible purchasers – rogue states, terror groups and freedom fighters, well-funded arms dealers – you know the likely people. I am sure we have both got the same list.

"We will see how you get on, negotiating with one of them, when they have a three-hundred-kilo-tonne bomb back home." Toprak paused to let the impact of his statement sink in. "How are the Doha talks with the Taliban going, by the way? Making progress?"

Mike's dark face glistened in the intense afternoon sunlight and sweat ran down his temples. Not even the breeze that blew across the harbour could relieve the build up of heat that seemed to bear down on him. The parade ground was flagged with smooth, pale limestone slabs that bounced it back up. In its time, the square had inflicted misery on countless military men, from many backgrounds and countries; today, it was Mike Lloyd's turn to suffer. Hakan Toprak stood erect in his buttoned black wool suit, soaking up the searing rays, seemingly unaffected.

Mike seethed with anger.

"Who are you, Toprak? What authority do you have? My guess is you're just small fry, trying to make a name for yourself. Where're the grownups here? When do we get to meet them? You come spouting all this shit, why should we believe a word of it?"

Toprak remained calm, eyes trained on the American's mirrored shades. He could see from the muscles in Mike's brow that the eyes behind them were pulled into slits, as tension gripped him. Mike, in turn, realised that Toprak had carefully planned this meeting and location to put him under maximum stress. He could not help himself from swiping back at the Turk.

"You're chicken shit, aren't you? Trying it on with the big boys. What if I told you to beat it, right now?"

"You are perfectly at liberty to do so. But, be aware, if you do, our press release goes out immediately and Al Jazeera, CNN, the BBC and TRT World, Turkey's main news programme, will all receive a package for airing this evening.

"You seem interested in my authority for being here? Well, you know my CV. I have had roles in several strategic posts, in industry, energy and finance. But I have always been part of Turkish military intelligence too and proudly carry the rank of General. I already sit at the top table and, with my brave and resolute fellow Generals, can tell you I am totally committed to bringing about change in my country. Think yourself lucky I am bothering to talk to you, Mike Lloyd, small fry Company man.

"You have got three days to get yourself back to Washington

and sort this out, otherwise you know what is going to happen. Do not mess me about or I will prove how serious we are."

Mike decided to take this on the chin.

"If we do all this and the conversations work out, when do we get our missile back?"

Toprak snorted a laugh.

"Don't be ridiculous! That stays with us, as a token of your commitment to the new spirit of co-operation between our nations. You trust us, we trust you. That's how it works."

The lines on Mike's brow deepened.

"You talk about trust when you've got one arm up our backs?"

"Yes, that about redresses the balance of power, would you not say?"

"You've got some balls, Toprak. They're going to hate you in Washington."

"Remember, I am not alone in this, in case you get any ideas about how inconvenient I have become."

With that, he turned his back on Mike and walked off the parade ground. The service road led him down towards the short bridge across to Gizra, where Bohdan was waiting with a cold drink and an air-conditioned S-Class Mercedes. Zuma III did not have a chance of linking his whereabouts to the long black car that shortly afterwards slid out of a carpark beneath a twelve-storey apartment block.

# ARTICLE IN MALTA TELEGRAPH

*Reporter Amy Halliday*
*21 September 2020*

### Israel launches air and ground attacks on Iran nuclear facilities

*In a serious escalation of the long-standing tensions between Iran and Israel, yesterday saw Israeli airstrikes on the two prime Iranian nuclear-development sites at Fordo and Natanz. The airstrikes were followed up by an airborne assault at Natanz by Israeli special forces.*

*The Israelis hailed the assault as an unmitigated success that would set back Iranians nuclear ambitions by several years. A spokesperson for the Israeli government reported one fatality from the raid, with three soldiers being slightly wounded.*

*It appears from US satellite imagery that so-called 'bunker-blasting' bombs were used in the attacks. These are advanced US military weaponry. Experts say the raids would only have been possible with American assistance and suspect that Israeli planes, adapted to carry the bombs, were launched from the Al-Udeid US base in Qatar, across the Persian Gulf.*

The Iranian Foreign Minister said: 'The Zionists want to take revenge because of our progress in developing a peaceful nuclear capability. But we will take our revenge on them. Iran does not recognise Israel's right to exist and this attack is an act of war by the Zionists, against the Islamic Republic of Iran.'

An American State Department representative said, in what was a turnaround to their previous position: 'Iran has failed to honour its obligations under the 2015 treaty obliging it to regulate its nuclear ambitions and limit its production of weapons-grade uranium. We understand Israel's action in pre-emptively striking at a dangerous and aggressive neighbour, which persistently acts beyond the bounds of treaty obligations and international law."

There are signs Iran has started mobilising its armed forces and has moved several brigades of their elite Republican Guards from the north-western town of Urmia, on its border with Turkey, to the south west of the country, threatening an attack on Israel, through the corridor of Syria and Lebanon. Given the present crisis, Iran has in recent days dialled down the rhetoric against the new, pro-western Turkish regime, much to the relief of those in Ankara, who feared an Iranian intervention on behalf of deposed President Bilal Kirmizi.

# CHAPTER 69
# GEORGE ZAMMIT
## THE LION BAR, MARSA, MALTA

THE LION BAR had a neglected frontage on the corner of a little-used road off the western end of the Grand Harbour. Since the Malta Shipyard and the old Marsa oil-fired power station closed, several years earlier, the inlet had become a shabby and forsaken part of the harbour. Moribund abandoned ships, awaiting a final trip to the breakers yard, were tied up against the quay. The rutted tarmac road was awash with spilled oil, casting rainbows over the puddles. Broken pallets, lengths of timber, disused vehicles and a buildup of litter, accumulated over the years, bore witness to the general abandonment.

Looking at the darkened, locked-up warehouses and smaller stone-built units, it was difficult to say which of them were in use and which had been abandoned. But what was clear, was that the Lion Bar was thriving. Its position, away from the main thoroughfare, the unattractiveness of its surroundings and the fact the it lay on a street that ended at the chained gates of the old power station, meant that few people accidentally stumbled upon it, and those who did, were rarely tempted to venture inside. Its location was what made it popular with its regular clientele.

The Lion Bar was the haunt of the immigrant community,

who worked in the docks and businesses around the Grand Harbour. The early arrivals from North Africa mostly settled in Albert Town, a district of Marsa where casual employment was often available. The first immigrants had found shelter in a church-run hostel and formed the basis of a new wave of residents, who replaced the ageing local population and those who left the district, when the large employers closed their gates. When the hostel itself was closed, it was no surprise that the rooms and cheap apartments of Albert Town were filled by the immigrants who had gradually made the area their home.

George parked the car a little away from the bar and he and Denzel slowly walked down the middle of the empty street, to announce their presence. Sure enough, half a dozen patrons scattered like rabbits at the sight of Denzel's uniform. Apart from selling cold beer, this was a place where a variety of drugs were readily available and where the dealers met their wholesalers. It had been subject to several high-profile raids by narcotics officers in the past, but any success was only temporary. As soon as the *Pulizija* left, the dealers slowly filtered back into the bar and business resumed.

Denzel put his hand on his father's arm and directed his gaze towards a long, thin, very dark-skinned man, in baggy denims and a ragged brown T-shirt. He had a wispy, goatee beard on his long, thin face and wore an off-white, lace prayer cap on the back of his head. He sat outside the bar, at a white plastic table, with one of his long legs wrapped around a chair leg. He was smoking a hand-rolled cigarette and had a small can of beer in front of him. He watched them approach and slowly got to his feet.

A slight smile crept over Moussa's face, as his eyes met George's. They shook hands and then, slowly nodding his head, Moussa put one hand to his brow and then touched it to his chest over his heart.

"Sergeant Zammit! You remember me? You were a friend, when I needed one most. How are you? Still doing good things, I hope?"

George nodded along with him, racking his brain, trying to recall their meeting. The man smiled at Denzel.

"You have a fine son. Now, I can say there are at least two good men in the Maltese *Pulizija!*"

George was embarrassed. He could not remember this man to save his life, but Moussa knew him as a sergeant, so their last meeting must have been six or seven years previously. George returned the greeting, as if they were a pair of long-lost friends.

"Moussa, it's good to see you again and it's good you are working with the Mission. The new people need all the help they can get."

Moussa sighed, deeply.

"Too true, my brother, too true. We are all finding things hard these days. Nuthin' gets easier. So, you want to speak to my shy friend? You know, we only bring this to you because it is a charity boat that we think is doing bad things. If the government learn the charity boats are bringing drugs, then they will have more excuses to stop them and people will suffer. If we help you, you will tell the government, yes?"

George nodded; he understood the point. The Maltese government were routinely berated by the charities for their handling of the migrant crisis and would certainly seize on any negative publicity to justify their own hard line.

"Of course, we will."

Moussa led them away from the bar, down the oily pavement, to a narrow alley between two high buildings, where a young man sat on a step, anxiously glancing at his phone. He wore a hooded top, a hi-visibility vest and, despite the late-afternoon heat, a thick woollen hat. Siaka was in his early twenties and had arrived from Mali six months earlier. A friend had got him a job cleaning on the boats that docked in the Grand Harbour. It could be casual work, from rubbing down the gel-coats of yachts in the marinas, to scrubbing out commercial fishing vessels. The company that employed him had a contract to clean and disinfect the decks of the *Samaritan,*

between voyages, a practice required by the public health
authorities.

Although French was the official language of Mali, less than
ten percent of Malians bothered with it. Siaka and Moussa spoke
Bambara, the language of the predominant ethnic group in the
country. Moussa translated as Siaka retold the story of the *Samaritan's* life jackets being taken from the ship, dumped alongside a
rubbish skip, then being quickly collected by another group of
workers. Siaka said he did not recognise the men involved, but
thought they could be Syrians or Afghans. Out of curiosity, he
had followed them. Now he offered to take George and Denzel to
where they had taken the jackets.

Siaka walked two hundred metres ahead, peeking around
corners, then beckoning them to follow, if all seemed clear. After
a walk of five minutes, they saw him squatting on the pavement,
resting his back against a wall, looking at an old, semi-derelict,
single-storey building. It had a roller-shutter door that was
secured with a heavy padlock, clipped firmly around a substantial hasp. There was no signage over the door, only a building
number, two hundred and nine degrees centigrade.

George and Denzel poked around the building, as Moussa
and Siaka moved away, to keep watch from the top of the street.
To the rear of the building was a flimsy wooden door that hung
loosely on its frame.

"We need to get a warrant," Denzel said. "Shall I wait while
you go? You've got more authority."

George looked over his shoulder and then, satisfied they were
not being observed, gave the door a stout kick with the sole of
his boot. The door flew open.

"Dad! What're you doing?"

"Nothing, we found it like this, after we had a report that
screams had been heard inside. Didn't we? Moussa told us he
heard screams, remember?"

They ventured into the dark, stuffy building. Where the
sunlight streamed weakly through the filthy windows. They

could see workbenches, packing cases and a stack of metal drums. Clouds of dust motes gently floated in front of them, suspended in the heavy, stale air. The place was completely silent. It had a concrete floor, stained and greasy. The roofspace was open, with wrought-iron trusses supporting a corrugated, asbestos-sheet roof. A makeshift plywood-panelled office occupied one wall, with a transparent plastic sheet serving as an internal window.

George entered the office and rummaged through the empty drawers, rattling the steel filing cabinets. There was nothing to be found except an old calendar from a chemical company and some delivery notes from previous years, dropped on the floor.

He left the office to poke around the warehouse itself and found Denzel prodding a pile of empty boxes.

"Nothing! Absolutely bloody nothing! Whoever was here has disappeared."

"We'll get forensics in and see what they can give us," said George.

"So frustrating! I thought we were on to something."

Denzel kicked a metal drum, that bounced along the floor with a loud clank and rolled away into a corner. After it had come to rest, there was a second clang as a metal disc rolled free from it. Denzel was already making his way out of the warehouse, when his father called him back.

"Wait up. What's this?"

George took the disc and slid it back inside. He tipped the drum and removed the insert again. Seeing a better patch of light from one of the windows, he manoeuvred the drum on its base towards it and peered into it.

"Well, well! They have bosses welded inside and I think this," he stooped to pick up the thin metal disc, "is a false bottom, waiting to be welded in place!" He waved the disc in front of Denzel. "Why would they need drums with false bottoms, I wonder?"

His son returned and looked into the drum, then took the disc from George, rubbing his thumb around the edge and noting how perfectly it sat on the bosses, some inches above the true base.

"I think you could be right, Dad."

"Well done, Denzel! You've discovered how they're moving, whatever it is that arrives in those life jackets."

"You discovered the false bottoms."

"I helped you work things out, but your willingness to listen to a tipoff brought us here. And look – here's a stack of new pallets and nylon strapping for banding. The drums were transported by road. So, all you need do now is some real police work. Ring round all the local hauliers, find out which ones picked up from here, and check the despatch notes. You'll soon see where the load was going! Looking around this place, there won't have been many pickups in the last six months, the dust is taking over.

"Denzel, we'll make a detective of you yet!"

AFTER HIS GETAWAY from Manoel Island, Bohdan drove Hakan Toprak steadily through Malta's anarchic traffic to the airport's VIP terminal. After the most cursory of formalities, he was aboard Natasha's Dassault jet.

Hakan was unaware that the plane alongside the Dassault Falcon was the bigger and considerably more expensive US Navy Gulfstream that, only hours before, had brought Mike Lloyd across the Atlantic.

Natasha was lounging in one of the cream leather-upholstered seats, laptop open. She watched Toprak duck inside and make his way down the aisle towards her. She gave a half smile of greeting and he eased himself down into the seat opposite her, with a deep sigh.

"All good?" she asked, raising her eyebrows.

"Yes, I think so. Life has been hectic lately."

"You've done brilliantly. You've got my full respect, Mr Toprak, and that's not something I say often."

He bowed his head slightly, in response.

At that moment a smartly dressed cabin attendant appeared with hot towels and two glasses of champagne on a silver tray.

Hakan took the towel and waved away the champagne. Natasha protested.

"No! Take it, I insist. We need a toast."

"If I drink, I'll fall asleep."

"Hakan Toprak, pick up that glass!" Natasha commanded.

Wearily, he raised it.

"What are we toasting?"

"Here's to you! Welcome to the Family!"

True to his word, within twenty minutes of lift off, Hakan's eyes closed and his head gradually slumped to his chest. Natasha watched him as he slept and wondered if there could ever be anything between them. He was annoyingly inscrutable; while most men immediately devoured her with their eyes and made clumsy conversation, she was intrigued by the Turk's air of over-riding calm and patience. She could never tell what he might be thinking, but his sharp intelligence and maturity made a pleasant change from Nick Walker's foppish youth and Luke's animal brawn. Maybe, she thought, maybe…

Natasha turned her attention back to her laptop and the two of them only became aware of their surroundings once more when the wheels touched down at Vienna International Airport. They were quickly processed in the VIP arrivals suite and stepped into the waiting car for the thirty-minute drive south to Schloss Alters-dorf, nestling in the undulating hills of the Burgenland wine district. As they approached the town of Rust, Hakan commented on the acres of vines that covered the inclines and depressions of the landscape, gently folding themselves into the topography.

Natasha turned to him.

"I didn't take you for a wine drinker."

"I am not, I don't drink really. But I always learn a little about my destination, for the sake of conversation."

Natasha smiled.

"You're so punctilious!" She paused then asked, "Are you nervous?"

"Not particularly; more interested, I would say. Should I be nervous?"

"No, you'll eat them up for breakfast."

Moments later, they were pulling into the grounds of the Schober home, Schloss Altersdorf. The drive wound through some woodland that masked the schloss from the road, then cut between formal gardens that greeted visitors on arrival. The lawns were a vivid, sprinkler-green, broken only by low box-edged parterres, designed so that nothing so crude as a fence should detract from the majesty of the house. In the middle of the turning circle before the front steps, was a centrepiece featuring a wide variety of seasonal plants in an explosion of colour.

At first glance, the schloss appeared to be more of a Palladian mansion, with two distinct wings set either side of a Classical façade. The wings were roofed with traditional red pantiles and the plastered exterior painted a brilliant white. Autumn had yet to take hold and the early-evening sun still cast a clear, sharp light over the scene.

Natasha said: "My God, what a beautiful place. I'm not surprised they didn't want to lose it."

Hakan craned his neck to take in as much as he could, as the car came to a halt in front of the house.

"Yes, it is certainly special. What exactly is the arrangement here?"

"We agreed to pay him a decent monthly retainer from his father's capital. I took all his cash when we... moved him to one side."

Hakan glanced at her, well aware of the circumstances of Herr Schober's murder by Natasha's uncle, Sergio Rossi.

She continued: "It wasn't very generous of me to deprive his family of it. So, with the retainer, even this bunch of spendthrifts should have enough to live on comfortably."

"He is very fortunate."

"Yes, it has all worked out well for him. Considering."

The car drew up in front of the house but, before they could open the doors, three male servants, all wearing the formal *Kniebundhose*, suede lederhosen that finished below the knee, trotted down the steps to welcome them and take the little luggage they had brought with them.

Natasha looked them up and down. She turned to Hakan.

"If I was strapped for cash, I know where I'd start making savings!"

He smiled.

As they climbed the short flight of stone stairs, Matthäus Schober burst through the main door and flourished his hands in the air, to welcome them like long-lost friends.

"You've made it! Good journey? The others are all here; we're ready in the reception room."

Natasha thought of the beaten and bleeding figure Simon had bundled into the car in Vienna, not so many months ago. She approached him and they stood face to face, only centimetres apart. She scrutinised him closely, her head so close to his, Matthäus could smell the sweet scent of her hair and a faint note of her perfume. His smile faded as, without a word of greeting, she slowly extended one hand towards his face and gently ran her middle finger along the side of his eye socket then down his face to his jawline, tracing the extent of the fracture he had suffered in Vienna.

"That seems to have healed up nicely. Now, show us to our rooms; we'll freshen up and meet you by the staircase in fifteen minutes. Does that suit you, Mr Toprak? Please extend our apologies to the others."

Natasha entered her room and took a moment to lie on the immense mahogany bed. She gazed up at the deep, ornate plaster cornices. The walls were hung with deep pink embossed velvet and the drapes around the bed were of pale blue silk. She thought how nice it would be to own this house and the estate. It did not take long to reach Vienna in the jet and the estate would make a magnificent summer retreat, to escape the humidity and crowds that ruined Malta in the summer months. It crossed her mind that they should have made it a condition of the retainer that she bought the house, along with the estate, and ejected the wretched Schobers. This was certainly far too good for them.

With a sigh, she sprang off the bed, freshened up in the bathroom and headed out of the door. Matthäus and Hakan were standing at the top of the grand staircase.

Matthäus said: "We thought we'd meet in the *sala nobile*, on the other side of the house. In Mother's days it was where we held the balls and Christmas parties. Nowadays, well – not much goes on there."

The house was built around a large interior courtyard, with a trickling fountain and Roman terracotta urns set to each corner, sprouting giant ferns. Looking through the long windows to the opposite side of the courtyard, Natasha could see the dozen or so most important members of the Family standing around in the corridor, waiting to begin the meeting.

As they turned the corner, the men, for they were all men, fell silent and stood back to form a line so Natasha, Hakan and Matthäus could pass. Natasha smiled and nodded her head in recognition, as she passed each member, lightly touching Bernd Kruder on the shoulder as a mark of special approbation. He glowed with pleasure.

At the door, she turned back to face them.

"Gentlemen, my apologies for keeping you. Please, let's be seated. Matthäus, thank you for your hospitality but you may leave us now, you're not Family yet."

And never will be, she thought to herself.

Matthäus's head and shoulders visibly slumped. The other members of the Family kept scrupulously straight faces, but Natasha knew that, as a group, they liked nothing better than to see someone who had over-stepped the mark being publicly slapped down. It made the others feel more favoured.

The *sala nobile* was a grand room with enormously high ceilings, pale *boiseries* and gilded detailing. The pine panels were marbled in a pale blue eggshell finish. The tall chairs, deeply upholstered with red velvet cushions, were arranged theatre-style. A shallow dais supported a mahogany occasional table with a chair to either side of it.

Natasha and Toprak mounted the dais and took their seats. Toprak was cool and relaxed, and absorbed the scrutiny of the curious Family members, without the least sign of losing his composure. His dark, unblinking stare took in the dozen dark-suited, white, middle-aged men, all calmly appraising him. Natasha had prepared short profiles of all the Family Committee members for him, adding her personal observations on their character and motivations. He felt well prepared to take his seat amongst them.

Natasha began.

"Please welcome the latest addition to our illustrious *Familia con pane*, Hakan Toprak. Or, as they call him in Turkey, Hakan *bey*."

There was a light smattering of applause and wide beaming smiles. Hakan was not fooled. Natasha smiled at him and raised her eyebrows. At the signal, Hakan stood and raised a hand to stem the applause.

"*Asalamu alaykum*. It means peace be with you. I am aware of the Family's heritage and, as a Turk and a Muslim, my being amongst you must be a new experience. Rest assured, I have left my scimitar at the door and I promise to curb my neo-Ottoman tendencies." As Hakan had anticipated, there was a polite ripple of amusement. "That said, all businesses must renew themselves and, in these times, when the East increasingly offers better prospects for growth and enrichment, I hope my local knowledge and connections will contribute to the long-term growth of the Family I am honoured to be able to call myself part of."

Natasha got to her feet.

"You probably know of Hakan *bey* as a shrewd businessman in the key Turkish industries of energy and finance. What you may not know besides is that, as a leading member of military intelligence, he also carries the rank of General in the Turkish military. He is now one of the leading figures in the new regime. The Generals realise they need to provide for their future as, in politics, there is no certainty of what tomorrow might bring.

"So, with Hakan's help, they have privatised part of their upstream oil and gas businesses and sold it to the Family. We have, at a stroke of Hakan *bey's* pen, been granted a multi-billion-dollar, twenty-five-year exclusive licence to exploit all Turkish maritime Exclusive Economic Zones, including the territory subject to the Turkish-Libyan Maritime treaty. I don't have the agreement with me, as it runs to fifteen volumes of paperwork, but our London and Ankara lawyers confirm it is watertight.

"The money we pay the government for the privilege of exploiting their oil and gas resources, will be held in a Turkish Sovereign Wealth Fund, for Turkey's further development. To give some context: over the term of our agreement, we expect the amount to comfortably exceed the one trillion US dollars held in Norway's Sovereign Wealth Fund. So, the Family and the government of Turkey are now in a long-term symbiotic relationship.

Like all good deals, his arrangement has only winners and Hakan Toprak is to be congratulated in piecing it together. Hakan will continue to serve the Turkish state, but we're honoured to also welcome him as a Family member. Of course, all our usual rules of confidentiality apply, but doubly so in the case of Hakan's membership of the Family. If the regime in Ankara were to suspect his loyalties to them were anything less than absolute... well, we'd probably lose the benefit of his advice, wisdom and service. That's something I would not tolerate. I'm sorry to be so blunt. Is that understood?"

A murmur of assent went around the room.

Hakan sat, legs crossed, looking totally relaxed. Being a part of the new Turkish government and, simultaneously, a Family member would certainly present challenges, but he was the Hawk and he knew how to defend himself and his territory.

Meanwhile, Natasha continued her address.

"We will, of course, continue to show our gratitude for this opportunity to the Generals, privately of course, and calculated as a percentage of the profits from our enterprise. But don't be alarmed. There is plenty left for all concerned!"

There was a short burst of laughter, then a low murmuring around the room, as the assembled group took in the enormous import of the news. Natasha clapped her hands to regain their attention.

"Furthermore, the Americans will release a statement tomorrow, giving their support to the new Turkish government and recognising the Exclusive Economic Zone created by the Turkish-Libyan treaty of 2016, in which we, the Family, now have a vested commercial interest. This will bring NATO members, particularly Greece, to heel and clear the way for a huge step forward in our oil and gas exploration business."

There was a much more enthusiastic round of applause.

Bernd Kruder was the first to question Natasha.

"How on earth did you manage to persuade the Americans to change their position so dramatically and in so timely a manner?"

She replied: "That's a testament to Hakan *bey's* strategic vision and his political adroitness. He knows how to make these things happen. You'll understand, there are things we cannot share with you, but rest assured: Hakan Toprak has more than earned the right to sit amongst us. Over the coming years, it will become apparent how valuable he is to us. But for now, trust me and trust him."

The questions flowed and Hakan and Natasha provided reassurance, batting away those enquiries they did not care to answer and instilling a sense of enthusiasm and excitement in the assembled Family.

After an hour, Natasha called a halt and told them they should retire and prepare for dinner as guests of the Schober family. She reminded them that discretion was of the utmost importance and that the Schobers were no longer to be considered privy to the affairs of the Family. With laughter and chatter, the group pushed back their chairs and left the *sala nobile* in small groups, heads together, speculating on what the future might bring.

NATASHA AND HAKAN TOPRAK lingered behind, waiting for their fellow Family members to make their way around the courtyard. When the last suit had cleared its marble floors, Natasha led Toprak out, down a small servants' staircase and onto the gravelled area behind the kitchens.

They walked around to the front of the schloss, across the belt of smooth, undulating grass, skirting stands of trees and a serpentine ornamental water course. A musty, cooling breeze from Lake Neusiedl blew across the town of Rust and up over the house, before becoming becalmed in the foothills of the Leithia range. Natasha stopped and shielded her eyes against the dropping sun, as three cumbersome storks flew low over the garden, their enormous wings gliding down towards the lake. After passing through an artfully maintained wilderness area on the edge of the formal gardens, a cobbled road led them through an ornate white arch into the stone yard, which served as the visitor entrance to the Schloss Altersdorf Winery.

The winery was older than the house, dating back to the seventeenth century, and its low white buildings with red pantile roofs extended around three sides of the yard. The vineyard produced the Rust Ausbruch, a local speciality, a nobly sweet wine with a centuries-old tradition. Behind the winery's façade were concealed modern, steel-framed buildings that housed the rows of stainless-steel tanks, in which the honey-coloured nectar sat maturing.

Once bottled, the wines were stored in racks, in cool cellars under the winery. These had been dug centuries before refrigeration had been thought of, to form a complex of tunnels that ran under the Leitha Hills. Matthäus's father had installed a large commercial lift and a small set of narrow-gauge rails, so boxes of expensive, long-aged wines could easily and smoothly be brought out of the tunnels on trolleys, up into the winery.

At the back of the tunnel system was an all but forgotten iron door, with ornate wrought iron hinges. Behind it, a shaft disappeared deep into the ground, where it accessed an old well. This had long-since fallen into disuse and had been blocked off generations before. The oldest worker in the winery said he could not remember the last time the door had been opened.

He had been surprised, therefore, when a team of contractors appeared a few weeks earlier, with a range of heavy equipment and instructions to cap the shaft and place a formidable steel structure behind the original door. The cellars were closed for a week, for safety reasons, but the visitors worked cleanly and caused no lasting damage. Most importantly, the wines had not been disturbed. After a week, their visit was all but forgotten.

Natasha and Hakan stood in the evening gloom, the sodium spotlights throwing yellow cones across the cobbles. Hakan had no idea what they were doing at the winery, but knew Natasha would have a good reason for bringing him there.

She had linked her arm with his, as they walked down the cobbled road towards the winery, her shoulder pressing close against his.

"Wrong shoes for these cobbles! You don't mind if I hold on?"

He found he did not mind at all and struggled to repress the pleasure he felt when her body was close to his. He had been close enough to Natasha to know that the last thing he wanted was to fall under her spell.

He was patient enough not to question her and was rewarded when she turned towards him and said quietly: "Would you like to see something extraordinary?"

Hakan's eyes widened.

"You mean, you have it here?"

Natasha kept her gaze on him for a moment, savouring the hint of shock on his face. She reached into her bag and, cocking her head to one side, produced a bristling key ring. She jangled it inches in front of his face.

He stood perfectly still, unable either to move or speak.

Natasha broke into a smile and said, still waving the keys: "I can't show you the thing itself, but I can show you where it is. We've stored it behind a special protective door for our protection. Radiation is nasty stuff and we wouldn't want the wine to become contaminated, would we? Coming?"

# CHAPTER 72

# ARTICLE: MALTA TELEGRAPH

*Reporter: Amy Halliday*
*21 September 2020*

**US shocks Greek government by acknowledging Turkish maritime claims**

*In an announcement likely to have far-reaching consequences in the eastern Mediterranean, the US Department of Commerce has said it now recognises Turkey's sovereign claim to explore and exploit resources beneath the seabed on its continental shelf.*

*In a dramatic turnaround of its position, which is contrary to currently accepted legal opinion, US spokesperson Dan Whittle said: 'Due to the uniquely complicated situation in the area, it was equitable to create an exception to current treaty interpretations that recognised Exclusive Economic Zones around hundreds of Greek islands, some only a few miles off the Turkish coast. As the law currently stands, Turkey is effectively blocked out of the Mediterranean by a series of tiny and sparsely populated rocks. This is manifestly unfair.'*

*Immediately after the announcement, MalTech Energy, which holds drilling concessions from the Turkish government, issued a NAVTEX notice, warning other vessels to steer clear of part of the contested area, where it intends to recommence exploration activities with its drillship, Ocean Vantage.*

*The Greek Foreign Minister said the actions of the Turkish government and MalTech Energy were unlawful and a mere statement by the US government carries no weight in international law. He said Greece would file papers at the International Tribunal for the Law of the Sea, in Hamburg, to prevent Turkey acting illegally and to seek legal clarification on the extent of Greece's sovereign rights under current treaties. Turkey has, in the past, acted with impunity when Greece has brought similar actions before the court.*

GEORGE AND DENZEL climbed the stairs to Assistant Commissioner Camilleri's corner office on the first floor. When he was a young officer, any visit to the Assistant Commissioner's office had George nervous and perspiring. In the past, Camilleri had blackmailed him, bribed him, lied to him, threatened him and generally manipulated him in any number of ways. George knew Camilleri enjoyed the application of power, especially in the subtly cruel forms of which he was a master. There was nothing physically threatening in the way he terrified his subordinates, but his ability to see into the beating heart of a person did not just extend to those he interviewed under caution; it applied equally to all who served under him.

As a junior officer called before Camilleri, George would find himself desperately trying to retrieve a pleasant memory or do some mental arithmetic, in a vain attempt to deflect the Assistant Commissioner's mystical mind-reading powers. He knew, however, no mistake could go unconfessed, no weakness remain hidden, no fear unrealised. George always hoped his intense focus would be mistaken for concentration but, invariably Camilleri would find his mark: that spot where he could insert his metaphorical stiletto and slowly twist, until he had caused sufficient pain, or gained the advantage he sought.

George could see Denzel, too, had that growing feeling of unease, as they turned onto the landing and approached the office at the far end of the corridor. George was amused. These days, he felt he could hold his own with Camilleri. But this was not quite the case, of course; George had simply ceased to resist him. He had capitulated to the irresistible force of Camilleri's will years ago and now did his bidding, without complaint or too many questions asked.

Apart from the whole issue of the B61 missile. Here, George had to compartmentalise the knowledge he had and throw away the key. Keeping his knowledge of that whole story secret was an intolerable burden to him and he worried incessantly about what had become of the missing bomb. He scoured the papers and listened avidly to news broadcasts, but had heard nothing about a US missile being either lost or discovered. The only compensation was the pleasure of knowing one thing the assistant commissioner did not, and George had to battle hard to resist the urge to feel a little smug.

That was why the link to the *Samaritan* was so sensitive. He had been sworn to secrecy by Mike Lloyd, who had threatened to take him to a black ops site and tear his fingernails out, one by one, if he said anything out of place, but especially to Camilleri. The American was a bull shitter, but you could never be quite sure.

As usual, Camilleri's office was totally clear of the piles of papers, coffee cups, photographs, sporting trophies, potted plants and other knickknacks that other officers surrounded themselves with. He would not want there to be any distractions from what happened within his lair. Neither would he want to disclose any unnecessary personal details about himself or his likes and dislikes. Making statements of that sort was a mistake, in his view.

As they entered George could see the AC was in his usual

position, looking out of the corner window, studying the activity in the marina below. He said nothing, merely waved them towards the large, highly polished rosewood conference table that dominated the room. George knew this short period of waiting was supposed to unsettle more nervous visitors, such as Denzel.

"Well, this is pleasant." said Camilleri finally, moving away from the window to take his seat at the head of the table. "Having the pleasure of a visit from two Zammits." He treated them to a burst of his reptilian smile, for a brief second. Then his long, pale face seemed to collapse, the smile disappearing as quickly as it had arrived. "So, what is this all about?"

George looked at Denzel, who had hoped to sit quietly and keep his head down. Realising he had to start the conversation, Denzel took a breath and began stammering and spluttering his way through the story of the *Samaritan* and the dumped life jackets. George had advised that they skirt around the illegal entry into the warehouse, so Denzel focused on the two hundred litre drums with the false bottoms and his trawl of the haulage firms of Malta. This had led to the ultimate discovery of the identity of the haulier, an international firm with a branch based on the Hal Far trading estate. A few phone calls later and they knew that a pallet of twelve drums, purportedly containing a clarifying agent, widely used in the food and drinks industry, was collected monthly and taken to an address in Austria.

"So, in short, sir, we want to question the owner of the *Samaritan*, a Mr Luke van der Westhuizen, and ask Interpol to pick up inquiries in Austria."

Denzel shut up and shot a glance at George, to seek reassurance on how he had done. George nodded back his approval.

Camilleri got up and walked towards the window, without saying a word. He buttoned his jacket, then unbuttoned it again. He returned and looked directly at George.

"Luke van der Westhuizen?"

George remained calm.

"So the records say, sir."

"Have you come across this man before, George? No, do not answer that." He stared across the table at Denzel for a moment, then snapped, "Good policework, officer. You have made a promising start with us and I will make sure my thanks are passed down to your superior. Now, leave us, please. You will hear from me shortly on next steps."

Denzel was shocked by this turn of events. He scrambled to his feet and, like so many young officers before him, exited Camilleri's office as fast as he could. As the door clicked shut, Camilleri addressed George.

"Well, this is a bag of snakes we have to deal with! There are all sorts of considerations here."

In many ways, George was relieved; so he knew about the bomb!

"Sir, I know, I'm just glad I could get it off my chest. Frankly, having to keep it to myself... it's been a burden to me and I'm sorry it's put you in such an embarrassing position."

"Well, it's not the end of the world. We can sort it out. It's nothing I can't manage..."

"Well, that's the point, isn't it? It *could be* the end of the world! I'm glad you're so confident you can get this sorted. I'll certainly sleep a lot easier!"

"George, I applaud your diligence, but the fact that Luke van der Westhuizen, the man you suspect of running an international drugs-running business, is Natasha Bonnici's boyfriend, does make things a bit complicated."

"Shit! Sorry, sir, I didn't mean..." Oh, God, Camilleri *did not* know! And George had nearly told him! For a moment, the steel door to Mike Lloyd's black ops site flashed before his eyes. But Camilleri was still talking.

"No, George, you are perfectly correct. Shit! That is exactly what this is."

"Sir," George tried to cover his retreat, "there's one more thing you ought to know. The address where the drums are sent is also a bit... well, unusual. I Googled it and have these images."

He rooted in the leather portmanteau that Marianna had bought him the previous Christmas, in anticipation of his return to a superintendent's position, and produced a series of photos of Schloss Altersdorf. Camilleri's eyebrows rose.

"My word, this *is* a hornet's nest. Who owns this little pile?"

"It's been in the Schober family for nearly two hundred years. Old nobility, Austro-Hungarians – pre-1918 that is. Then, after the war – World War I that is —"

"I know what happened to the Habsburgs, I am not uneducated."

"Of course not. Well, they still live there, apparently. An interesting fact is that Herr Schober, formerly the senior male member of the family, was murdered a few years back, in Milan. A helpful assistant inspector in Vienna recalled he might have been the victim of an organised crime assassination. Nothing came of the police investigation."

"And you want Interpol to kick the castle doors down?"

George glanced down at the photographs of the schloss.

"Looking at these photos, I'm sure the Schobers will have people employed to open them, if asked."

"Hmm. Probably." Camilleri was back on his feet. He took a few paces one way, then a few back the other. "Leave this one with me, I need to think. And, George, good work, both of you. And you were absolutely right to come to me."

George left, happy to leave Camilleri with the headache of working out the politics of it all. Relief flooded through him. He had managed to keep his secret to himself! He smiled, as he felt the weight of the monkey climb off his back and drop onto Camilleri's.

Camilleri was perplexed. He hated only knowing half a story. Van der Westhuizen had tried to bribe him, undoubtedly because he was starting up the new route, smuggling drugs through Malta. Van der Westhuizen was Natasha Bonnici's boyfriend and she currently had Camilleri delivering cryptic messages to Mike Lloyd, about God knows what. The drugs went to an old family in Austria, and the head of that family had recently been murdered in Milan. A murder in Milan? Marco Bonnici had told him of Natasha's and Sergio's clear out of the Wise Men there. Surely not! And George was behaving strangely... what exactly had happened while he was away, assisting Belkacem in Libya? Camilleri decided it was time for him to do a little digging. It would do no harm to drop van der Westhuizen's name into the mix with Mike Lloyd and see what reaction it got.

Camilleri did not like it when he was not fully informed. That was the way the reins of power would start to slip from his hands.

LANGLEY HAD TOLD Mike Lloyd to remain in Malta and liaise with the Turk, while trying to locate the whereabouts of the missile. The days had turned to weeks, then months. General Howard H. Howard and Nick Cole had asked the President to green light an ambitious plan to lure Toprak back onto Manoel Island for another meeting. The wide-open parade ground was perfect for a surprise, high-speed helicopter extraction, where they would ambush Toprak, lift him to the VIP terminal of the airport, bundle him onto the Gulfstream and take him to El Udeid Air Base in Qatar. From there, it was only thirty minutes' drive to a US black site. After a few days there, the pair assured the President, they would know everything Hakan Toprak knew.

The plan was perfect, except for the fact that Hakan Toprak had disappeared again. The spooks in the three-storey basement of the US Embassy in Malta had trawled all departures from the island, watched hours of satellite and CCTV footage and monitored more electronic communications than could possibly be imagined. Nothing. It seemed he had vanished into thin air.

The US had made contact with the new regime in Ankara, where relations were developing well, particularly after the Israeli attack on Iran and the US recognition of the Turkey–Libya maritime treaty. However, the regime steadfastly denied any knowledge of any officer, or government servant, called Hakan Toprak, or any knowledge of a B61 missile missing from Incirlik.

There had been a senior executive in the Turkish Oil and Gas Organisation of that name, but he had retired some months previously and his whereabouts were unknown. CIA agents in Turkey tried to trace family and friends and former work colleagues of the mysterious Hakan Toprak. They found only a few people who admitted to knowing him and even they had only the sketchiest memories of the man. All that was left of him was a wisp, a rumour, the ghost of his existence.

The spooks were asked to compile a history from the digital footprint he must have left behind, but even that yielded thin pickings. Apparently, as a youth he had won medals for wrestling in his home town of Gebze, south of Istanbul. While completing his National Service in the military, he had won yet more medals in wrestling competitions. Apart from this record of his prowess on the mats, there was no further mention of Hakan Toprak.

So, when Camilleri telephoned Mike Lloyd for a chat, he was more than happy to pick up. He knew, OK hoped, that the Maltese policeman had something for him. Something, anything, he could grasp onto would be worth having. As he had admitted to himself over a week ago, he was all out of ideas. His agitated nights were spent prowling the corridors of the hotel where they had set up his base; his mornings desperately shouting instructions and orders into the secure telephone and his afternoons fielding endless requests for updates from persistent and self-important project managers, planners, secretaries to the various committees, both military and governmental. This was not what he was made for and his impatience showed.

He had been forced to confide in Camilleri that he was looking for a Turkish national who had been involved with the military and the highest levels of government. He had provided Toprak's name and a grainy photograph, downloaded from

Zuma III. Camilleri knew exactly who Hakan Toprak was, as Abdullah Belkacem's son had tried to kill him and George had petitioned Natasha for help in obtaining his release. Camilleri filled in Mike Lloyd with what he knew, but other than providing more background, Mike saw little connection with his area of interest.

Mike picked up the phone full of hope.

"Tell me, Gerald! What have you got for me?"

"Not much, I am afraid. But you might be able to help with something that niggles me."

"Well, maybe. Spill it."

"Does the name Luke van der Westhuizen mean anything to you?"

"Yes, go on." Mike held his breath.

"Well, you know he supposedly runs a maritime rescue charity, with a ship called the *Samaritan*?"

"I know that much."

"We think it is a front for a drugs-running operation. Two of my officers have discovered how the product is moved on and are keen to bring in Interpol and Austrian Federal Police."

"Austrian?"

"Yes, this is the strange part. There is evidence to suggest the drugs are shipped to a castle south of Vienna, owned by some blue-blooded Austrians."

Even as the words 'blue-blooded Austrians' passed his lips, the penny dropped and Assistant Commissioner Gerald Camilleri realised what it was that had been bothering him. Van der Westhuizen, Natasha Bonnici, Austrian blue blood – the Family! It had to be, yet he knew drugs were not something the Family were into. They had bigger fish to fry than that.

"Mike, I might be onto something here but I cannot tell you yet. I need to know what I am looking for. If you will not tell me, I cannot help you."

The CIA man nearly exploded.

"You *will* tell me! You've no idea what I'm dealing with here.

I need the President's authority to say anything about this operation to anybody, and that includes you! The President of the United States… you've heard of him? He's a big shot!"

"Come, let us not be too dramatic, Mike. Help me and I will help you. How long have we known each other? You understand my methods. Tell me, what on earth is going on?"

Mike Lloyd thought about what would happen if he requested permission to bring Camilleri into the loop. The debates, the arguments, the papers to be drafted, protocols, the phone calls all hours of the day and night; he could not hack it.

"You know this Hakan Toprak, the Turk?"

"Yes, I have told you I do."

"He stole a nuclear device from our Incirlik airbase in Turkey. Well, to be plain, it's a damn' big nuclear bomb. Blow the fuck out of any city you could name and all the countryside for a hundred miles around. It's bad news, Gerald, and he's blackmailing us on behalf of the new Turkish regime – *us*, the US government!

There was a stunned silence on the line. Mike went on: "We boarded the *Samaritan* in the Gulf of Sirte, over two months ago, on a tipoff, as it was coming out of Libya. All we got was an empty crate; someone was yanking our chain. If this ever gets out, so help me, your ass will be in a hole in the ground before you know it! We're keeping the whole thing super schtum. Please don't pass this up the line."

Camilleri was stunned. He felt embarrassed at the drama that had been played out under his nose, while he had been excluded. He pulled himself together and put on his most aloof professional air.

"Well, well! That explains one or two recent political events. So, could it be that this missile followed the same route as the drugs?"

"It followed the same route from Turkey to Benghazi, then an empty crate was put aboard the *Samaritan*, to throw us off the trail. So, yeah! It's a distinct possibility."

"The destination in Austria is not your standard drugs trafficker's lair. I will send you photographs and such information as we have. This is all most interesting."

"You do that, Gerald. Send me anything you got, now! We're tearing our hair out here. If something comes of this, you've just immeasurably furthered the state of US-Maltese relations. Forget the Brits' George Cross in World War Two, we'll give you an aircraft carrier. Hell, have two!"

Camilleri picked up his phone and wandered across his office to the window. He noticed an old blue double-decker tourist boat, commentary blaring from its speakers, ploughing across the harbour. They always ignored the speed restrictions. Their wash shook the yachts on the pontoons. He should do something about it.

But there was something he needed to ask Mike Lloyd, first. He could not quite put his finger on it, but it concerned what he had just heard. Then, it dawned on him. Could this have a connection with George's trip to Libya?

"One more thing, Mike, does Zammit know about this?"

"Of course! We sent him to Libya to find the darn' thing. He was the one who found the crate being loaded onto the *Samaritan*, when he was undercover in Benghazi, but it was empty! Made us all look like fools, though he wasn't to know. He seems a little dim sometimes, but it looks to me like you've got a good officer there."

"Hmm. I applaud your faith in him."

They ended the call and Camilleri walked back to his desk and sat down. For a moment, he considered the expensive black Mont Blanc fountain pen, with its 18-carat gold nib, that he used to sign his mail. He took off the cap, held the pen in his fist, nib down like a dagger, and with one fast, furious movement, slammed it into the surface of his desk, covering his hand and shirt cuff in deep blue ink.

THE CHATTER of the US Black Hawk helicopters, from Brumowski Air Base, north west of Vienna, were heard over Rust on the morning of 23 September, just as the sun was rising. The clear, cool autumn skies had caused a low mist to rise from Lake Neusiedl that had enveloped the town, but had not managed to creep up the winding backroad that led to the more elevated ground occupied by the schloss.

At first, the four helicopters resembled a flight of blackbirds, aiming straight and low over the undulations of the vineyards and wooded crests of the low hills. They moved as one but, as they neared Rust, the ugliness of their black bodies and the harsh jibber jabber of their cries became ominous and threatening. Each Black Hawk carried ten combat-ready troops, bristling with weaponry, communications equipment and protective Kevlar body armour.

The road from the town heading towards the schloss had been closed by the police and a convoy of trucks and vehicles, belonging to EKO Cobra, the police tactical unit of the Austrian Federal Ministry of the Interior, was nose to tail along it. Right at the back of the line, in a plain blue minibus, were the American and Austrian scientists and security officials, including an increasingly tense Mike Lloyd.

A monitor hanging above the dashboard of the minibus showed the same feed that was being displayed in the Situation Room in Langley, where the host of spectators included the President, himself.

Mike watched, as the Black Hawks swooped onto the lawns of the schloss. Before the rotors had even slowed, the helicopters spilled their troops, who spread left and right, taking tactical positions behind the low hedges and making their way to the rear of the building.

A small group of men and women appeared at the front door, in nightwear and dressing gowns, clearly bemused by what was happening around them. A younger man clad in a long dark robe dropped the hand of an elderly woman and strode across the lawn to confront the soldiers. Mike could only hear the feed from the comms between the troops, but from the visuals, he could tell this man was livid with rage. He was flailing his arms around and shouting. Two soldiers brusquely bundled him to the ground and secured his arms behind his back. As they dragged him towards the schloss and the waiting ensemble of distressed residents, the man's dressing gown fell open to reveal a pair of crested and monogrammed pyjamas.

It took the troops thirty minutes to find the tunnels under the winery. Mike's anxiety turned to hope as the feed showed the men slowly and methodically exploring one section after another. There was some indecipherable chat on the audio and an order to halt was given. An Austrian EKO sergeant produced a wizened old man with wispy white hair. He was wearing an overcoat on top of striped pyjamas and talking rapidly, explaining something in German and pointing down the tunnels. After a few minutes the troops moved on purposefully, led by a diminutive figure in an oversized coat and leather slippers.

It took a specialised team of military engineers half an hour to dismantle the two leaves of the black gloss steel door. There was then silence, as they stared at the formidable stainless-steel structure revealed behind it. It was a substantial second door, recently installed and secured with a combination lock a regional bank would be proud of. Mike was on the edge of his seat with excitement.

One of the engineers tapped and scratched at the surface of the door and pronounced that it was a bank-vault design, made from specialised concrete poured inside a steel casing. The only way through was to drill a series of holes with a thermal lance, that burned steel rods in pure oxygen, reaching a temperature of four thousand degrees centigrade. After a brief discussion, he scurried off to try and find the equipment.

There was an air of anti-climax as the wait began and Langley announced they would take a short break. Nick Cole spoke to Mike and told him the President had gone back to bed.

"Good job, Mike. I stuck by you, knew you'd come good."

Mike considered the reverse of this statement.

"All right! So, others didn't?"

"You're a hero now. Only good things can come of this. Let's take a break. Get back to me when it's show time."

Mike sat back in the van and started to plan his approach to the occupants of the castle, who were apparently making quite a fuss. His plan had been to have the proof in front of him, a dirty big missile. But looking at the impenetrable vault-door, that was just as good a starting point. It had not arrived by itself, had it?

He was about to leave the van and get some coffee from the mobile canteen, when something caught his eye. A static feed had been set up in front of the door, so it was in the top right-hand section of the monitor at all times. Two of the engineers were standing by the door, taking measurements and chatting. One had put his hand on the handle next to the combination lock and it had moved a fraction. The engineer's body language changed and the two men crouched down by the door, shining a large torch along the edges of the jamb, where it met the frame.

The engineer turned and shouted down the corridor: "*Es ist offen!*"

Mike's German was non-existent, but his heart leaped at the announcement. His mouth had gone dry and he had forgotten to breathe. His fingers started to tremble slightly, as the engineers, centimetre by centimetre, edged the door ajar. They inserted a thin optical wire that gave them a visual inside the vault, checking for triggers or traps. Then, a Geiger counter was held near and quickly discarded, with a shake of an engineer's head.

Finally satisfied that there was no danger in opening the door, they swung it a little wider so that they could enter the vault behind. At first Mike could see nothing, the door was not open far enough for him to see right inside. He could see the twin beams of the engineers' torches.

In less than ten seconds, they were out, contemptuously pushing the door fully open to reveal the hewn stone walls within. Mike did not need them to say a word, he knew what they had found. One shrugged and said directly to camera: "*Es ist leer, nichts! Scheisse!*"

It is empty, nothing! Shit!

Which was exactly how Mike Lloyd felt at that moment.

IT HAD TAKEN Denzel over a month to secure the co-operation of
the Turkish Police in arresting Luke van der Westhuizen. The
*Samaritan* was registered under the flag of Malta and shipping
registers gave the owner's details as a Turkish company in
Ankara. The address of the company turned out to be a small
legal office, who initially stonewalled all enquiries.

Denzel persisted in badgering the Maltese authorities to press
the Turks to help. Nobody was more surprised than he was
when, some weeks later, he received a message that the beneficial
owner of the company that had registered the *Samaritan*, Luke
van der Westhuizen, was being held in custody and the Turkish
authorities would look sympathetically on any request for
deportation.

When the *Samaritan* and its crew were released from Souda
Bay by the Americans, Luke had flown straight back to what he
believed to be the relative safety of Turkey. But he arrived back at
his home, in Istanbul, to become tangled up in the military coup
and to find his wife had, without a word, returned to Azerbaijan,
guessing his star was about to fall. As someone who had spent
the last ten years cultivating friendships amongst the deposed

regime, his plan was to wait for the dust to settle, then set about rebuilding his network. Within days of putting his head above the parapet, however, he found himself arrested on drugs-smuggling charges. He was currently being held in a small, single-occupant cell in Turkey's highest-security prison, the concrete jungle that is Silivri, along with seventeen thousand other inmates.

That was where Denzel arrived to accompany Luke and his Turkish guards on their journey to Istanbul's old Atatürk Airport. There, they were due to board a Maltese Armed Forces plane, which would bring Luke back to Malta, to face trial for drugs trafficking. Denzel had got as far as the prison's imposing entrance gantry, supported by triangular red concrete pillars, when a polite official asked him to step into a small white car for a journey to the administration block. It was there that it was explained to him that the prisoner had committed suicide.

Denzel was so shocked, he sat and listened to the brief explanation without a word. Apparently, Luke had torn his bedding into strips and fashioned a makeshift noose. He then turned the steel-framed bed on its end and managed to choke himself to death from a bar. He had been found this morning. They apologised for not being able to spare Denzel the journey.

The next day, he and George sat in Camilleri's office digesting the news. A shaken Denzel was assured that he was not to blame for the turn of events in Silivri. Camilleri moved from his usual position by the window, to lay a paternal hand on Denzel's shoulder. But not for too long, as the assistant commissioner hated physical contact of any sort and knew he did not do empathy very well.

"You know, the Turkish prison system has a reputation for being, let us say, robust. Do not blame yourself, Denzel. You just did your duty, trying to bring him in. And remember, this man was not only an international smuggler of heroin. He traded illegal African diamonds and systematically exploited the migrant crisis for his own ends. I mean, how much more blood can a man have on his hands?"

George sat quietly. He was disappointed for Denzel, who had wanted to nail a big scalp early in his career. It was easy to say there would be other opportunities and George knew that to be true, but it would provide little immediate comfort to his son.

Camilleri finished: "I cannot say too much, but I suspect our Mr van der Westhuizen was involved in a lot more than we will ever know about and that, when the political winds changed, he was left exposed. Whenever a new regime comes into power, there is usually a certain amount of tidying up, shall we say? Well done anyway, Denzel. This episode has served you well, so do not be glum. I can imagine how proud your mother is of you."

Denzel raised a smile.

"She's been making a bit of a fuss!"

Seeing that Camilleri was wrapping up the meeting, George had one more question to put.

"What about the Austrian side of things? May I ask what happened there?"

"Oh, yes. I passed it over to the Austrian Federal Police and they raided the castle. Made some big drugs-related arrests. They have formally expressed their thanks to Malta for the information. Apparently, the count or baron or whoever he is, was operating a substantial distribution operation, all over Europe – in fancy wine bottles. Ingenious really."

George was suspicious.

"So, that's it?"

"Yes. What more do you want? We have run out of medals to give you. But, George, I need a quiet word. Denzel, give us a moment, will you?"

Denzel left the room. George was not expecting what came next, as Camilleri resumed his usual position by the window.

In a low voice, he began, "How dare you undermine me, keep

me in the dark, disrespect me, make a fool out of me... and in front of foreigners! Such disloyalty is something I will never forget."

Camilleri turned his head to glower at George. There was white spittle in the corners of his mouth.

"Ah! So you know now?"

"It was humiliating that I was literally the last person to be informed. But, yes, finally I know."

"I'm sorry but I had no choice. Mike Lloyd made me sign this document and I promised..."

"Do you work for Lloyd? For the American government? Or do you work for me?"

"I work for you."

"Yes, you do. Anyway, I would have liked to think you trusted me enough to let me know what the hell was going on. I have been worried, confused. But, George, though it pains me to say this: well done! You have been a credit to the *Pulizija*. Mike Lloyd said I should be proud of you, though the delicate circumstances mean your actions cannot be publicly acknowledged and, of course, I will not be able to recommend your promotion back to superintendent. So, you'll have to make do with my thanks, for what those are worth to you. Now leave, before I decide to fire you!"

George and Denzel left the station and the afternoon heat hit them like a brick. Denzel was quiet and George knew from experience there were things on his mind.

"It's nearly winter and yet it still feels like summer. Anyway, is there more to this than he's letting on?"

"Oh, definitely! But I'm not sure we'll ever get to know about it."

"Do me a favour, Dad. Can we go down to the Lion Bar on the way home and tell Moussa what's happened? He'd like to know he was right and that things have sorted themselves out?"

George looked at his watch.

"OK, it is about the time he makes an appearance there."

They drove down to the Grand Harbour and parked a little way along. As before, they walked down the middle of the deserted road leading to the bar, like a pair of gunfighters, giving the locals notice of their arrival. Moussa was sitting alone, a phone in front of him. He spotted the two policemen and stood up expectantly. They briefly touched hands, in the Malian way, and Moussa finished the greeting, putting his hand to his head and then his breast.

Denzel filled him in on what had happened and Moussa nodded along, his face showing neither happiness nor disappointment, just acceptance of the facts.

"So, one less boat now, out in the rescue zone. One bad man is dead, but more innocent people will die. Maybe I should have said nothing."

Denzel was disappointed.

"But think of those you have saved; those who would have died because of heroin addiction or a life on the street. You did the right thing."

"Those who die from drugs can choose, or in Europe, there is the medicine. Those in the sea are trying to save starving children or them escaping death from militias. They have no choice. No, we need more ships like the *Samaritan*, not one less."

"Listen, Moussa," said George. "I know this is bad news for you. But there might be an answer. What I'll do is see if we can get the court to sequestrate the ship, as property obtained using drugs proceeds. The court could choose to donate it to a charity. If that charity can raise the money to fund the running of the operation, then maybe we can get the *Samaritan* back out there. What do you think?"

"It costs a lot of money."

"*Mela*, we can try anyway, no? It'll take time though."

At that moment Denzel's radio crackled and he heard a request from HQ for anyone near the western end of the Grand Harbour to check in. He duly responded to the call. There was a report of two bodies floating near to Victoria Quay, only a few hundred yards away from the Lion Bar.

George had heard the message and nodded to Denzel to accept the callout.

He clapped Moussa on the shoulder and said: "We'll try to sort something, I promise. I have some ideas. Remember, I've been on a boat from Libya and came pretty close to being lost in the water myself. I know what you're saying."

With a dismissive wave, Moussa watched them leave, certain it was all talk. He vowed next time to keep his mouth shut and never voluntarily tell the *Pulizija* anything.

They drove the short distance to the junction with the road that ran around the north side of the Grand Harbour. The bodies had been found floating next to a little-used quay, adjacent to where the high-speed catamaran for Sicily docked. The high paling gates were open and a motorbike patrol officer waved them through.

The sun had fallen behind the high ground to the west of the harbour and an autumnal coolness had finally settled over Valletta, dispersing the unseasonal heat. George and Denzel walked across the concrete sections of the quay, where a small crowd stood chatting and looking down into the calm, blue-green water. Mainly workmen from the nearby warehouses, they fell back when they saw Denzel's uniform. George could not help remembering the last time he had been called to investigate a body found floating in the Grand Harbour.

That had led to his first meeting with Abdullah, his encounter with Abu Muhammad's ISIL militia and his perilous crossing of the Mediterranean in a people smuggler's inflatable boat. As he had told Moussa, he knew exactly what the maritime migrants experienced during those terrible voyages from Libya.

Denzel was squatting looking at the bodies. One was a white woman, young and slim with an almost boyish figure. She was lying face down, as do most fresh corpses in water. George had learned that a body gradually fills and stays beneath the surface, until the bacteria in the gut and chest cavity produce enough gas to float it up again, like a balloon. The weight of the arms and the legs initially causes it to lie face down, until the gasses build up. Then, the body will flip onto its back and lie there, with every appearance of staring at the sky it can no longer see.

The woman was wearing a printed blue dress, which floated around her above her waist, showing her pert backside and white bikini-style pants. Her hair was blonde and cut short. George guessed her height at around one hundred and sixty centimetres.

He turned to study the man, who was only two metres from the woman, and his heart skipped a beat. He knew instantly who this was. The pale, slim fit chinos, the thin torso in a light blue shirt with the sleeves rolled tight above the elbow... and to put the identity beyond any doubt, the floppy mass of blond hair that fanned out around the skull, like a crown of straw.

George turned around and stared into the middle distance. The crowd facing him sensed something had happened and reacted to his distress, exchanging glances and muttering to one another.

Denzel approached him and laid a hand on his arm.

"Dad? What's wrong? Do you know them?"

George swallowed hard to dispel the shock that had locked his throat solid. It was not grief, of course. In fact, the dead man meant nothing much to George, but the sight of him lying there in the water awoke memories of the time they had spent together. They had not been friends, but for a brief while they had been allies, trusting one another in adverse circumstances, and they had prevailed. He turned and made eye contact with his son.

"Yes, I do. Or, correctly speaking, I know the man. Ring the maritime police and get them over. We'll need a diver with a net to retrieve the corpses. We also need them to search for a possible weapon."

"Who is it?"

George sighed.

"One of the men I met doing the crossing – he's an Englishman, who works in the gaming industry. He's called Nick Walker. You'd better also ring the assistant commissioner. Camilleri will want to be informed before anyone else."

GERALD CAMILLERI HAD DECIDED he could keep quiet no longer and arranged to call on Natasha. He needed to confront her with the knowledge he had about the missile and the stark truth of Luke's murder in Turkey. He also wanted to inform her officially of the discovery of the bodies of Nick Walker and Cristina Cassar, which he suspected would be less of a surprise.

She had listened in silence, eyes down, picking at the skin on her cuticles. She was not wearing makeup and her hair was gathered back and tied on top of her head. Her black velour leisure suit completed a very informal look, but Camilleri did not judge, he was here to lay things out

He could tell she was shocked by the news of Luke van der Westhuizen's death. Her head had jolted, when he informed her and there had been a pause, while they sat in silence for almost a minute, as she gathered her emotions.

When they moved onto the deaths of Nick and Cristina, her expression changed. Any trace of pain or sadness drained out of it. She sat looking at him, face distant, almost daring him to make an accusation. Camilleri told her the details and they lapsed into another period of silence. Seeing he would not proceed without a response from her, she said, "That is unfortunate. There was a time I was very fond of Nick. But now I find myself strangely indifferent. As to his – friend, I never met her."

Camilleri noted her hard, defensive stare and sighed.

"The third thing I need to do is clear the air about you having any possible involvement with a stolen US missile."

She clapped her hands together and a grin spread across her face.

"You worked it out! You're so clever, Gerald!"

"Clever or not, I am only as effective as the information I receive, and what I have received from you has not helped me in the slightest. I need to know what your interest in this matter is, the Family's interest, otherwise there is a very real possibility I could become the instrument of your undoing, which would be, to echo your word – unfortunate."

She looked at him. He had become like an old uncle to her and she had started to take him for granted. She realised she had underestimated him and it would be negligence on her part if all that had been achieved were to be lost because she had misplayed the assistant commissioner.

Camilleri broke into her thoughts.

"For example," he said, "it was George Zammit who worked out how Luke van der Westhuizen was moving drugs and that led to the raid on the schloss in Austria. Van der Westhuizen ran the *Samaritan*; you were in a relationship with him. You had me going through that elaborate charade, getting messages to Mike Lloyd, when all the time there was something I was missing.

"So, I told Mike Lloyd about the *Samaritan* and Luke, and it all came spilling out. The theft of their missile. My own officer's covert involvement in the search. I had no idea Zammit was up to his neck in a Libyan operation to recover this bomb. No idea, either, that the schloss was owned by a Family member.

"Had I been fully in your confidence, as I would have been in your father's, the raid could have been avoided. So, you see, I have every reason to feel frustrated about being excluded. And, naturally, I am mildly interested as to whether this abomination of a weapon is on our island?"

Natasha graciously capitulated and asked him to tell her everything he knew about Mike Lloyd's and Hakan Toprak's involvement. From what he said, she gathered he knew a lot more than she had intended him to. She then took a deep breath and filled him in on the details of the Family's plan and Toprak's involvement in it.

She finished her explanation by saying: "It's just business, Gerald. I'm leaving all the politics to Hakan and Mike Lloyd. So far, it's working out OK. Be assured, this missile is not in Malta, it has never been in Malta and it never will be in Malta. I hate them. Filthy things!"

Camilleri listened to her, his mouth downturned, as if he was hearing something distasteful. Once, she had finished, she sat back and folded her arms. The pair of them took a moment to weigh up where their relationship now stood. Camilleri was certain things would be different from now on. He did not trust her, he did not like her and he certainly didn't respect her. Natasha had the cold, self-serving instincts of a cat and she sensed everything he felt. He pushed back his chair to leave, saying: "Well, well! I have heard some stories in my time, but never anything quite like that."

A FEW DAYS after his show-down with Natasha, Camilleri found a message on his desk, asking him to arrange a visit to Castello Bonnici, together with Inspector Zammit.

George and he were in the back of a police BMW, being driven to the castello for their meeting with Natasha. On getting into the car, George had asked the assistant commissioner the purpose of the visit, but Camilleri merely shrugged his shoulders and said: "We'll know soon enough. She asked to see us."

"And we jump up and run to her?"

Camilleri fixed George with watery pale blue eyes and said calmly:" Yes, that is how it usually works."

The assistant commissioner looked tired. The lines on his face had become deeper lately and George couldn't decide whether this was due to increasing age or the weariness brought on by years of playing one side against the other. He was no longer a young man and, for the first time HQ gossip had it that the 'R' word had been mentioned. George had no love for the man, but wondered who else could possibly hold the island together in the way that Camilleri did.

A small Eastern European, with a head as smooth as an egg, ushered them onto the rear terrace where Natasha sat, a heavy woollen shawl draped around her shoulders. The searing heat of summer had faded to cooler, damper weather. The freshly tilled earth from the terraces below the castello gave off a rich, musty, vegetal scent, very different from the citrus summer bouquet. George noticed Natasha was starting to develop thin lines around the corners of her eyes and her jawline was not quite as firm as it once had been. She had lost none of her beauty, but, he realised, even Natasha Bonnici could not stall the advance of time for ever.

She rose to greet them, folding the shawl over the back of her chair. Despite himself, George could not but help break into a smile of pleasure as she grazed his cheeks with hers, her faint musky scent flooding his senses. Who would not smile when they had been graced with a kiss from the Lady Mantis herself? They sat and Camilleri spoke for them both, refusing refreshments.

Natasha's face became serious, as she addressed the business of their meeting. She looked at George, but spoke to his superior.

"How much does he know?"

"I told you last time. Almost all of it."

She kept her eyes on George.

"Can he be trusted?"

"He has behaved impeccably so far. So discreetly, in fact, he did not even think it necessary to confide in me."

George looked suspiciously at them both and said, "Are we talking about what I think we are?"

"Of course, George," his superior confirmed.

George realised both Camilleri and Natasha were scrutinising him. He immediately became edgy, his glance flickering between them. It was hard for him to decide which he distrusted the most.

"Relax, George." Natasha Bonnici eyed him coldly. She was making a decision.

"You and I have been through a lot in the past few years. I don't care what you think of me but, in a strange way I think I do trust you." She paused, before taking the final step on the road to full disclosure. "George, I'd like you to go to Libya for me and visit your friend Abdullah. You two need to finish a job for us – making the B61 missile safe. But this time, you work for me and the assistant commissioner, not Mike Lloyd. He must never, ever know what we've done. Ever! You and the Arab ... well, you are a good team."

"He's a Berber."

"Sorry? A Berber, is he? Whatever. You work well together; you know how to get things done."

"Mela! *You've* got the missile. Why?"

She smiled and crossed her legs, making herself comfortable in her chair.

"To make MalTech Energy the most powerful energy company in Europe, of course. But don't get me wrong, I don't want to use the damn' bomb. I and the regime in Ankara want a few select people, most of them Americans, to *think* Turkey has it. I want access to Turkish oil and gas and their pipelines, and Ankara wants the US to be their bosom pals, making them the number one playmaker in the eastern Med and Middle East."

"So Hakan Toprak has it?"

"Ah, the Hawk! That's what they call him, you know? But no. He's too obvious a suspect. The Americans are all over him. The missile is far too dangerous to be left lying around in Turkish hands. The Americans have mounted an undercover search. If it were in Turkey, they'd find it. The world today is a dangerous place and there're all sorts of people who couldn't be trusted with it. God knows, you've met some of them!"

George looked at Camilleri, hoping he would appreciate the irony of the statement.

"That's why you have to go to Libya and meet your friend. To make sure he does what I've asked."

"So that's where the bomb is, in Libya?"

"Yes, it never left there. A day or so after the *Samaritan* sailed and all those soldiers returned to barracks, a small fishing vessel opened its hold in Benghazi. A long thin box was buried there in half a tonne of ice and a selection of fresh fish. No drama, no fuss. It was unloaded in Marsabar, at our oil and gas terminal, by Abdullah Belkacem, who has been hiding it for me ever since. He's terrified of it. You'll have to tell him, by the way, he owes me for the fish. I know he sold them."

George paused to absorb what Natasha was saying.

"So, the weapon is with Abdullah?"

"Yes. Has been for weeks. It was a risk, but it was safer than bringing it to Europe."

"And it arrived in Marsabar at the same time as we got back from Benghazi?"

"I suppose so, more or less."

George was disturbed that Abdullah had said nothing to him. He remembered how many times he had risked his neck on Abdullah's behalf; how many times Abdullah had emotionally blackmailed him. The trip to Gavdos, the visit to hellish Duésa and then the crazy gaol-break. When they went through the charade on the docks at Benghazi, hiding behind the generator from the Libyan security detail, he had known the crate was empty. He had kept George in danger from the il-Bibi brothers, hanging around Benghazi for a week. Abdullah had taken him for a fool, the whole time. It was not disappointment George felt; it was anger.

He said to Natasha: "What are you going to do with it anyway?"

"Abdullah Belkacem has been given clear instructions, which I'll copy to you when you fly out."

"What if I get there and he's got other plans for this missile? Or what if I refuse to go and want nothing more to do with this whole thing?"

"Well, first, if you find he's turned into Frodo, with the Ring, you tell me straight away. In that case, I'd probably tell a mullah in Qatar I know. Word would soon get back to some of the more radical militias in Libya. They'd take it from him." She played with a coffee spoon, twirling it between her thumb and first finger.

"Or, more likely, I'll tell the Americans that Abdullah Belkacem stole it and where they can find him. And if you get clever with me, George, Gerald has a direct line to Mike Lloyd and we could even suggest you were involved in that little trick that made their navy look so stupid. I've a few options. But let's not be negative. This is an easy give, George. Let's make the world a safer place, plus you'll have my thanks."

George's anger flared at the threats, brightly but briefly.

"I've seen your thanks. I was the one who pulled Nick Walker and his girlfriend out of the Grand Harbour. It wasn't pretty."

Camilleri instantly shot him down.

"George, how dare you! You have no evidence on which to base that accusation."

George fired back at him.

"It's true – sir! You know it, and I know it."

Natasha was quiet for a moment, studying the tabletop. Finally, she raised her head and her dark eyes looked deep into George's, cutting straight through his petty defiance.

"Well then, it seems we understand each other perfectly."

# CHAPTER 79

# GEORGE ZAMMIT
## NAFUSA HILL, LIBYA

TWO DAYS LATER, Abdullah was driving George through a narrow gorge, that snaked deep into the Nafusa Hills. They had left the tarmac and the Land Cruiser was bumping along the hard pack dirt road, a cloud of dust rising behind it. The hills rose from the coastal plain, to an escarpment seven hundred metres high, incised with steep narrow-sided valleys. Abdullah had been born and bred in one such steep-sided valley. When he married, he decided he could do better for his new family than scraping a living from the thin soil of the family farm and had headed to the city of Marsabar.

Abdullah knew the roads and tracks through the hills, as well as he knew the streets of his adoptive city. And, for information on any cracks or crevices he did not know, he could turn to Rania's brothers, who herded goats across the top of this rocky, bare escarpment.

They eventually left the hardpack and the SUV started slowly climbing a rough track through the yellow grasses and sparse scrub of the high ground. It appeared that the original, single track had been broadened and flattened in recent days. Shrubs had been squashed and lay prone in the dirt, while larger rocks were either scattered or crushed into small pieces. What had been an ancient track for man and goat, had been widened by the repeated passage of heavy, commercial vehicles.

After twenty minutes of cautious progress, they reached a small flat plateau, just big enough to accommodate two rusted, Isuzu five-tonne trucks, one of which had a small crane neatly folded behind the driver's cab. The trucks stood backed up to the rock face and a series of wooden battens formed a ramp from the first vehicle into a four-metre-high, zigzag fissure in the rock face.

As George had feared, they had been arguing ever since his arrival. He had told Abdullah how he felt and Abdullah's reaction was to go into a protracted sulk. As they sat in the car, neither of them moved to open a door. Abdullah had a face like thunder. Natasha had been smart to send George. Abdullah had got it into his head that he wanted to keep the weapon and had become reluctant to destroy it. Natasha had foreseen the problem. The power of the weapon had got under his skin.

"Mela, I do not believe you are doing this to me, George. You are my brother and now you tie one hand behind my back."

"Mela, this thing has corrupted you! It's turned your head! If you don't do as she says, I promise you, I'll call the Lady Mantis and she'll tell ISIL or the Americans, probably the Americans, what you're doing. This thing must be put beyond use! You know that!"

"It can be kept safe in this cave; Rania's brothers will never speak of it. I have their word."

"No! Why would you want to keep it, if not to try and use its power? To threaten people with it? No, it's got to be destroyed."

"If it were not you, and the debts I owe you, I would deal with you the old way and use it for good."

"Huh! So that's what you've been thinking, is it? How to get rid of me and still keep a clear conscience. And you call me your brother? These last months, I have seen what that means! Pah! What has happened to you?"

Abdullah looked at him, fury on his face. He struck the dashboard with the palm of his hand, causing a cloud of dust and cigarette ash to rise around them. He opened the door and jumped out, spitting noisily.

George heard him say, to no one in particular: "It is worse than arguing with Rania. And her father warned me, she is as stubborn as a mule!"

Sticking his head back into the vehicle, he shouted angrily at George: "Are you coming? There is work to be done if the Lady Mantis is to have her way."

Inside the fissure, the walls and roof opened out to form a cave, high enough for a man to stand and wide enough for them to walk, three abreast. The floor had been smoothed, with larger rocks broken and cast to one side, while hollows and cracks had been filled with pools of blue resin. Steel plates lay on the roughest sections. At the back of the cave was an old yellow cement mixer and a huge stack of cement bags. Next to it were several one thousand kilo bags of sand and aggregate. A motorised pallet truck stood idly by, while a hose snaked out to a series of two hundred litre drums, strapped upright in the back of one of the Isuzu trucks that provided a water supply.

A small oily generator rattled away in the fissure's entrance, powering the string of lights that ran the length of the cave. Twenty metres from the entrance, a tunnel branched off to the left. The floor of this spur was also lined with steel checker plate. At the end of the tunnel, attached to the ceiling with steel bolts, which had been drilled into the rock, was an electric winch. Its thick steel cable and heavy-duty carabiner dangling above a two-metre-wide black hole in the tunnel floor.

Abdullah led George into the cave.

"It has taken the three of us many weeks to prepare this place. The old well is dry and we have sealed the base with many tonnes of concrete. Now we bring in the demon missile. It weighs four hundred kilos, but the floor is smooth enough to push it on the trolley. We must be careful – it would not do to drop it!"

George heard the engine of the Isuzu start up and power the

hydraulics to unfold the crane. Rania's brothers pulled back a tarpaulin from the bed of the second Isuzu. They attached the four-metre-long box, with the yellow triangular warning logos and the USAF markings, to a series of slings. George and Abdullah took the folded stainless-steel trolley from the other truck and set it up at the mouth of the cave.

George grabbed Abdullah by the arm.

"Open it."

He stared at George, his facial muscles tense.

"What for? You do not trust me, eh?"

"I want to see it – with these eyes." He raised two fingers in a mockery of Abdullah's favourite gesture, pointing to his own eyes.

George's first sight of the B61 came as an anti-climax. The long thin, grey metal tube had a short black nose-cone and a red band painted around its centre. The tail fins were also painted red, but otherwise it was unremarkable. They all peered inside the crate in silence. It was impossible to get any sense of the awesome power of this weapon from the nondescript item that confronted them.

Finally, George shrugged and said: "OK, that's it. Box it up and let's get rid of it."

After forty minutes of heaving and pushing, the four hundred kilo box was suspended vertically over the mouth of the well. The webbing slings around the base of the crate were bound tightly with nylon strapping to prevent slippage. Abdullah held the winch control in two hands and slowly lowered the missile, down into the pitch darkness of the shaft.

Not taking his eyes off the winch above him, he said: "It is eighty metres to the bottom. I know, because I have been down there. It is dry and cool."

George shuddered at the thought. The box reached the bottom, with a soft thud that echoed up the shaft. Abdullah watched as the line went slack, then he let what remained on the drum, spool off and follow the crate down into the well.

He turned to George.

"There! Tell the Lady Mantis millions of dollars have been buried under the Nafusa Hills. Now, the hard work begins!"

They toiled for the remainder of the day, making load after load of concrete, tipping it from the mixer into the well. No sooner had one batch disappeared than they set to with shovels, loading more cement, sand and aggregate into the mixer. After many hours, Abdullah lowered a length of marked rope into the shaft, to measure their progress. He proudly announced they were a quarter of the way up the shaft. George fell to his haunches, his back aching and his naked torso running with sweat.

"Do not worry, George, we will only fill the well halffull. So, the same again, come on. You can tell our Lady Mantis how we sweated for her!"

All afternoon, the trucks ran back and forth. They left empty and returned filled with bags of material to make concrete. Their tired arms shovelled and shovelled, as the well gulped down barrowload after barrowload of wet concrete. The diesel fumes from the mixer made their heads ache. George's hands blistered through his heavy canvas gloves. They stripped to their underwear, as sweat drenched their clothing. Finally, Abdullah lowered his rope and declared himself happy that the B61 was totally and irrevocably encased in its safe concrete grave.

To finish the job, they tipped several tonnes of aggregate on top of the concrete, giving the impression to anybody investigating the well, that the shaft naturally bottomed out onto a bed of shale and loose rock. Finally, satisfied with their work, they hurried out of the cave and George watched, resting, as Abdullah moved the trucks to the edge of the flat area, away from the entrance.

The brothers brought out the mixer and several boxes of tools and slung them into the trucks. George went back into the cave and removed the bulbs and shades from the lighting cable and yanked the wires from the clips in the cave roof.

Abdullah said: "There must not be any sign of the work that has been done here."

When there was nothing left to bear witness to their labours, Rania's elder brother exited the cave, unfurling a wire behind him, which he attached to a small metal box. George realised they were going to blow the cave, sealing the mouth of the well for ever. He saw the sense in destroying the entrance and encasing the missile under even more tonnes of rock, but he was concerned.

"It won't set off the bomb, will it?"

Abdullah took the detonator from Rania's brother and turned to George, taking the cigarette from between his lips. He smiled and said: "Do not worry, my friend, there are no sad endings for those who trust in Allah!"

Screwing his eyes shut, he pressed the detonator.

HAKAN TOPRAK WAS SITTING under a yellow branded umbrella, in the fashionable village of Bebek, on the European bank of the Bosphorus, midway between Istanbul and the mouth of the Black Sea. The waterway in front of him was busy with all manner of vessels, from small weekend pleasure boats to the commercial shipping that constantly made its way up and down the narrow channel. He sipped from a cup of thick, powdery Turkish coffee, foam clinging to his moustache. It was late in the year and the cold continental winds that ripped south from the Arctic had started to funnel their way down the Bosphorus passage.

He raised the fur collar of his coat and pulled his scarf a little tighter around his throat. Hakan looked at his watch and counted down the seconds until the appointed time, when he knew his phone would ring. Exactly on 2 p.m. Eastern European Time, which was about 7 a.m. in Washington, it rang.

"Mike, prompt as always. Thank you for the action this morning, good work!"

The Straits of Hormoz was a narrow maritime pinch-point in the Persian Gulf, which ran north of Dubai and south of the tip of Iran. All traffic from Iraq, the Gulf states, the big Saudi ports such as Al Jubail, had to pass through this ninety-kilometre-wide stretch of water to reach the Indian Ocean or the Suez Canal.

The Iranians constantly made a nuisance of themselves, with gunboats hassling the massive tankers and the occasional drone attack on ships operated by 'hostile' governments. Hakan had asked the Americans to put an end to the low-level harassment. The Americans had obliged, using their Reaper drones to blow a small Iranian RHIB, armed with rocket launchers, out of the water, also downing two Iranian Shahed drones. The Iranians had got the message and Tehran had remained strangely quiet about the morning's setback.

"Yeah, Hakan. Pleasure, as always, to be your bullyboy. You give us a free pass to do what we like around here these days, it's great! But now it's payback time. Have you got the envelope?"

Hakan had the envelope, which had been dropped on his metal table, moments previously, by a well-dressed woman in a long navy-blue woollen coat and matching hijab. She had glided past him, walking a small, fluffy white dog.

"Listen, Mike, you cannot push this thing too far, otherwise we'll kill the goose. Is that not what you say?"

"Kill the goose that lays the golden egg, you mean. But you can't sit there and enjoy one-way traffic. That's not how it works."

Hakan was frustrated.

"We've apologised for the Armenian genocide, agreed to take another million Syrian refugees and compromised on an autonomous Kurdish area. What more do you want?"

"We want the Russian navy bottled up in the Black Sea. That's what we really want. That's the big boys' game. You gonna play?"

The envelope contained a copy of the 1936 Montreux Convention, which guaranteed the free passage of civilian vessels and Russian naval ships up and down the Bosphorus. It had been a thorn in the side of Turkey's sovereignty for years, but the Turks had reluctantly accepted there was no getting around it.

Hakan grimaced as he surveyed the waterway in front of him. It was thirty kilometres long, between one and three kilometres wide and thirty metres deep, in its central channel. Its size, congestion, strong winds and eddies made it a nightmare to navigate.

Mike Lloyd spoke bluntly. With the Americans everything was about money.

"We'll give you the money for the new Kanal Istanbul."

Hakan sat very still. He could see exactly what the Americans were thinking. Since the time of the Ottoman sultans, there had been dreams of building a twenty-kilometre canal between the sea of Marmara and the Black Sea, to the west of Istanbul, near to Istanbul airport. Such a canal would run parallel to the Bosphorus, some thirty kilometres to the west. This would enable shipping to avoid the treacherous Bosphorus Straits, and it would free Turkey from the constraints of the convention.

"So, you give us the fifteen billion dollars; we build the new canal and, not being bound by the treaty and being a peace-loving nation, we restrict access to Soviet naval traffic. We then do something to restrict traffic in the Bosphorus. We stop dredging, or we build a low bridge, or God forbid, there is a collision, which blocks access. Am I close?"

"Hakan, you're way ahead of me, but it all sounds great, yeah?"

Hakan shook his head.

"You are pushing us into a war with Russia, do you not see that? What with Crimea, Georgia and now the Ukraine, all they need is the smallest excuse to expand their influence by force.

"Well, you've got to break a few eggs to make an omelette! You're NATO members – entitled to the full service of the Seventh Calvary!"

"No, this is not on. I will not back it. It is too provocative."

"Hey, hey! So, being provocative is OK when it suits you? Getting the Israelis to do your dirty work, having us take out Iranian assets, stealing the Greeks' oil and gas. You guys gotta to grow up! You don't get it all your own way. You want to be in the Super League, you got to stand up and be counted! "

There was a pause on the phone. Mike's tone changed. There was menace in it.

"This is how it's going to be. Understand? Don't wave the B61 at me either, 'cos you know what? I think you're bluffing about it and I'm calling you out.

"We've been watching you, the Bonnici woman and half of the Austrian nobility. You've not put a foot wrong. Well done! But this nuke is somewhere and I think you've put it beyond use. I don't think it ever made it out of Libya!

Hakan swallowed hard. He hoped the sound had not been picked up by the phone.

"Really, Mike? Your evidence for this is?"

"The fact that I can't produce evidence, is evidence enough. We've been all over marine-traffic reports and know the missile went to Benghazi. From there the trail goes cold. Those fake leads: the *Samaritan*, the winery tunnels in Rust. All bullshit bluffs. Pissing us around.

"But you know what? When you analyse satellite feeds, real-time vessel-tracking sites, electronic harbour authority records, it's amazing what you find. There was one boat that left Benghazi soon after the circus that made asses out of us. One boat! It pops up, from nowhere, then turns around in a matter of an hour, or so, and goes – where do you think it goes?"

"I've no idea."

"It goes to Marsabar, but not the port or the marina. Oh, no! It goes to the MalTech oil and gas terminal. Why did it go there? Nobody knows! Nobody has any record of it being there. But we have satellite photos. Strange, don't ya think?"

Hakan was feeling distinctly uncomfortable. He replied in his most controlled, flat tone.

"As you say, you have no proof, but I grant you it is very interesting."

"You know Abdullah Belkacem, don't you?"

"Yes, of course."

"And you know his links to Natasha Bonnici of MalTech Energy, the beneficiary of our recent strategic assistance? You know she owns the gas terminal at Marsabar, don't you?"

Hakan remained silent, so Mike continued.

"There's a groundswell of opinion in Langley that this nuke, our nuke, is somewhere in western Libya. Now, that's a dangerous place, right? Even Natasha Bonnici knows that. So, right-thinking people, like that bitch and you, won't have left this thing lying around for some Islamic State militia to get their hands on. None of us would want that, would we? Neither would we want it in the hands of Abdullah Belkacem. Well, not for long. He's a man with a volatile temperament, in a country surrounded by people who could easily make him lose it."

"Where are we going with this, Mike?"

"Hold your horses, Hakan, I ain't finished yet. Which brings me to a 'big bang' in the Nafusa Hills. We picked up this small, seismic disturbance from an Italian lab in Tunisia, and located the site, roughly of course. Middle of fucking nowhere! Would you believe it? No quarries or towns nearby. It was an explosion on an open hillside, ten miles from the nearest village, and guess what? That's the village Abdullah Belkacem calls home.

"So, we think this nuke is at the bottom of some cave in the Nafusa Hills and has been buried under tonnes of shit. Which is a good outcome, as far as we're concerned. Maybe not so good for the locals, who'll be drinking radioactive water for the next two hundred years, once the thing starts leaking, but hey ho!"

Hakan sat very still and said nothing. He even slowed his breathing, in case Mike Lloyd should pick up on any change to its rhythm. But Mike had more to say:

"You and Natasha Bonnici can get rich stealing the Greeks' gas and oil, I don't give a rat's ass about that, but you'll dig that canal! Got it?

"You've heard of 'state capture'? It's what the Mafia did to Sicily and Southern Italy in the nineteen seventies and eighties.

That's what you've done. You, the Generals and the Bonnici woman. You're criminals, nothing more, nothing less. I know you, Hakan Toprak.

"But here's something else. We'll play along with you for a bit. You know why? Because the old assholes on the Hill are crapping themselves and we've got them where we want them. The boys in Langley and the Pentagon have free rein to strike at all the bad guys in the eastern Med, and they're loving it. So, get ready, we're going to make you the biggest bogeyman since Fidel!"

Mike Lloyd gave a full-throated guttural laugh.

"Yeah, you sure made us all laugh. Thinking you could pull one over on us! But, remember, any time we like, we can tell your Generals what a double-dealing piece of shit you are. I bet they still think they're the proud owner of a nice big bomb, don't they? So, play ball and get us what we want."

Hakan Toprak sensed the line go dead. He relaxed back in his chair, in contemplative mood. He looked down the Bosphorus, his bottom lip tugging at the thick hair of his bristly moustache. He tried not to be shaken by what he had heard. He'd had just had a going over. But so what? He was alive, the game was still on and all the American had achieved was to vent some personal anger. The man was always angry about something or another. It was always going to be a game of bluff and counter bluff.

Hakan's back was to the West; that was fine. He was happy that he was now part of the Family in Milan, and certain no harm would come to him from that direction. Ahead of him, looking towards the Asian side, he thought of the opportunities to be had in chaos. Oil, war, strife in the Middle East, and, beyond that, the wide-open countries of Central Asia, across the Caspian Sea: Turkmenistan, Kazakhstan, Uzbekistan. All rich in oil and gas and all looking to Turkey to pipe those riches to the west. Yes, he was happy with the view east.

To the north it was different. His eyes narrowed, as he cast his gaze up the channel where, after a few short kilometres, the

Bosphorus opened out into the Black Sea. The biting Russian wind was chilling his bones and it was only October. If the Americans were really going to make a play in the Great Game and prod the bear, who was he to stop them?

Creating the Kanal Istanbul would mean new tariffs, bigger tankers, more leverage over the Russians. Yes, he should not close his mind to the prospect.

He had to keep the Generals happy, but he imagined their hooded eyes behind their favoured thick, black-framed spectacles, always suspicious, always calculating. He was due to meet them in a few days and smiled, as he imagined the looks on their puffy faces, with their heavy jowls folded over stiff military collars, when he told them he had extracted fifteen billion dollars from the US for their pet project.

Then, his gaze wandered south and he immediately felt more relaxed. The Blue Homeland had been established; it was a reality. Turkish rights extended across their continental shelf in the Aegean and southern Mediterranean. The Greeks were furious but, without American support they were impotent. The Americans had signed a mutual defence and assistance treaty with Turkey, effectively throwing a protective shield around its newfound friend in the east. It was working well in the south.

From his place at the crossroads of Europe and Asia, all looked well to the Hawk. The prey was plentiful and there was enough to last for many years. He hunted alone, which was how he liked it, but now he had to think of the Family also. Once you joined, you could never leave. That had been said to him. Everyone needs Family. He would wait and see if that was true.

# CHAPTER 81
# DANKA AND SAVI
## MALASAÑA, MADRID

THE FAÇADE of the Bar Dos Tiempos was an explosion of yellow and blue ceramics, with a mosaic image depicting a classical Bacchanalian scene of drunkenness and debauchery. The café was off the Plaza del Dos de Mayo, in the edgy, bohemian Malasaña district of Madrid.

It opened early and closed late. The breakfast crowd took its coffee very seriously and lingered at the tables, until they were replaced by students from the nearby university, together with 'in-the-know' travellers. In the evenings, the clientele of the bar was young and loud, with a love of strong sangria, hard cider and craft beer. All this made the two-bedroomed apartment above the bar noisy, but very cheap.

Danka worked in the bar, serving drinks, cleaning tables and sweeping kilos of olive pits and napkins from the floor. Savi told her it was totally 'not cool', he had money, lots of it, but she said it was good for their cover and she needed something to get up for. Danka's bar job gave them the option to rent the apartment, access to which was through the small and chaotic kitchen. During opening hours, this gave Danka an added sense of security.

Their departure from Malta had been surreal. Neither of them could quite believe they had left Simon lying in a pool of blood on the castello's drive. Savi's first hysterical reaction was to call the *Pulizija*, but Danka knew enough about Natasha Bonnici to quash that idea. Instead, they drove to Danka's apartment, where they had grabbed passports, a bag of Danka's clothes and, most importantly, Savi's laptop, together with a number of hard drives, including his 'cold wallet' with his holdings of crypto currency.

The first flight out of Malta was to Catania, Sicily. From there, they leap-frogged their way, across Europe, to Madrid. Some things were just too important and, for Savi, the chance to line up with SnakeByte, at Madrid Games Week, was one of them. As it turned out, it had never entered Natasha's head to have them followed out to Madrid and the team never made the final. But Savi could live with that, he had not let the boys down. He knew it would be the last time they would play together.

They had rented two rooms in a hostel for the first three weeks, where Danka felt the effects of shock kick in. For several days she said little, locking herself away, fuzzy-headed and heartbroken. Then, her grief was punctuated by bursts of anger. Her moods swung between the two, screaming, then crying, crying then screaming. Savi spent most of the time in his small bedroom, with the curtains closed, his noise-cancelling earphones on his head and his fingers brushing the keys of his laptop. He had no idea how to respond to Danka's distress and so he kept out of her way.

Savi's sense of loss ran just as deep, but he lacked the means to express it. Over the days that followed their arrival in Madrid, he felt cheated and angry that Simon had been taken from him. Only later did he accept that he was indirectly to blame for his protector's death. He vowed, then, he would step up and act like a man. He would make it up to Simon by taking care of Danka. He had lost the man who had befriended him; the thought of losing her as well, made Savi very edgy.

A fortnight after their arrival in Madrid, Danka caught

Savi by the wrist, as their paths crossed in the corridor between their rooms. She was pale, eyes puffy and blonde hair plastered to her head. She put her arm around him and took him into her room, sitting him down on her unmade bed.

"They've found Simon's body. He was tangled up in a fish farm net off St Paul's. I don't want to think about it, it's too horrible. There's a WhatsApp group of Poles in Malta and someone left a message about the funeral. It was yesterday. They buried him in Addolorata." Addolorata was Malta's enormous neo-gothic cemetery that boasted elaborate family chapels and funeral monuments. "He'd have been disappointed. He'd have wanted to be buried back home."

Savi looked at his feet.

"We should have been there."

"Yeah, I know. But we couldn't. He would have understood. He wanted us to be safe. And we are – for now. Anyway, he's where he belongs, now.

"So, listen, I'm back. I'm not hysterical anymore. I'm all cried out. But I'm not going to get over this for a long time, you know? So, the plan is that I'll look for a job, bar job or anything, I've got a little bit of Spanish, so that should be OK. We'll stick together, rent a flat, change our look and settle here for a while. It's as good as anywhere. Agreed?"

Savi was relieved. A plan! That was good. Somebody was doing something. He sucked his bottom lip, as if considering things carefully, and nodded his head.

"Yeah, sounds cool. That works for me."

"So, how you doing? What've you been up to while I've been crying the weeks away?"

"Yeah, it's interesting. I felt pretty down, you know?"

"Yeah, I know. I'm sorry, I haven't helped. I'm so…destroyed."

"But, like, it's all my fault. If I hadn't been so fucking stupid about Natasha and all that, none of this would have happened.

You wouldn't have had to come get me out. Simon would still be here. I feel shit about it."

Savi's eyes filled up. Danka squeezed him tight.

"Leave it, Savi. 'If only, if only, if only' – don't. It'll drive you crazy! That's where I've been, right? If only we'd left when Simon told us to, yeah? But we'll get over it, together. No blame, no recriminations. That's no good."

"Yeah. I'll try. But I've been doing some stuff too. Listen to this. I've bought a package of malware from some really creepy Koreans. This stuff is super-wicked. Not, like, wicked good. I mean, wicked, really nasty."

"Yeah?"

"It's expensive, but next level. It's so fuckin' clever. And we're going to fuck up Maltech Energy so bad! There will be no way back from it. No ransom, no contact, we're going to drop a digital bomb that will frazzle and fuck up everything, all of their IT, straight down the toilet. It'll ruin that bitch!"

Danka frowned and grabbed his wrist.

"Wait a minute. Hang on. Let's not do anything now, while we're angry and screwed up. Leave it for a month or so and see how we feel then. We don't want to make a big mistake here. Let's get our heads right first. Yeah? I haven't got the energy for this, you know? I'm exhausted, I can't think straight right now."

So, they left it. Danka washed dishes and Savi started hanging around the Universidad, toying with the idea of starting a course or something. He took Spanish lessons, twice a week, from a young good-looking female undergraduate, called Mia, he met in the bar and on whom he had developed a serious crush. In the kitchen, Danka learned Spanish dialect, slang, and how to curse in Castilian, Catalan, Galician and Basque. In return she taught the kitchen porters the language of the Polish gutter.

One Sunday morning, after several months of living in Malasaña, Danka was sitting on the sofa, legs curled beneath her. Her hair was now over her collar and framed her face, softening her features. No longer spending her days in her kettle bell studio had reduced the pronounced musculature of which she had once been so proud. But the set of her jaw, her stocky build and the heavy tattoos that covered her arms and shoulders, signalled she was still a woman to be reckoned with. She had to remain strong, physically and mentally; she knew she could never again take their safety for granted.

The memory of Simon's murder and the constant state of low-level anxiety about their security, kept her mentally attuned to the arrival of new faces in the bar, unfamiliar sounds during the night and unexpected encounters on the street. If Savi had similar concerns, he was very good at not showing them.

When winter arrived, they realised it was warmer outside the flat than inside. Other than what seeped up from the kitchen below, there was no source of heat and the electric fire they found in a cupboard was ineffective. So, later that Sunday, after a miserable lunch scavenged from the kitchens, sitting in their newly bought winter coats, they had decided to go for a walk to the park.

On Sundays Danka's shift did not start until the evening so, in the early days after their arrival, they joined all the other Madrileños, doing circuits around El Retiro Park, or walking the Golden Mile in Salamanca, pressing their noses against the high-end boutique windows and grabbing tapas at the Platea food hall. As they became more familiar with the city, they gradually ceased exploring its outer districts and often went to the nearby Parque del Oeste. This space was one of their favourites, a spacious tract of grassy knolls, winding tracks and small wooded copses.

It was cold and a strong north-easterly wind blew down the paths, stirring the leaves and making Savi and Danka pull on their matching woollen beanie hats. They had found some shelter on a seat near the monument to Simon Bolivar, where Savi huddled, trying to roll a *porro*.

Danka had crossed her legs and thrown an arm around the back of the bench. She felt relaxed for the first time in months.

There was no reason, it was just something she had started to feel – good again. Confident. Now she was ready, there was something she had been waiting to say to Savi. This seemed like as good a time as any.

"You know that nasty program you said you had fixed up when we first arrived? The one I said not to use?"

"You mean the Korean malware package for MalTech?"

"Yeah. Do you think now might be a good time?"

"Sure. It can go any time. But I'm telling you, it's serious shit."

"How bad?"

"Hard to describe. They compare it to a digital electromagnetic pulse, a flash of electronic lightning. It rips through the systems and the network, and fries anything connected. I mean, it's not an EMP, 'cos that's a high-energy nuclear thing. But this is a quantum-based, lightning-fast virus that will instantly destroy all their security and corrupt all MalTech's financial and management information, all their operational stuff, their pipelines, shipping, drilling rigs, even the fire alarms and access programs. You name it, anything that's connected to the home servers, even backups, they're totally fucked. When I press 'Return', she won't even be able to get her car out of the garage!"

"No way! Really? Is it traceable?"

"The Koreans say not. I can't see how we would get any blowback. But, Natasha is going to know who did this. It's Natasha, right?"

Danka turned to face him and smiled.

"It wouldn't be any fun if she didn't. You still up for it?"

Savi thought for a moment.

"Yeah! We need payback for Simon."

"You feel good here? Safe? Because, if we do this, we'll have to keep looking over our shoulders for a long time and she'll try to hunt you down online. You'll have to dump your phone and go dark for a while and then be really careful, or you could lead her to us."

"Yeah, I suppose." He paused, to nibble at what was left of the nail on the first finger of his right hand. Danka had long-since stopped being disgusted by Savi's habits.

"Screw her," he said finally. "She's a cold-hearted bitch. I'm not scared of her. Well, I am a bit, but that's only sensible, right? She's got this coming!"

"Good, being scared of her *is* sensible. OK. Let's do it then, shall we?"

"Yeah! Let's! Really? Are you sure?"

# EPILOGUE

Two years ago, Amy Halliday had promised herself she would stop drinking. She had made the resolution at about the same time as Natasha Bonnici and her various companies had suspended the many SLAPP actions they had brought against Amy. The dozen or so court cases were in no way an attempt to secure justice for a wrong done, but a crude and effective measure designed to silence and harass an opponent. They forced her to spend money she did not have, defending baseless actions for criminal defamation, libel, as well as on suits to protect her professional reputation.

So, she was disappointed in herself when she opened a bottle of wine that evening. The sun was going down, but her sixteenth-floor apartment was on the east coast so she missed the glory of a sunset over an ocean horizon.

She sat outside, wrapped up against the strong north-easterly wind that swept the salty, damp air across the exposed terrace. Her laptop was open, on her knee, and for the tenth time she was reading the notes that Simon Michallik had given to Nick Walker. The stories were incredible: oil smuggling, money laundering on an epic scale, corporate skulduggery, murder, links to international terrorism, corruption of government officials and the *Pulizija*... and behind it all, a powerful ancient gang, club, guild – whatever they were – known as the Family.

She had shown her editor the document a few weeks earlier. He had read it in silence. When he had finished, he put his head in his hands for a moment. Finally, he looked up at her.

"And they are both dead? The author and the source who gave this to you?"

"Yes, and the source's girlfriend. All murdered in the last two months."

The editor shared the document with the paper's owners and their lawyers. The response was not good. They were categoric about refusing permission for the *Telegraph* to begin any investigation into the truth of the allegations made in the notes. In the past, the *Telegraph* had also been the target of Natasha's army of lawyers and did not want to become involved in another time-consuming, expensive legal tussle with one of the island's leading figures. Amy was distraught. People were dead, for God's sake! Nick had given her the document as insurance for his and Cristina's future safety. Now, they were both dead, and she was unable to make good on her promise.

What Amy did not know was that a junior member of staff at the *Telegraph*'s lawyers had overheard the shocked partners talking in a corridor about the contents of Simon's notes. This young lady had a ruthlessly ambitious side to her character and saw an opportunity to ingratiate herself with the island's leading corporation. She put a call through to one of MalTech Energy's in-house lawyers, for which she was rewarded, and soon the news that the notes were in play reached ears within the castello.

In desperation, Amy had turned to a group of London-based journalists, who specialised in collaborating in large-scale investigations of international importance. At first, they too felt that the fact the two individuals who could corroborate the allegations were dead, was a major obstacle to taking on the project. However, they had asked Amy to come to London, where she told them the story of Natasha Bonnici, her corporate entities and the Family, who squatted on Malta like a giant octopus.

They had then told her that, if she were prepared to leave her post at the *Malta Telegraph*, and take on the investigation fulltime, they had a fund that could indemnify her against the costs of any SLAPP-action legal fees. They could pay basic living expenses and give her the professional resources and assistance to conduct the investigation. An undertaking of this sort could easily take two to three years which, they said, was a long time to be looking over your shoulder. She had said she would think it over.

Just as she refilled her glass again, she heard the faint chimes of the doorbell. Visitors were not common in the evenings but sometimes the office called round to drop off a layout or an article that needed a second opinion, before the presses started to roll. So, she went to the door and fitted the security chain. Opening it a crack, she saw a short, bulky, middle-aged man, in a soiled blue jumper and baggy jeans. The strange thing was not that he did not immediately speak, but the strong smell of the sea that seemed to emanate from him.

It reminded her of rock pools, buckets of seaweed and low tide adventures from her childhood. She also noticed the glittering particles that stuck to his thin, plastered-down hair. Silver flecks, with dancing rainbows inside them. She recalled the sleek, oily skins of North Sea mackerel and torpedo herring, which her father brought home, wrapped in newspaper. For a moment she was almost overcome by a wave of nostalgia. Memories of times far back, in the innocent days of her childhood.

The man seemed to be gazing down the corridor, as if looking for something, far away. She said: "Can I help you?"

# ABOUT THE AUTHOR

AJ Aberford is a former corporate lawyer who moved to Malta several years ago. He is enthralled by the culture and history of the island that acts as a bridge between Europe and North Africa. Its position at the sharp end of the migrant crisis and the rapid growth of its tourist and commercial sectors provide a rich backdrop to the Inspector George Zammit series.

To keep up to date on AJ Aberford's fiction writing please subscribe to his website: **www.ajaberford.com**.

Reviews help authors more than you might think. If you enjoyed *Hawk at the Crossroads*, please consider leaving a review.

You can connect with AJ Aberford and find out more about the upcoming adventures of George and Abdullah, by following him on Facebook or, better still, subscribing to his mailing list.

When you join the mailing list you will get a link to download a novella, *Meeting in Milan*, a prequel to the Inspector George Zammit series.

# ACKNOWLEDGMENTS

The Inspector George Zammit series is my debut work and I have too often been blind to my many mistakes. I thank my wife, Janet, for gently pointing them out, the time she has spent working on the various drafts and for her encouragement and support. I also thank my editor, Lynn Curtis, who has worked patiently with me, giving sage advice, steering the plots and refining the prose.

# THE GEORGE ZAMMIT CRIME SERIES

# MEETING IN MILAN

Short-story prequel available for free: www.ajaberford.com.

What is a family?

Two very different cousins, one from Malta and one from Sicily, are brought together to embark on their university studies in Bologna.

While spending time with their uncle and dying aunt in Milan, they learn some truths about themselves and realise that family is not what it seems.

In the space of a few short weeks, they have a decision to make. It is a choice that could change their lives forever and, once made, there will be no going back …

# FIRE IN THE MOUNTAIN

George Zammit returns in *Fire in the Mountain*.

George is sent to Sicily to investigate a kidnapping in the shadow of an erupting volcano. Mystical monks, murderous criminals and an erupting mountain of fire await him.

Subscribe to AJ Aberford's website to keep up to date on the release date of *Fire in the Mountain* and news of further books in the series to come: www.ajaberford.com

# HOBECK BOOKS – THE HOME OF GREAT STORIES

We hope you've enjoyed reading this novel by AJ Aberford. To keep up to date on AJ Aberford's fiction writing please subscribe to his website: **www.ajaberford.com** and you will also be able to download the free novella *Meeting in Milan*.

Hobeck Books also offers a number of short stories and novellas, free for subscribers in the compilation *Crime Bites*.

- *Echo Rock* by Robert Daws
- *Old Dogs, Old Tricks* by A B Morgan
- *The Silence of the Rabbit* by Wendy Turbin
- *Never Mind the Baubles: An Anthology of Twisted Winter Tales* by the Hobeck Team (including many of the Hobeck authors and Hobeck's two publishers)
- *The Clarice Cliff Vase* by Linda Huber
- *Here She Lies* by Kerena Swan
- *The Macnab Principle* by R.D. Nixon
- *Fatal Beginnings* by Brian Price
- *A Defining Moment* by Lin Le Versha
- *Saviour* by Jennie Ensor
- *You Can't Trust Anyone These Days* by Maureen Myant

Also please visit the Hobeck Books website for details of our other superb authors and their books, and if you would like to get in touch, we would love to hear from you.

Hobeck Books also presents a weekly podcast, the Hobcast Book Show, where founders Adrian Hobart and Rebecca Collins discuss all things book related, key issues from each week, including the ups and downs of running a creative business. Each episode includes an interview with one of the people who make Hobeck possible: the editors, the authors, the cover designers. These are the people who help Hobeck bring great stories to life. Without them, Hobeck wouldn't exist. The Hobcast can be listened to from all the usual platforms but it can also be found on the Hobeck website: **www.hobeck.net/hobcast**.

## OTHER HOBECK BOOKS TO EXPLORE

### The Rock Crime Series by Robert Daws

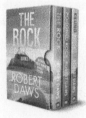

The magnificent Rock crime series from acclaimed British actor Robert Daws – includes free bonus story *Echo Rock*.

'An exciting 21st-century crime writer.'
**Peter James**

'A top crime thriller.'
**Adam Croft, crime writer**

Detective Sergeant Tamara Sullivan approaches her secondment to the sun-soaked streets of Gibraltar with mixed feelings. Desperate to prove herself following a career-threatening decision during a dangerous incident serving with London's Metropolitan Police, Sullivan is pitched into a series of life-and-death cases in partnership with her new boss, Detective Chief Inspector Gus Broderick. An old-school cop, Broderick is himself haunted by personal demons following the unexplained disappearance of his wife some years earlier. The two detectives form an uneasy alliance and friendship in the face of a series of murders that challenge Sullivan and Broderick to their limits and beyond.

The Rock Crime Series transports readers to the ancient streets of the British Overseas Territory of Gibraltar, sat precariously at the western entrance to the Mediterranean and subject to the jealous attention of neighbouring Spain. Robert Daws shows his mastery of the classic whodunnit with three novels rich in great characters, tense plotting full of twists and turns and breath-taking set-piece action.

**The Rock**

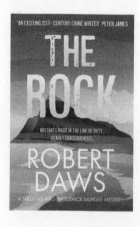

Exiled to Gibraltar from London's Metropolitan Police after a lapse of judgement, DS Tamara Sullivan feels she's being punished – no matter how sun-kissed the Rock is.

But this is no sleepy siesta of a posting on the Mediterranean. Paired with her new boss, DCI Gus Broderick, Sullivan will need all her skills to survive the most dangerous case of her career.

A young constable is found hanging in his apartment. With no time for introductions, Sullivan and Broderick, unravel a dark and sinister secret that has remained buried for decades.

Are they prepared to face the fury of what they are about to uncover?

**Poisoned Rock**

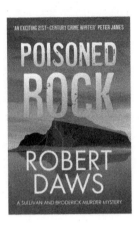

As the bright lights of a Hollywood movie production shine into the dark recesses of Gibraltar, murky secrets emerge from the shadows of the Rock's past.

It seems the legacy of wartime spying, sabotage and treachery runs deep on the Rock.

Past and present collide plunging detectives Tamara Sullivan and Gus Broderick into a tangled web of intrigue and murder, and their skills and uneasy working relationship are about to be tested to the limit.

**Killing Rock**

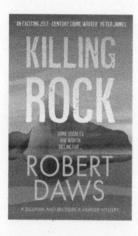

A wealthy household massacred in Spain.

Unidentified mummified remains found at the foot of the Rock.

A US Congressman's run for President hangs on events in Gibraltar.

What's the connection?

Detectives Tamara Sullivan and Gus Broderick face the most dangerous and elusive murder investigation of their lives, and for Broderick, it's about to become all too personal, with his career in real peril as his past comes back to haunt him.

Will Sullivan and Broderick's partnership survive this latest case, as killers stalk the narrow streets of Gibraltar?